THE EXILED QUEEN

A Roman Era Historical Fantasy

Roxana Arama

Dhawosia Publishing

For Smaranda and Zamfira

Andrada the Witch,
Andrada the Whore,
Andrada the Wicked,
Andrada Evermore.
—from a Dhawosian nursery rhyme, second century LE

Note: The Lucretian Era (LE) owes its name to the Roman poet Titus Lucretius Carus. The publication of his poem *On the Nature of Things* marked its beginning, and the Lucretian Era continues to this day.

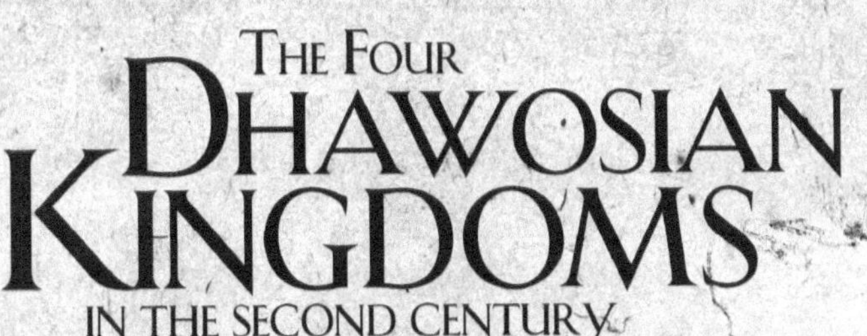

THE FOUR DHAWOSIAN KINGDOMS
IN THE SECOND CENTURY OF THE LUCRETIAN ERA
N
SARMATIA
TWIN WILLOWS
THE CARPATES MOUNTAINS
PYRETUS
STEPPEWYND
HYPANIS
THE GREAT PLAINS
EREBON
ZALMODAVA
OZANA
SANAPA
HIERASUS
TYRAS
THE NORLAND PASS
KERTA
ALBANOR
THE WHITE FORTRESS
SEHULDAVA
THE DANUBIUS DELTA
THE RED TOWER
THE TAURIS PENINSULA
VALDAVIA
ALUTUS
TOMIS
THE IRON GATES
THE BLACK SEA
DANUBIUS
THE ROMAN PROVINCE OF MOESIA
TO ROMA

MAIN CHARACTERS

Andrada, princess of Kerta and King Cothelas's daughter
Andrada's nursemaid
Apollonius, Roman architect from Damascus
Avezinas, King Cothelas's first councilor and Andrada's tutor
Boruistas, King Cothelas's treasurer
Brasus, Valdavian bard
Calidrones, guard in the Six-Sided Tower
Citera, Valdavian high priestess
Comosicus, King Cothelas's field aide
Cothelas, king of Kerta and Andrada's father
Dapyx, prince of Valdavia and King Nicetas's younger brother
Dokina, Andrada's handmaid
Gerulas, Kertan chieftain from the Bear-Hunters tribe
Ismarus, Kertan guide
Kosingas, Valdavian scribe
Lucius Flavius Magius, Emperor Vespasianus's diplomatic legate
Meda, princess of Steppewynd and King Scorilus's daughter
Moskon, prince of Steppewynd and King Scorilus's son
Nicetas, king of Valdavia and Andrada's husband
Oroles, King Nicetas's blood brother
Pegrina, queen of Kerta and Andrada's mother
Piepor, Chief Gerulas's brother

Quintus Domitius Cispius, Roman citizen from Moesia
Rada, medicine woman from Twin Willows
Rescuporis, prince of Steppewynd and King Scorilus's stepson
Rescuturme, queen of Steppewynd and King Scorilus's wife
Rubobostes, Kertan chieftain and owner of salt mines
Scorilus, king of Steppewynd
Syrmos, heir to the Bear-Hunters tribe
Tarbus, Valdavian chieftain
The Cartographer, mapmaker from Valdavia
Tymnes, envoy for the Traders' Guild
Una, the youngest of the medicine women of Twin Willows
Wodan, King Cothelas's army chief
Zia, the oldest of the medicine women of Twin Willows
Zyraxes, high priest of Beleizis and King Nicetas's older brother

MAIN GODS

Azemel, El's younger brother and ruler of the Underworld

Beleizis, god of thunder and rain

Bendis, goddess of hunters, forests, and wild animals

Ea, great earth mother goddess

El, sky god and creator at the beginning of time

Enoz, goddess of the crops

Heusos, goddess of the night's guiding stars, one of the Three Light Divinities

Mehnot, moon god, one of the Three Light Divinities

Napat-Dehnu, deity uniting Napat, god of rain, snow, and dew, and Dehnu, river and sea goddess

Samca, Azemel's wife and goddess of the night spirits

Sehul, sun god, one of the Three Light Divinities

PART ONE

"*Andrada the Witch...*"

—from a Dhawosian nursery rhyme

118–127 LE

CHAPTER ONE

The Book of Andrada

Every year on midsummer day, Princess Andrada waited for King Cothelas to come and wish her a gods-blessed birthday. Every year, he was too busy ruling Kerta to visit his daughter. But this year was different because she was turning ten, and the gods had given mortals ten fingers and ten toes for a reason.

The morning before her birthday, Andrada and her nurse shared a light meal in the women's wing of the king's house. Andrada gobbled up her bread and cheese, staring at the grand balcony outside the dining hall. Her father could be in the square right now, drinking from the fountain of Mount Kogalan or talking to people. Yes, she'd meet him tomorrow, but tomorrow was so far away. If she could catch another glimpse of him, she'd be better prepared for him on her birthday. She had seen him from afar at public gatherings, but her nurse had always kept her from going near him.

Andrada took one last bite and bolted to the balcony, ignoring her nurse's call to finish her milk.

She flung herself against the stone parapet, catching her breath. On tiptoes, she surveyed the sunny square for a sign of her father. Then she searched the stepped terraces of Sehuldava, all the way down to the fortified city walls.

People crowded the streets as always, but there was no sign of their king. Andrada clasped her hands together and prayed to the sun god

Sehul to shine a ray of light and reveal her father to her in the bustling city below.

She waited, twirling a ringlet of hair around her finger.

Nothing happened. Andrada looked away, a painful knot growing in her throat, tears blurring the snowy mountaintops in the distance. Maybe her father was in the throne chamber, listening to his subjects on Petition Day. Maybe he was in his council chamber, preparing for an attack from Emperor Nero's Roman legions. Maybe—

A gentle touch on her shoulder made her flinch. The nurse had joined her on the balcony. And someone else was there: a man, his sandy hair wild under the bright sun. He wasn't her father though, so he didn't matter.

Andrada wiped her eyes while the nurse nudged her toward the stranger. He stood by a trestle table covered with parchment sheets, charcoal sticks, and clay jars marked with colored brushstrokes. He didn't wear a cloak or the forward-bent felt cap of a chieftain.

"Princess Andrada," he said, bowing. "I come from a land named Valdavia, beyond the Carpates Mountains." He spoke her native Dhawosian but with an unfamiliar sound. "People call me the Cartographer because my work reveals the hidden face of the earth goddess Ea. I take places too big for the naked eye to see—watersheds and mountains and seashores—and I capture their likeness on my maps. Would you like to see a map, Princess?"

No, she wouldn't. She already had a map of the four Dhawosian kingdoms in her chamber. She studied it every day so her father would be impressed.

She found a new ringlet to play with and said nothing.

"He's here to capture your likeness," the nurse whispered in Andrada's ear. "King Cothelas sent him."

Her father wanted her portrait? Then she shouldn't make him wait. Hands trembling, she parted her thick, curly hair and brought it over her shoulders.

"Oh, no, no, no. It needs combing."

"Your hair looks fine, child," the nurse said.

"No, it doesn't," Andrada said, her heart beating in her throat. "Bring me my comb. It's in my horse-box."

The nurse sighed. "Cartographer, watch over the princess, will you?" In that light, the scar on her right cheek looked like a streaming tear.

Andrada waited for the nurse to disappear into the dining hall before she approached the man. He had already drawn a few black lines on a sheet of parchment that was held flat on the table with pebbles.

"My father wants my portrait?" she said.

"He needs it, yes." He glanced at her and back to his parchment.

"Where is he now?"

"In the king's chamber." That was in the men's wing, on the other side of the king's house, past the great hall with the throne chamber.

"Doing what?" Andrada said.

"Drawing, as I do now." His breath smelled nice when he spoke.

"Drawing what?"

"Something he lost ten years ago."

"What did he lose?"

The Cartographer laughed. "You ask a lot of questions, Princess." He dug into one of his belt pouches, took out a few green leaves, and tossed them in his mouth. "You remind me of a little girl back home in Valdavia. Her name is Una."

Andrada caught that pleasant scent again as he chewed. "What kind of leaves are those?"

"Water mint. When you travel as much as I do, you want something to remind you of home." He swallowed. "The medicine women of Twin Willows tell me it's also good for my stomach."

Andrada realized she didn't have time to waste before the nurse returned. "Can you draw my father's portrait for me?"

"Your father's? Why?"

"Because—"

Just then, the nurse stepped onto the balcony, holding Andrada's horse-box. Fast as a night spirit, that woman.

"Ah, let me look at that," the Cartographer said, taking the box from the nurse's hands. "Beautiful carving of a horse. Whitewood from the northern forests. Good for pigments."

Andrada didn't dare ask him again for her father's portrait with the nurse there. "Can you make my horse's hair blue?" she said instead. "With a golden harness?"

"As soon as we finish our work here." The Cartographer gave the horse-box back and returned to his sketching.

Andrada opened the whitewood box—always hard for her small hands to handle—and dug through her treasures, looking for the bone comb. Her fingers touched the gold coin stamped with her father's profile. She couldn't quite tell what he looked like in real life, but she was sure to recognize that shaved head tomorrow. It had to be tomorrow.

She stiffened her neck as the nurse forced the comb's wide teeth through her unruly hair. On the next pass, it caught in her gold hoop earring. She yelped as a dark hair fell on her embroidered skirt. "One day, nurse, I'll hurt you back."

"Of course you will, child. Though not for a while."

Once her hair was tamed and pinned up, Andrada put on a piece of jewelry from her horse-box: a gold necklace with a crystal pendant.

"Queen Pegrina would've liked that for your portrait, yes," the nurse said. She turned to the Cartographer. "Before she died, the queen left this necklace for the princess."

Andrada whipped her head toward the nurse. Her beautiful crystal necklace had belonged to Queen Pegrina? The woman her father still mourned? He'd been shaving his head since the day she died, as a promise to wait for their reunion in the god Azemel's Underworld. Andrada couldn't understand why that woman deserved such devotion. When Azemel's wife, Samca, the goddess of the night spirits, had come to Queen Pegrina's deathbed with Her twin cups of life-giving water and deadly water, the queen had chosen the one that took her to the Underworld—not the one that would have kept her here, with her newborn daughter and her husband.

"No, don't take it off," the nurse said.

Andrada dropped the necklace in the horse-box, then climbed onto a high stool to pose for her portrait.

"May I borrow that necklace?" the Cartographer said.

Andrada shrugged. The Cartographer picked it up and looked at it. Light passing through the pendant speckled his sunburned face with many colors. He drew the crystal and the chain on his parchment, added more details, then returned the necklace to the box.

Andrada sat up straight, posing. She listened to the voices in Mount Kogalan's Square below and to the water trickling in the fountain, and after a while, she felt warm and sleepy.

"We'll do colors now. First your eyes, then your hair," the Cartographer said, picking up a jar. "This is malachite green, the favorite color of the goddess Enoz of the crops." He scraped a good amount of pigment onto a wooden plate and took daubs of yellow, blue, and brown from other jars. He mixed and added, and smeared the result on that plate. Then he stared into Andrada's eyes, squinted, frowned, and mixed some more.

"Will you see my father today?" she whispered to him.

"Yes," he whispered back.

"Tell him not to forget tomorrow's my birthday. I can't wait to meet him."

The Cartographer scratched his sandy beard. "Wait, you've never met your father?"

"Never." Before she knew it, she was in tears.

The Cartographer looked at the nurse. "This child needs her father. Without him, she's lost. Not just now, but always."

The nurse squeezed Andrada's shoulder. "Tomorrow, child...Maybe tomorrow."

On midsummer morning, Andrada climbed into the warm washtub without her usual splash. The chamber looked unfamiliar somehow, even though the beds, shelves, and tables were the same, as was the hearth in the center with the smoke hole above it. Then she noticed the large wooden screen blocking her sight of the door. Was that there for her birthday?

"What's that?" she asked but received no answer.

The nurse poured water over Andrada's head and rubbed scented oils in her hair. "Keep still now." She wrapped the wet hair around her fist. "May the gods forgive me."

Andrada felt something cool and thin on the nape of her neck. She pulled away with nowhere to go, heard a hiss, and her forehead slammed against her knees.

"What have you done?" she cried.

Her beautiful hair was in the nurse's hand.

"Why?" Tears already rolled down her cheeks.

"King Cothelas's orders," the nurse said. "May the gods forgive him."

She covered the severed hair with the fine linen meant for sacred offerings and carried it beyond the wooden screen. She exchanged a few words with a man waiting there and came back.

"The Greek physician is ready for you."

Andrada's chest tightened with sobs. "Who?"

The nurse handed her a damp cloth for teeth cleaning, but Andrada wiped her eyes with it instead.

The nurse patted her on the back. "Your mother, with her last breath, made your father promise you'd be like a son to him. So now the king believes he must cut your hair short, dress you in boy's clothes, and send you to school for the next eight years. Girls' apprenticeships end at sixteen so they can marry soon after. You'll be with a tutor for two more years." She shook her head. "I tried telling him that your mother meant he should *love* you like he'd love a son, but he wouldn't listen to me."

"Then...this...is all her fault," Andrada said, crying.

"No, child, it's not. He's just a man who can't understand a mother's love."

"And what would you know about that?" Andrada whispered through tears. "You're no mother either."

The nurse touched the scar on her cheek but said nothing. She took a towel and draped it over Andrada's trembling shoulders. She then helped her out of the water and walked her to the edge of the screen.

The Greek physician's hairy hands reached out from the other side to inspect the limbs Andrada extended to him. He counted her fingers and toes and listened to her chest and back through a twisted horn.

Andrada kept touching the bare skin at the back of her neck. No hair there. No ringlet long enough to loop around a finger. She told herself she'd be more like her father now—less hair—but she couldn't stop crying.

"The princess has no bodily flaws," the physician announced. "By the grace of the Three Light Divinities, she can enter an apprenticeship."

The door opened and closed a moment later.

"What kind of apprentice...ship?" Andrada asked through sniffles. She didn't want to go to school with the boys.

"King Cothelas never told me," the nurse said. "He just ordered me to get you ready." She tucked Andrada's short hair behind her ears and removed her earrings. "You won't need these anymore."

A handmaiden brought new clothes, and Andrada put them on. First, there was a linen tunic with tight sleeves. It only covered part of her legs, ending just above the knees. Then there were woolen trousers, tall leather boots, and a leather belt with pouches. She wondered if that was why the Cartographer had done her portrait the day before, drawing her long hair and her dress.

"Am I supposed to pretend to be a boy now?" Andrada said.

"You be yourself, child," the nurse said. "But you'll be learning and doing things that only highborn boys are allowed to."

She held up a black shawl with a hole in the center and slipped it over Andrada's head. "This is your apprentice's apron." She tied a tasseled rope of red and white thread around Andrada's waist. "The king is taking you off Ea's path of womanhood, may the gods take care of you both."

The nurse gave her an unwanted hug. Andrada breathed in the familiar bittersweet scent of sage, and it comforted her. Then she pulled back, wiping another tear off her cheek.

She'd be with her father soon enough.

Andrada, her nurse, and her royal retinue arrived at the school on a lower city terrace. It was a stone building with many chambers that opened into a square. Highborn apprentices in black aprons filled the air with shouts and laughter. With no hair ringlet to twirl, Andrada took the nurse's hand and squeezed it. Her father must be there somewhere. It was her birthday, after all.

A man raised a draco, the Kertan wolf standard, at the top of a spear. The brass tongues of the wolf's hollow head rang in the wind, claiming power over the realm. The linen bag that was the wolf's body swelled in the breeze, adorned with flapping ribbons. At the wolf's call, the boys headed for the doors of the school chambers.

"You may leave now," a guard told the nurse, but Andrada wouldn't let go of her hand.

"I'll pick you up later," the nurse said. "And I'll have walnut honey cakes waiting for you at home."

Andrada watched through tears as her nurse disappeared into the crowd. She reached for a ringlet but touched only the skin below her ear. Her hand smelled of sage though, which made her feel better.

The guard nudged her through a doorway. She wiped her eyes because she'd meet her father now, and that was all that mattered.

Inside, she saw ascending rows of stone benches and shelves full of scrolls. There was a round hearth in the middle of the chamber. A man in dark robes sat at a narrow table, but he couldn't be her father because his head wasn't shaved and he had a gray beard. He was a tutor then, judging by the gold chain around his neck.

"Princess Andrada," he said, "take a seat."

With every step she took, her scratchy wool trousers rubbed against her thighs. She sat in the lowest row of benches, beside a wooden frame with strings of colored glass beads and a folded pair of wax tablets topped with an iron stylus.

"When's my father coming?" she said.

"Do not speak unless spoken to, apprentice."

"What kind of apprentice am I?"

"Quiet, or you'll be sorry."

No, he'd be sorry when her father learned how he had spoken to a princess—and on her birthday, no less.

She turned her attention to a map of the Dhawosian kingdoms hanging on the wall. Unlike the small map in her chamber, everything was big and drawn in vivid colors. At the center, the Carpates Mountains curled like a brown snake powdered with snow. Everything to the left of the mountains, all the way to the green fields at the edge of the map, was Andrada's country, Kerta. To the right of the mountains were the kingdoms of Valdavia and Steppewynd, separated by the Pyretus River. Valdavia was painted in light and dark green because of its forests and fertile valleys. Steppewynd was shown in yellow and brown because its fields had long been dead.

"How much longer until my father arrives?" Andrada said.

The tutor looked up from his work, his eyes dark and cold. "By the Three, apprentice, I just told you to keep quiet." As he opened his mouth for further scolding, a messenger walked in.

While the men talked, Andrada went to the map. The Danubius River flowed through six blue branches into the Black Sea. South of the Danubius, the former Dhawosian kingdom of Moesia—now a Roman imperial province—was marked with small pins, mostly along streams and lakes. What did those pins mean?

After a moment, she knew the answer: Roman forts, which had cropped up everywhere since Moesia had been conquered. She looked at the tutor to tell him of her discovery.

He was already approaching, a wooden rod in one hand. On his gold chain, a large crystal pendant swung against his dark robes to protect him against evil spirits.

"King Cothelas sends word that we are to begin at once," he said.

Andrada clasped her clammy hands together. Her father had sent word? That meant he wasn't coming. He wasn't coming...

The tutor stopped before her. "Name."

"Andrada of the Andori tribe, princess of Kerta."

"And I am High Priest Avezinas, your tutor in everything from numbers to sacred formulas to weapons. I'm the king's first councilor, and you're my only apprentice." He frowned. "By the Three, what's this? Tears? Tears won't save you from the Romans if they come here." He held out the rod. "Palm up."

Andrada obeyed, not knowing the significance of that.

The rod struck her hand. Its bite sank into the bones of her fingers. She shrieked and pulled away.

"Now the other one," Avezinas said.

She presented her other palm, shaking. The rod burned a bright line of pain across her hand. New tears sprang up, and she wiped her face with the back of her burning fists.

"That's for crying like a little girl," Avezinas said. "Now tell me why you're crying."

She tried to sound calm, but her voice wavered. "I...want to see my father."

"The king will make time for you someday, apprentice. But not today."

He laid a hand on Andrada's head. She stood still, afraid to breathe.

"Andrada of the Andori tribe," he said, "today, you begin your journey from ignorance to wisdom as wished by your mother on her deathbed. Today, you become an apprentice warrior like the highborn boys of our land. Today, I, Avezinas, high priest of Sehul and first councilor of King Cothelas of Kerta, take custody of your heart and mind in the name of the great mother goddess Ea and Her three divine children. May Sehul, god of the sun disc, Mehnot, god of the moon, and Heusos, goddess of the night's guiding stars, watch over you during this sacred journey."

Chapter Two

The Book of Andrada

Twenty moons had passed since the beginning of Andrada's apprenticeship. It was now the middle of winter. Her time at school was filled with parchment and ink, horse manure, blades and grindstones, bows and arrows, and—too often—her tutor's wooden rod. The boys mocked her when they practiced riding and fighting together. But despite that hardship and having to wear chest bindings during vigorous physical exercise, she liked training as a warrior and didn't miss wearing skirts. She hoped her father would be proud of her when they finally met.

One afternoon, Andrada waited for a chance to ask her tutor an important question, while Avezinas went on and on about the Roman Empire's growing threat to the three remaining Dhawosian kingdoms. Even with the fire crackling in the hearth and the smoke rising to the hole in the ceiling, their school chamber was as cold as a cellar.

Avezinas sat at his table, wrapped in a fur cloak, his breath a haze before him. "That's it for today, apprentice," he said at last.

Andrada scribbled on her wax tablet, her fingers stiff. "So...will my father stand with Valdavia or with Steppewynd as they quarrel over laborers and fair prices?"

If Avezinas turned her question around, she was prepared with facts. When the gods had first created the four Dhawosian kingdoms—Kerta, Valdavia, Steppewynd, and Moesia—Steppewynd had been a realm of bountiful gardens crossed by thousands of irrigation canals. The soil in the other three kingdoms was either too wet and heavy or too dry and light for crops. But Steppewynd's soil was the gods' gift to all of Dhawosia. That blessed age had ended a hundred years ago with Queen Seba, who had allowed deadly waters to turn her fields white with salt. With Steppewynd's decline, famine and strife hit all four kingdoms, and Gaius Iulius Caesar, Roma's dictator for life, set his eyes on Dhawosia.

As the Roman campaign was about to begin, the great mother goddess Ea and Her divine children rained down daggers on Caesar in Roma. Safe for now, the Dhawosian kingdoms made a pact. Steppewynders would travel to Kerta and Valdavia each spring, and their work would provide for their families in winter. With their labor, Kerta opened more mines in the Carpates Mountains. Valdavia cleared the trees in its valleys and planted grain. Moesia built outposts on the shores of the Black Sea to trade goods with Roma.

The pact between the Dhawosian kingdoms was flawed though. The price of Steppewynders' labor had been firmly agreed on, but not so the price of the goods it produced. As Roma's appetite for gold, lead, wool, and grain grew, so did the wealth of the three Dhawosian kingdoms that sold them. The chieftains of Valdavia and Kerta grew to favor their Roman merchant friends over their Dhawosian kin. And when Roma had attacked and conquered Western Moesia fifty years ago—and Eastern Moesia thirty years later—those chieftains had chosen not to intervene.

Even now, with three Dhawosian kingdoms left and the Roman Empire more powerful than ever, Steppewynd remained at the mercy of Kerta and Valdavia, providing the labor that kept the Roman merchants happy. Every year, Steppewynd demanded a new trade pact between the three kingdoms, and every year, Valdavia found reasons to delay. Now Steppewynd threatened war to break the stalemate.

"Will King Cothelas stand with Valdavia or Steppewynd?" Avezinas said. "That's a thorny matter, apprentice. A king must consider many things when his neighbors quarrel. And it's almost time for supper."

Andrada had a good reason to press the question. "If my father fails to stop the war between our two neighbors, won't Emperor Nero see that as a chance to conquer the rest of free Dhawosia? Divide and rule, says the

Roman. When Valdavia and Eastern Moesia quarreled twenty years ago, Emperor Claudius pounced and brought all of Moesia under his control."

"And why would Nero come here when he has enough trouble in Britannia and Parthia?" He had taken the bait.

She pointed at the map on the wall. "To fortify his northern border and control the Danubius River and the Black Sea. And to add Caesar's ambition to his own victories." Andrada rolled her iron stylus between her cold hands. "So...will my father pacify his neighbors or watch Nero bring his Pax Romana to Valdavia and Steppewynd? And then, of course, to our own Kerta."

Avezinas frowned. "A thorny matter indeed, even for a clever apprentice like you."

Andrada had her opening. "Then let's go ask my father."

Avezinas stroked his gray beard. "By the Three Divines, apprentice, I see what you're doing. No, the king has no time for your questions. That's my job."

Andrada feared he'd reach for the rod to punish her for asking yet again, in a different way, to see her father.

"Let me point you to the answer," he said instead. "Think about our defenses if the Romans attack us. Think of the resources we have here, around the Carpates Mountains. Think of what binds us together as Dhawosian kingdoms and what tears us apart. Write me at least ten tablets, due tomorrow morning."

He gathered his scrolls and rod, chuckling. Then he left. He probably thought he had punished Andrada, but she didn't mind writing that exposition and argument. Most subjects in school were straightforward. She couldn't argue on matters of sacred literature because what the gods had said and done couldn't be questioned. Numbers were just numbers, to add and subtract, but history and politics, with their many sides to each conflict, were alive and exciting.

The school day was over, but Andrada knew not to go out into the snow-covered square just yet. The boys were still around, laughing and screaming and throwing snowballs at one another. She waited inside, pacing around the warm hearth, cleaning specks of black wax off her apron, and peering outside for her nurse.

When the square fell quiet, she stepped out—

A snowball hit her shoulder. She turned and spotted Syrmos of the Bear-Hunters tribe and a few other boys, all grinning at her. Syrmos was a year older than Andrada, had straw-colored hair and dark brown eyes—and the most infuriating smirk.

"Poor little girl," he said. "Nobody came to pick her up today."

The boys in the square cheered him on. One day, Andrada would be their queen. What would her father say if she didn't stand up to them now? Biting her lip to hold back tears, she stomped toward him over the crunchy snow, her hands balled into fists.

"You want to fight me?" Syrmos drew a short leaf-shaped blade.

Andrada would rather bleed than let him see her cry. She came up to him and spoke in a commanding tone. "You will now teach me the blade trick you showed them today, after the sword-fighting lesson. Go on."

He frowned and pulled back. "You watched us?"

"I always watch my enemies."

He threw her a side glance. "I'm not your enemy."

"Then show me your trick."

He laughed. "Do you even know what this is? Go on—knife or dagger?"

"A knife is for cutting; a dagger is for killing. This is a Roman dagger. The raised midrib here makes the blade stronger. Good for thrusting at bones and slashing through muscle."

A few boys whistled in admiration.

"Now show me your trick," Andrada said, keeping her voice low to sound more like them.

Syrmos looked her up and down. "Fine. Here, slip it under your belt." He turned away from her. "Now come closer and grab me while I'm not paying attention."

As she grabbed him, Syrmos took half a step back, his left hand grabbing the hilt on her belt. Then he turned, dagger in hand. He held it a few inches from her neck, his breath warm against her cheek.

"Kiss her, Syrmos," a boy shouted.

Andrada freed herself. "Show me again."

He pushed her aside and gave her back the blade. She slipped it under her belt again. Now she'd be ready for him.

Andrada heard her nurse's voice. "What in the gods' names are you doing here?"

"Nothing," Andrada said, as the boys scattered. "Where have you been?"

"Doesn't concern you, child. Let's go." The nurse started ahead.

"My blade," Syrmos whispered, and Andrada flung it into the nearest tree trunk with a zing.

"Poor Queen Pegrina..." The nurse shook her head. "To see what has come of her dying wish."

Chapter Three

The Book of Andrada

Summer returned, then another arrived. Andrada sat on her stone bench at the front of the otherwise empty school chamber, watching Avezinas pace in front of her with his hands clasped on the wooden rod behind his back. She was hungry and ready to go home for the day.

"It's been three years since you started your apprenticeship," Avezinas said. "Let's hear the creation story." He set his rod on the table.

Andrada cleared her throat. "In the beginning, there was no sky, no sun, no moon, no stars, no earth. Nothing but the hot breath of the god El. He spoke, and the goddess Ea was born. He spoke again, and the sky appeared, and the sun, and the moon, and the stars, and the earth, the mountains and the valleys, the sea and the fish, the trees and the birds, the animals and the people, the disease and the cure. He then marked Dhawosia on His map and the other realms, all the way to the big ocean."

Avezinas nodded in rhythm with her words.

"As El admired His creation, His shadow on the ground took a life of its own and became Azemel, El's younger brother, whom El tasked with guarding the dead in the Underworld. At last, when the world was to El's liking, He put His creation in Ea's care, planted the seeds of His divine children in Her womb, and rested. But in His absence, mischief flourishes among mortals and gods alike, whom El has given free will. To this day, He sleeps, but the Great Awakening will soon come. El shall rise and behold His creation. He shall ask not only His divine children about the state of the world entrusted to them, but us mortals too. Dhawosians and barbarians alike. No one knows what El will do if He is displeased with our work, and that's why we should all strive to better our world so He will—"

A messenger burst through the door. "Your Holiness," he said, out of breath, "war broke out between Valdavia and Steppewynd. The Steppewynder prince almost killed the Valdavian king. He set the Valdavian camp on fire at night and stabbed the king in the gut. The Night Attack, they call it..."

"Let's go," Avezinas said, following him out.

In his hurry, he had left his rod behind. For three long years, Andrada had lived in fear of that rod, and now there it was, on the table, forgotten by its master. She stared at it, waiting for Avezinas to come back for it. She waited and then waited some more, just to be sure.

The boys were now playing outside in the square. School was over, and Avezinas wasn't coming back.

Andrada went to the table and picked up the rod. By itself, it held no power. It was light and smooth and harmless, but in Avezinas's hands, it was a weapon. Weapons were to be ritually destroyed when no longer needed. Andrada gripped the rod with both hands and pressed it against her knee. That hurt, and the rod bent but didn't break. There was no more fire in the hearth, so she couldn't burn it either.

She let out a groan of frustration, and with it, the rush of vengeance passed. She set the rod back on the table. Even if she destroyed this one, Avezinas would get another and punish her. No, it was better to wait until she met her father to ask him to stop Avezinas from using the rod.

But her father still hadn't come to see her. Not for all her right answers to Avezinas's questions, not for all the tasks finished before they were due, not for all her knowledge of weapons and talent with horses. Not for all her prayers, night after night, to Sehul, Mehnot, and Heusos—the Three Light Divinities—and to Their mother Ea, to bring her father to her. She wiped the tear at the corner of her eye.

She packed her tablet and stylus in her satchel before she stepped outside. Her nurse wasn't there yet, but the boys were, and that meant trouble. Today they focused their jeers and whistles on another girl, one who stood alone in the middle of the square. She didn't look like an apprentice though. She was taller and a bit younger than Andrada, and she wore her black hair in two short braids.

"That's all you've got?" she yelled, her hands on her hips. "I've seen the likes of you, and you're not worth a frozen cabbage."

An angry tutor came out of his school chamber shaking his rod, and the boys scattered.

The girl set eyes on Andrada and came running. "Auntie said I'd find you here. I'm Dokina." She slipped her hand under Andrada's arm. "I'm here to walk you home. I'm your new handmaid." Her eyes were brown and her nose stubby, and she appeared to smile even when she wasn't. "Who's the boy with golden hair and dark eyes? The good-looking one."

None of the boys seemed good-looking to Andrada, but the girl probably meant Syrmos.

"I don't know you." Andrada shook her off.

"I told you, I'm Dokina. Your nurse is my mama's little sister. Here, look. Auntie gave me her headscarf to prove she sent me."

Andrada recognized the black scarf but still buried her nose in it. It smelled of sage.

"I've just arrived from Albanor, you see," Dokina said, "and Auntie said I should make myself useful while she sees to supper. Though I got lost twice already on the way to this school of yours, so you lead the way home, and I'll just keep you company. Can I call you *Andrada*? It's such a beautiful name."

"No one calls me *Andrada*."

Only *princess* or *child*. Or *apprentice*...

"Then I'll be the first," Dokina said with a big smile.

Andrada shrugged and headed up the stone steps to the next terrace, where the city's vegetable gardens were.

Dokina caught up with her and locked their arms again. "I was so happy when Mama got word from Auntie. That was two days ago, just after our priest in Albanor called the new moon. Mama packed me up and sent me here right away. It didn't take long to pack since I don't have many things, and the things I have were already in a bundle because I was going to Chief Rubobostes's windmill for work. To grind salt and grain. I had a plan to charm that old goat, get him to marry me, and become the mistress of his chiefdom. Or marry one of his sons." She giggled. "It's much better that I'm here though."

How could anyone talk so much? "If you don't keep quiet," Andrada said, "I'll tell my nurse to send you back to your mother in Albanor. Or to that Chief Rubobostes's windmill."

"Why would you do that, Andrada?" Dokina clasped something she had around her neck. "Divine Sehul, Mehnot, and Heusos, please protect me from such misfortune."

Andrada had never frightened anyone before, not even a servant. She didn't like the feeling. "What's that at your neck?"

"Oh," Dokina said. "My mama gave me a crystal shard to keep in this pouch here. It protects me from evil spirits because it's real crystal, from the sky god El. You must have big crystals in the king's house, don't you? I have just this small shard."

"I have..." Andrada stopped herself before telling Dokina about the crystal pendant she never took out of her horse-box.

If that girl had to keep talking, maybe Andrada could learn a few things from her. She must know a lot about her auntie. "Do you know how my nurse got that ugly scar on her cheek?"

"Oh, your father gave it to her."

A jolt shot through Andrada's stomach. "My father? Why?"

"His soldiers caught Auntie in the Sanctuary of the Dead years ago. That's what Mama says. The king saw the column of smoke from afar and sent them to search the place. They found Auntie watching over the smallest of the cremation tables. Over her dead baby boy."

Andrada flinched. Her nurse had had a baby? She had been a mother? Why hadn't she said anything all these years? And how was she still alive? A commoner setting foot on royal sacred ground would be sentenced to death. "Who was the father?"

"We think Tzintus the woodcutter, but Auntie has always kept her mouth shut. After my baby cousin died, she brought him here from Albanor and used the royal cremation table to send him to the highborn realm of the Underworld so he could have a good afterlife. When the soldiers brought her in, the king was already mad with grief because your mother was dying of childbed fever. Auntie wouldn't utter a word, for she'd taken the mourning vow of silence that lasted thirty days. But when your mother smelled the smoke on Auntie's clothes, she knew Auntie would be a good mother for you. She asked her to be your nurse, and your father had to spare her life. But he marked her cheek as punishment."

Andrada imagined her father using his blade on a cowering woman. No, the nurse wouldn't have cowered but looked him straight in the eye. Still, hurting a bereaved mother...could her father really do that? No, it must have been his soldiers, when they caught her in the Sanctuary of the Dead. Dokina's mother must have had that part of the story wrong.

"Supper better be soon," Dokina said. "I didn't get a bite to eat since I got here, and I didn't think to save some of the flatbread I had with me for the cart ride because I was going to King Cothelas's house, and I thought they must eat like kings there. But Auntie didn't give me a crumb when I arrived. She sent me to fetch you on an empty stomach."

Poor nurse, surrounded by soldiers with drawn swords after she had just lost her baby. Before she knew it, Andrada was in tears, the sort that always made Avezinas reach for the rod.

"Did you cut your hair short because of head lice?" Dokina said, panting as they climbed the last steps to the terrace of the king's house.

Andrada wiped her eyes with the nurse's sage-scented scarf. "What did you say?"

"See, my hair was much longer, but Mama sheared me like a sheep when I got lice a few years back. But princesses don't get lice, do they? So then why is your hair so short?"

They were in Mount Kogalan's Square now. People milled around the fountain or chatted in small groups.

"That's the king's house?" Dokina said, pointing. "When I arrived, I went in through the servants' door, but look at this now, all these stairs and fires in those braziers. That's the wing where the great hall is?"

Andrada realized that, for the first time since she had become an apprentice, the nurse or someone else wasn't around to guard her. She looked at the entrance to the great hall atop the granite steps. If her father was in the throne chamber, all she had to do was walk past the guards, stop at the foot of his chair, and say, *Father.*

He wouldn't know her though, and she wouldn't recognize his face either, just his shaved head. The last time she saw him had been during the Festival of the Renewed Sun at the end of last year, and he was far away, leading the ceremonies. He stood above the crowd, at the top of the stairs outside the New Temple of Sehul, wearing the king's wolf mask and pelt cloak, while Andrada watched from the king's house balcony with the nurse. She couldn't even hear his voice over the wolf howling of dracos and the bleating of sacrificial goats.

"The king has brown eyes," the nurse had told Andrada when she gave her the gold coin stamped with King Cothelas's profile, years ago. "He has a tall forehead, like the kings of old. But unlike them, he doesn't bring a sword everywhere he goes. He carries a whitewood codex stuffed with parchment." Another reason not to believe Dokina's story about the nurse's scar.

Andrada looked around the square and spotted a big man in a cloak.

"Dokina, wait here."

"Now, don't be long. I'm so hungry."

Keeping her head low and hiding behind the man in the cloak, Andrada walked right past the great hall guards, like an apprentice sent with an important message. No one paid attention to messengers, and no one knew her as the princess because she had never been introduced to her people.

The great hall buzzed with voices. She saw a few shaved heads here and there, but no whitewood codex. She arrived at the throne chamber, where more people stood or sat around the hearth, talking about the Night Attack and the king of Valdavia, either dead or dying of a gut wound. Andrada rounded the fire, to the right of the chamber, toward the dais.

The gilded chair at the top of the steps was empty, but those people were waiting for the king. So where was he? She noticed a closed door at the far end of the hall, flanked by torches in gold brackets shaped like wolf heads. Could that be her father's council chamber?

She started toward that door, but something caught her eye. Between two flaming braziers was the largest painting she had ever seen, a huge wooden panel mounted on the wall. It was the image of a beautiful woman in a red dress, seated in a gilded chair, a crystal pendant on her chest. The necklace looked just like the one in Andrada's horse-box.

Queen Pegrina. Andrada had never seen her mother's likeness before. The queen's skin was pale, her long hair light like Syrmos's, her eyes green. But there was something about the way those eyes stared down at the chamber, smiling but not smiling, that terrified Andrada. She followed their eerie gaze. They were watching the king's throne. And whenever her father sat there, that was what he saw: those bewitching green eyes above the flames of the hearth.

"By Sehul's flower," someone's deep voice rang in Andrada's ear. "What business does an apprentice have in the throne chamber?" A guard towered over her, spear in hand, his brows knotted over fierce eyes. He grabbed her by the arm and dragged her away.

"How dare you? I'm the princess!" Andrada's voice was nothing but a squeak, and she looked nothing like a princess, with her trousers and her short hair. "Let me go." She jerked her arm away, and the guard lost hold of her.

She ran through the crowd, around the hearth, and bumped into a man. He didn't budge—another guard blocking her path. Then she saw the whitewood codex, the shaved head, and the dark, adoring eyes gazing up at Queen Pegrina's portrait. Around him, everyone fell silent.

The guard reached for Andrada. "Forgive us, my king."

After years of waiting and praying, Andrada was just one small step away from her father.

The guard grabbed her, his arm over her chest, his hand over her mouth.

"Father!" Andrada's cry was muffled under the guard's thick fingers.

Her father never turned, his eyes fixed on Queen Pegrina. Or were those evil green eyes fixed on him, keeping him from seeing anything else, even his own daughter?

Before she knew it, Andrada was out of the throne chamber, out of the great hall, falling on her face at the bottom of the granite stairs in the square.

"Do you know who I am?" she yelled back at the guard. Tears burned the rims of her eyes, and her lower lip trembled.

"A troublemaker who deserves a good flogging," the guard said, closing in.

Andrada scrambled up and dodged his slap just in time. He was coming after her again when Dokina shoved him aside. Together they ran toward the women's wing of the king's house. She could hear the tapping of the guard's spear on the cobblestones behind them, his heavy boots, his panting, his curses.

A boy in an apprentice's apron appeared, barring their path.

It was Syrmos, grinning. "Lost without your nurse, little girl?" He punched Andrada in the shoulder, spun her around, and locked her back against his chest.

"Let her go, you scoundrel," Dokina cried.

"Hold him right there," the guard yelled from just a few steps away.

"Who's that?" Syrmos whispered in Andrada's ear.

"Hold him, by Sehul's swelter—don't lose hold of him."

"Let me go," Andrada said, kicking Syrmos in the shin.

"I'll get you back for that, little girl. But you're our little girl to hurt, not his." He freed Andrada and pushed her away. "Run," he ordered.

And she ran and ran and ran.

That night, Andrada came up with a plan to banish the evil sorcery that held her father captive, away from his daughter. She tiptoed to check on the nurse and Dokina in their beds. They were both fast asleep after a busy day, a soft snore coming from the nurse's mouth.

Andrada put on her trousers and tunic, careful not to make a noise. She filled a long-spouted clay lamp with oil, slipped it under her cloak, and sneaked out. Trying to make her way to the throne chamber through the king's house was sure to get her caught, so she left the women's wing and went out into Mount Kogalan's Square.

It was dark but for Mehnot's half-moon and Heusos's eyes twinkling among the stars of the Small Dog, pointing north. Andrada walked around the wall of the king's house until she arrived at the granite stairs to the great hall. The doors at the top were never locked, and she went inside. Along the empty hall, mounted torches burned low, dappling the floor with pools of light. The fire still burned in the throne chamber's hearth, but no one was there.

Andrada looked up at Queen Pegrina. In the low firelight of the braziers flanking the portrait, the queen's red dress was a dark brown. The crystal pendant on her gold necklace looked dull, but her eyes were still green, alive and staring. She could stare all she wanted. Her evil spell didn't work on Andrada.

Her entire life, Andrada had prayed to the gods and Their mother Ea to send her father to her, and the gods had never answered. Now she could set things right on her own. Still, she whispered a few words to Heusos, patron goddess of night travelers, to bring the cover Andrada needed to finish that task.

Stretching on her toes, she tipped the spout of her oil lamp onto the panel, drawing zigzags as high as she could reach. Drops of oil fell on the floor and her boots, but most stuck to the wood. She took out the wick of her lamp, dipped it into a brazier, then flung the blue flame at the painting.

One of the oil lines lit up, a slash of light from the tip of Queen Pegrina's sandal, up her long skirt, to the thin fingers resting in her lap as if holding something now lost. Colors brightened in the firelight, then shriveled. The dry layers of pigments crackled. Smoke stung Andrada's eyes, and she stepped back.

She stared with dry eyes at the blue-yellow flames, at the burning spirit who had held her father captive for years. The fire licked the panel, pigments melted, and the gesso underneath turned black. Flames dripped onto the floor in puddles of burning oil—

A blow to her rib cage knocked Andrada down, the lamp in her hand shattering against the flagstones.

"What have you done, boy?" Firelight was bright on a guard's bewildered face. He tried to smother the flames with his cloak, but it caught fire, and he flung it away. He dashed out, yelling, "Fire!"

Queen Pegrina's arms and bosom were gone, but the green eyes were still there, where the lamp oil hadn't reached.

Andrada pulled back up at the sound of approaching footfalls. She ran to the dais and hid behind the throne.

The guard had returned and was now shoving his shoulder against the panel and straining to lift it from its hooks on the wall. But the painting was twice as tall as he, and it rained fire down on his face. He leaped away, and the panel settled back on the wall with an echoing thud.

Townspeople rushed in, passing buckets of water from hand to hand. A man grabbed one end of the burning panel but let go, cursing, and wrapped his hands in his cloak before trying again. Two more men grabbed the portrait from each side and yanked it off the wall. The chamber thundered, then sank into dimness with one last bucket of water splashing.

"Put up the portrait," a man said. It was Andrada's father in a night tunic and a woolen cloak.

She stepped out from her hiding place behind the throne and crept to the edge of the small crowd. A few men lifted the burned panel and propped it against the wall. Most of the painting was blackened—including the lower half of the queen's face—but her eyes, wet as if she were crying, were as bright and alive as ever.

Andrada's father stared at the scorched wood, his back to the people. Silence fell around him.

Andrada held her breath. Had it worked? Had she released her father from the spell?

"What happened here?" he said.

The guard stepped forward, shaking. "My king, I—"

"You were sleeping instead of guarding the throne," a woman next to Andrada barked at him.

The guard snapped around, and his and Andrada's eyes met.

"That boy," the guard said, turning to the king. "It's all his—"

Andrada's father dropped to his knees in front of the burned panel. His shoulders trembled. He caressed the blackened, soaked wood.

"Why, my love?" he asked the painting. "Haven't I done everything you asked of me?"

"The queen has sent him a sign," whispered the woman who had accused the guard. "Maybe the fire is no one's fault."

Andrada's father rubbed soot all over his shaved head. And when he turned around, he looked like an angry night spirit, his face blackened and streaked with tears.

Something was going on in his heart, something so huge that Andrada had no way of understanding. She didn't dare to go nearer. She had oil on her boots and clothes. He'd know what she had done and would never forgive her. So she sank into the crowd and disappeared.

The next morning, Andrada watched Avezinas for signs he might know what she had done to the queen's portrait. His words and glances unsettled her, as if he were waiting for a confession.

Better to distract him. "If Roman men can wear togas and skirts, why don't Dhawosian women wear trousers like mine? They're far better garments for...well, everything."

Avezinas looked at his own dark robes before answering. "This is the way of our ancestors, which the gods gave us at the beginning of time." He shrugged. "The Romans and the Greeks have lost their way."

"As when they renamed El and Ea and Their divine children in their language?"

"And when they imagined new gods that aren't real."

Andrada pushed on. "Still, they can see how useful a pair of trousers is when you ride a horse. Wouldn't that small change help them in battle?"

"Do they look like they need help in battle, apprentice?" a man asked from the doorway. "What are you teaching my child, Avezinas?"

Andrada's heart leaped into her throat. Her father was there, in her school chamber. He had come to see her, after all those years. Oh, no, he was there because of last night. He was there to punish her, though his face was clean of soot and his voice calm.

As he walked in, she squirmed in her seat, thinking of the rod. Her father was blocking her path to the door. Was this a trap? She glanced at her tutor, but his face offered no clues.

"Avezinas tells me you're an outstanding student," her father said, "and that the Three Divines are pleased with your work. So I came here to see for myself."

A few snooping faces, Syrmos among them, vanished from the doorway.

"What are you studying today?" her father said.

"History," she said, her hands trembling on her knees.

"Very well, apprentice." He took a few steps around the hearth fire. His fingers, holding the whitewood codex behind his back, had soot-encrusted nails. "Let's start with a simple question. I see you've heard of the Romans."

She closed her mouth and nodded. This was really happening—her father was talking to her.

"Tell me, are we meant to become another one of their provinces?"

Andrada had to make a good impression, so she chose her words with care. "When Roma conquered Moesia, Kerta sent no troops to stop them. Now we don't have Moesia to help us."

"So we're meant to become a Roman province."

"It's...a thorny matter," she said.

Avezinas smiled, stroking his beard.

"If the three Dhawosian kingdoms don't band together soon," Andrada said, "we could fall to the golden eagle's claws." She felt proud of her last turn of phrase.

Judging by his grin, Avezinas was bursting with pride too. But did her knowledge please her father? A ball of worries filled her stomach.

"Are we meant or not meant to become a Roman province?" he said again.

"Neither," she said. "The future is not written in stone, not even by the gods. But the future is perilous for the free Dhawosian kingdoms. We must all come together and prepare to fight."

At last, her father smiled. "Avezinas, you did a fine job here."

"I told you, my king. Blessed be your queen for sending you here today."

Oh. Andrada wished she could tell them that Queen Pegrina hadn't sent him there, but one glance at the rod changed her mind. Another glance at her father and her worries melted away. He was smiling at her. Seeing her. He looked happy.

She was glad she had burned the portrait.

"I'll see you again soon, apprentice," her father said, starting for the door.

"Father," Andrada called after him. His grimace made her correct herself. "My king. May I ask a favor?" After all that had happened, she felt confident.

He nodded.

"Would you please tell my tutor to stop using that rod on my hands?"

It was a long moment. The two men exchanged glances.

"Give that to me," her father said at last, his hand extended to Avezinas, who had no choice but to pass the rod.

Andrada knew she had made a terrible mistake. The flesh of her palms hurt in anticipation.

Her father strode to the hearth and threw the rod in the fire. "Avezinas, my friend, you'll have to use persuasion from now on."

Andrada wanted to run to him but didn't. She knew how to wait for him, so she'd wait until the day he'd welcome her in his arms. Until then, she'd be a dutiful daughter. She'd make him proud.

She watched him walk away. Her heart was so full, she had no words for how she felt. If she were to cry now, Avezinas wouldn't punish her, not today.

She waited for the tears to come, but they didn't.

Chapter Four

The Book of Andrada

Four good years passed for Andrada without Avezinas's rod or much taunting from Syrmos. When her father had time, he came to see her at school and praised her in front of her tutor. He sometimes excused her from her lessons to have her sit through Petition Day with him, when the people of Kerta asked their king to be their judge and protector. He even took her to his council chamber on occasion, where he discussed matters of the state with his trusty chieftains.

Meanwhile, she had grown to know him better—her childhood dream come true. She had learned he liked sheep's cheese spread on flatbread sprinkled with white salt. He admired Hannibal Barca's strategies in the Punic Wars between Roma and Carthago, centuries before. And he sometimes lost his temper if Andrada didn't have the right answer to his questions. When that happened, she feared losing his newfound affection, so she studied harder to make him proud of her again.

On a cloudy fall morning, Andrada waited outside the great hall for her father to call her in. Her hair had been cropped the day before, and the icy air on the nape of her neck worsened the ache in her belly. To distract herself, she walked around, trying not to step on the cracks between the flagstones. Had she been home, the nurse would have placed warm stones on Andrada's belly to help with the pain that tormented her every moon, making her insides bleed. The hearth fire in the throne chamber would have helped, but that meant standing under the half-burnt portrait of Queen Pegrina. At least Andrada's embarrassing tears had disappeared on the night of the fire, so she could keep her aches and sorrows better hidden.

A guard called her in and bowed as she passed. In the throne chamber, she couldn't help peering at the wall. The green eyes still glared down from their scorched panel, though they no longer held power over Andrada's father. She hurried to the council chamber ahead.

Guards stood outside an open door flanked by torches in golden wolf-head brackets. The pile of blades on the floor—no weapons allowed during council—was higher than ever.

The chamber stank like a den of wolves. Dozens of men draped in heavy furs sat shoulder to shoulder on benches around the stone table. Andrada's father was at one end, and she recognized Avezinas and a few others around him. Chief Wodan, in charge of the army; Chief Comosicus, Wodan's field aide and faithful companion; Chief Boruistas, the treasurer; and Chief Rubobostes, owner of the largest salt mines and former target of Dokina's marriage schemes.

"What's she doing here?" a man whispered as Andrada took a chair in the corner, behind her father.

The logs in the hearth crackled with the sweet scent of pine resin. The white pain in Andrada's belly kept her from listening to Chief Boruistas, who read aloud the tally of taxes for the year. Andrada found comfort in counting the carved wolf heads on the candle wheels hanging from the high beams. She then counted the table candles crackling in their wolf-headed holders around jugs of wine, flagons of firewater, and wooden cups. Gone were the days when the king had gold cups at his table.

Andrada's father held up a gold coin. "Whose profile is this, my lords?"

No one looked at the shiny disc with uneven edges, its center stamped with the familiar profile of a shaved head.

"So where are my taxes for the year?"

The chieftains looked angry and cornered.

"Chief Rubobostes, your mines haven't brought in any salt this year," Avezinas said.

Chief Rubobostes, an old man with watery eyes, raised his arm. "By Sehul's flower, I've got no one to send to the mines. My men are up on the slopes, replacing the Steppewynder shepherds we lost after the Night Attack."

Someone else cut in. "I can't find a family in my chiefdom willing to mine my gold unless they're paid more than it's worth."

Andrada perked up. Four years ago, after the Steppewynder prince had almost killed the Valdavian king during the Night Attack, all trade and travel between the two neighboring kingdoms had ceased. Because Kerta lay to the west of Valdavia, it had lost all its migrant Steppewynder laborers. Now it struggled to feed its people and fulfill its trade obligations with Roma. Two years ago, Andrada's father had been negotiating the reopening of the trade routes between its neighbors when the old king of Steppewynd died. His son ascended to the throne, and the Valdavian king refused to engage with the man who had almost killed him. The standoff had persisted since.

Chief Comosicus spoke next. "For the Steppewynders to reach my mines, they must cross through Moesia in the south. They'll risk falling into the hands of the Roman slave merchants, and they're not that desperate yet. But I am. Training new iron ore miners brought an untimely death to many households in my land—"

"Even your own, Chief Comosicus?" Andrada's father pointed at the men around the table. "Or yours, my lords? Have you no strong-armed sons to send down my mine shafts?"

The chieftains murmured to each other. Some busied themselves with their wooden cups.

"Easy for him to say," someone whispered nearby, the same man who had questioned Andrada's presence earlier. "He has no sons to call his own."

Anger at the man who had dared insult her father took Andrada's mind off the pain in her belly.

"Even so, my king," Chief Wodan said, "how much salt would my two boys bring up? How much gold? How much lead? How much iron?"

Men nodded around the table.

Chief Boruistas pointed to his treasury parchment. "The Germanic tribes of the Great Plains could mine your mountains."

A few men protested. "For thrice the Steppewynders' price!"

"None of this matters." The man who had been whispering sat up in his chair, and Andrada could see him now. He had light hair and a fur cloak. "Even if we somehow pull all the gold and salt from our mountains, as Roma wants, it's not what we need right now. We need grain to feed our people. Roma doesn't have enough to trade, and Valdavia's harvest has suffered without its Steppewynder farmhands."

"Yet somehow, Chief Gerulas," Avezinas said, "our chieftains' wives have been trading grain with the merchants of Moesia for olive oil and silver mirrors."

Andrada remembered that Gerulas belonged to the Bear-Hunters tribe, same as Syrmos.

"That's not true." Protests erupted around the table.

A divided country was a perfect target for the Romans' next campaign of conquest. Andrada glanced at her father. His jaw twitched. He whispered something to Avezinas, who rose from his chair and slipped out.

"My lords," Andrada's father said, his wolf-pelt bracers crossed over his chest, "the Valdavian king put us on this path of strife and scarcity when he closed the trade routes with Steppewynd after the Night Attack. But you're marching on it with great fervor. Wherever I look, I see chiefdom turning against chiefdom, priests and temples fanning the flames of discord, people raising their voices against their king. Meanwhile, Roma is looking for the next temple to plunder after the one in Ierusalem last summer. The New Temple of Sehul, perhaps? Because if we can't mine our own mountains as free men, they'll make us do it as their slaves."

The people of Dhawosia had never been slaves—the gods forbade that barbaric custom. Did Andrada's father truly believe that could happen?

The chieftains were all quiet now. No one touched the wine.

"From this day on," her father said, "not paying taxes to the king's treasury is punished by seizure of property and redistribution among the next of kin, who'll then be responsible for their share of taxes."

Panicked glances darted across the table. Hands rushed to the belts where daggers used to hang, but some of the younger men looked pleased. With one decree, Andrada's father had made enemies of landowners and friends of their next of kin—a shrewd move that would keep the chieftains from banding together against their king. But would this move refill his coffers?

Avezinas walked back in. "Messengers have been sent across the land with the king's new decree about the collection of taxes—"

"A bad decree that won't outlive this king," Chief Gerulas muttered.

Andrada leaned out of her chair to glance at him, though it hurt to move.

"Guards are waiting for my call," Avezinas said, "in case you want to express your displeasure with your...bare fists." He returned to sit next to his king.

"For many years," Andrada's father said, his shaved head glistening with sweat, "I hoped that when I was gone, my chieftains and priests would come together to keep my kingdom safe. But I've lost faith, my lords, and so, to provide for future unity, I give you my heir to the throne."

He extended his arm toward Andrada and motioned for her to rise, to face the wolfmen down, as he had, and show them she could be their queen.

She gently stood up from her chair. If she disappointed her father, she'd lose his hard-won affection forever. She gritted her teeth and stared at the men.

"A woman?" Chief Rubobostes said. "The gods once trusted Queen Seba, and she turned Steppewynd's gardens into a wasteland. The priests of the ancestral shrines would never give their blessing to another woman ruler."

Avezinas's familiar look of disdain reappeared on his face. "The same gods who forbid us to put you in chains and force you into mines as slaves bestowed Their blessings upon our chosen heir. We've received many propitious omens—"

Chief Wodan cut in. "A king can have ten healthy sons and still end up heirless—war, plague, you name it. That's why we have the King's Challenge. We'll choose the worthiest of us when the time comes, the way your grandfather was chosen."

The King's Challenge, created after the tragic reign of Queen Seba to prevent another woman from ever claiming a Dhawosian throne, was invoked when the old king left no sons behind. The contender who passed the trial took the throne. The others received a cup of deadly water so their dreams of ruling perished with their last breath.

Andrada's father stood, his fists propped on the tabletop. "Am I to believe you'll come together when I'm gone and do right by the King's Challenge? Just look at what happened in Roma after Nero's death: civil war between ambitious military leaders. They came and went: Emperor Galba, Emperor Otho, Emperor Vitellius, and now the newest one, Vespasianus. No, my lords. Without an heir, you'll fight each other like rabid wolves while Roma mounts the golden eagle over Sehuldava."

"Adopt an heir then, my king," Chief Gerulas said over the others' protests, "as the Romans do. The high priest of Heusos in the Bear-Hunters' temple has received a sign that our own Syrmos, the best of all apprentices—"

"Princess Andrada is a better apprentice than Syrmos," Avezinas said.

It felt good to hear that, but her father's next words felt even better. "This apprentice here is my heir."

The chieftains grumbled and whispered around the table while Andrada watched, her hands clasped together, her breath shallow, the pain in her belly irrelevant. If she were to become the future queen, she'd spend all her time with her father, learning from him how to rule Kerta. She was a hardworking student. She'd make him proud.

At last, Chief Wodan spoke. "Avezinas says the princess is a good apprentice and the gods approve. But Avezinas's word is not enough. If we're to break Queen Seba's taboo and allow another woman to rule us, then Princess Andrada must pass the King's Challenge. The chieftains will choose a worthy opponent for her."

Andrada felt dizzy, tiny white sprites dancing before her eyes. Could she pass the King's Challenge? Books, horses, blades—she had mastered them all. The gods willing, her father would live a long and healthy life before she'd have to face Syrmos or one of his ilk on a battlefield.

"And if she fails," Chief Rubobostes said, glancing at Andrada for the first time, "she drinks a cup of deadly water."

No, she wouldn't fail. Her father believed in her.

"Because we need unity now," Chief Gerulas said, "the challenge should begin on the midsummer of next year, when Princess Andrada turns eighteen years of age."

So soon? Andrada's heart beat so fast, it hurt.

At last, her father nodded in agreement. "Until then, go home to your tribes and prepare to send your sons into the mines when the weather turns. Send me black salt and white salt, and the gold I need to hire Germanic laborers to smelt your iron and shear your sheep. Then we can bid for grain on Roman markets. The first two chiefdoms to send in their taxes will have them cut in half next year. May the Three Divines help us all."

Wood benches screeched on flagstones, and grumbles rolled off tongues. Outside the doors, blades clanked when retrieved, but there was no sound of fighting.

"Chief Gerulas, a word," Andrada's father called after the chieftain, then turned to her. "You'll be their queen one day. Tell me, what would you do with Gerulas? Because if you just let him go, you'll look weak. You'll have to kill him to show them who's queen."

Andrada's insides turned cold. "Can't I just send him away? In exile?"

"Exile, you say? Very well...Chief Gerulas, you're still wearing your riding clothes, so you can leave the soonest."

"I don't understand..."

"Go to the Valdavian king and convince him to start talking to Steppewynd."

How in El's slumber was he supposed to do that? Was he a friend of King Nicetas of Valdavia?

"By Sehul's flower, my king," the chieftain said, "I know nothing of diplomacy."

"Oh, but you do, Chief Gerulas. You've just proven it by turning a chamber full of chieftains against their king—if only for a moment. I can't think of a better man to send to King Nicetas on my behalf. Twenty soldiers will see you all the way to the Iron Gates."

Chief Gerulas looked terrified. "The...Iron Gates?"

"Snow is already falling in the mountains, over the Norland Pass and the Red Tower Pass, so you can't take those routes. Surely you're not afraid of crossing the Five Gorges at the end of fall?"

Now it all made sense to Andrada. She had heard of the Five Gorges and their rough waters over the jagged riverbed of the Danubius. Sending a man downstream through the Iron Gates was a death sentence. And it had been her idea to exile Chief Gerulas. She felt weak in the knees.

"Not afraid," Chief Gerulas said, "but what about my township and my mines?"

"As your next of kin, your brother Piepor will watch over them while you're gone. Guards, make sure Chief Gerulas is safely on his way. At once."

Andrada's father gave her a nod on his way out. He seemed proud of her, but that was no comfort.

She slumped into her chair, doubled over, and hugged her belly. Pain she'd been keeping at bay crept up to the hinges of her jaw, solid pain that scorched. She forced herself to breathe. All pain would pass, and she'd once more be the son—and now the heir—her father wanted.

Chapter Five

The Book of Andrada

On midsummer day, the morning of Andrada's eighteenth birthday, she said a prayer to the Three Divines before she even opened her eyes. As the days had counted down to the King's Challenge, she had focused on her studies and practice, but now her stomach was up in her throat.

"You've received a linen shift from the New Temple of Sehul," Dokina called, and Andrada turned to look. Dokina wrinkled her nose, holding up the ugly garment. "Is this your King's Challenge? Wearing this scratchy sackcloth for all of Sehuldava to see?"

"I wish." Andrada dragged herself out of her bed.

Past challenges in the four Dhawosian kingdoms had involved sword fights, horse races, and escaping from dungeons. She could do all that, though wearing a shift instead of trousers would make things harder. The only thing she had never mastered was swinging a mace, but her father had taught her how to dodge one and fight back with other weapons. The royal blacksmith had even made her a special sica sword that had the usual long curved blade but also a hilt that fit better in her small hands.

"Chief Rubobostes asked my father to return me to women's clothes for the challenge. Now that my apprenticeship is over, all those men want their trousers back."

Dokina laid the linen shift on the bed. "I'm sure Master Syrmos will like you no matter what clothes you wear." Her wink annoyed Andrada.

"He's only helping me prepare for the challenge."

She had spent winter and spring with him, sparring in the armory and racing horses, while Chief Wodan had taught her to be fast on her feet and nimble to make up for her shortcomings with the mace.

"I don't know," Dokina said. "Master Syrmos is a full-fledged warrior, but he sure spends an awful lot of time with a mere apprentice. I bet he wants to marry the king's daughter—"

Andrada threw a pillow at Dokina. "You're the one in love with him." She would have said something wittier but didn't know what being in love meant and didn't want to give Dokina another reason to make fun of her.

Dokina flung back the pillow, but the nurse caught it as she entered the chamber. "Sitting on your arse and jabbering, Dokina? Go draw the bath. There's a ceremony waiting."

"Oh, Auntie?" Dokina said, heading for the door. "A messenger from Albanor stopped by the kitchen. Tzintus the woodcutter sends his greetings and hopes you visit Albanor this summer." She ran out laughing.

The nurse shook her head in disapproval. For a moment, the weight on Andrada's shoulders lifted—until she remembered that if she failed the King's Challenge, she'd have to drink a cup of deadly water.

"This is my birthday present for you," the nurse said. "An embroidery frame, like we had eight years ago." She held out a piece of linen stretched between two wooden frames. "I hope you still remember how to thread a needle."

Andrada accepted it, though she hadn't missed embroidering at all.

The nurse took the gold chain with the crystal pendant from the horse-box and brought it over. "Your mother would've wanted you to wear it today." The necklace hadn't left the box in years, but Andrada wouldn't hurt the nurse's feelings, so she let her clasp it on. "And now the earrings. Gold filigree hoops sent by the king." She held up a silver needle.

Andrada gave it a glance and steeled herself. The King's Challenge was sure to be harder than ear piercing.

"This will make the wound heal faster." The nurse ran the tip of the needle through the flame of a candle, then pulled Andrada close and rubbed her right earlobe until it went numb.

The needle pierced the flesh, burning its way through. Andrada winced but didn't cry. The gold tip of the earring stabbed her wound, and it was done.

She braced herself for the second piercing, but somehow it hurt more.

Guards opened the path to the ceremony site, and more of them followed Andrada, but she walked alone on cobblestones, under the curious gaze of the people of Sehuldava. The gods watched from Mount Kogalan and from the snowy peaks surrounding the fortress, and she prayed to them to keep her alive. She cherished life, despite the dull pain from her new gold-hooped ears and the ball of fear in her chest.

The fragrance of new grass and upturned soil filled the warm summer air. Andrada passed a group of women dressed in festive colorful clothes, feeling exposed in her rough-spun linen shift and thin woolen cloak. Her hair had escaped the blade today and was instead adorned with a garland of pine shoots and Sehul's yellow flowers.

On an upper terrace where an orchard grew, she saw Avezinas praying at a terra-cotta altar of Ea and El. He seemed troubled as he motioned for her to kneel next to him. The earth goddess stood taller than the sky god, their necks adorned with crystal beads, their heads hollow and smoldering with burning incense. Seeing their calm faces quieted Andrada's squirming heart for a moment.

"May the Three Divines watch over you, Princess," Avezinas said in a tone that worried her anew.

Through the cool shade of trees, Andrada arrived at the top terrace, with its circle of standing stones. Over the years, she and Dokina had sometimes come to that ancient sanctuary to listen to the spirits whisper, their sweet voices just beyond words and comprehension.

The guards stepped aside and let Andrada enter the stone circle. In the center of the sanctuary stood a wooden arch wrapped in flowers. Beyond it, where the standing stones grew taller, Andrada's father waited. He wore a low, bent-forward felt cap on his shaved head.

Andrada darted to him.

"Wait there." He didn't shout, but the stone circle carried his voice.

People's chatter around the sanctuary filled the air with tremors felt in Andrada's tender earlobes.

"Little girl, little girl…" Syrmos's voice called from nearby. There he was, with his boys, grinning at her, pretending to drink from an imaginary cup and choke to death. She never knew when he was her ally or her enemy.

She turned away and spotted the chieftains, now dressed in ceremonial clothes. Wodan and Comosicus kept to themselves, Boruistas was arguing with Rubobostes, but she knew she wouldn't find Gerulas in the crowd. People said he had drowned trying to sail across the Iron Gates last fall. Andrada begged the gods not to punish her for his misfortune.

Those men were there to watch the woman fail, but with the help of the Three Divines, she'd be the next queen of Kerta, erasing Queen Seba's taboo from the Dhawosian royal chronicles. Unless…She wondered what deadly water tasted like. She didn't want to know. She wondered who the other contenders would be. She didn't want to know that either.

One famous King's Challenge had sent its contenders to retrieve a stolen treasure from a Germanic tribe in the west. Another had sent them east, across the Black Sea, to the Tauris Peninsula, to learn the secret of being invincible in battle. One had sent them north, over the Carpates Mountains, through thick forests full of wild bees and beasts, to bring back word from a famous prophet. Andrada's great-grandfather had destroyed a Roman fort south of the Danubius River, in the new imperial province of Moesia, and thus founded the royal Andori bloodline. Would his line end in the snake- and mosquito-infested Danubius Delta? Or at the Iron Gates? Andrada's heart raced as she thought of all the ways she could face death.

Shadows were short and dark on the grass, which meant the ceremony was about to begin. At last, Andrada's father motioned to her, and she advanced to the flower gate. On its other side stood two dark-robed silhouettes: on the right, Avezinas, holding a torch, and on the left, the nurse, carrying an apprentice's apron and a bundle of boys' clothes Andrada had worn until yesterday.

Drums rapped, alpenhorns bayed, and people fell quiet. The crystal on Andrada's gold necklace was warm with sunshine. At her father's nod, she stepped through the flower gate. She turned to her right and extended her trembling hand to Avezinas, but he didn't offer her the torch as she had expected. Instead, he showed her the left side of the gate, where the nurse stood. Blood rushed to Andrada's cheeks and pain to her earlobes. Of course, today she returned to Ea's path of womanhood. From now on, she turned left instead of right during ceremonies and stood with the women, watching in silence. Only men were allowed to set things on fire.

Avezinas brought his torch to the flower gate, and after the flames engulfed it, the nurse threw the bundle of clothes into the fire. They both guided Andrada to her father, by the tallest standing stones. She heard the crackling of the burning gate behind her, felt its heat on her back. Around her, colors became louder, sounds stronger, smells coarser, textures hotter—a sign that the guardian spirits of the sanctuary were present. Had she turned her head, she would have surely seen them dancing under Sehul's sun.

"We are all here," her father said in a loud and clear voice, "to witness the end of an apprenticeship. Andrada of the Andori tribe, today you begin your age of maturity. From this day on, you will stand in front of the great mother goddess not as a child but as a woman."

She stood still as he rubbed damp black salt on her forehead.

"Sehul, god of the golden disc, lord of light and life," he said with eyes to the sky, her left hand in his right, "this child is no more. Mehnot and Heusos, guide this woman through the night and keep her safe from harm and pain."

At her father's sign, Syrmos entered the stone circle and came to stand at her side. That could only mean one thing.

"Syrmos of the Bear-Hunters tribe and Andrada of the Andori tribe, you are now equals in the eyes of the gods, as you have both finished your apprenticeships. You are now contenders in this new King's Challenge."

Syrmos threw her a glance as if he hadn't expected to be there. She didn't believe him but was relieved he was her opponent. Better Syrmos than a seasoned chieftain. Then she remembered that one of them would have to drink the deadly water. If she prevailed, Syrmos would die, just like Chief Gerulas.

Her father's voice echoed around them. "Your challenge is to find the heart of Sehuldava and to reveal it to us on the last day of the year, during the Ceremony of the Renewed Sun."

Andrada's whole body trembled from the relief she felt. No cup of deadly water for either her or Syrmos for half a year. At least not until the ceremony that marked the middle of the Festival of the Renewed Sun—those twelve sacred days encompassing the end of the old year and the beginning of the new one. No horse races, no sword fights, no wild bees and snakes, no Roman forts, no Iron Gates. She took a deep breath and let it out. She didn't have to worry about her skirts slowing her down.

"There is one commandment you both must obey. On the highest terrace of the city, in the north, the Old Temple of Sehul still stands beyond ancient trees, forgotten by most. You may search anywhere in Sehuldava for its heart, but you're forbidden to enter that temple during your quest."

The Old Temple of Sehul? Until now, Andrada had never wondered why the New Temple of Sehul was called *New*. But why forbid her from something she hadn't even known existed?

"The king and his contenders," Avezinas announced, "will not meet or send messages to each other until the Festival of the Renewed Sun at the end of the year. The King's Challenge has begun."

Between the pain in her tender earlobes and her frenzied thoughts about Syrmos and the King's Challenge, Andrada couldn't settle for the night. She paced around the hearth, staring at the red embers, thinking through the many possibilities.

The sounds of music, laughter, and cheering from Mount Kogalan's Square echoed through the open windows. People were still out, celebrating under the midsummer night sky. The nurse hadn't returned either.

Dokina sat up in her bed, listening to the cheerful panpipes.

"The heart of the city?" Andrada said, tapping her chin. "What do you think that means?"

"To me, the heart of a city is its people," Dokina said. "Like those in the square, wishing you a blessed birthday."

"Its people, huh? Then why order me to stay away from an old temple? No people there."

"Eh, what do I know?" Dokina said, slipping down onto her pillow. "I'm just a girl from Albanor who can't read or write. And who's tired and would like to go to sleep."

Andrada walked another circle around the hearth. "Does my father want me to obey the edict and stay away from the temple, or is he sending me in? Is there a third choice, you think?"

Dokina shrugged.

"The first time I met him," Andrada said, still pacing, "he asked me an either-or question, and the answer was neither. And did I tell you about that time when he asked me who was the hero of the Night Attack?"

"No," Dokina said, yawning.

Andrada pretended not to see that. "The Night Attack was when Prince Scorilus of Steppewynd almost killed King Nicetas of Valdavia, who was only nineteen at the time."

Dokina pulled her woolen blanket up to her chin.

Andrada ignored that too. "During the Night Attack, Prince Scorilus of Steppewynd set the Valdavian camp on fire and ambushed King Nicetas in his tent. The two fought with blades, and Scorilus stabbed Nicetas in the gut. He would've killed him too, had it not been for a commoner who shot an arrow at Scorilus's unprotected armpit and stopped him from stabbing Nicetas again. Oroles, son of Zonaras, then took his king to the village of Twin Willows, half a night away on horseback. The medicine women there drained some of Oroles's blood through green glass tubes and gave it to the king—"

"And made Oroles the king's blood brother," Dokina said, yawning again. "I know the story. Women sing it around the hearths of Albanor while spinning wool."

"They do?" Andrada said.

"Mm-hmm. His name means *eagle* in Old Dhawosian. Everywhere he goes, people give him a hero's welcome, and he tells them to prepare for El's Great Awakening—"

"Anyway, one morning, my father asked me who I thought was the true hero of the Night Attack: Nicetas of Valdavia or Scorilus of Steppewynd? It was a hard question. I knew my father admired Scorilus for trying to secure a better lot for his people. I knew he despised the young and stubborn Nicetas, who cut off the trade routes between Steppewynd and the rest of Dhawosia. But Scorilus is the reason our own Kerta is hurting."

Dokina nodded and slipped her hand between her cheek and the pillow.

"In the end, I named Nicetas because he'd won the war. My father told me he was disappointed. I said I was sorry, and he became even more cross because a true king never apologizes. Only later did I grasp that neither Scorilus nor Nicetas was a hero. Instead, the hero was the commoner who had saved his country and his king with a single arrow. Oroles, King Nicetas's new blood brother."

"Uh-huh," Dokina said, her eyes closing now.

"My father has tried to trick me before. He now says not to go into that temple, but what if it houses the guardian spirits of Sehuldava? They could tell me where to find the heart of the city…Tomorrow morning, I'll ask Avezinas to let me read the scrolls and codices he keeps in his library. I must learn all there is about that temple—before Syrmos does. Dokina? Dokina?"

So easy for Dokina to fall asleep. "Sweet dreams," Andrada whispered and blew the candle on the small table by the bed.

The more she thought about it, the more it looked like her father hadn't warned her off a forbidden path but given her a cryptic clue.

Chapter Six

The Book of Andrada

Over the summer, Andrada had come to appreciate the Roman codex, with pages that could be turned and marked, compared to the Greek scroll, which had to be unrolled and read through the small window between the two rods. It took a long time to find something in a scroll and only a moment to check a bookmarked page in a codex. While Syrmos was out in the streets, asking people about the heart of the city and getting nowhere, Andrada sat in the library of the New Temple of Sehul, studying.

The Old Temple of Sehul had been built by the founders of Sehuldava to capture the light of the sun on a high holy day. The light would enter the temple through a small window and reach the inner chamber. Mortals were refused entrance except on the sacred day when the sun unlocked the inner chamber with its beam of light. But the parchments were silent about that day. It couldn't have been midsummer. There hadn't been enough time for Andrada to discover she had to go to the temple on the very first day of the King's Challenge. There were only two high holy days left before the Festival of the Renewed Sun: midfall and midwinter. So Andrada waited for the sun and moon to balance at midfall to make her first trip there.

At first light, while Dokina and the nurse were still asleep, she put on boots and threw a thick woolen cloak over her new women's clothes. To defend against evil mountain spirits, she filled her pockets with black salt. She lit a lantern in the kitchen and sneaked out of the king's house through the servants' entrance.

The air grew cooler as she climbed terrace after terrace, passing dwellings and gardens. At the north gate, she spotted the gatekeeper in his house, watching the road through a window hole. The Artisans' Quarter around them was quiet, and any movement would attract his attention. So Andrada hid behind a thick tree, covered her lantern with her cloak, and waited.

She was shivering by the time the keeper yawned and went inside. Andrada sprung to her feet and ran past the gate as fast as her long skirts allowed, until she was up on the cobbled road beyond the Artisans' Quarter—the forbidden path to the old temple. The city of Sehuldava was now hidden behind pine trees, and the path ahead smelled sweet and unsullied in the quiet hour before dawn. She climbed by the light of her lantern, still getting reacquainted with the sensation of her legs touching under her woolen skirts.

The road turned, the trees thinned, and the slope leveled. Against the dark blue sky, the Old Temple of Sehul appeared. It looked nothing like the new temple, with its Greek-style sandstone columns and pediment. This was a low mound covered in slabs of limestone, built into the mountain like a cave. Around it, the city walls stood in good repair, topped with sharp spikes to keep out the beasts of the forest.

Andrada walked past standing stones, some fallen on their side, all carved with spirals, swirls, and circles that evoked the air spirits that dwelled in sacred places. She brought her lantern close to the carvings. If the stones had ever been painted or varnished, the rain, snow, wind, and sun had bleached them clean ages ago.

From everything she had read, the entrance of a sun temple should point east, and a well-placed standing block should shield its entry corridor from direct sunlight. She found the standing block, carved with swirls. And there was the square opening above the entrance, admitting Sehul's light into the inner chamber on the temple's high holy day. Two steps separated the standing block from the entrance. Andrada could peer in, but she worried she'd anger the guardian spirits.

She waited for the dawn, until roosters began crowing in the city below. As she watched, the right side of the temple turned a deep yellow, but the rising sun didn't hit the small window.

For a moment, Andrada couldn't breathe. The temple didn't capture the rising sun on midfall day. Midwinter day was her last hope before the Festival of the Renewed Sun. If the temple didn't unlock its secrets then, she'd be forced to drink a cup of deadly water. Even worse, she'd let her father down. Now that she had his love, she couldn't lose it, not ever. She wished she still had tears to ease her heartbreak.

At last, she caught her breath and was able to think. She'd come back on midwinter, yes, but she needed a fallback plan. She'd follow Syrmos's example and talk to the people of Sehuldava in the meantime.

For three moons, Andrada split her time between the temple library and the people of Sehuldava, who told her stories and legends and nursery rhymes. They shared their worries and their hopes with her but couldn't point to the beating heart of the city. She looked everywhere: the marketplace, the square, the workshop.

One day, she sat in the courthouse, where the judge listened to a merchant and a shoemaker. Their grievance was about a sack of grain bought from Moesia but not delivered because the price had gone up. While Andrada saw justice delivered, she didn't find the heart of Sehuldava in the courthouse.

Another day, she crossed into the Artisans' Quarter and walked to the city brothel, an establishment many wanted closed but that always paid its taxes. She hoped the place where people went for love, as Dokina had explained, would also know something about the heart. The keeper welcomed her in and asked if she preferred a man or a woman companion, or perhaps both. Mortified, Andrada forgot all about the heart of the city and bolted out.

One morning, she went to the New Temple and prayed with the sick for divine healing. But when she saw the dead taken out of the temple's infirmary, she knew she wouldn't find the beating heart of the city there.

She returned to the library. One evening, she found a poem by Sappho of Lesbos, whose words spoke of a woman and a man embracing, while the poet watched them. *The sweetness of her voice as she talks, the sweetness of her laughter...makes my heart shake inside my breast... A look at that beautiful woman, and I can't speak any longer, as my tongue goes silent...*

Andrada kept reading, a sudden flush on her face.

...all at once a subtle fire races under my skin...

...my eyes can't see a thing, and a whirring whistle thrums at my hearing...

...cold sweat covers me, and a trembling takes hold of me all over...

...I'm greener than the grass is and appear to myself to be little short of dying...

There was a heart beating behind those words, of a nature unknown to Andrada yet familiar. But it wasn't the heart of Sehuldava.

The only place still left to search was the Old Temple of Sehul. Before dawn on midwinter day, Andrada and Dokina set out for the highest terrace of the city. They took a roundabout way through frozen orchards and along the fortress wall, avoiding the prying eyes of the north gate-keeper. The snow crunched under their boots, and the air smelled of wood smoke rising from the lower terraces.

When the temple mound came into sight, Andrada ran up to the entrance. "No, no, no...It's not a midwinter temple either." Yet the rising sun hit closer to the square window above the entrance than it had at midfall.

"You roused me from my warm bed for nothing," Dokina said, "and on a morning when Auntie lets me sleep in on account of Sehul's holy day. If we go back now, I might get some shut-eye before she wakes up."

Andrada kicked at the snow in frustration. Whatever the guardian spirits would do to her if she disturbed them in their home, it couldn't be worse than a cup of deadly water in ten days. Her father would see how hard she had tried and would still love her when they met again in the Underworld.

"No, Andrada, don't go in!" Dokina yelled. "It might be full of rats. Oh, dear gods, I hate those squirmers."

"Rats?" Andrada said. "You can't be scared of rats. They're like birds with no wings. And they're everywhere."

A twig snapped under her foot in the snow. The same sound echoed from the temple mound but also from behind her. She spun around. There was no one there, but her stomach balled up in an icy knot.

Dokina pulled out her mother's small crystal from the leather pouch around her neck and gave it a kiss. "Can we go now? Please?" She flinched and turned around. "Who's there?"

A voice came back from the temple's entrance. "Who's there?"

"Let's go." Dokina grabbed Andrada's arm. "Evil spirits have taken over this gods-forsaken place."

"It's only an echo, Dokina."

"And what's an echo if not the voice of mischievous spirits?"

Andrada's pockets were full of black salt to protect her from them. "Here, have some." She took a pinch and rubbed it on their foreheads with spit.

Dokina wasn't soothed though. "You said it yourself. This isn't a midwinter temple. This isn't the day for us to be here."

"Then when? The King's Challenge is upon us, and there are no more holy days left in the year. I don't yet have the answer for my father."

"But you do; you've learned so much about your people. That's the heart of the city. The chieftains won't make you drink deadly water when you have the people of Sehuldava on your side."

Andrada wanted to believe that.

It was early morning, six days before the end of the year, and the beginning of the Festival of the Renewed Sun. Andrada stood at the window, downhearted, watching the servants clean the snow in Mount Kogalan's

Square and decorate the leafless trees with lanterns. She didn't know the answer to the King's Challenge, and she could almost taste the deadly water on her tongue. She assumed it was bitter, though she couldn't quite imagine being dead and going to the Underworld, where Queen Pegrina dwelled. Her best chance now was to proclaim the people of Sehuldava as the heart of the city and dare the chieftains to punish her for it. Syrmos would do the same. What happened next to both of them would be the gods' will.

A group of men entered the square, with Andrada's father leading the way. Her heart jumped. She had to see him, to get a sign from him about the King's Challenge. She stumbled over the embroidery frame on the floor, avoided the chamber pot by a hair, threw her cloak over her shoulders, and ran out the door.

Outside, men in fur coats gathered in the center of the square.

"Careful, careful!" Several hands strained to lift the top of the fountain of Mount Kogalan. They set the limestone piece to the side.

Andrada stepped closer and caught her father's eye. He gave her the warmest smile she had ever seen from him, a sign she must be doing well on the King's Challenge. She nodded back, relieved.

She glanced at the fountain. It seemed it had been altered. A lead pipe rose from the center of its base, with a wick sticking out.

"With this new mechanism," a young man said, "the city of Sehuldava will be ready for the Festival of the Renewed Sun." He was but a few years older than Andrada, had dark skin and curly hair cropped short, Roman style. His Dhawosian sounded different from the Kertan dialect.

"I don't understand, Master Apollonius," Avezinas said. "How will this fire burn for twelve days with no one watching over it?"

"As long as there is oil in the underground reservoir we built, it will, Your Holiness. And at the beginning of the new year, after we put out all the lights, the king will use this wick dial here to rekindle the fire. Please allow me to demonstrate."

Andrada wondered if this fountain could be the heart of her city. In summer, it gave its people clean, fresh water. And starting this winter, thanks to this Master Apollonius, it would give them light too, holding the sacred flame needed for the Festival of the Renewed Sun.

"If anything goes wrong with this fire," Avezinas said, "the Three Divines won't bless us into the new year." He turned to Andrada's father. "My king, we've used the brazier in the temple for so long—"

"And last year, we almost set the temple on fire. This is progress, Avezinas, and the gods love people's ingenuity. Master Apollonius, you've traveled the Roman world from Damascus to Ravenna. Tell Avezinas your gods are pleased with the Roman people's love of contraptions."

"Indeed, Your Holiness." Master Apollonius turned to one of his men, who passed him a small oil lamp. He brought the flame close to the wick in the center of the bowl but stopped short of lighting the fire, staring at Andrada. "This is a fountain of sacred fire. I must first ask the woman to leave."

"Father?" Andrada waited for a long moment, her cheeks and ears burning.

Her father waited too, his smile gone. All she could do was shake her head—the gold hoops in her ears trembling—and turn away. She despised those men who saw her as just another woman, not the future queen of Kerta. This Master Apollonius, she would punish him or, better still, forgive him—after he begged for mercy.

She wandered through the snowy streets of Sehuldava, her breath loud inside her head and visible before her. Through her skirts, the cold gripped her calves, and she missed her woolen trousers.

When she looked up at last, she found herself in front of the north gate of Sehuldava. The air smelled of roasted meat and incense from the Artisans' Quarter. A fire burned in the square, where the gatekeeper and his son turned a boar on a spit, too busy to notice Andrada heading up the mountain.

No one followed her. When she reached the path between the pine trees, she started hiking. On the highest terrace of the fortress, she walked to the temple mound, and there was Sehul Himself, breaking through the clouds.

The snow-lined window above the entrance was bathed in sunshine. Which meant the inner chamber was now lit with sacred light. Andrada couldn't believe her eyes. The sun temple had come to life now, six days before the end of the year, midmorning. It was the start of the Festival of the Renewed Sun, when Sehul revealed Himself as an invincible god after being at His most diminished for three straight days.

Andrada felt that blend of awe and terror she had read about in sacred texts but had never experienced. She sensed the gods' presence around her. They wanted her to go in now, before the sun shifted, to find the heart of the city and complete the King's Challenge.

Sifting through the black salt in her pocket, she rounded the standing stone in front of the entrance and stepped into a narrow, dark corridor. The stone outside blocked most of the daylight coming in, leaving the small window as the brightest source.

A swarm of yellow and green sprites danced in front of Andrada's eyes, showing her the way. She took a pinch of black salt from her pocket, mixed it with spit, and rubbed it on her forehead. Her first steps were slippery. Then the snow was gone, and the ground turned dry under her boots.

The corridor was low and climbing into darkness. She followed the ascending slope, feeling the cold stone walls with her hand. She looked behind to see that the temple entrance was now a dim line in the distance, but the lintel window above it was still bright. Sehul's light reached her, drawing a big spot on her chest. She stepped to the side, and the light shot past her, along the rising passage. She continued up, and when she turned around again, the beam of light touched the hem of her skirt.

At the end of the corridor, she found the narrow entrance to the temple's inner chamber. She stepped inside into complete darkness. Her heart sank. She had missed the light by just a few moments. And she didn't even have a lantern with her.

The sacred chamber couldn't be big because the walls whispered close by with a faint buzz, like a swarm of bees. She wasn't scared though. Evil spirits wouldn't sound like that.

She took a few steps into the chamber, and the place lit up. Of course. Her long skirts had been blocking the light. Where she had stood before, the beam of sunshine entered the circular chamber, just above the ground.

She didn't have much time. As the sun shifted, the beam would no longer hit the small window, and the inner chamber would fall dark again. She had to find the heart of the city.

Zigzag and spiral carvings decorated the chamber walls. The ceiling was high, a corbeled vault narrowing to a point like a beehive. Three alcoves opened into the rounded wall.

In the left alcove, on a stone drum, was a familiar terra-cotta altar with the hollow-headed Ea and El wearing crystal necklaces. Before the altar lay a clay urn engraved with gilded spirals. Small black statuettes of Sehul's sun, Mehnot's moon, and Heusos's twin stars hung on chains from the edges of the urn's painted lid. It was an ash urn, but whose? Kerta was the only Dhawosian kingdom that burned its dead. Flat stretches of land for graveyards were hard to find, but there was plenty of wood on the mountain slopes. So these must be the ashes of a Kertan. No matter; the urn couldn't be Sehuldava's heart.

Andrada backed away to the third alcove, opposite the first. On the stone drum, a dozen heads made of painted marble were stacked like cabbages at the market. On the floor and against the alcove's walls, wooden panels in all sizes showed colorful variants of Queen Pegrina's face. The last time Andrada had destroyed the queen's likeness, she had won back her father. Was she supposed to do something with one of those portraits? She looked at each of them. No, there was no life in any of them, let alone a heart.

She turned to the central alcove. On the stone drum, a crystal bell as big as her fist scattered the sunlight. She glanced around. Nothing moved. With unsteady hands, she picked up the bell. There was no dust mark left in its place. The stone drum was as clean as an ancestral shrine. Inside the bell, a small crystal sphere hung from a crystal chain, and on the lip of the bell, the word ONE was engraved in Greek script.

"Are you the heart of Sehuldava?" she whispered.

In her hands, the bell rang—not a tiny clink, but a loud sound that bounced around the chamber, behind Andrada's back, above her head, beneath her feet, deep into her bones. The air vibrated like a heartbeat as the chamber grew dimmer.

Yes, that was the true heart of Sehuldava, no doubt about it.

The sun slipped away, and in the darkness that fell, Andrada listened to the bell, still ringing like a whisper in her hand.

Yet something was wrong because she now felt dizzy. Her stomach balled up as though she had drunk from a cup of deadly water.

She remembered what she had read about this temple in the library. Mortals couldn't be here in the absence of sunlight. She was sure the guardian spirits had gathered around her. They'd grab her and drag her to the Underworld because she was trespassing. She shrieked, terrified, and the bell slipped from her trembling fingers.

She patted the stone drum, searching for the bell, which she could still hear whispering from everywhere. Something that felt like the claw of a night spirit touched her. She shrieked again and stumbled back.

Her father had warned her to stay away from this place. Not to trick her but to protect her. More claws grazed her in the dark. With clipped breath, she followed the wall around the chamber to the opening of the dark corridor.

In the dying echo of the crystal bell, she begged the gods who had brought her here, "Forgive my trespassing."

She ran along the descending slope to the growing daylight, until she was outside again, her eyes hurting from the sudden brightness.

The sun was now gone, and the sky was covered in gray clouds. A blizzard gained strength with Andrada's every panting breath.

She ran down the path between the pine trees. At the bottom of the slope, a young man studied the ground, looking around, covering his face against the harsh wind. Andrada ducked behind a tree. What was Syrmos doing here? Had he followed her, tracking her prints in the snow? It looked like he had lost her trail because of the blizzard.

A thick flake landed on Andrada's nose. Another clung to her eye-lashes, and another, and another, until the snow was falling so fast, she couldn't see around her. She could only hear the rhythm of her own ragged breath. Had the gods heard her words? Were They not just forgiving her trespassing but also erasing the signs of it?

Awe and terror descended upon her again. If this blizzard was the gods' doing, it would be the first time They had ever answered her prayers.

On the morning of the last day of the year, Andrada was summoned to a meeting with Avezinas. At first, she thought the temple servant would take her to the New Temple of Sehul to prepare her for the Ceremony of the Renewed Sun. She was ready with her answer about the people being the heart of the city. Instead, they took the path to the temple library.

The fire burned in the hearth, and Avezinas sat at a table. Everything looked so familiar, yet there was nothing ordinary about this meeting.

Avezinas looked dour.

"How did I fail?" Andrada whispered as she stopped before him.

He shot her a bitter glance. "How do you think? You entered the Old Temple of Sehul."

"Did Syrmos tell you I went there?"

"The guard in the vault under the temple heard the bell and saw you leaving on the day of the snow blizzard. When an intruder makes a sound, the whole inner chamber trembles in unison."

A quivering chamber. That would explain the dizziness she had felt that day. "Why did my father have to mention that temple at all?"

"That was part of the challenge, to see if his future heir would obey his orders. A good ruler always listens to wiser voices. As a girl, it should've been easier for you to follow instructions."

In the back of her mind, Andrada knew she should be terrified about her impending death, but anger prevailed. "You're telling me the challenge was to *not* stray from the beaten path? My father admires people who take chances and do bold things. His beloved Hannibal won impossible battles, didn't he? Scorilus went to war for his people, right? And the King's Challenge was to see if I could just sit on my arse and do nothing?"

"It wasn't nothing, Princess. The challenge was getting to know your people, the heart of the city."

Andrada felt like throwing up. It really had been as simple as Dokina had said. No false choices, no hidden meanings. "You just revealed the answer," she whispered.

"It doesn't matter now," Avezinas said. "Your place in the challenge is forfeit."

"But I have the answer! The people of Sehuldava will agree with me when I proclaim them the heart of our city."

"And that's why King Cothelas won't allow you to speak today. We can't have our people and our chieftains fighting over you during the sacred ceremony. The prosperity of the new year depends on the gods' benevolence during the Festival of the Renewed Sun." He sighed. "I'm sorry, Princess. You failed the King's Challenge."

"And Syrmos won?"

"If he delivers the right answer, yes."

Andrada stared at her former tutor for a long moment. "So, what now? A cup of deadly water? Today?"

"Chiefs Rubobostes and Comosicus must be present when the deadly water is passed to those who deserve it. Lucky for you, they failed to arrive before the snow blocked the mountain passes. So you have until the beginning of spring."

Andrada knew how to ride fast, how to lose her chasers, and how to fight them. She had prepared for the King's Challenge.

Avezinas stood up. "Don't even think of running away, or your nurse will be put to death. And you'll spend the rest of your short life in prison."

Dokina's story about the nurse's scar didn't seem so farfetched now.

"I won't go anywhere," Andrada said. "Just leave her out of this."

Avezinas nodded. "And if you think of taking your own life, not only will you end up in the worst part of the Underworld as someone who angered the gods, but your nurse will still be put to death."

"I won't," Andrada said, exhausted. "Can I see my father now?"

As he had done years ago, Avezinas shook his head. "The king is now in seclusion, preparing for tonight's ceremony. You must wait until he sends for you."

Syrmos had delivered the right answer to the King's Challenge, Dokina told Andrada. During the Ceremony of the Renewed Sun, Syrmos stood before the people of Sehuldava, declared them the heart of the city, and was celebrated by cheering crowds as the chosen heir of Kerta. The taste in Andrada's mouth was bitter, and her heart pumped like that of a chased rabbit.

During the first days of the new year, she went around the city as before, waiting for her father to send for her. Everywhere, people looked at her as if she were already on her way to the Underworld. Some even asked her to take messages to their loved ones. Andrada listened, swallowed her pain, and promised to deliver.

But hope grew in her heart as the days lengthened. She spent more time in the temple library, ignoring Avezinas's pained glances and learning about the crystal she had found in the old temple. People used it in amulets throughout Dhawosia, but could it do more than ward off evil spirits? Could it help her avoid a cup of deadly water?

One manuscript said crystal came from the tears of the sky god El, shed during His Small Awakenings, when He looked down at the world and saw the wrong in it. Another spoke of a crystal amulet that took the words of a mortal to a divine being's ear. If crystal could do that, who had answered Andrada's prayer? The terrifying powers that had brought down a blizzard over the city in the blink of an eye belonged to only a handful of gods.

Andrada had nothing to lose. So, on the first day of spring, she headed to the old temple. If the guardian spirits let her in, she hoped to ring the crystal bell again and pray to be saved from death by poison.

She had planned to go alone, but Dokina would have none of it, though her courage waned by the time they arrived at the Old Temple of Sehul.

"What if a guard comes while you're inside?" Dokina said, standing in the fresh snow.

"Then…howl like a wolf. I'll hear you," Andrada said, holding a lantern.

Dokina clasped the amulet pouch hanging from her neck. "What if a real wolf attacks?"

Andrada rounded the standing block and entered the narrow corridor.

"Don't be long," Dokina called, "or we'll be late for the midday meal and right on time for a tongue-lashing from Auntie!"

The ground in the corridor was dry, the walls cold, the air stale. Holding the lantern, Andrada headed to the temple's inner chamber and then to the central alcove. The bell was back on the stone drum. The guard in the vault had likely set it back in its place. Everything else was as before: the terra-cotta altar, the ash urn, Queen Pegrina's portraits.

Andrada waited in the center of the chamber for the guardian spirits to appear as before, buzzing like bees around her. Her breath was shallow, her heart hammering. After a while, she understood. She was already marked for the Underworld, so the spirits wouldn't bother with her now. She caught her breath and set the lantern down.

She picked up the bell, the word ONE engraved on it. One what? One wish? One divine being to hear it? The bell glimmered with reflected candlelight. She shook it, and it rang that clear sound that looped around her. If her father's guard was still around, Andrada didn't care.

"Take away the cup of deadly water…" she whispered.

The bell kept ringing, and the chamber quivered. The shadows on the walls and floor trembled with it, and Andrada felt dizzy again. She put the bell back in its place on the stone drum, then closed her eyes, knowing she'd been heard.

"You can't sleep here," Dokina was saying, holding the lantern. "Get up, Andrada, get up!"

The howling of not one but dozens of wolves surrounded the temple.

Andrada held on to Dokina's hand and pulled herself up. She rubbed her sleepy eyes. They were alone.

She followed Dokina outside to the bright snow, where birds circled the sky, squawking and cackling. Dokina dragged her along to the back of the temple, where the mound became one with the mountain. There they climbed on the mound, grabbing branches and rocks, as wolves kept howling down in the inner city.

"At least Auntie won't be angry with us for missing her meal," Dokina said, standing on the icy temple roof.

From there, Andrada watched the north gate over evergreen treetops. The air rang with iron-tired cartwheels and iron horseshoes on cobblestones. Dozens of howling dracos flew high at the top of spears.

"Chiefs Comosicus and Rubobostes are finally here?" Andrada said, knowing the answer.

The bell hadn't answered her prayer. The chieftains were there for her execution. For the first time, she panicked.

There was still time for her to run away. She could jump from the temple roof over the city wall and hide in the forest. She had nothing with her though—no weapons, no food, just a lantern. But that would have to do. Then she remembered her nurse would be put to death.

"Princess Andrada," a man called from below. "We've been looking for you."

She looked down and saw Chief Wodan, the army commander, with a group of soldiers.

"King Cothelas sends for you, my princess."

It was over. Unable to utter any words, Andrada climbed down, holding her skirts. Chief Wodan helped her land on her feet, and together they started on the path back to the city. Dokina followed them, wiping her eyes.

Andrada didn't know how long she had walked in silence, with only one terrifying thought looping through her mind. *I'll die today.*

At the north gate, she saw a convoy of riders and carriages bearing the Valdavian blue standard adorned with a charging aurochs. *His hooves heavier than hammers, his body larger than the largest bull's, his horns deadlier than daggers*, the songs went. The convoy rolled up the ramp into Sehuldava. Townspeople gawked at the strangers, with their untrained Valdavian horses snorting and neighing at the pretend wolves of the Kertan standards.

"That's King Nicetas," Chief Wodan said, pointing to a black walnut carriage. "We're giving him a royal Kertan welcome."

It wasn't the chieftains then? "Where are you taking me?" she finally thought to ask.

"To sit at the head of the feast hall and greet our guests," Chief Wodan said.

CHAPTER SEVEN

The Valdavian Chronicle

King Nicetas dragged his feet behind his blood brother Oroles. They followed the Kertan servant through a crowd of courtiers, past a blackened wall adorned with a scorched wooden panel. He couldn't tell if the green eyes in the painting belonged to a man or a woman. But he wondered why Cothelas the Bald wanted to look at that strange remnant of a face from his throne across the chamber. Not the first strange thing he had seen in Kerta, after those howling dracos that spooked his horses. He had heard of them from songs and legends, but feeling their eerie voices pound his chest earlier had unsettled him.

They stopped before a door flanked by torches in wolf-head brackets of Kertan gold.

"No weapons in the council chamber, King Nicetas," the servant said.

"There's still time to turn back, my lord," Oroles said.

"No, it's time to choose peace of mind," Nicetas said. "For me, for everybody." He unbuckled the belt that held his sica sword and his Roman dagger and left it with his brother.

As the door thumped shut behind him, he saw Cothelas the Bald alone at a grand stone table, studying a whitewood codex. The Kertan king raised his piercing dark eyes.

"Nicetas of the Carpi tribe," he said, "son of Anartus. You've answered my call." His Dhawosian was as crisp and clear as a cold stream in the woods. "Which means you want to marry my daughter Andrada."

"Indeed."

"Come join me."

Nicetas sat at Cothelas's right. A map of Dhawosia and its neighbors lay on the table. It was a rough piece of work with entire swaths grayed out in crosshatch over Sarmatia in the east and the Great Plains in the west.

Cothelas poured wine into gold cups.

The scent hit Nicetas—it was Moesian wine, the same wine he'd had in his tent during the Night Attack. In an instant, he saw himself again waking up to clatter and smoke and the smell of spilled wine. The flames licked his skin through his clothes. Scorilus, clad in bronze armor, broke into the tent, wielding a falx pole arm with both hands. The ground trembled under his heft.

Nicetas grabbed his sica and fought back with all his strength. His shorter, curved blade even hooked and yanked the falx from Scorilus's hands. But then the Steppewynder grabbed Nicetas's beard, forced him to his knees, twisted his wrist, and squeezed the sica from his hand. Scorilus pushed him down, trapping him under a mountain of armor. Nicetas wanted to punch, but Scorilus gripped his arms. He wanted to bite, but Scorilus was covered in scales. He wanted to shout, but Scorilus was crushing his throat.

A horse with its mane on fire tore through the tent's canvas, and Nicetas grabbed that chance to throw Scorilus off. He groped around in the grass for a blade. There had to be a weapon on the ground—a shard from the broken wine pitcher, a bread knife, anything. He glanced back up and saw a dagger stabbing down at him.

He rolled away from its path, but a blaze had ripped through his left side.

Nicetas hated remembering that cursed night—and he had grown better at keeping the memories at bay. But sometimes, like now, all it took was a whiff of Moesian wine to throw him back into that nightmare.

"King Nicetas," Cothelas said, raising his cup. "To your health!"

Nicetas held his breath and gulped some wine, then wiped his mouth with the back of his hand. Short stubble scraped his skin—he'd never grow his beard again.

"As you might know," Cothelas said, "your war with Scorilus—and most of all, your retaliation—have left my mountains without Steppewynder miners and my flocks without Steppewynder shepherds. Sending my iron, gold, lead, and wool to Roma grows harder every year."

Nicetas didn't need an explanation. Back home, the lack of Steppewynder farmhands had left Valdavia hurting for grain. He had his own chieftains to appease, but he'd never slacken the noose around Scorilus's neck. He'd never reopen the trade posts along their border.

Cothelas crossed his arms; his leather bracers were incised with wolf heads. "Why not return us all to the times before the Night Attack?"

Nicetas shook his head. "Those days are over."

"But you've been starving your own people," Cothelas said, sounding annoyed. "Your grain rotted in the fields after the war. Now your fields are left untilled. If we're weak, Roma will swallow us all."

"There's another way." Another way to bring his kingdom back to prosperity while still keeping Scorilus locked out of the Dhawosian world. But Nicetas needed Cothelas's help. And Cothelas the Bald needed a husband for his only daughter.

"The armies of the new Emperor Vespasianus," Nicetas said, "aren't yet ready for more lengthy campaigns. Not after laying waste to a kingdom on the shores of the Levantine Sea less than two years ago. So the emperor wants me to defend his northern borders against barbarian tribes."

"Barbarian tribes?" Cothelas seemed puzzled. "Isn't that what they call us?"

Nicetas nodded. Valdavians whose lives had been upended by the closing of trade routes crossed the frozen Danubius River in winter to plunder the Roman settlements of Moesia. Nicetas's people were the barbarians Vespasianus wanted protection against—and he had to get it from Nicetas. The Romans, who couldn't control all the tribes they fought against on their ever-expanding border, had to accept this poor state of affairs. It was a political reality Nicetas had been taking advantage of, unsure how long the Romans would tolerate it.

"Roman gold will start coming in as soon as our soldiers—Valdavian and Kertan—start patrolling the northern banks of the Danubius River for the empire to see. Then you can hire the Germanic tribes of the Great Plains as miners and shepherds. You might even get Roman laborers in from Moesia—as long as we keep the northern border of the empire safe from us barbarians."

Cothelas's face didn't betray any emotion. "How much gold are we talking about?"

Nicetas tapped the map on the table. "The Danubius is a long river, and the forests on its northern banks are hard to patrol. The emperor understands that."

"Yet I fear you'll use the Roman gold and my soldiers not only to protect the empire's borders but also to keep Steppewynder laborers from ever reaching us here in Kerta."

Nicetas took a sip of that awful Moesian wine. "Our alliance will allow you to deliver the ore Roma expects from you. You won't need Scorilus anymore."

Cothelas scratched his chin. "The king won't like our alliance."

"May he soon join the god Azemel in the Underworld." Nicetas downed his cup.

Cothelas emptied his too. "When we're family, you'll have my soldiers. And maybe things will return to normal. To be honest, I prefer Kertan salt from my own mines to the Black Sea brine I'm now buying from Roman Moesia."

Nicetas pushed back his chair. "Then we're agreed."

"Not yet," Cothelas said. "I'm claiming your firstborn son."

"My...firstborn son?" Bedding the Kertan princess wasn't something he planned to do anytime soon.

"My first grandson. You'll send him to me to be brought up as a Kertan. The gods willing, my daughter will give you other healthy sons." Cothelas smiled. "Don't make me wait too long."

Nicetas didn't have a choice, caught between Vespasianus and Scorilus.

"Agreed..." he said.

"Then let's drink to this day," Cothelas said, pouring more wine. "To the tribes of Andori and Carpi coming together." He handed a full cup to Nicetas. "Time for you to meet your bride."

The Book of Andrada

Andrada hurried to prepare for the Valdavian guests, still shocked by the turn of events. Her nurse helped her put on an embroidered dress and the gold chain with the crystal pendant. After a quick hug, Andrada ran out the door, a sudden joy at the feeling of air reaching her lungs. She was still alive, and it felt great to run.

She entered the feast hall still pushing in her gold-and-emerald hairpins, just as her father and King Nicetas arrived. The Valdavian king was shorter than she had imagined from stories about the Night Attack. The sadness in his blue eyes spoke of his fall under the dagger of a stronger man.

After introductions, he addressed her. "Princess Andrada, word of your beauty and grace has crossed the Carpates Mountains..." His Dhawosian was mellow, like a song. His voice was deep and gentle but as listless as the look in his eyes. "...and brought me here today to ask for your hand in marriage."

"Marriage?" Andrada turned to her father, who nodded.

King Nicetas looked confused at her obvious dismay. "King Cothelas...allow me to present my gift to the princess. Oroles, bring it here."

The hall was spinning around Andrada. Oroles, the hero of the Night Attack, brought a black walnut box with silver fittings. He propped the lid open to reveal a silver diadem encrusted with round sapphires. King Nicetas lifted the diadem over Andrada's head. Her own gold-and-emerald hairpins were in the way, but she guided his hands and stiffened her neck to keep the silver band in place, though it was too large for her head.

She was now betrothed to King Nicetas of Valdavia. Horns blasted, and courtiers burst into cries of joy. Her father took her arm and led her to the tables ahead.

"This is my cup of deadly water?" she whispered to him.

"Yes." He stared ahead. "The chieftains disagreed at first, but the potential of a lucrative alliance with Valdavia changed their minds."

Marriage instead of poison—had the crystal bell answered Andrada's prayer and taken away the cup of deadly water?

"I'd rather have the real thing," she said.

"The time for the Underworld is later. There's much you can still do for your country and for me. And I for you, if ever you find yourself in need."

They reached the royal table laden with baskets of bread and jugs of wine. Andrada's father sat down first, then King Nicetas at his right, and Andrada at his left. The hall filled with chatter and the clinking of knives and cups as the guests settled around trestle tables.

To start the feast, Andrada's father took a swig of wine from a gilded horn bearing the images of Ea and the Three Divines. He then passed it on to King Nicetas, who drank and passed it on to his blood brother Oroles.

The evening meal lasted forever. The panpipes sounded like a lament in Andrada's ears. Her father talked only to King Nicetas while peeling strings of roasted lamb and drinking wine. Andrada's neck was sore with the burden of the sapphire diadem that kept slipping. The fish on her plate looked dry. She kept reaching for the raisins and the flatbread instead and was grateful when the servants cleared the table.

"King Cothelas, may I have a moment with my bride?" King Nicetas said.

Andrada hated that word, but she followed him through the crowded hall, holding on to her diadem. Candles swirled in the corner of her eye in ribbons of incandescence.

They sat on a bench outside the hall, and she waited for him to speak first.

"I hope you'll like Zalmodava, my city," he said, sounding awkward. "You can see the two peaks of Mount Ea-El from everywhere in the fortress."

Andrada could still hear the tambourines, the panpipes, and the drums coming from the depths of the feast hall. She'd wait for the end of that merry tune, and then she'd excuse herself and return to her chamber. Maybe her tears would return that night and offer her some relief from the day's madness.

"My younger brother, Dapyx," King Nicetas said, "I hope he'll be a worthy companion."

Andrada didn't need another companion—she had the nurse and Dokina—but she pretended she cared. "How old is your brother, King Nicetas?"

"Fourteen, an apprentice warrior."

Andrada hoped the tune would end anytime now, but each note toppled the previous, and the melody regrouped and took off again.

"I, too, lost my mother," King Nicetas said, "though not as early in life."

Of all the things he could speak of...

"With your permission..." Andrada sat up and turned to leave. The sapphire diadem slid off her head and fell, clinking against the flagstones.

King Nicetas picked it up and held it out to her. But he seemed unwilling to part with it, just as she didn't want to wear it. She snatched it from his hand and walked away.

On the way to her chamber after that dreadful conversation with her future husband, Andrada ran into Syrmos.

"I was going to enter that old temple too," he said, his eyes downcast. "Because I was desperate. My last hope was for our people to save me if I proclaimed them the heart of the city. But the blizzard stopped me..."

"Don't apologize, Syrmos. You'll make a great heir and king."

Andrada felt better when she reunited with her nurse and Dokina. The fire in the hearth crackled under the smoke hole, warm and welcoming.

The air smelled of sage and burning resin, and the window shutters were closed, dampening the sound of the party.

"Sit here." The nurse showed Andrada to a chair and began pulling the emerald pins from her hair.

Andrada took off the crystal pendant and dropped it in the horse-box.

Dokina picked up King Nicetas's diadem. "Queen of Valdavia." She put the sapphire diadem on Andrada's head, but it sank down to her eyebrows. "Hm. Not a good fit though." She tried it on. "Perfect fit." She twirled around the hearth, her braids flying, the diadem's blue stones sparkling in the candlelight.

"Dokina, stop that," the nurse admonished her.

With a soft knock on the door, two handmaids came in, bringing a red trunk painted with gold wolf heads.

"We must pack now," the nurse said. "The king wants you to be ready tomorrow morning."

"So soon?" At least she'd have Dokina and the nurse with her on the road.

"He said it's better if we don't give the chieftains a chance to change their minds."

The nurse began sorting through garments and old toys, while Andrada watched. She felt like a plant pulled from its dirt, roots and all. The handmaids went through drawers, taking out clothes, folding them, and putting them in the red trunk. Andrada told them to keep a couple of dresses for themselves.

The nurse picked the embroidery frame off the floor and the basket with the thread and needles from the shelf. "Maybe you'll finish a piece of needlework someday."

"Why bother?" Andrada slumped in her chair. "I was supposed to learn that before getting married."

"Dokina," the nurse said, "the princess is upset. Go to the kitchen and bring her a cup of warm milk."

"I have to pack too, you know," Dokina said but left.

"Girls, go wait outside," the nurse said, and the handmaids shuffled out. She closed the door behind them. "Things will be fine, child."

Andrada couldn't see how.

"You're safe now, with your whole life before you." The nurse fidgeted with her black headscarf, a habit she had when feeling anxious. "There's something I must ask you though."

Andrada waited. "Yes?"

"Please let me stay."

"Stay?"

The nurse looked pained, the line of her scar dark on her cheek. "Here in Kerta. Return to Albanor."

Another blow. There was no end to them today. "I don't understand…"

The nurse had always been there to hold Andrada's hand and tell her stories and feed her warm broth when she was sick. To touch her forehead every night with sage-scented fingers so Samca's night spirits wouldn't torment her with bad dreams. To hold her head while she threw up when the food was tainted. To place hot stones wrapped in a towel on her belly when her painful moon affliction returned. Andrada remembered a bad knee scrape after falling from the saddle once. The nurse had been there to dress it with a soothing salve. The nurse had always been there.

"I knew this sad day would come…" The nurse took the horse-box to the red trunk. "But it still hurts."

Andrada followed her, now panicked. "Then come with me. Please."

The nurse kept rearranging things in the trunk. "I can't. I must stay here. The Great Awakening might be upon us."

"What about me?"

"You'll have Dokina…"

Andrada understood at last. "You want to stay with him?"

The nurse frowned. "Not that nonsense about Tzintus again—"

"I meant your dead son…You want to stay here because this is where the wind spirits scattered his ashes. You think you'll see him again after the Great Awakening." Andrada felt betrayed. "You deserved the scar the soldiers gave you."

"The soldiers?" The nurse seemed surprised. "Oh, no. This scar, I gave to myself."

"What? Why would you do that?"

The nurse sighed. "When Samca snatches a baby from the cradle, the gods give the mother something in return so she won't go mad with grief. They call it the gods' mercy: to forget how the pain felt. But I didn't want to forget, so I carved this here, to remember every time I touched my face."

That story was worse than Dokina's, and Andrada didn't quite understand it. "But I need you more than he does. The Great Awakening won't be tomorrow." She opened her arms. "Please come with me to Valdavia, just for a little while..."

"You'll have Dokina with you, child." The nurse's words felt like a blade through the heart.

Andrada wanted to cry. What would a world without the nurse be like? A world without her father? A world with King Nicetas.

"Very well," she said at last. "Go back to your village if that's what you want."

"It's not, child. It's not." The nurse cleared her throat. "Before we part, I must teach you the farewell ceremony for tomorrow morning. That's when your groom will slash through a red-and-white twine tied outside your childhood door. And I must also tell you about that first night...after the wedding."

"I have no need for your advice now," Andrada said.

People were fickle—they died, they left, they stayed behind. Not so the gods. They were there. Always.

With a traveling cloak on her shoulders and the white headscarf of the betrothed tied at the back of her head, Andrada stood in front of the Old Temple of Sehul one last time.

"Please let me in," she asked the guardian spirits. "I swear, I won't bother you ever again."

She held up her lantern, rounded the standing block, and entered the corridor.

The same yellow and green sprites danced ahead, and no one stopped her. In the inner chamber, she caught a glint of crystal from the central alcove. The terra-cotta altar of Ea and El was still in the left alcove, on the stone drum with the ash urn. Andrada took out an incense pouch, opened the strings, and poured half the powder inside the goddess's head, half inside the god's. She lit the incense with the candle in her lantern.

"Forgive me for stealing Your bell," she told Them.

The two censers sputtered and hissed, the smell heavy and sacred, blending sweet basil with pine resin. Ea, the taller head in the crystal necklace, belched a puff of aromatic smoke. The short head crackled and sighed. It sounded as if the gods had forgiven her.

The bell glimmered under Andrada's lantern. Her two earlier wishes had come true, though not how she had expected. The snow blizzard had erased the signs of her trespassing. The cup of deadly water had turned into a wedding convoy. Those wishes had come true in the blink of an eye. If she now asked the bell to make her the queen of Kerta, would a bolt of lightning hit her father and Syrmos on the spot? She wouldn't tempt the gods, no.

She picked up the bell and put it in her pocket. It rang again, that long, clear sound, making the chamber tremble in unison, and she hurried out before growing dizzy. She didn't know if the bell had to ring inside the temple for the divine being to hear her words, but she uttered no new wish. For now, she'd go to Valdavia, where her marriage would be her new apprenticeship. There she'd become a true queen. And one day, she'd return home as the heir her father had once named in a council chamber full of grumbling chieftains.

Andrada and King Nicetas left Sehuldava with their royal retinues. Hers—in wagons and on horseback—was ten times larger than his. Courtiers and diplomats, physicians and priests, artisans and merchants, handmaids, servants, and cooks. Some of them would return to Kerta as soon as their princess was settled in Zalmodava, some would stay for the wedding ceremony, and some would begin a new life in Valdavia together with their queen.

They traveled for days through forests and valleys in the foothills of the Carpates Mountains. Andrada and Dokina spent their time in their bumpy carriage, talking and sleeping. At night, they camped around fires, where Nicetas was always busy with his horses, his people, or his brother.

On the eleventh day, they took a narrow road winding up the rise. It had been almost springtime when they pulled out of Sehuldava, but as they approached the Norland Pass, they headed back into snow.

The pass was a busy carriage route during the summer, one of the only two roads between Valdavia and Kerta wider than a footpath. Now the horses' hooves and the carriages' iron tires echoed alone between the mountain walls.

Andrada opened the carriage shutter and looked out, while Dokina chattered. She smelled the crisp, cold air. She heard no birds in the trees, no critters rustling through last year's brush under the snow. Even the stream that carved the gorge was silent under a sheet of ice. It was as if the mountain spirits glared down at the convoy for disturbing the pass too early in the year.

"Why are we stopping?" Dokina said.

Andrada looked out. Fort Norland stood before them, a massive fortification between the two mountain walls, complete with ramparts and arrow slits.

There was a knock, and King Nicetas opened the carriage door. He wore an overcoat of gray lambskin.

"Time to make an offering to the Valdavian goddess Bendis." He held out his hand, a few falling snowflakes melting on his skin.

Andrada hopped on the dirty snow, just as Nicetas pulled a dagger from his belt. She recoiled, wishing she still had the sica she had left behind in Sehuldava.

Nicetas smiled, his blue eyes cold. "Bendis, the patron goddess of hunters, forests, and wild animals, asks for a lock of hair from each betrothed girl passing through here, as a sign of her purity."

He let go of Andrada's hand and coaxed a short lock of her hair from under her headscarf. The hair didn't resist the blade.

"Now bury it in the ground, Princess Andrada." He placed both the blade and lock of hair in her hands. "Oroles, watch over the princess."

Oroles stood by Andrada as she dug a hole in the frozen ground and buried her lock of hair. She had never spoken to him before. He was taller than Nicetas, had brown hair and eyes, and seemed nice.

She was ready to return to her carriage when Oroles pointed to the mountaintop, where a flittering red dot descended in bounds against the steep limestone wall. It turned into a small bird with a long beak, which then landed and hopped toward them. Its dark back and tail made it hard to spot against the muddy snow when it didn't move, but when it opened its wings, it looked like a huge butterfly with red feathers and white spots around the edges.

"The goddess Bendis is sending us a sign," Oroles said. "Seeing a wall creeper here usually means good luck for the mountain traveler."

"But wall creepers are afraid of people," Andrada said. "This one must be hungry. Or lonely after a long winter."

The bird turned one bead-like eye to Andrada, inching closer with its wings spread a little, ready to take flight. It opened its beak and let out a drawn-out whistle of high and low notes. A sharp echo rang from all directions, like the crystal bell's in the old temple.

"She's telling us we're invading her home," Oroles said.

Out of nowhere, a black eagle swooped in and snatched the wall creeper in its claws. It flapped its wings a few times before disappearing over the trees into the gray clouds.

"Are you harmed, Princess?" Oroles said, looking worried.

"No, no…"

A drop of blood fell on the snow between them.

"A bad omen," Nicetas said, returning. "Bendis isn't happy with our offering." He took Andrada's hand and dragged her toward the west gates of Fort Norland. "We must make amends then. You and I, Princess, we'll cross the pass on foot to show the mountain spirits the respect they demand."

Andrada didn't understand how she had offended the Valdavian deities but was eager to do whatever was needed to appease Them. She followed her future husband into the fort with the rest of their retinue following at a good distance.

Inside the courtyard, soldiers watched them from the ramparts. Laborers tending the cooking fires, the rainwater barrels, and the drying racks moved out of the way in silence.

Andrada and Nicetas left Fort Norland through the east gates. The pass itself was a couple of Roman miles long. Nicetas strode ahead, squeezing Andrada's hand, and after a while, she began walking in lockstep with him. In the west, Kerta moved away with each hairpin turn between the walls of the gorge.

Chapter Eight

The Book of Dapyx

From the depths of the main hall, Prince Dapyx of Valdavia studied the guests who had just arrived at the king's house. Legions of servants hauled trunks in from the carriages lining the Twelve-Pier Bridge. Dapyx told himself again that when he met his brother's bride, he'd keep his changing voice under control and try to stop that silly blush of his from spreading like a rash from cheek to earlobe to neck. Good thing he had just turned fourteen because he could now say he was fifteen without lying too much.

When Princess Andrada of Kerta stepped into the main hall, Dapyx knew her by the white headscarf of the betrothed. She had a pretty face. He'd been hoping she'd be plain—not ugly, but plain—so that, just this once, his brother wouldn't have it all. He approached, hoping she wouldn't be as pretty up close.

A Kertan handmaid took the princess's cloak. There—underneath the gold thread of her high-waist dress, she barely had any breasts at all. She pulled her headscarf off and passed it to her maid. Another flaw: her curly dark hair was short, down to her shoulders, some strange Kertan fashion, no doubt. He'd expected a woman with curves and flowing hair. Instead, he was staring at a tomboy in princess clothes.

It seemed Nicetas wasn't too pleased either. "Princess Andrada, here's my brother Dapyx," he said in passing and went over to see High Priestess Citera, who was in charge of the wedding preparations.

The princess smiled, and dimples formed just above the corners of her mouth. She extended her hand. "Andrada of the Andori tribe."

Only men shook hands, but Dapyx reached out. Just before their fingers could touch, she pulled back, frowning, as if catching her mistake.

She pressed her hand over her heart, on her flat chest—a proper greeting. "Pleased to meet you, Prince."

Her handmaid brought a silver tray, and the princess tore a piece of bread and dipped it in white salt.

"Have a bite, Dokina," the princess said, and her handmaid followed the welcoming custom too.

As the princess chewed, she glanced at Dapyx, and he felt his blush spread all over his face. She wasn't beautiful, at least not like the girls in the Ozana Valley, who sometimes let him sneak a trembling hand under their clothes. But her eyes, the color of emeralds, had a perfect shape, with long eyelashes. And those small breasts...they were alluring, even though they were hard to notice at first.

She licked her lips and smiled. Definitely pretty. Her front teeth pushed against each other, just a little, in the cutest way.

"The king tells me you're an apprentice warrior," she said.

Dapyx had heard the Kertan dialect before, spoken by merchants, but never with such clear diction, like the controlled trot of a beautiful stallion.

"My father sends a gift." She motioned to a servant who held up a huge oval object wrapped in wool cloth. "From his armory."

The servant pulled the cloth off to reveal a ceremonial shield made of Kertan gold encasing a wooden plank the size of a grown man. The servant set it down with a grunt.

Dapyx could never lift that shield, so he didn't even try.

By the twinkle in the princess's eye, she knew it too. "This shield is for after you become a consecrated warrior, my lord." She motioned for her servant to take it away.

The hot rash spread over Dapyx's face. "If only Nicetas had such a shield during the Night Attack," he said, the low tone of his voice leaping to an uneven, girly shrill.

"Princess." Nicetas walked back up to them, cutting Dapyx a side glance. "High Priestess Citera awaits you now. I won't see you until the new moon, for the...wedding."

Dapyx felt pleased by his brother's hesitation at the word *wedding*, but he was sad to see the princess go.

Dokina tried to follow her mistress, but a temple servant blocked her way. The handmaid had dark eyes and a round face. She was pretty like the girls of the Ozana River Valley, but not like Princess Andrada. She squinted around, looking lost, still holding the tray and the princess's headscarf.

Dapyx watched his brother's betrothed follow Citera out of the main hall, to the Temple of Concord. He had never before felt this urge to run after a girl, to stay close to her. They were locking her away for almost a moon to prepare her for the wedding. He had to have something of hers until then. Without a word, he snatched the white headscarf from Dokina and dashed off to his chamber in the men's wing.

The Valdavian Chronicle

Nicetas had made a mistake, and he needed the Valdavian gods to deliver him from it. Since his meeting with Cothelas the Bald, he'd been praying to his favorite goddess, Bendis, to send a sign so he could call off his wedding to the Kertan princess. The dead wall creeper alone wouldn't convince the high priests, who knew Valdavia needed Cothelas's soldiers to keep the Romans peaceable.

On the night of the full moon, Nicetas joined them in the clearing outside the Temple of Concord. They gathered around the limestone bowl to learn the Kertan gods' will. Low clouds blew in from the forest beyond the temple. With the torches extinguished, the priests couldn't divine the signs of Mehnot's moon and Heusos's eyes on the surface of the holy water. They prayed until Sehul's dawn but couldn't catch a glimpse of the Three Divines, as if the Kertan gods didn't want a union that carried the ungodly price of a firstborn son. Nicetas left the clearing with a spring in his step.

Now, if only Bendis could convince Her brother Beleizis—lord of thunder and rain, patron god of Valdavia—to send a bad omen, Nicetas would invoke the will of all the gods and call off the wedding. Cothelas wouldn't be able to claim wrongdoing. He'd be angry, but maybe Roman gold would soothe his bruised honor as soon as their two armies started patrolling the Danubius banks together.

A few days before the new moon, Nicetas added another three hundred troops to the patrol squads watching over the thousands of guests roaming the Ozana Valley. The guests brought wedding gifts in fragrant wooden chests and trading goods in hay-padded crates. They brought the colors and perfumes of Roma, the textures of Sarmatia, and the crafts of Germania, but they also quarreled among themselves and harassed the girls in the Ozana River Valley. Inside the fortified city, under the open skies between the king's house and the Temple of Concord, they sat around campfires, dipping bread in Kertan white salt and pouring Moesian wine from glazed jars. They told stories of land, honor, and kin from the Great Plains in the west to the Tauris Peninsula in the east, but they also relieved themselves all around the temple's sacred grounds.

The gods willing, that madness would be over soon.

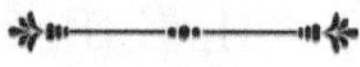

The Book of Andrada

Andrada lost track of day and night under the soot-black ceilings of the Temple of Concord's windowless sacred vaults. The food was always the same: unleavened bread, white salt, and mountain stream water, but the duration of the baths changed, as did the fragrant oils the temple servants rubbed on her body. She was grateful she couldn't cry in front of those stern Valdavian women who forced her to spend her waking hours cleansing, learning, and praying—cleansing her spirit for the sacred union to come, learning how to welcome her husband into her bed and make him laugh with pleasure, and praying to the Valdavian gods to bless her womb with healthy children.

Her dream of becoming the queen of Kerta seemed distant now. She didn't even know which gods to pray to here. Would the Kertan gods listen to prayers uttered on foreign soil? The whitewood box with the crystal bell was inside the red trunk, and she had yet to see it since her arrival.

She missed Dokina more than she had thought she would. Dokina was chatty, yes, but she was a familiar and friendly face. What if she got bored waiting and decided to return to Albanor, to be with her mother and her aunt?

The only light in that darkness came from the moments spent with High Priestess Citera. She had deep, dark eyes that seemed to see into people's hearts. When she rubbed scented oil in Andrada's hair and brushed it with care, Andrada's whole body melted. Citera's warm, soft touch left a faint perfume on Andrada's skin. Not sage like the nurse's hands, but rosewater. When Andrada's painful time returned with the moon's waning crescent, Citera didn't lay warm stones on Andrada's belly but brewed a potion that took the pain away.

Citera's Dhawosian was sweet and soothing, and her words were wise. "While the fertility of Valdavia's crops depends on the correct performance of the sacred royal duties, and while it's your duty to bend to the man's strength, to please him and turn him from a warrior into a father, you must also remind him to honor Ea's womanly essence that lives within you."

Citera's father was a Steppewynder merchant who had moved his household to Zalmodava. To become a high priestess, she'd been cut off from her family as a young boy, made a eunuch, and pledged to the Temple of Concord at the high priest's advice. Citera was grateful for the good life she had here, honoring her true nature. "Sometimes, even the gods don't know how to divide us into two distinct camps," she once said. But she still missed her sisters and her mother, forever out of reach.

Maybe for that reason, she seemed to understand the homesickness ailing Andrada's heart.

"Do you have regrets?" Citera asked one evening after prayers, her dark hair framing her pale face.

Andrada thought of the time when Chief Gerulas had been sent to his death at the Iron Gates because of her. She thought of failing the King's Challenge. "A few," she whispered.

"Forget them." A light smile parted Citera's lips. "The gods have bigger plans for you. Soon, you'll be the queen of Valdavia."

"I want to be a good queen," Andrada said. "Can you teach me how?"

Citera was quiet for a moment. "Though our king pretends otherwise, Valdavia needs all its Dhawosian brothers. Roma is marching. Cities and temples are falling, and we're in Roma's path, more so than Kerta is. We need Scorilus of Steppewynd too."

"But he tried to kill Nicetas."

"Scorilus attacked us because his people had been hurting for a long time. Now Nicetas is trying to starve them. There's no work for them in Sarmatia in the east, only here, with us." She looked into Andrada's eyes. "If you persuade King Nicetas to reopen the trade routes with Steppewynd, you'll strengthen Valdavia against the Roman menace. You'll be the queen this country needs."

The Valdavian Chronicle

On the morning of his wedding, Nicetas hoped for word from Beleizis to call it off. Dressed in silver-threaded clothes and a blue wool cloak, he strode through the crowd gathered outside the Temple of Concord, whispering another prayer. He arrived at the sundial, where his older brother Zyraxes, high priest of Beleizis, waited to deliver his god's omen.

With his gnarled aurochs-headed staff, Zyraxes didn't just look ten years older than Nicetas—he looked ancient. He wore dark robes cinched with hemp cord and tied his gray hair on the nape of his neck in a thin ponytail.

Nicetas climbed on the sundial and greeted Zyraxes, who today had a smile in his gray-spiked beard. The shadow of the sundial's central pole lined up with the dusty groove. It was time. Zyraxes faced the crowd, his staff raised. A temple servant took out the sundial's pole, and another brought linen towels and two silver trays and set them on a barrel table.

The crowd parted. A man holding a basket filled with grass led a white bull to the sundial. The bull was as majestic as its cousin, the aurochs of the mountains, and it obeyed its master. Its loose jaw swung from side to side, its eyes huge and at peace.

The bull master climbed first on the sundial, and his beast heaved itself up next, its hooves clopping on stone. The man set the basket down and from under the grass pulled a hatchet, holding it down along his leg.

Zyraxes raised his staff and chanted, "Lord Beleizis, look down on us with mercy, receive our humble offering, and give us the sign of Your blessing for our king and the woman he wants to marry."

The bull master caressed the beast's forehead, and the bull closed its huge brown eyes before it could see the hatchet's hammerhead hit. A crack. The bull staggered, its knees gave way, and as it fell to the ground, its master flipped the hatchet to the axe blade and slit its jugular with a backhand swing. Blood erupted from the wound. The bull master forced the white beast down, the gash in its throat against the sundial, into the central hole. He threw his shoulders and legs across the jerking mass and pinned it down.

The grooves on the sundial filled with red streams parting under the bull's head and rejoining in a large drain around the base. A temple servant put a clay urn to the mouth of the drain to gather the warm blood. The bull's body twitched, and rivulets of blood advanced in small waves to the rhythm of the pumping heart, weaker and weaker each time. The smell of fresh blood reminded Nicetas of hunting in the forests around Twin Willows.

The bull's tongue hung to the side, bits of grass still sticking to its raspy surface. The eyes, wide-open and brown, grew cloudier until they froze, reflecting the sky.

Temple servants began beating large drums with wooden mallets. The bull master got back on his feet and raised his hatchet. With a few blows, he severed the bull's head, grabbed it by the horns, and set it on a silver tray. He wiped his hands on a linen towel and laid the offering at Zyraxes's feet.

"Mother Ea," Zyraxes said, "accept our humble offering." He sprinkled a fistful of Kertan black salt over the tray before a temple servant took it away.

With a long knife, the bull master cut open the beast's belly. He sank his arm inside and pulled out the heart—red and huge, dripping blood—and dropped it on the other silver tray. He wiped his hands and arms on linen towels and took the tray to Zyraxes.

Again, Zyraxes sprinkled black salt over the tray. "Lord Beleizis, please accept our humble offering and give us Your sign."

The bull master slit open the rest of the stomach. The pink and gray and yellow innards flopped out of the white belly. The temple servants silenced their drums as Zyraxes leaned over the bull's innards.

Nicetas held his breath but kept praying. Just one more ill omen, and there'd be no wedding. He hadn't asked Zyraxes to provide it no matter what the bull's entrails revealed, because he knew his brother wouldn't grant him the favor. Zyraxes wouldn't forgive Nicetas for taking the throne from him, as their parents had consecrated their older child to Beleizis's temple after he had fallen ill. Their mother had been so afraid that ten-year-old Zyraxes could die of gray fever, like her firstborn daughter, that she offered him to Beleizis if the god saved his life. But Zyraxes always complained about the arrangement. No sacred text he had ever read—and he had read them all—mentioned removing a first-born son from his father's line of succession just because he fell ill once, when he was ten.

After Nicetas had become king, Zyraxes retreated to Mount Ea-El, where his servants carved a small hut inside a giant boulder. He spent a whole year at the Boulder Hut, playing the panpipes for the gods and waiting for a divine sign. When he came down at last, he let the world know he was now a prophet, which suited Nicetas just fine. Prophets were useful to kings. The Roman emperor Vespasianus was now using them to convince his people they needed a royal dynasty again. He had even performed healings during a public appearance in Egypt—as prophesied—to prove his divine nature.

Nicetas looked at his own prophet with hope and apprehension. They had argued about the wedding before because Zyraxes wanted the Kertan alliance, but a high priest wouldn't lie about the gods' signs.

Zyraxes raised his arm. "Beleizis has accepted our offering. He has shown us His sign." He stared at the bull's innards. "And the sign is..." He chewed on his beard as if hiding his smile. "The sign is propitious!"

The crowd erupted with cheers.

Nicetas felt sick. "Are you certain?"

"No doubt, brother." Zyraxes even looked sincere. "And now it's time for your bride."

The Book of Andrada

In a sleeveless linen shift, Andrada stood barefoot, surrounded by busy temple servants. They had bathed her in goat's milk that morning and perfumed her with rosewater. Now they parted her shoulder-length hair and braided it into thin tresses put up with silver hairpins. Then they brought a silver-threaded robe with embroidered aurochs and laid it over her shoulders. Nothing was made with the familiar Kertan gold here. They cinched her waist with a bejeweled silver belt, hung heavy silver hoops from her earlobes, and adorned her with a silver necklace encrusted with crystal. They clasped spirals of silver around her wrists and forearms. On the left side of her belt, they hung the silver knife she'd use during the ceremony. They gave her silver sandals fastened with silver anklets and set the sapphire diadem in place with hairpins so it wouldn't slip.

Her new queen apprenticeship had begun. She walked from the sacred chambers, holding her head high under the burden of Valdavia's sacred silver. She followed Citera along torchlit corridors and spiral staircases to an enclosure with a stone door outlined in daylight. The air trembled with the rhythm of drums outside.

The door opened, and Andrada saw countless faces peering up from a sunny rotunda. Citera walked out onto a dais overlooking the crowd and spoke to an older priest who carried a wooden staff. Nicetas came into view, also dressed in silver, his dark hair slicked back, his face shaved clean.

Andrada followed Citera's gentle pull into the bright light of the Temple of Concord, while the crowd gasped and murmured. The drums picked up. The air boiled with the dense smell of incense, wine, leather, and sweat.

Andrada knew her part. She turned away from the crowd and kneeled in front of the temple's giant granite statue. It was Ea, seated with a god-child in her lap, against the crook of her left arm, her right hand raised in blessing. The child was Beleizis, the patron god of Valdavia. The image reminded Andrada of being little and sitting in the nurse's lap. Her heart ached with longing, and she pushed that memory away. She started praying to Ea, who might be the only divine being to answer her pleas here in Valdavia.

The drums fell quiet. Nicetas kneeled at Andrada's side and took her hand. Citera wrapped twine made from two strands of wool—one white, signifying purity of heart; one red, for the blood of the ancestors—around their wrists, and with each loop, she praised a god of the Valdavian realm.

"The gods have received our offerings," she said, "and Their signs are propitious. Does anyone dare stand against this sacred royal union?"

Andrada felt Nicetas's hand tensing on hers.

Citera lifted her arms. "Then it is—"

"Just give it a moment," Nicetas whispered to the high priestess. "I want this done right."

Andrada's hand was sore in Nicetas's grip. Silence stretched to uncomfortable murmurs. What were they waiting for?

Citera took a long time to rub the black salt on his forehead, then on Andrada's. "It is the gods' will," she said at last, "that this man and this woman be united as one."

Andrada risked a sideways glance. Nicetas looked defeated. She didn't understand why, but she shared his misery. Citera went around the statue and reappeared carrying a glazed urn. Andrada and Nicetas grabbed the handles, and together they brought it to the feet of the goddess. They poured what smelled like sacrificial blood over a drain. Citera disappeared behind the statue again and brought back a torch, which she put in Andrada's and Nicetas's joined hands. She then led them down into the rotunda.

Young Dapyx stood in the front row by the dais, all dressed up and pouting. Oroles was there too. People stepped aside and made a path. And there was Dokina, flowers in her braided hair. Andrada thanked Ea her companion hadn't left her.

In the center of the temple, a mound covered in a white bull's skin filled the round hearth. The head and the hooves of the bull lay on top of the mound of fat and bones. Andrada and Nicetas lit the brush around the offering with their torch. The fire spread, roaring and hot against their faces, the smoke of sizzling fat rising through the opening in the domed ceiling. The fistfuls of black salt Citera threw into the flames sparkled and hissed with colored light.

"The gods receive your offering and welcome you now as husband and wife. Go forth and prosper, King and Queen of Valdavia."

With her left hand, Andrada pulled out the silver knife, cut the red-and-white twine on her wrist, and threw it in the fire. She offered her freed hand back to Nicetas. He kissed it and brought it to his forehead.

Citera held out a crystal bell not very different from Andrada's own and rang it. The crowd cheered. Then the drums, whistles, and panpipes joined in, each echoing a specific bird call, each the favorite sound of one or another god or spirit.

Andrada's chest filled with sound but no joy. The howl of a lonely draco rose outside, scaring away some of the other sounds. There hadn't been a war between Valdavia and Kerta for ages, and the Valdavians had forgotten the Kertan battle call. People chuckled and renewed their bird trills. Through it all, Andrada kept hearing the clear ringing of Citera's bell.

After the ceremony, Andrada and Nicetas sat under a blue canopy at the head of the feast hall in the king's house of Zalmodava. In the din of laughter and music, an endless stream of people approached the royal table—hats in hand, servants in tow—to present gifts to the newlyweds. A scroll of *Medea*, a tragedy written by the Greek poet Euripides. A dagger for the firstborn son and a comb for the firstborn daughter, made from the tusk of a beast that had lived in the times of Queen Seba. A round crystal from the fabled mine in the east. And other wonders of nature and craft from all over the known world.

Andrada accepted the gifts with a smile and half a nod weighed with silver adornments. She ate bull-meat stew with a silver spoon she shared with Nicetas, and they drank wine from the same onyx-encrusted silver cup. The wine took her mind off the looming hour when she and Nicetas had to go to the bridal chamber and put to use what she had learned at the temple. She kept reaching for the cup for courage, and the servants kept it full.

"Emperor Vespasianus's diplomatic legate, Lucius Flavius Magius, at your service." The young man addressing Nicetas was tall and thin, his skin dark, a red toga over his left arm. His slave held out a box full of glittery things. "My emperor wishes a long and fruitful marriage upon his cherished friend. He hopes Your Highness sees the wisdom of maintaining Pax Romana within and without the empire's borders. He also wishes to...remind Your Highness of your pledge to protect the Roman settlements south of the Danubius River. The emperor would hate to have to send in our legions."

Andrada put down the wine. A threat at her wedding from a Roman legate?

"My lord Magius," Nicetas said, "I assure you there've been no incursions south of the Danubius."

"My people tell me Dhawosian outlaws crossed the frozen Danubius at the end of winter and made it back to Valdavia safely with their plunder."

Nicetas took a deep breath. "If that indeed happened, it won't happen again."

"I will communicate this excellent state of affairs to the emperor." Legate Magius smiled a toothy grin. "To show how much Emperor Vespasianus values our friendship, I bring the queen a gift of fine Roman jewelry and, for the king, a magnificent Arabian stallion."

"Thank the...emperor," Andrada said with an unexpected giggle. The wine made everything merrier.

Nicetas threw her a hard look. "And I'll repay his generosity with a gift of bears and boars from our forests for Roma's circuses."

The legate retired, and the box of jewelry was taken away. Andrada reached again for the onyx cup, only to watch Nicetas gulp down the wine to the last drop.

For the time being, there were no guests waiting to be introduced.

"May I be excused for a moment?" she said.

Dokina helped her from her seat. Andrada felt unsure on her feet, and she leaned on Dokina's arm as they headed through the crowd to the latrines.

When they returned to the hall, Andrada spotted a man standing in front of the king's table. He wore a dirty headdress and a cloak of undyed wool. He talked while Nicetas shook his head. More threats? Nearby, Oroles watched the same scene with a preoccupied look on his face.

She approached him. "What's that about?"

Oroles fingered the silver chain around his neck—the mark of the king's first councilor. "I don't know, my queen." He knew but wouldn't trust a stranger with his king's matters.

Andrada had to make him her friend first. She whispered in his ear, "People all over Dhawosia sing your praises for the Night Attack...You

saved my husband's life...Without you...I wouldn't be so blessed today."
She realized her words came out slurred.

Oroles frowned. "Anyone else would've done the same."

"True...but the gods chose you, my lord." She lost her balance, but
Dokina caught her in time.

Her charms hadn't worked, for Oroles bowed to her and walked away.
Another day, perhaps. She felt confident to walk alone, but Dokina stayed
right behind her, with a hand on her back.

Andrada noticed young Dapyx staring at her from the side, so she
went straight to him. "Who was that man..." Her tongue was heavy. "With
the king...just now?"

"The Steppewynder emissary," he said, turning red.

"What were they fighting about?"

"Scorilus is angry about the wedding."

Unlike Oroles, Dapyx seemed eager to talk.

"And Nicetas?" Andrada said.

"He told Scorilus to curl up at the foot of Azemel's throne in the
Underworld."

Dapyx was a wonderful ally to have here in Zalmodava. Overpowered
by gratitude—or wine—Andrada leaned over and kissed him on the cheek.
His skin was hot and sweaty, and a few short hairs tickled her lips.

Later that night, a few temple servants took Andrada to the bridal chamber, where she found a small gathering of courtiers outside the door.
Their role was to wait for Nicetas to come out later and confirm the
union. Andrada winced as she went in.

The chamber had a simple bed and a hearth in the center. While
muffled merriment still rang from the feast hall, the temple servants took
off her sapphire diadem, then the adornments from her neck, hands, and
feet, then her wedding robes, and placed everything inside a dark chest
painted with silver aurochs. They undid her short braids, but her locks
were all twisted and sticking out.

Despite the fire in the hearth, Andrada stood shivering on a bearskin rug. Her sleeveless shift, soaked with sweat from the feast hall, was now cold against her back. A servant set a silver tray with linen towels on the table. Another brought a silver pitcher full of steaming water and a silver washbowl. "Remember, my queen," he said, "the fertility of the seasons depends on the fertility of the royal couple."

As Nicetas opened the door, the hallway noise grew loud for a moment, then muffled again. He wore his silver-threaded tunic and blue woolen cloak. At his sign, the servants left.

Andrada and Nicetas were alone at last. He put his hands on her shivering shoulders. She tried to remember what Citera had taught her, but the wine fog was still thick. The wife's first duty to her husband was…Nicetas's cloak clasp was a silver fibula in the shape of an aurochs with ruby eyes. Andrada fumbled with it, trying to pull its pin free from the cloth.

He took her cold fingers in his warm hands. He found the pin and unclasped his cloak. What if he didn't know what to do either? Andrada's head was swimming, and she felt nauseous. She shouldn't have drunk so much wine.

Now she remembered: unbuckle his belt, take off his ceremonial sword, and lead him to the bed by the hand. But he took off his belt and sword on his own and pulled his tunic over his head. Andrada gasped and covered her mouth. On his stomach, scar marks spread out from a healed wound on his left side.

All warriors had scars, but Nicetas seemed embarrassed about his. "Ea spared my life that night, but I remain branded."

Andrada stepped closer. Her fingers touched the wiry hair on his chest and slipped lower, feeling the crests and creases in the skin slashed by Scorilus's blade during the Night Attack. She touched the seams where the medicine women of Twin Willows had stitched the wound. She moved her hand up, back to his chest, and felt his heart beating under her fingertips.

Nicetas sat down on the edge of the bed. He wrapped his arms around her waist and pressed his head against her breasts. The damp fabric of her shift was between them, and he pulled her closer and tighter between his legs.

He looked up at her, the whites of his eyes streaked with fine red veins. She leaned down to kiss that stranger, forehead first. But in the moment, she threw another glance at the striking scar on his belly.

He saw that. His upper lip curled, and his jaw clenched. He pushed her away, and she staggered back against the wall.

She watched him put his clothes back on in silence. Citera wouldn't be happy, but Andrada was relieved. There'd be other nights for sacred royal duties.

Nicetas unsheathed his short bridegroom's sword, closed his left fist around it, and pulled the blade through. He thrust the sword back in its sheath and stepped close to Andrada, so close that she could smell his breath through her own, heavy with wine. He pinned her shoulder against the wall, grabbed the fabric of her shift in his bleeding hand, and wadded it up between her legs.

That was not what Citera had told Andrada to expect. She had said there might not even be blood.

Nicetas let go and went to the table to get a linen towel from the silver tray. He wiped the blood off his hands and threw the towel on the bed. He ripped a piece of linen with his teeth and wrapped it around his hand. He went around the bed, tossing around the fur blankets. He then reached into the chest and took out the sapphire diadem.

"Talk to me," Andrada whispered, frightened.

He threw his cloak over his bandaged hand holding the diadem and headed out.

"It's done," he told the courtiers outside.

Soon after that strange episode with Nicetas, Andrada arrived at the queen's chamber. The place was large and welcoming: carved Valdavian-oak panels on the walls, fur rugs, and woolen blankets everywhere.

Dokina had lit the fire and set the table with a wine pitcher and a bread basket.

"You're free to get drunk," Andrada told Dokina. "I know I want more wine." She stepped out of the fur slippers and the cloak the temple servants had brought her after the bridal chamber.

Dokina poured the wine, and Andrada downed the whole cup. It was sourer than what they'd had at the feast but strong. She hoped it would take her mind off that strange day, if only for a while.

"That man was a beast," Dokina said, pointing at the dark spots on Andrada's shift. "Did it hurt?"

"Only my pride..."

"You need clean clothes." Dokina led the way.

The red trunk with wolf heads waited at the foot of the bigger of two beds. Andrada shrieked with joy and dug in, pulling out bundles of linens and woolens, even the nurse's embroidery frame, until she grabbed the four legs of her whitewood horse-box. She then took out the crystal bell.

"That's the bell from the Old Temple of Sehul, isn't it?" Dokina took it from Andrada's hand and rang it. The sound was so clear, like snow and ice and a heart that kept beating. The ringing went on and on and on, looping through high and low notes. Dokina silenced the bell in her hand. "Why did you take it?"

"I think it grants wishes..." The new wine was working. "Not sure how or why..."

"Does it now?" With the bell in her hand, Dokina walked around, searching for something. She stopped in front of the writing tray on the table, with its blue glass inkwell. "Dear bell, make this inkwell crack. Spill its ink right now." She rang the bell, but nothing happened.

"It's a sacred bell, Dokina, not a magic wand. I told you...I don't know how it works..."

"There's a word carved on it, but I can't read it."

"ONE."

"One what?"

"I don't know..." A wave of weariness came over Andrada. "That's the word on the bell."

"Maybe the bell grants only one wish?"

"It's granted me two so far...but in a strange way..."

"Maybe the bell only works for one person?"

Andrada sat in a chair by the hearth, and the world steadied around her. "Maybe it doesn't even work here, only in that old temple."

Dokina sat on the rug and crossed her legs. "I want to see how it works, so make a wish."

"It has to be something worthy of a divine being's ear...Something important, like that affair with the Steppewynder..." She snapped her fingers, trying to remember the word.

"Emissary? No, that'll bore your divine being to tears."

Andrada laughed, then sighed. As the Valdavian queen, she could hold power in the king's house without the bell's help. But she needed to impress her new husband, who might then trust her with some court duties. She'd grow her power, then—

"Do you love Nicetas?" Dokina said.

"What an odd question. Of course not." How to gain his trust though? Andrada's father had promised his help if she needed it. She could use his architect, Apollonius of Damascus, to build a magnificent Roman garden, here in Zalmodava. She'd show Nicetas she could handle such a massive task.

"That'll make the little prince happy," Dokina said. "Did you see how he blushed when you kissed him?"

The wine fog was worse than Andrada thought. "Wait, I kissed Prince Dapyx?"

"You sure did—on the cheek, in front of everybody." Dokina put the bell in Andrada's hand. "Why not ask for true love?" She pushed back when Andrada shook her head. "Yes, go on. True love."

Andrada could almost see her Roman garden, going up the hill between the king's house and the Temple of Concord, where only bushes and weeds grew now. She'd partition the space with terraces after the model of Sehuldava. She'd make it look more like home—

"What are you waiting for?" Dokina said.

"Yes, yes...True love," Andrada said and rang the bell.

Chapter Nine

The Dynastic Scrolls

A few days after the Valdavian royal wedding, Una, the youngest of the medicine women of Twin Willows, held Nicetas in her arms again. She embraced him tighter than ever, glad for the noise of hammers and saws outside. She was grateful for the house he was building for her—the newest king's house, up on the hill above her village—and she kissed him on the lips harder than ever. He kissed her back, but he wasn't in a hurry like her. He smelled her hair and caressed her forehead, while her breath turned more and more ragged.

Una remembered the door. She let go of Nicetas and went to latch it. This chamber alone was larger than the roundhouse where she lived with her mother and grandmother—and sometimes a patient or two behind wooden screens. She then went to close the shutters, pausing for a moment to take in the beautiful view Nicetas had gifted her. Beyond the forest, the waters of the Pyretus River glimmered in the sun, with Twin Willows on their southern bank. In the center of her village, she spotted her roundhouse with its weather vane.

Una closed the last shutter. She turned to the darkened chamber where Nicetas waited for her on the white fur rug by the hearth. The king of Valdavia—who had died and gone to the Underworld after the Night Attack, who had been rescued from Samca's claws and restored to life, who had seen Ea's face of light and had heard Ea's voice that healed wounds—that king was waiting for her.

"Don't look," she said, and he hid his face in his hands.

She pulled her brassbound wooden box from her satchel, found the cylindrical sponge soaked with resin and lavender oil, lifted her skirts, and slipped it inside. She would not carry Nicetas's child—not yet.

"Now you may look." She kneeled next to him on the rug and kissed him on the ear. "And even touch...if you wish." She began to undo her sandals' laces.

"Let me..." He took them off and clasped her ankle, then moved up against the fine hairs on her leg, his touch tickling the back of her knee. A kiss on the inside of her thigh made her giggle.

He undressed her while she hummed for him the ballad of the goddess Bendis, who had fallen in love with a Valdavian prince and turned him into a great aurochs to keep him near. The aurochs still roamed Bendis's forests and dwelt in a mountain cave where the two lovers met on the full moon in human form.

Una kneeled naked on the rug, watching her beloved, the trust in his eyes as he undressed for her by the fire. He was building a home for her on this hill above Twin Willows, and she sat on a rug made of white hare pelts he had hunted for her the year before. It was his way of thanking her for healing his war wounds, vanquishing Samca's evil spirits from his nightmares after the Night Attack, and teaching him how to love. How to love her.

Una stopped humming. She was dying of thirst, and he was her water. She pulled him closer to her, guiding his fingers to her breast. He kissed it, kissed her lips, then caressed her thick braid and brought it over her shoulder. He undid the knot of her tie, unbraided her hair, and spread her wavy locks over her breasts.

She loved that he was never in a hurry with her. He kissed her forehead, her eyes, her mouth. He kissed the nipple poking through the curtain of golden hair. His face glowed with the fire, and his fingers worked her body with ease.

She lay back on the rug, pulling his warm embrace to her. Soft pressure parted her thighs—his hand, cupped like an offering of honey to the gods—and she opened. She knew the touch of his fingertips, the rough hand of a hunter. She knew the shape of the scar on his stomach, knew his smell of dampness and dust and desire, and she felt him right in the middle of her, where the entire world now was. He was there, and she was there, and she seized him for herself and held him, his tongue warm and tasting of wine and of their meal's tart remnants, and she felt like a goddess herself when she had him in the palm of her hand, in the warmth of her mouth, in the softness of her belly.

It seemed like a moment of no words, coiled time, keen senses, but it must have been longer because the hammers and saws outside had fallen quiet. Una felt Nicetas's soft kiss on her shoulder, and she turned her head to watch him bring out the silver comb he had given her years ago. She sat up, lowered her head, and hugged her knees. She felt his hand beneath her hair, and the comb on the skin of her head, sliding down in one long stroke.

Again, she hummed the ballad of Bendis and Her great aurochs. She felt Nicetas's gentle tug separating strands from tangles he had made earlier, when he had grabbed her hair and pulled her head back to kiss her. She watched his shadow at their side, the arched shape of his body swimming into a river of rhythm, working the comb up and down while she hummed.

He cleaned the comb, and she smelled the hairs burning in the hearth. He ran two fingers through her hair, separating it in three, and began plaiting. When the knot was tied again, he returned the braid over her shoulder, as he had found it earlier.

"That could've been our wedding night," he whispered in her ear.

Her stomach turned cold. "You know I can't."

She was from the line of Ea's medicine women, who never married and had only one child, a girl, who carried forth the secrets entrusted to them by the goddess. The few times over the ages when the youngest medicine woman had died without having a child, the others mended the line by transferring their blood to someone chosen by Ea. Marrying and breaking the covenant would bring a thousand years of darkness over the known world, and Una couldn't be the first medicine woman to risk it, not even for her beloved Nicetas.

"You could've at least accepted the silver diadem I made for you. Sapphires the very color of your eyes—"

"It wasn't right for me to wear it. Give it to your wife."

Nicetas groaned. "I hate Her…"

Una knew he meant Ea and not his new wife he didn't care about.

She put her shift back on, her hands shaking. "How can you say that? She pulled you from the Underworld after the Night Attack. We gave you Oroles's blood, but She gave you life again." She rubbed her temples to relieve a sudden headache. "And She'll expect you to do your part when I ask you."

Nicetas stood up and gathered his clothes. "I gave you my word." He had sworn to be the father of Una's daughter when the time came, still more than a year away.

She finished dressing, then opened the shutters. The chamber was bright again. Against the blue sky, a flock of swallows was returning to the Pyretus Valley for the spring.

"I wish we were more like those birds," Nicetas said. "They build their nests wherever and mate whoever they want."

"But we aren't," Una said.

PART TWO

"Andrada the Whore..."

—from a Dhawosian nursery rhyme

127–129 LE

Chapter Ten

The Book of Dapyx

Dapyx loved uttering Andrada's name. She had given him permission at the beginning of spring, when she asked him for a courier to send to her father. Twenty-three days later, a small army of gardeners arrived in Zalmodava, streaming up the Twelve-Pier Bridge with shovels, hoes, and buckets piled into wheelbarrows. They covered the length of the stone bend, from the first pier on the north side of the fortress to the last pier, where the bridge leveled up to the east gates. Their young chief, one Apollonius of Damascus, had had some unpleasant business with Andrada back in Sehuldava, for he apologized to her in his stilted Dhawosian the moment they saw each other. She forgave him, but there was no warmth between them, and Dapyx liked it that way.

In another ten days, the tangled thicket between the king's house and the Temple of Concord had been thinned, with lines drawn, stakes hammered into the ground, and ropes stretched to map the plans Andrada had been working on with Apollonius. Andrada wanted different terraces for a flower garden, a water garden, an herb garden, and a vegetable garden. Around them, she planned terraces for grapevines and orchards, and in a few places, she wanted outhouses with deep pits and cedar roofs.

When Oroles asked about the disturbance of the temple's sacred woodland, Dapyx told him the gardens were Andrada's gift for Nicetas, and the councilor didn't press the matter further. It seemed to Dapyx that Oroles felt bad for the queen, who didn't know her husband was with Una in Twin Willows.

Dapyx wasn't sure Nicetas would like the changes done to Zalmodava Hill, but he knew Zyraxes would hate them when he returned from the Boulder Hut on Mount Ea-El. Dapyx didn't care about Zyraxes though. Andrada needed him at her side, and that was worth his oldest brother's anger. He liked that his opinions were important to her. When he had drawn an arrow in black ink on her parchment map, the herb garden had moved to a plot closer to the kitchen, bordering the vegetable and the flower garden.

That morning, Dapyx woke up feeling sore all over. Yesterday, he and Andrada had helped scoop out the frogs and fish from a woodland pond and carried them in buckets to a makeshift pool.

There was a dirty rag on his pillow, and he tried to think if it had anything to do with the frogs. Then he realized it was Andrada's white headscarf of the betrothed—crusty and not white anymore. It had lost her delicate scent and only stank of his seed. He remembered her kiss again, and his whole body ached in a different way.

When he met her in the new gardens, she said, "They're cutting down the big tree."

"What big tree?"

"The one above the aquifer. Apollonius says that if we build a water-wheel and an aqueduct there, we'll have all the water we need to irrigate the new terraces. Come, I'll show you."

Dapyx didn't care to see a tree being felled, not even a big one, but Andrada grabbed his hand and pulled him along. The blisters left by the rope handles of yesterday's frog buckets burned, but he didn't complain.

When he saw where they were headed, his heart filled with dread. "You said we wouldn't be touching that part of the woodland." He stopped walking.

"Why do you think that tree is so big?" she said. "Because it's sitting on all that water."

"But that's Zyraxes's sanctuary, where he plays his panpipes and prays to the gods. No one may disturb it, not even Nicetas. Andrada, you can't fell Zyraxes's sky oak."

"Where else will we get water for the gardens?"

Dapyx thought about other options. "The Ozana River. Its water is brought through tunnels into the reservoir. For the well in the courtyard of the king's house. There's plenty of water there."

"You didn't say anything about a reservoir," she said with a frown.

"You didn't ask. Andrada, trust me, we must stop Apollonius from cutting down that tree."

They started running, and now he outpaced her. The wind brought smoke from the clearing ahead, smoke that had been rising from that part of the woodland for days. Not once had he wondered about it, busy as he'd been with the frogs and getting in Andrada's good graces.

Axe blows grew louder as they got closer. Through the trees and the smoke, Dapyx made out three gardeners, clearing smoldering brush from around Zyraxes's sky oak. On the other side, four men with axes worked through the fire-shriveled bark.

A gardener blocked Dapyx's path. "You can go no farther, my lord. It's not safe."

"Don't fell that sky oak," Dapyx cried, fighting the gardener's hold. "Stop now!"

"You'll get hurt, my lord." The gardener kept Dapyx in his grip with little effort.

Andrada arrived, panting. "Let him go! Find Apollonius...and tell the axes to stand down."

The gardener nodded, released Dapyx, and took off.

"Good thing Zyraxes's tree is so big," Dapyx whispered. "It can withstand all this..."

The axe blows fell silent a moment later.

Through the brush and the smoke, Dapyx saw a robed man approaching. He couldn't believe Zyraxes was back home. He was supposed to sit with the gods up on the mountain until the last new moon of spring.

Dapyx nudged Andrada, and they both rushed to meet Zyraxes, putting some distance between them and the scene at the clearing.

"What's happening here?" Zyraxes said. "I could see the smoke from the Boulder Hut."

"We're planting new gardens, Your Holiness," Andrada said, looking flustered.

Dapyx took a step forward. "We'll have a flower garden, and an orchard, and—"

A cracking sound came from the clearing beyond.

Zyraxes gaped. His tree's head of branches drew a slow arc against the sky. When it hit the ground, Dapyx felt the thud in his chest and the soles of his feet.

"No, no, no..." Zyraxes cried. "My sky oak..."

"There's water underneath it," Andrada said, sounding contrite, "for the aqueduct..."

"My tree..." Zyraxes's eyes turned red with tears. "It linked heaven and earth. It was my sacred ladder..." He thrust his staff into Andrada's face. "How did Nicetas let this happen?"

"King Nicetas's house is in my care now," she said.

Dapyx felt proud of the way she squared her shoulders and stood up to Zyraxes.

"I'm the queen, and these gardens are a gift from my father to my husband."

"Yes, that's right," Dapyx said, his voice slipping.

"Wretched Kertan..." Zyraxes wiped a tear. "You'll pay for this sacrilege."

Dapyx had never cared that Zyraxes hated Nicetas, but now he worried that his oldest brother might hurt Andrada.

The Book of Andrada

Andrada slammed her chamber's door behind her. Her breath was shallow after running here from the gardens and from a whirlwind of anger and humiliation. She longed for her nurse's sage-scented embrace, her rough fingertips against Andrada's cheek.

"What happened?" Dokina said, wiping her hands on her apron.

Andrada went to the table, light-headed, her hands shaking. She'd write to Nicetas at his hunting camp in the Blue Highlands, and she'd explain everything. She had asked Oroles who was in charge at the court when both the king and the high priest were away. He had told her she was the queen of Valdavia, and she ruled here in Zalmodava.

"I'll tell him what Apollonius told me about the aquifer," Andrada said.

She sat down, drew the writing tray near, and picked up the inkwell. It slipped through her trembling fingers, weightless in the air for a moment, then shattering on the floor the next. Shards of blue glass landed everywhere. A puddle of black ink grew on the flagstones.

"By the Three Divines," Dokina cried.

She undid her apron and dropped to her knees. The black ink had stained the leather of Andrada's boots. Dokina folded her apron and wiped the boots and the floor, again and again, the amulet pouch at her neck swinging on its string as she scrubbed.

The significance of that moment left Andrada speechless.

"It won't come off," Dokina said, after scrubbing with water. "This stone soaked up the ink like a sponge."

Andrada leaned back in her chair. "It's fine, Dokina..."

"No, it's not fine. It's a bad omen. A broken inkwell, a stain that won't come off, very bad signs indeed." Dokina looked up. "Why are you smiling?"

"Because it worked, Dokina. You remember your wish on my wedding night?"

"What wish? I had a lot of wine that night." Dokina rubbed her forehead with the back of her stained hand. "Oh...you think the bell's god answered my wish to break this inkwell?"

"Looks like it." The crystal bell had answered Andrada's other wishes in an instant because they were cries for help. But the divine being had let Dokina's silly wish wait until the end of spring. "And He's answered it here, in Zalmodava. He must be a god whose patronage spans kingdoms, like Ea."

"You said *He*." Dokina stood up from the floor. "You don't think it's Ea?"

"No...When I was little, I used to pray to Ea and the Three Divines to bring my father to me, but They never answered."

"Then who?" Dokina frowned. "You know, we can ask the bell to reveal something about its master to us. Like, if we're wrong to be praying to *Him*, then *She* could, maybe, break the next inkwell?"

"What if it's someone like Napat-Dehnu of the Steppewynders? Both god and goddess."

"Wait!" Dokina's eyes widened. "Do you think I can ask Him to teach me how to read and write?"

Andrada smiled. "No need to bother Him with that. I'll teach you."

"You will? That'd be wonderful." Dokina's face changed. She pointed an ink-stained finger at Andrada. "Do you remember your wish from that night? Soon, He may grant you true love, not just a broken inkwell."

Chapter Eleven

The Book of Scorilus

In the great hall of the White Fortress of Steppewynd, Petition Day went on and on through the hot and humid summer day. King Scorilus paced before his throne, stretching his neck and rubbing his shoulder. His war wound had long since healed, but the spot under his armpit where Oroles's barbed arrow had hit six years ago still hurt when his muscles tightened. Scorilus had that dull pain to remind him that the gods could toy with mortals in the cruelest ways. Why else would Nap-at-Dehnu, the patron deity of Steppewynd, send him to war only to put an arrow in his side?

No day went by without letters from around the country about the shortages of grain, wool, and iron caused by the loss of the border trading posts since the Night Attack. It angered Scorilus that he couldn't help his people. Steppewynder laborers put their lives in smugglers' hands, risking death from Valdavian soldiers at the border, only to return to low-paid work in the west. The priests and the lords of his realm carped about it but did nothing to help the people. How could this ruin be Napat-Dehnu's divine plan for Steppewynd?

Scorilus had been there when his father received the deity's blessings for their ill-fated war with Valdavia. As a prince, he stood at the top of the Tyrine Tower that morning, searching the horizons for signs of his older brothers' return. They each had gone to find the fertile land Napat-Dehnu had promised to Steppewynd after generations of being poor and at the mercy of the other Dhawosian kingdoms.

Scorilus stared at the blurred strip where the green-blue of the Black Sea and the muddy blue of the Tyras River met. No sign of Eptalas's ships approaching the harbor. Over the eastern hills, no cloud of dust announced the return of Phradmon's army.

"Why you?" King Thiaper said, his white beard trembling in the wind. "Why did Napat-Dehnu send your brothers away and leave me the youngest and weakest of my sons?"

Scorilus knew to remain silent. It didn't matter to his father that Eptalas had lost Steppewynd's fleet and Phradmon the cavalry in their quest for Napat-Dehnu's promised land in the east. It didn't matter that Scorilus had married the fertile widow Rescuturme when he was barely out of his boyhood, which had provided the royal offspring the kingdom needed.

King Thiaper closed his eyes and turned his ear to the sky. "Our deity is speaking again."

Scorilus tensed, straining to hear. Between sky and water was the sacred place where the god Napat had once joined with the goddess Dehnu. A voice in the wind whispered something Scorilus couldn't comprehend. Could it really be Napat-Dehnu? In *Odysseia*, the Greek goddess Athena made Her divine voice heard to mortals.

Scorilus waited, his mouth dry, his knees weak.

"They command me to build an army," King Thiaper said. "And They command you to lead it west, against Valdavia. Our promised land lies west, not east."

Scorilus heard the voice in the wind again, but he couldn't make out the words.

"But young King Nicetas is our friend, Father..."

"There are no friends when the gods speak."

Scorilus knew it was wrong to doubt. "But what about Emperor Nero and his legions?" he shouted against the wind. "He'll attack both us and Valdavia."

"Why are you still questioning Them?"

It was wrong to question Napat-Dehnu, yes. "But what will happen to my children if I die?" His son Moskon, the next in line to the Steppewynder throne, was nine. His daughter Meda was ten. His three adopted children from Rescuturme's previous marriage were between twelve and seventeen. They all needed a father.

Then the voice in the wind roared, "Bow!"

Scorilus fell to his knees, shaking with awe and terror. Napat-Dehnu had spoken. Yes, he'd go to war. All his life he had dreamed of being an explorer like his brothers and Odysseus—a dream his father had forbidden. Now he'd become a warrior and make his father proud.

"Bring me victory," King Thiaper ordered, "under the black banner with the two-headed white snake."

Scorilus had been close to victory when that barbed arrow hit and pierced his lung. Then he'd been close to death, drowning in his own blood. The night Oroles saved Nicetas, a Greek physician had also saved Scorilus, draining his right lung with green glass tubes. Now Scorilus ruled over a struggling Steppewynd, a king unable to feed and clothe his people, stuck in the great hall with his complaining subjects.

While the guard let in another petitioner, Scorilus walked over to his fifteen-year-old son Moskon, who sat at a table with a stack of wax tablets and a pile of parchment pages. The boy looked pale as always, though he was busy jotting down notes about his father's work.

The new petitioner bowed to the king. "May Napat-Dehnu smile upon you and your family, King Scorilus. The Traders' Guild sends its wishes of prosperity."

"Prosperity, Master Tymnes?" Scorilus said, walking back from Moskon's table. "Never mind. Have you brought me any books?"

Tymnes, a Greek trader, circled the mosaic on the floor: the image of Napat, god of rain, snow, and dew, holding in His arms the river and sea goddess Dehnu, the two united as one at the waist, Their lower body that of a white snake. In the old days, the two water deities had blessed Steppewynd with fertile fields. Then Napat-Dehnu had turned garden into wasteland during the reign of Queen Seba to punish a country that had grown too proud of its divine gifts.

"The books weren't easy to come by," Tymnes said, "not with the trade routes cut off. But I did bring a few Greek scrolls from Moesia and even a Latin codex." He pointed to a cart brought in by his servant. "First, Homeros's *Odysseia*." He motioned to a gilded wooden box.

Scorilus picked it up and chose a scroll from a set of twelve on double rods. He inhaled the perfume of fresh parchment: thick hide, earthy lime, and sooty ink, all blending into the rich promise of a story from a faraway land—a story locked for now behind a spider's nest of Greek script, too tangled for his poor eyesight. He needed one of his children to unlock it for him.

"My Greek nurse used to recite from it," he said, a touch of longing in his voice. His favorite lines were about exploring faraway lands like Odysseus and seeing the world with his own bad eyes...

From realm to realm, a country to explore,
That never knew salt or heard the billows roar,
Or saw a vessel stem the watery plain,
A painted wonder flying on the main.

"What's your favorite part of the story, Master Tymnes?" Scorilus said.

"When Odysseus escapes the Cyclops tied to the underbelly of a sheep."

That was Scorilus's least favorite part, where the Cyclops ended up blind and alone. "Thank you, Master Tymnes." He swatted a fly. "The Traders' Guild has been most resourceful."

Tymnes grinned, revealing a missing tooth. "And how did my king like the last book I brought, Publius Ovidius Naso's *Lamentations*, if I'm not mistaken?"

Young Moskon had loved Ovidius's dazzling descriptions of Roma, written sixty years ago. But Scorilus had been bothered by the poet's descriptions of Dhawosia, on the western shores of the Black Sea. A *wild barbarian world*, he called it. Its people *are more beast-like than the wolves*. But Tomis, the Moesian harbor where Ovidius had lived in exile, wasn't much different from Scorilus's own White Fortress in Steppewynd. And while the local farmers may have looked fierce to Ovidius at first, with their helmets and their blades at the ready, those same *barbarians* had been kind to the poet after Emperor Augustus exiled him there.

Tymnes was waiting for an answer. A Greek trader would likely agree with a Roman poet—at least in his heart, if not in his words.

"I liked it well enough," Scorilus said. "My son Moskon did too."

"Then my king will love Lucretius." Tymnes picked up another box from his cart. He removed the lid to reveal a Latin codex with painted wooden covers. "More than a hundred years ago, this Roman poet showed us the true nature of things and soothed our fears of death and gods." He brought the codex closer. "But for us to fully comprehend his words, we must first open our minds to the idea of something tiny and eternal, a prime body we Greeks call *atom*. Has my king heard of Democritus?"

Scorilus nodded, unsure.

"I can't wait to read it, Master Tymnes," Moskon said, bringing him a large coin purse. He then returned to his chair to record the transaction on a tablet.

"Always grateful to do business with the Tyrageti tribe," Tymnes said, weighing the purse in his hands.

Yet he still stood there, his wind-burned cheeks stretched in an obsequious smile.

"Spit it out, Master Tymnes." Scorilus clasped his hands behind his back. "What does the guild want from me this time?"

Tymnes cleared his throat. "Due to the hardship brought by the loss of our trade routes to West Dhawosia and to the Roman provinces south of the Danubius River, the guild asks permission to open a new passage between Steppewynd and Roman Moesia through the Danubius Delta."

"The delta? What about the snakes and mosquitoes? The marshes can't be tamed."

"We don't have much of a choice, my king. We've always relied on the markets at the Valdavian border for trade with the Romans, and thanks to King Nicetas, the trade posts are now gone. We tried crossing the Upper Pyretus River, but the king is now building a fortress in the hills above the village of Twin Willows. We can hardly lay our passage under the king's nose, so we had to search down south for a new route."

"But you need something else," Scorilus said, skipping ahead. "Not just my approval for crossing the delta."

"We need protection, my king. We won't be the only ones in the marshes. Rogue bands of traffickers use ferries to cross into Moesia. We must protect our boats and convoys."

Scorilus cocked his head. "You want me to give the guild its own army?"

"A small one...Since my king's laborers have been banished from Valdavia, the Traders' Guild offers them honest work as soldiers. And Steppewynd's treasury gets a fair share of our profits."

It wasn't the worst offer. "But an army?"

"Black marketeers kill our traders and then flaunt their newly found affluence."

Like Tymnes, Scorilus wore a dull-brown tunic of undyed wool. Dyes had become expensive and rare in Steppewynd. His belt buckle was bronze rather than Kertan gold. But now that Tymnes had mentioned it, Scorilus realized that not everyone dressed down. Some chieftains, and especially their wives, still glittered like water under the sun.

Scorilus nodded. "I want a plan. How much it costs me at first, how much it brings to my treasury after."

Scorilus's stepson Rescuporis brushed past the hall guard. He had a smirk on his youthful face framed by long hair and a dark beard. "My father always appreciates a good plan, Master Tymnes."

Scorilus waited for Tymnes to leave—never quarrel with family in front of strangers. Rescuporis behaved as if he were the heir to the throne of Steppewynd, never mind his younger half-brother Moskon.

"You have something to say, my dear stepson?" Scorilus said.

Rescuporis treaded around the mosaic with deference. "Napat-Dehnu is still waiting for your victory over Valdavia, Father. Our promised land."

"Then They shouldn't have allowed that barbed arrow to fly."

"The gods work in mysterious ways. Father, please let me build you a new army so we can finish what you started six years ago."

Scorilus wondered if Rescuporis had spoken with Tymnes about this. "Build me an army? With what? The bickering chieftains who retreated after the Night Attack, pleased with their plunder? And you want to build this army now, when we should be filling our silos for winter?" Scorilus lowered his voice. Rescuporis had a way of incensing him every time he opened his mouth.

At the table, Moskon plucked a sheet of parchment from an orderly stack. "Buying grain from the Romans of Moesia is now pricier than ever, brother. The chieftains have no coin to pay their soldiers, and those who do are profiting from the closing of the old trade routes. As Master Tymnes has just confirmed. Those chieftains won't want to go to war and lose their windfall."

"Who asked your opinion?" Rescuporis said, turning his back to Moskon. "Father, just borrow from the Romans and pay them back with Valdavian plunder."

"Borrow?" Scorilus said. "And risk the future of Steppewynd on the success of one military campaign?"

"Roman citizen Quintus Domitius Cispius," the guard announced, and Scorilus motioned him in, glad to abandon his quarrel with Rescuporis.

Cispius was a tall man with light hair, and he looked healthy and well-fed, unlike many of Scorilus's people. He wore a bright crimson cloak and a whitened toga. The Romans had conquered the world south of the Danubius, including Moesia, but had no good sense for clothes. Why they insisted on wearing yards of linen instead of a pair of sturdy woolen trousers, Scorilus couldn't fathom. Even that sullen Roman poet Ovidius had understood that trousers ward off the cold and the blade.

"My dear Cispius," Scorilus said, "you haven't shown your face around here since you forced me to buy foodstuff from you at triple the price."

Cispius pressed his thin lips together. "Our gods have a strange sense of humor, Your Highness. I'm here because Emperor Vespasianus has begun work on a new Temple of Peace near his forum. Some call it the Coliseum because of its size. The loot from the temple in Ierusalem isn't enough for this new colossal building, so his subjects must contribute. From us, the merchants of Moesia, he wants more sea salt."

Scorilus could see where this was going but said nothing.

"I couldn't help but overhear earlier," Cispius pressed on, "and I might have the answer to Steppewynd's troubles."

Scorilus waited.

After a long pause, Cispius said, "Salt pans, Your Highness."

Rescuporis scoffed. "I'm already twenty-three years old, Father. I want to bring glory to my country. Letting brine dry in the sun, then scraping off the salt—where's the glory in that?"

"Salt pans..." This might be just what Scorilus needed to keep his people from starving. "But why ask me for sea salt, Cispius, and not Cothelas the Bald for his rock salt?"

"King Cothelas's mines have lost their Steppewynder labor since King Nicetas's decree to close the trade routes. Kerta still sends some salt to Roma but doesn't have any to trade."

Time to extract the best deal. "I still don't see why I should help you."

"We can help each other, Your Highness. My salt pans can't keep up with the emperor's demands, but if Steppewynd supplied me with salt, we could satisfy Roma and keep its legions from meddling in our affairs—both yours and mine. In return, I'll ship grain to the White Fortress at the old price."

"Half the old price."

"I can't go lower than three quarters."

Scorilus nodded. "Now...have you given any thought to cutting a new trade route through the Danubius Delta?"

"That place is full of snakes and mosquitoes," Cispius said, grimacing.

"Nothing our brave people can't handle." Scorilus patted Rescuporis on the back. "Son, take Cispius to Tymnes, and you might still have your glory. Build that new army of yours. Help the Traders' Guild secure a new route that'll bring my sea salt to Cispius in Tomis. With enough coin, we could then rebuild our fleet. How many people have you gathered already?"

Rescuporis shrugged like it was nothing. "Four hundred."

"That would be a great start, Your Highness," Cispius said. "The city of Tomis and I owe you our gratitude."

"Princess Meda," the guard announced.

Scorilus's sixteen-year-old daughter walked in. Slender and tall, she had taken to dyeing her hair red with chestnut sap on the eve of every full moon. On her arm, she wore the bracelet he had given her on her last birthday—six coils of Kertan gold ending in snake heads with crystal eyes. His daughter would never be without royal jewelry, regardless of how plain his own clothes were.

"Time for supper, Father," Meda said, "and some well-deserved rest."

Scorilus felt grateful. He turned to Moskon. "Petition Day is over, son. You've done well today."

The prince had worked harder than ever before. Maybe he was growing stronger.

After supper, Scorilus settled in his chair to listen to his daughter reading from Tymnes's codex. The Latin hexameter was a heartbeat wrapped in Meda's sweet voice. He listened to the sense inside the sound, trying to sort through the swirl of impossible thoughts unleashed by the words of the poet Lucretius.

"*What man is there whose heart with fear of gods does not cringe, whose limbs don't cower in terror when the parched earth rocks with the mighty thunder and trembling rolls through the great heaven? Don't people and countries quake, and proud kings shrink, when they see lightning, dreading that the gods will punish them at last for their acts of injustice and their words of pride?* Should we keep reading this, Father?" Meda had an intense look on her face, her finger still on the page. "I fear Napat-Dehnu's wrath. This Roman poet says that the thunderbolt's seeds of fire are just atoms. Atoms that reach first our eyes and then our ears—no gods involved. That can't be right, can it, Father?"

Scorilus needed to contemplate this awful revelation before he could explain anything to his daughter. "It's late…We'll stop for now."

Meda left. Scorilus paced around his chamber, trying to make sense of what he had just heard. Here was a poem by Titus Lucretius Carus called *De rerum natura—On the Nature of Things*—that answered questions

Scorilus had grappled with for years. The certain death of his brothers, the failed Night Attack, Moskon's delicate nature, and Rescuturme's failure to bear more children—how did they advance Napat-Dehnu's grand plans for Steppewynd?

If Lucretius was right, they didn't.

Nature, free in a world without lords and masters, does everything by herself, without the gods.

Stardust stirring in the void. Everlasting atoms, swerving, colliding, and flying off, making and unmaking the world. Scorilus wished he had read this book when he was younger. It might have spared him countless days and nights of pleading with fickle gods who didn't exist.

His faith in Napat-Dehnu had been steadfast when he had donned Valdavian clothes and sneaked into Nicetas's camp at night, undetected by eyes better than his. He had worked out the location of the king's tent, the number of guards outside the entrance, the shortest route in and out for when he'd return with his troops. His plan of attack seemed flawless against a tired Valdavian army forced to set up camp on territory chosen by Scorilus. His men had even had time to dig holes around that campsite, stick spears into the ground, and cover them with branches for later, when the panic would start and horses would charge out. Nothing could go wrong.

But in a world of colliding atoms, everything could go wrong. One man with a barbed arrow had taken the victory away and saved the Valdavian king. In a world where Oroles had stopped Scorilus's sacred mission, there was no Napat-Dehnu.

Scorilus's heart jumped. Was he angering Napat-Dehnu at that very moment with his blasphemous thoughts? But if Lucretius was right, Scorilus's racing thoughts were locked inside his own head. No one was listening from the outside. His doubt was his and his alone to ponder. That fateful day at the top of the Tyrine Tower when he had thought he heard the voice of Napat-Dehnu, it was just atoms vibrating in the air.

He opened the drawer where he kept Oroles's barbed arrow. Three prongs of sharpened bone made the tip. He sighed, remembering how he had pulled it from the bleeding flesh in his armpit.

If Lucretius was right, the sad truth was that Scorilus had survived the Night Attack by chance, not because of the gods. One day, death would come for him as it already had for Eptalas and Phradmon, and for King Thiaper. Scorilus shouldn't fear death though. *Death is nothing to us,* Lucretius said. *Concerns us not one bit, since our souls are mortal.*

Scorilus shouldn't fear death because he'd never witness being dead. His mind would cease to exist and to observe the world and himself.

Yet death, in killing things, does not extinguish their atoms, but only scatters the stardust, which then joins anew in different shapes and colors.

He took a deep breath, his right side a little tender. Against small odds, his atoms held together, and he was still alive. For how long, he didn't know. But while he was alive, he'd better live. He'd better see what happened when he tried new things.

Yes, he'd play that game of chance to its fullest, while atoms minded their own dance in the void, indifferent to mortals' dreams.

We have no power to shorten our imprisonment in death. Live on, then!

If and when he got hurt, he'd handle it. But could he bear to watch Moskon get hurt? Moskon, who tried so hard to overcome his sickly nature and make his father proud? Or his beloved daughter Meda, who cheered her father up and read to him? Or his two stepdaughters? Even Rescuporis, with his annoying behavior? Freed from fear for himself, Scorilus still feared for his children. And how long would he be able to protect them, before turning into Lucretius's atoms, seeping into the cold dirt of a shallow grave?

In the morning, he'd mount that barbed arrow on the wall of the great hall, pointing up to a heaven devoid of gods, to remind himself of the true nature of things.

Chapter Twelve

The Valdavian Chronicle

Before midnight on the first day of fall, Nicetas and his men arrived at the hunting quarters of the king's house. Servants began unloading freshly killed game, pelts and furs, and smoked meat from the wagons. This summer, the goddess Bendis had delivered the best quarry in years. Too bad She hadn't delivered the one thing Nicetas wanted most.

Zalmodava didn't feel like home though. The night smelled of upturned earth and was loud with the croaking of angry frogs.

Nicetas wished he were back in Twin Willows with Una in their house like newlyweds. All summer long, he had brought up the new queen of Valdavia to make her jealous. Una would remind him of her duty to Ea, but then throw herself at him like there was no tomorrow.

In truth, she had nothing to fear. Because she was in the good graces of the goddess Enoz of the crops, he didn't need to perform the sacred royal duties to protect the harvest. He'd take Andrada to bed one day to produce heirs for Cothelas and himself, but right now the thought of touching another woman the way he touched Una balled up his stomach.

He stomped on the floor to knock the caked dirt off his boots, stretching his arms and his stiff back. He'd have to deal with the saddle sores later. He yawned until his jaw popped.

When he opened his eyes, Zyraxes stood before him, gripping his staff. He didn't look happy, but then, he never did.

"It's past midnight, Zyraxes. I'm going to bed." Nicetas spread his legs slightly to ease the discomfort.

"I'm here to ask for your forgiveness, my dear brother." It was the least sincere tone Nicetas had ever heard.

"Whatever for?"

"I was away at the Boulder Hut on Mount Ea-El, fasting and playing the panpipes for the gods. So I wasn't here to stop the queen from razing the temple's sacred woodland." He pointed through a side archway into the darkness.

"I can't see a thing right now. Can we talk in the morning?" Nicetas yawned and turned around, but Zyraxes blocked him.

Nicetas walked to the archway and stared into the night. The crescent moon and the handful of stars that shone around the clouds revealed nothing, though the smell of raw earth hinted at the truth. He scratched his stubbly cheek. "How bad is it?"

"She felled my sky oak." Zyraxes choked on his words. "My sacred tree. You must lock her up in the Six-Sided Tower. Nothing else will appease the gods."

Nicetas sensed the danger. "Andrada is the queen, Zyraxes, the queen you wanted, remember? You're the one who read the entrails of the white bull." He couldn't help feeling a twinge of satisfaction. "Were you wrong then...or are you wrong now?"

"You must punish her!" Zyraxes slammed his staff against the floor.

"No, I mustn't. Answer the question." Nicetas was fully awake now.

The frown between Zyraxes's bushy eyebrows deepened to a scar-like line. "You know the gods work in mysterious ways."

"I know. And They favor me. I even died once and went to the Underworld. The reason I'm here now is that Ea rescued me and sent me back here to be your king."

"My sky oak helped me feel Ea's touch on our world. You're letting Her down—"

Oroles came in from the darkness through the archway. "Welcome home, my lord. I brought you some fresh water."

Nicetas drank the cool, sweet water of home, grateful for the chance to stop and think. For as long as he could remember, Zyraxes had blamed him, doubted him, humiliated him.

"Zyraxes has some troubling news, Oroles. What happened to his woodland?"

"The queen and the prince hope you'll like King Cothelas's gift, my lord. The gardens are a work of marvel, blossoming all summer long."

"A gift from Cothelas the Bald?" Nicetas said. "That changes things."

Zyraxes pointed at Oroles. "You left this commoner in charge here, and he failed us."

Nicetas raised his voice. "I didn't need to leave anyone in charge because I've been ruling my kingdom from my new king's house in Twin Willows. As you've probably noticed, your temple has been receiving Roman coin of late—"

"This is not about your border arrangement with the emperor—it's about him."

Nicetas had had enough of Zyraxes's bile. Oroles was his chosen first councilor. A man with a trade, a builder who had finished his apprenticeship, knew how to read and write and how to work with numbers. A man who kept the gods' words close to his heart.

"Oroles is no ordinary commoner," Nicetas said. "The goddess Herself spoke to him once, up on Mount Ea-El."

"You don't believe that," Zyraxes said with a smirk.

Nicetas believed that story more than he believed in his own descent into the Underworld. He couldn't remember seeing or hearing the goddess and being saved, though Una and everyone else said it had happened.

But Oroles's story felt true. He'd been lying in bed half dead during the last pox outbreak, when Ea appeared to him and told him he'd live. When he was well again, he thought it had been a fever spirit toying with him, so he went up on Mount Ea-El to pray for clarity. One night, he saw the fiery eyes of Samca's spirits around his campfire and heard Samca's thundering voice: "Go back to your village. Live and die like a builder." He was frightened, but he stayed—the fire kept him safe. Later that very night, Ea spoke to him in a soothing voice: "The Great Awakening is upon us, yet parts of El's beautiful garden have turned into a wasteland. Oroles, son of Zonaras, bring this message to all my mortal children: It's time to right your ways, or you'll face El's wrath when He awakes. Teach them, Oroles, to help those in need, respect their neighbors, and never repay evil with evil—and El's gardens will be restored." Those were the true words of a goddess to Her chosen mortal—Nicetas didn't doubt that.

"Once and for all, Zyraxes, Oroles is my brother."

"I'm your brother," Zyraxes said, "and I have to remind you of it every day."

"No, you don't." Nicetas turned to leave.

"Your queen," Zyraxes called after him, "turned my sky oak into gallows and water boxes for her waterwheel. My sacred tree, brother!"

Nicetas threw Oroles an inquiring frown.

"We now have a waterwheel, my lord," Oroles said. "Built by a Roman architect and turned by the tread of beast or man."

"I see." Nicetas turned to Zyraxes. "So, the queen you've blessed me with helped our most treasured friend and ally turn Zalmodava Hill into a garden worthy of a Roman emperor. I don't see how this is not cause for celebration. Brother."

"By Beleizis's thunder," Zyraxes yelled, "it was a sacred tree—"

"For which, tomorrow morning, the queen and I will bring offerings to the Temple of Concord. Make sure Citera knows we're coming."

Zyraxes slammed his staff again. "I'll tell your wife about Una. She'll be hurt and humiliated. And she'll tell her father."

Nicetas weighed his threat. "I'll lock you up in the Six-Sided Tower if you do."

"The gods cherish honesty," Oroles whispered, and Nicetas cut him a hard glance.

"No, the queen is not to be disturbed."

"You're not punishing her at all?" Zyraxes sounded defeated.

"What's done is done, brother," Nicetas said. "Next time I'm in Twin Willows, I'll ask Una to handpick a sky oak sapling for you."

Zyraxes now had tears in his eyes. "Don't you dare," he whispered, then walked away.

The Book of Andrada

The day after the king's arrival in Zalmodava, Andrada brought Dapyx and Apollonius with her while her husband examined the new waterwheel. It was her first chance to gain the trust of the man she hadn't seen since her wedding. While he was gone, Oroles and Zyraxes ruled the city, though never together. They weren't friendly to Andrada, but they weren't friendly to each other either. Zalmodava would do better under one constant ruler, as Andrada would now argue. She'd make the case to Nicetas by showing him her new gardens, which had flourished all summer long.

The air was sweet with the scent of fire-dried Valdavian sky oak. Nicetas had arrived with Oroles at the site of Zyraxes's felled tree, but he didn't look angry, just preoccupied. He walked around the honey-colored timber frame, patted the turnstile, and shielded his eyes against the sun as he studied the toothed drum fixed on top of the pillar. Oroles pointed to a hinged piece that fell between the drum's teeth and kept it from slipping backward when it turned.

"It's so simple," Nicetas said. "Oroles, you're a builder. Why didn't you think of a contraption like this?"

"This machine took our engineers centuries to perfect," Apollonius said.

Nicetas followed along the horizontal post with its smaller toothed drum at one end and the axle of the waterwheel at the other. He arrived at the well. He lifted one of the wooden boxes and swiveled it around its iron hinges. "Why move our water uphill when the gods have given us a land crossed by rivers?"

"Steppewynd could put this machine to better use," Oroles said.

Nicetas squinted at his blood brother. "Always thinking of Steppewynd, aren't you?"

"The Steppewynders are Dhawosian folk, just like us. They want a better life for their children, just like we do. We've been keeping that from them for years—"

"Enough," Nicetas said.

Both men had intense looks in their eyes. Andrada thought to say something to cut through that tension, but what could she say to those two strangers? Yet from their curt exchange, she gathered it wouldn't be easy to convince Nicetas to show mercy to Steppewynd, as High Priestess Citera had hoped. They'd have to become closer before she could bring up the Steppewynders' plight.

"Would my king like to see how it works?" She gripped one of the crossbeams of the turnstile and pushed. It didn't budge. She shoved her back against it.

Dapyx ran to help her, but she shook her head. "No, let the king do it."

Dapyx blushed and slinked away. Nicetas stepped into his little brother's place and leaned against the turnstile. The whole frame resisted and creaked for another moment, then the beam in Andrada's hands slipped forward. She planted her heels against the grooves on the wooden floor and strained with her entire body to keep it moving. With each step, the beam grew harder to push as the buckets filled with water, until two gardeners joined in, and they all settled into a rhythm marked by the clanking of the gear lock on the toothed drum at the top of the turnstile.

"Keep the wheel turning," Nicetas told the gardeners as he stepped away.

Andrada and Apollonius followed him to the other end of the structure, where the loop of empty buckets sealed with pitch and beeswax dunked into the well, while the full, dripping ones soared above their heads. Water splashed into a trough at the top of the wheel.

"And the aqueduct?" Nicetas said.

"We have not started working on it yet," Apollonius said, "but when it is built, we will have running water in Zalmodava. The days when people hauled buckets from the well in the king's house courtyard will be over. No more maintaining the underground tunnels that bring water from the Ozana River to the well. And this water is cleaner than that of the river, where villagers wash and bathe upstream."

"Not until the gods are appeased," said a voice Andrada had missed for the last few moons. Citera stood on the other side of the waterwheel, her eyes shadowed by her black cowl.

"High Priestess Citera," Nicetas said, "I gather you're here to tell me what Ea demands of me and my queen."

Andrada didn't know what he meant, but she liked the way he had said *my queen*. If he was happy with her work, he might give her ruling duties soon. He certainly didn't seem to enjoy ruling, just hunting.

"Indeed," Citera said. "Ea has named Her price."

"Let me guess," Nicetas said. "She wants me to slay an ox."

"A dark bull, my lord."

Nicetas laughed without mirth. Andrada hated that she didn't know what was going on. Did Zyraxes send Citera to punish Nicetas for the new gardens? Was Ea angry with Andrada for planting them? If so, why had they flourished all summer long?

After the dark bull's sacrifice at the sundial later that day, Andrada watched Citera perform the atonement ceremony in the Temple of Concord. As the high priestess poured the blood for the gods to taste, she asked both Andrada and Nicetas to return to their chambers for a day of solitude, fasting, and prayer.

Andrada sent Dokina to stay overnight with the kitchen maids and began her assigned task of prayers for forgiveness. She didn't know if the Valdavian gods would accept her prayers, so she asked Sehul, Mehnot, and Heusos to plead with Their brothers and sisters on her behalf.

Before going to sleep that night on an empty stomach, she asked the Three Divines to keep her gardens free of pests and plight—and Zyraxes's curses.

In the morning, after a quick bite of bread and honey, she headed to the throne chamber to ask her husband to let her sit with him during Petition Day.

A guard stood by the door, a spear in hand, but no one else was there. Andrada hadn't seen the throne chamber of Zalmodava before. It was smaller than the one back home but more charming. The walls were covered in black walnut panels carved with profiles of Valdavian kings. The hearth in the center was made of marble, and the king's chair was polished silver.

"Tell the king I'm here," Andrada told the guard posted outside the council chamber.

"I'm afraid King Nicetas has left Zalmodava this morning."

Andrada's body stiffened. "It can't be." She had waited all summer to speak with the king.

She found a lock of hair but no comfort in twirling the short ringlet around her finger. Her mind flashed through the past day, from the waterwheel to the temple ceremony, but she couldn't remember any mention of another coming journey. Nicetas must have had a good reason to leave, but what and where?

She didn't quite know how she returned to her chamber.

"The kitchen maids said the king has gone hunting again, though the cellars are full," Dokina told her at the door. "Most animals are burrowing for the winter. The Blue Highlands may already be covered in snow..."

Andrada found her horse-box on the table, next to the new glass inkwell. It was still whole though Dokina had asked the divine being to crack it if they shouldn't call Him *He*.

Andrada clutched her crystal bell, choosing her words. "Fearsome god, please bring my husband back soon, alive and healthy." She didn't want Nicetas to return early because he'd been injured while boar hunting, but she wanted him in Zalmodava so she could start her royal apprenticeship already.

She rang the bell, bitter about the time wasted waiting for her husband over the spring and summer. Every passing day was another one her father stayed disappointed in her for failing the King's Challenge. Every day, Syrmos grew into his role as the chosen heir of Kerta. Andrada's whole body trembled with the bell's sound, and her anger faded. She had been heard.

By the end of fall, snow had sealed the shutters of the queen's chamber, and the king still hadn't returned home. To Andrada's disappointment, her governing apprenticeship would have to wait until spring. She had asked Oroles to call up a Petition Day for her to oversee, but he seemed pained to even talk to her.

"I can't do that, my queen," he had said. "As first councilor, I'm supposed to handle Petition Day on behalf of my king."

One evening, Andrada sat by the hearth with the embroidery frame in her lap and a new sensation of sweat on the nape of her neck, where her hair was at last growing longer. For once, Dokina was quiet, working on her own embroidery.

Andrada was forever grateful to Citera for that blessed painkilling poultice of hers. The high priestess had just sent a new one that morning. Maybe someday Andrada would return the favor by convincing Nicetas to reopen the trade routes with Steppewynd—if she saw him long enough to talk to him.

She wondered why the crystal bell hadn't answered her prayer to bring her husband home. Was her wish unworthy of the divine being? Did He ignore wishes sometimes? Gods were capricious, yes...Andrada pushed the needle in. The black thread looped and knotted over the emerging image of Mount Kogalan on her canvas.

Andrada pushed the needle in again, right into her finger. "Ow!" She licked the tip of her forefinger and tasted blood. "I. Can't. Do. This."

"Let me see." Dokina put down her work. "It's just a prick. Here." She took out her crystal shard and touched the red dot on Andrada's finger. "You could use a thimble..."

Andrada shook her head. "Embroidering just isn't for me, Dokina."

"Like everything else, it's hard at first. We'll work on it again tomorrow. The light is better in the morning anyway." Dokina stacked the two embroidery frames on the table and put the needles and the balls of thread back in the basket. "Teach me more Greek letters, maybe?"

Andrada shrugged. "I guess…It's not even suppertime…Gods, I hate this chamber. I wish the nurse were here with us."

"She wouldn't have time for us though, what with the baby and all." Dokina's hand shot up to her mouth.

The chamber turned cold. "What did you say?" Andrada whispered.

Dokina dropped her eyes. "I swear, I just found out from a Kertan merchant who had business here in Zalmodava. He knows Mama, and he's brought me news before. I was going to tell you. When the time was right."

"And when was this baby born?"

"Two moons ago. A little boy, fat and healthy."

"At her age, Dokina?" Andrada felt sick.

"That's what I thought too. Auntie is a year younger than Mama, and I think Mama might be forty years old. Auntie could be a grandmother by now. But if Ea blessed Auntie's womb, who are we to complain?"

The nurse hadn't spent any time missing Andrada. She had replaced her. Andrada's stomach knotted with tears she couldn't cry. The nurse had always been *her* nurse. The mother of a dead baby, yes, but not the mother of a fat and healthy boy. "Is she even married?"

"To Tzintus the woodcutter."

"But when…when did she have the time to move, get married, and have a baby?" Andrada tried to grab a ringlet, but it brought back memories of her nurse. She clasped her hands together instead.

"It was time for her to have her own family…" Dokina said. It sounded like an apology.

A kitchen girl knocked on the door and announced that supper was ready.

"I'm not hungry." Andrada could think of nothing now but the nurse and her baby.

"There's someone waiting for my queen in the dining hall," the girl said.

"The king?" A spark of hope.

"High Priest Zyraxes has returned from the Boulder Hut on Mount Ea-El and wants to share bread and salt with his queen."

Andrada didn't care about Zyraxes right now. "Tell him I'm not hungry." She waved the girl away. The door closed. "Dokina, can you talk to that Kertan merchant of yours and find out more?"

"He's gone back since we talked. The Norland Pass is always open, even in snow. He said something else..." She played with her amulet pouch and waited for Andrada's sign to go on. "Rumors that King Cothelas is planning to adopt Syrmos."

"As...his son?" Andrada stared at the limbs of fire in the hearth. To her nurse and her father, it was as if she had never existed. How could they have shape-shifted like night spirits the moment she had gone away? No, the nurse didn't matter anymore, only her father.

Andrada had been working hard to become the leader he had once wanted her to be. Since the wedding, she had built a garden and harvested its crops. She had read the entire *Valdavian Chronicle*, with its three centuries' worth of local history, in hopes she'd take over Petition Day. In due course, she'd convince Nicetas to reopen the trade routes with Steppewynd and return the three Dhawosian kingdoms to prosperity. And when the time came, she'd state her claim and fight her new brother Syrmos for the Kertan throne.

A jolt of dread hit her. In her haste, she had just made a mistake a real queen would never make. "Did Zyraxes just say he wanted to share supper with me?" It was important to make things right with him. After all, he was the high priest of Beleizis and a prophet.

She flung open the door and ran all the way to the dining hall. The table was set for two, steam rising from the broth in the bowls, but no one was there.

Chapter Thirteen

The Book of Andrada

It was bees, butterflies, and birds as far as Andrada could see, and she heard the burbling of irrigation canals everywhere. The king would return any day now, and her apprenticeship could finally begin.

She was proud of her work here in Zalmodava: the kitchen garden, with its dark and light green rows; the herb garden with purple and yellow blossoms; the flower garden, filled to the brim with patterns of scented color—the Valdavian goddess Enoz had blessed the new crops that spring even though the king and queen hadn't performed their sacred royal duties.

The air grew cooler as Andrada, accompanied by Dokina, reached the water garden in what used to be Zyraxes's sacred place. The gardeners had finished laying six small fishponds around the waterwheel. The wheel turned with the lazy tread of a mule, and the trough emptied into Apollonius's new aqueduct.

Andrada heard rushed footsteps behind them. It was Dapyx, running on the newly paved road.

"How does he always find us, Dokina?"

"I told you that old kiss was trouble." Dokina hid her giggles. "You should remind him you're a married woman and he's only fifteen."

"I know, but I must be gentle. He's a friend."

Andrada turned around and waited for Dapyx. He was dressed for riding, in woolen trousers and a short tunic, but he wore no hat, his cloak was drab, and from his belt hung the curved blade of a sica in a plain leather sheath.

"Dressed for the road, Dapyx?" Andrada said.

"May I walk with you?" the prince said, not glancing at Dokina.

"Dokina, return to the house," Andrada said. "Oh, don't look so sad. I won't be long." She took Dapyx's arm, and his eyes widened. To Dokina, she said, "I'll want some bread and honey, and some warm milk when I get back."

Dokina nodded. "Remind him today," she whispered before she left.

Andrada strolled with Dapyx at her side. The air was fragrant, Sehul's sun went in and out of the clouds, and shadows blurred and sharpened on the white river-stone pavers. She stole a glance at Dapyx. Maybe it was wrong, but it felt good to have him around. He was family now, certainly more family than her husband, who had been in the Blue Highlands since last fall. More family than her father, who had given up on her and chosen Syrmos. More family than her nurse, who now lived under a woodcutter's roof in Albanor with a little boy at her breast.

Dokina was right though. She had to make Dapyx understand there was no hope for his infatuation with her.

"Do you think Nicetas will like my blossoming gardens?" she said.

"I'm sure he will—if he stops by long enough to see them."

"Oh, I miss my husband so much." That sounded fake, but Dapyx cringed nonetheless.

They walked in silence alongside gurgling ceramic pipes laid on the ground, following the path of apple saplings to the king's house.

Dapyx cleared his throat. "Is there anything you'd like me to bring you from the valley?"

"The valley?"

"Sanapa and Erebon, the villages on the Ozana River. That's where Zalmodava's artisans and laborers live."

Andrada knew commoners didn't live inside the fortress, unlike her people in Sehuldava, on lower terraces. "What I meant was, what do the common folk say when Prince Dapyx of Valdavia comes to their village?"

"He doesn't." He pointed to his ordinary clothing. "To them, I'm Master Balius from the king's house kitchen. It's been working so far."

"Clever. And what does Master Balius do in the valley?"

"He steals kisses from girls." Despite his voice slipping a little, Dapyx looked defiant, as if he wanted Andrada to be troubled by his words.

She wasn't. "And when he doesn't steal kisses from girls?"

Dapyx began to blush. "I talk to the stall keepers at the market. I learn what's going on in all of Dhawosia, more so than I gather from my tutors."

A queen could use that kind of knowledge. Setting the boy straight could wait a little longer.

"You know, Dapyx, I've been here for a year now, but I've never set foot outside the fortress. I want to come with you. I want to learn more about my country, about my people."

"I can teach you about Valdavia—"

"No, not like that. Back in Kerta, I studied everything there was about Valdavia, Steppewynd, and Moesia. But I never even left Sehuldava until Nicetas took me away." She clasped her hands in prayer and turned to him. "Will you help me explore my new country, Dapyx? The valley is as good a place to start as any."

The prince looked pleased but took a long moment to answer. "Fine, I'll take you with me. But you'll have to follow my word in everything. We can't get caught."

"I'll do exactly as you say, Master Balius." She bowed her head. "So, how do I look?" She pointed at her clothes made of fine blue wool embroidered with silver thread.

"Very beautiful," he blurted, then turned red the next moment.

Andrada burst out laughing. "What I meant is I can't go dressed like this."

"Gods, no. Plain riding clothes would be best. Boy's clothes, no earrings. And you'll need a hat over that hair."

"But I don't have boy's clothes." She was about to say *here* but caught herself.

"I'll bring you some of mine. We're almost the same height."

"And who will I be?"

"Balius's apprentice...Lipoxais. He...doesn't talk much. In fact, he doesn't speak at all."

Andrada nodded. She'd discourage Dapyx's feelings another day.

The Book of Dapyx

The next morning, Dapyx paced around the stables' courtyard, a ball of nerves in his stomach. He had barely slept after he gave Dokina a change of his clothes and was left imagining Andrada's small breasts touching the linen of his tunic as she dressed. Had he known the entrance to the secret corridors of the king's house, he would have watched her through a peephole. Since her arrival, he'd been looking everywhere for that entrance. He had started with the kitchen, behind cupboards and piles of firewood—nothing. He had inspected the hallways at night, searched behind statues and inside hearths—no luck. He had even asked Kosingas, the current scribe of *The Valdavian Chronicle*, to bring any drawings he could find in the temple library—no secret corridors on the brittle scrolls. Still, he hoped.

The gates under the stables' archway creaked open. Andrada looked ordinary enough in Dapyx's faded blue cloak, properly clasped over her right shoulder with a bronze pin. His gray woolen trousers hugged her long legs, and she seemed taller in his scuffed riding boots. She wore Dapyx's brown fur hat, which he had chosen for its flaps that covered her pierced earlobes and her longer hair.

He pulled her draft horse from the barn, a short, black, easygoing gelding with hooves covered in tufts of hair.

"A man's horse, not a palfrey," he said. "If we're to go into the valley as Balius and Lipoxais, I must teach you how to mount and ride your horse like a man."

He let go of the reins and locked his fingers to make a step for her, but she didn't follow his lead. She put on her riding gloves and stood by the point of the horse's shoulder as if whispering in his ear. Her left hand rested on the crest of his neck. The horse stood still and smelled her gloves. Dapyx watched in amazement as she placed both hands on the horse's back, her elbows out, and pushed herself up. She swung her right leg over the croup, her cloak floating open on air, and she sank into the saddle without rattling her ride.

Dapyx couldn't have done it better himself.

She leaned forward and grabbed the reins. The horse lifted his head, inched forward, and let out a soft snort. Andrada's heel tapped in, just behind his girth.

"Shall we?" She nudged her ride and cantered out of the courtyard.

Dapyx closed his mouth. What else didn't he know about her?

He hurried to bring his own saddled horse from the barn, a dapple-gray stallion named Dapple, his brothers' gift for his tenth birthday. Dapple shook his head, nickering, asking for a carrot. Dapyx gave him his due, and while the horse munched, he grabbed a thick lock of mane and mounted, but not as smoothly as Andrada. He grunted with pain, clicked his tongue, and started after her gelding at a sharp trot.

"Let's not attract too much attention to ourselves," he told Andrada when he caught up with her.

The guard at the Six-Sided Tower pocketed a silver coin and lowered the drawbridge. Dapyx and Andrada loped over the Twelve-Pier Bridge and headed north, into the forest.

"You ride well," Dapyx said when they reached a clearing.

"I had good tutors."

What kind of tutors, he wanted to ask, but she took off again.

They followed the Ozana River upstream, and Dapyx halted at the fork in the road. "To the right, we have Erebon, with its master blacksmith. Left is Sanapa, home of a great carpenter and his warmhearted daughter." He watched Andrada but saw no sign of jealousy.

"I could use a blade," she said, and he couldn't believe his ears. "Erebon today, Sanapa tomorrow."

The path sloped down through the thinning forest. The sun glimmered through the leaves above their heads. A small village soon appeared—a few dozen thatched roofs spread in circles around a white oak tree. The sounds of the forest fell quiet, and the sounds of the village grew louder: a dog barking, the watermill cranking, goats bleating on the riverbank.

"Remember," Dapyx said, "I'm Master Balius, and you're my apprentice, Lipoxais." He dismounted at the barrelhouse and tied Dapple to an iron ring in the wall, next to the water trough and a block of white salt.

Andrada dismounted too and tied her horse, not waiting for Dapyx's help.

"Pull your hat low," he said, "walk half a step behind me, and let me do the talking."

The marketplace in Erebon lay under the white oak's shade. Most people were out tilling the fields, but some stalls were open, selling seeds, medicinal potions, and coops of goslings.

"The blacksmith is through there," Dapyx said, pointing Andrada to the muffled hammering beyond the square.

Across the road, toward the thick smoke drifting from the smelter, a lonely Sarmatian merchant had stretched a rug on the grass and was arranging his wares. He wore a headdress like a caravan driver and dealt in small statuettes of polished sandstone. As they drew near, Dapyx could make out the carved shapes and faces—including Nicetas and Una together.

Since the Night Attack, common people had been thinking of Una as the true queen of Valdavia. They made offerings to the statuettes of the king and queen they believed would perform the sacred royal duties demanded by Enoz. Though this year the crops would depend more on Germanic tribesmen paid with Roman coin.

Dapyx couldn't let Andrada see those statuettes. He grabbed her arm. "We must go."

"Now? What about the blacksmith?"

The Sarmatian merchant smiled, caressing his black beard. "Young masters, stay a while. Come look at my wares."

Dapyx felt a rush of panic. The merchant knew what Nicetas looked like. He might recognize Andrada too. "Zyraxes," he blurted out. "I just saw him talking to the blacksmith."

"Are you certain?" Andrada said.

"We'll come back another day. You promised to do as I say."

He pulled Andrada along, and together they retraced their steps across the square, to the barrelhouse and their horses. He looked back once in a while to keep up the ruse, but nobody followed or paid attention to them.

Dapyx realized he was still holding her hand. She was beautiful, with her flushed cheeks, her green eyes, her red lips parted as she panted. She was with him, and she trusted him. He wished she'd never let go.

Chapter Fourteen

The Book of Scorilus

On the top terrace of the White Fortress of Steppewynd, Scorilus watched his stepson Rescuporis struggle against the coil of rope tying him from shoulders to waist to the trunk of the holly oak tree.

The crowd pressed in close while guards pushed them back. More people gathered on the rooftops around the Tyrine Tower. At Scorilus's side, Moskon, his youngest, stared at the scene, his face flushed despite the cool breeze on that spring afternoon.

"You won't hurt me, Father," Rescuporis said. "You won't disobey the gods and murder your son."

That argument didn't work for Scorilus anymore. "Where's my daughter? Where's Meda?"

"She's gone." Rescuporis grinned. "Gone, gone, gone. That sweet ass of hers will buy us a powerful alliance with a Tauri lord and his fierce riding archers."

Scorilus balled his hands into fists. The thought of his seventeen-year-old Meda thrown on the fur rugs of a filthy chieftain from the Tauris Peninsula, passed from one barbarian to another—it choked him.

The Greek historian Herodotus had written about those faraway lands, where they made bowls from their enemies' skulls, arrowheads from their bones, waterskins from their hides. Where they fed human flesh to their dogs and bears, wove blankets from human hair, and buried living horses with their dead warriors.

Scorilus felt his blood boiling. If there was one thing he had done right in his wretched life, it was raising his daughter. Healthy, beautiful, loving. He knew he'd have to part with her soon, but not like this. Now her life depended on his staying calm.

"Where did you take her?" he said with dangerous evenness.

"You'll thank me one day," Rescuporis said, "when you have the army you need to conquer Valdavia, our promised land. My new Tauri allies—"

Scorilus groaned. "You and your wars. We don't need Valdavia, Rescuporis. We can restore our ancestral lands to their former glory. And we can do it through trade, not war."

Rescuporis and his mercenaries had been guarding the Traders' Guild's route through the Danubius Delta, bringing salt and pickled fish from the new Steppewynder salt pans to the merchants of Roman Moesia. The merchants kept their emperor happy while he built his Coliseum. With coin coming in from Cispius of Tomis, Scorilus was buying not only Egyptian grain to feed the hungry but also Levantine cedar to replace the fleet once squandered by his brother Eptalas. This spring, the first ships started sailing along the western shores of the Black Sea, replacing Rescuporis's mosquito-infested trade route through the delta.

Scorilus leaned into his stepson's face. "I would've let you run my new trading fleet."

"You think trade sounds heroic?" Rescuporis wriggled against the ropes. "Well, I traded Meda for riders for my army."

Scorilus took a deep breath. "Where's your sister?"

"Half-sister. You didn't mind marrying my other sisters to chieftains of your choosing. Why is Meda different?"

Because of her love for Scorilus. She kept him company, read to him, made sure he ate and rested, and never asked for anything in return other than to have a say in her own marriage.

Scorilus stepped back and gave the sign. One of the guards threw a rope over Rescuporis's ankles and cinched it around the tree trunk. The jeering of the crowd grew louder.

"Where is your sister?" Scorilus said.

Rescuporis looked away, defiant. "The view is great from here, Father. King Thiaper's Tyrine Tower. Eptalas's estuary. Phradmon's hills. And in the valley, one day, an army of Tauri riders at my command, thanks to Meda."

"You won't live to see that day if you don't tell me how to find her." Scorilus stepped back and took a longbow and a quiver from one of his guards.

The crowd retreated, but Moskon stayed put, a terrified look on his face. "Please, Father, don't hurt my brother."

"If you're to be king someday, you should stomach this."

Scorilus plucked an arrow by the feathers and fitted it on the bowstring. It was a simple arrow, not the barbed kind that had wounded him during the Night Attack, but it would still hurt. He squinted and aimed its blurry tip at Rescuporis's right leg.

If he missed, the crowd would laugh at him, and then he'd have to kill his stubborn stepson in front of them.

"Stop, stop," he heard his wife cry. "In the name of Napat-Dehnu, stop!"

He lowered his bow as Rescuturme ran to the holly oak, her new red robes billowing. It had been a while since the last time they talked. They lived separate lives now, but he was glad she had found him. Maybe she'd knock some sense into her stubborn son's head.

"I'm fine, Mother," Rescuporis said. "Now go away."

"How are you fine?" Rescuturme grabbed at the ropes. "You're tied to a tree." She turned to Scorilus. "And you, why are you pointing an arrow at your own son?"

"He sold our daughter to a Tauri barbarian." Scorilus's voice trembled. "He won't tell me where she is."

She turned to Rescuporis. "What have you done to Meda, you fiend?" She propped her fists on her hips. Her face was red and sweaty from running there.

"Father, make her go away," Rescuporis said.

Rescuturme slapped him. "You don't talk to your mother like that."

Her son groaned. "Go away, woman. People are watching us."

She turned to Scorilus. "Please don't hurt him. Put him in the tower for a day or two. He'll come around, you'll see."

"We don't have a day or two," Scorilus said. "Guards, take the queen away!"

The guards did as ordered. Rescuturme shrieked and cursed and begged until Scorilus could no longer hear her over the crowd's noise.

He fitted the arrow back on the string. "Where is she?"

"You're lost in the wilderness, Father, while Napat-Dehnu is guiding me to victory."

There was no Napat-Dehnu.

Scorilus loosed his arrow and pierced his stepson's right thigh. Rescuporis grunted but didn't scream. Scorilus dropped the bow. He couldn't believe he had hit his target.

Moskon turned around and threw up.

Scorilus stepped closer. Blood dripped from Rescuporis's leg, over his boot, on the dirt at the holly oak's roots. "Where's my daughter?"

Rescuporis struggled and cursed.

Scorilus motioned for a guard to pick up the bow, now that he had made his point. "The left leg now. Nock your arrow...Draw...Loose."

The arrow appeared through Rescuporis's left thigh. This time, he screamed.

"There's more of you to pierce, Rescuporis."

Scorilus waited while the archer nocked another arrow. "Where is Meda?"

"I'm here, Father! Here!"

Scorilus didn't know where to look, his heart beating in his throat.

"Meda?" Moskon called, wiping his mouth.

People stepped aside, and she appeared.

Her robes were stained, her red hair undone, but it was Meda, and she looked unharmed. On her arm, she even wore the coiling gold snake from Scorilus. A dozen Tauri archers followed, men and women.

Tears made Scorilus's world blurrier than before. "Meda...how?"

"Please, Father, untie him."

Meda and the Tauri archers stopped a few paces away, close enough that Scorilus could smell a trace of his daughter's sweet perfume.

"What did they do to you?" he said.

"Nothing at all," Meda said.

"What did you bribe them with?" Rescuporis said between grunts.

"A cartload of iron ore. A man named the Cartographer convinced them to trade me back to my father."

She sounded a little unsure as she pointed to a man among the Tauri. Not that the details really mattered. Scorilus would do anything to have her back.

The Cartographer wasn't dressed like a Tauri rider. His cloak was made of furry patches of bearskin. He wore no hat, and his sandy hair was unkempt. From his pilgrim's belt hung tools useful for the road, and he had a leather satchel across his chest.

"He is right," Scorilus told the Tauri archers in his stiff Sarmatian. "At sundown, I will give you two cartloads if you leave her here with me now." New ore had just arrived from Tomis on one of the new ships.

The Tauri leader, a woman with a fur hat low on her forehead, glanced at Rescuporis.

"We take him with us," she said. "And three cartloads of iron ore."

Scorilus nodded to his guards, who untied Rescuporis and held him upright, the two arrows sticking out from his legs.

"Once again, trade beats war," he told his son in Dhawosian, "but you and I are done. Never come back to the White Fortress."

"Father?" Meda said.

"No, he's betrayed us, and he must go." Before sundown, Scorilus would move to secure Rescuporis's old trade route through the Danubius Delta.

"Very well, Father," Rescuporis said. "Moskon, farewell, brother. Judging by your health, I may never see you again."

If Scorilus had felt any pity for his stepson, it vanished then. He pushed Rescuporis to the Tauri leader while she sent Meda his way.

The next moment, his daughter was in his arms, and the crowd burst into cheers.

At sundown, Scorilus and the Cartographer watched the Tauri riders leave with their three cartloads of iron ore. Rescuporis rested on a bed of hay in another cart, his leg wounds tied with bandages. As his cart pulled away, he glanced back one last time, but Scorilus didn't acknowledge him.

"How can I ever repay you, Cartographer?" Scorilus said after the fortress gates closed.

"One day, I'll ask for a favor, and I hope King Scorilus will grant it." The Cartographer spoke Dhawosian with a Valdavian accent, open vowels and smooth sounds. "Until then—"

He reached into his satchel and pulled out a parcel, something of an odd shape, wrapped in dirty linen.

Scorilus took it and found the edges of the cloth. He recognized the crystal hilt of a dagger. Then he gasped in horror. The dagger's blade went through a shriveled right hand. The skin was discolored and dry, the nails looked like tree bark, but even so, Scorilus knew whose severed hand that was. He dropped it, and it landed on the dusty ground, covered in white crumbs and stained linen.

"Kertan salt," the Cartographer said, "to keep the flesh from decaying further."

Scorilus pounced at the crystal hilt, feeling a moment of terror as he stepped on the twiglike remains under the sole of his boot—and pulled out the dagger. He locked the Cartographer in a tight grip and pressed the still-sharp blade against his neck. An unexpected cool smell came from the man's open mouth as he panted. Valdavian water mint.

The Cartographer kept his fists down. "I'm merely returning what's yours, King Scorilus."

"Where's my brother?"

"Judging by the dagger...Prince Phradmon is...dead."

Scorilus had known his brother had perished since Moskon was but a little thing riding on his knee and crying, *Giddy-up, horsey,* but it still hurt to hear the words spoken out loud. He released the man from his grip and rubbed tears from his eyes.

"Where did you get this?" He picked up Phradmon's severed hand in its linen wrapper.

"Sarmatia," the Cartographer said, rubbing his neck, "pinned to a well along the Old Salt Road, beyond the Borysthenes River. A warning to unwelcome travelers."

Scorilus wiped his eyes, the evening breeze drying his tears. He ran a finger along the dagger's crystal hilt, over the carving of the snake with two heads. The curved, double-edged steel blade was the perfect hand weapon for an explorer, great for slicing and stabbing.

He'd been jealous when his father sent Eptalas east in search of Napat-Dehnu's promised land, and a dagger similar to this passed from father to son. When Eptalas didn't return, Scorilus watched his father give Phradmon this very dagger. Later on, Scorilus asked his father for a third dagger for his own journey east, but the answer was no. No more explorers in King Thiaper's house. From now on, he needed warriors.

Odysseus would have been the perfect son for him: a king, a warrior, and an explorer. A son who returned home alive.

"Why didn't they keep this costly dagger?" Scorilus said. "Don't they care for a good steel blade and a large piece of crystal?"

"They care more if the world is terrified of them and keeps away."

"When did they...?" He couldn't say the words.

"The winds are strong in that part of the world. Judging by the dry skin on the bones, the trophy had been pinned there for a few good days before I found it, around the time of the harvest fair."

"My brother was alive as late as last fall?"

The Cartographer nodded. "I beg your forgiveness for not bringing it sooner. Winter was coming, I had a pressing matter to tend to in the Tauris Peninsula, and—"

"Don't. You found my daughter and brought her to me." Scorilus's voice trembled. "I'm forever in your debt. And asking even more of you now."

If Phradmon's body was out there, Scorilus's sacred duty was to bring him home and bury him in the family tomb, even with no gods watching.

"Bring me news of my brother's last whereabouts, and you'll be royally rewarded."

The Cartographer bowed his head. "My duties take me to Valdavia next, but I'll send word around and start the search."

CHAPTER FIFTEEN

The Valdavian Chronicle

Nicetas wiped the olive oil off his cheek with a wet towel. He picked up the razor while a servant held up his polished silver mirror. He started on his left side, close to the ear, and the blade slid down, taking with it the growth of the last day on the road. The beginning of summer in Zalmodava smelled different somehow—and it had to be the queen's new gardens.

The knock on the door was hurried and didn't wait for an answer.

"Welcome home, my lord," Oroles said, pushing in a wheelbarrow filled with scrolls, parchments, and tablets. "The letters since the beginning of spring."

Nicetas dipped the razor into the bowl. Bits of hair and circles of oil floated on the water. "I hoped to finish cleaning up first..."

"News from Roma speaks of an army growing strong again," Oroles said.

"Ah, you're finally home, little brother." Zyraxes appeared at the door, his staff in his hand and a scornful look in his eye.

Nicetas put down the razor.

"Your Holiness," Oroles said, but Zyraxes didn't acknowledge him.

"I have news for you," Zyraxes told Nicetas.

"What?" Nicetas said, instantly annoyed.

"As you were gone from fall to summer, you might not know that late this spring, Cothelas the Bald withdrew his soldiers from Valdavia. Now we don't have enough people to guard the emperor's northern border.

Some of our own tribes might return to plundering the Roman outposts in Moesia."

Nicetas glanced at Oroles, who motioned to the wheelbarrow. "I was about to—"

"Why did Cothelas do that?" Nicetas asked Zyraxes.

"The Kertan emissary said that you're not delivering on your part of the marriage alliance."

Nicetas bit his tongue and returned his attention to the mirror and the blade in his hand. This nasty surprise was his fault. At the end of winter, he had told Oroles he'd deal with his correspondence upon his return to Zalmodava. It wasn't Oroles's fault that Nicetas had put off his return, day after day, until summer arrived and he had no choice but to kiss Una goodbye and return to the drudgery of the Valdavian court.

Zyraxes narrowed his eyes. "Which part of the marriage alliance is he talking about?"

"For the love of all the gods!" Nicetas wasn't going to tell Zyraxes about promising Cothelas his firstborn son. "Oroles, I need to talk to the queen."

"At this hour, Queen Andrada is usually in the gardens—"

"Don't call the desecration of our sacred land a garden," Zyraxes said.

"Oroles, tell her to return to her chamber and wait for me," Nicetas said, and Oroles took off. "Zyraxes, didn't I ask you to make peace with the queen?"

"Believe me, brother, I tried. I climbed to the Boulder Hut, and I prayed to the gods for the strength to forgive her. But when I returned, willing to try, she refused to break bread with me."

Nicetas groaned. "I don't have time for this. Go!"

Zyraxes left.

Nicetas rubbed his palm over his cheek. The right side of his face was still rugged, but now his hand wasn't steady enough to finish the job, and he'd never let a servant shave him. No one had come near him with a drawn blade since the Night Attack.

"By Beleizis's thunder," he muttered as the servant held up the mirror again.

Nicetas had to keep Emperor Vespasianus happy, or else the next Roman campaign could be against Valdavia. He had no choice. He'd send word to Cothelas that the Kertan heir should be born early next year. Maybe the king would relent and send back his soldiers. But first, Nicetas had to do what he'd been dreading for more than a year.

"Bring me some wine," he told the servant. He'd need it.

The Book of Andrada

Andrada tied her horse to a rusty iron ring outside the barrelhouse in Erebon. Dapyx pulled Dapple to the water trough and rolled the salt block closer. Every time they visited the villages of the Ozana River Valley, they acted as Master Balius and his apprentice Lipoxais. To conceal her voice and accent, he did all the talking but asked the questions she was interested in. Over many moons, she had learned a great deal about the heart of Zalmodava.

As back in Sehuldava, people here feared their gods, worked hard to make a living, and followed the law of the land. Trade was hurting though. Andrada had ordered a sica with a thin hilt to fit her hand better than those in the armory, but each time she visited the blacksmith, he apologized for having no iron ore to make it. When she wanted to offer him more coin, Dapyx reminded her that a kitchen hand didn't have the means of a queen.

Andrada hoped she'd get her sica today, at long last.

"Good day, Master Balius," the innkeeper called through the window. "Busy day at King Nicetas's house today, no?"

"Busy how?" Dapyx said.

Andrada stayed near him, listening, her fur hat low on her head.

"Make sure you buy the freshest vegetables for the king's stew," the keeper said, "what with the great deal of game the carts hauled in. Must be all smoked so it won't spoil. I saw the royal convoy this morning when it crossed the valley. The goddess Bendis has truly blessed the king's bounty."

Andrada's breath caught in her throat. Nicetas was home, and she wasn't there to greet him. He might never allow her to run Petition Day after such a mistake. Whenever Oroles came down from the Blue Highlands, she'd spend time with him in hopes he'd help her with the king. All that work and patience could be in vain if she didn't return to the fortress right now.

"Hurry," she told Dapyx, who undid Dapple's reins with shaking hands.

"What about your sica?" he said.

She groaned. "The gods just don't want me to have that blade."

"Which gods? Yours or mine?"

They galloped all the way back to Zalmodava, cantered over the Twelve-Pier Bridge, and dismounted outside the gates. Dapyx left their exhausted horses and two silver coins with the gatekeeper, and they sneaked into the courtyard, where they parted ways.

"If you see him first," Andrada said, "tell him we were busy working in the gardens."

With Dokina's help, Andrada finished changing into her dress and was tying a red scarf around her tangled hair when the door slammed open against the wall.

"Leave us," Nicetas said, and Dokina shuffled out.

"What's the matter?" Andrada said. He couldn't be unhappy with her gardens. They were thriving. She hoped they'd be the reason he'd finally spend some time with her.

He lumbered across the chamber with a bitter look in his eyes. "We can't put it off any longer."

Oh, he was there for the sacred royal duties. Andrada's mind started racing. She couldn't remember Citera's instructions from last year, but she took his hand and pulled him to her bed. He followed her, whispering the beginning of the prayer to Enoz. She scooted back on lumpy furs, and he tumbled into the bed next to her. She froze there, not knowing what to do next.

"Please talk to me," she whispered. Their faces were so close now, she could see the stubble on his cheek and smell the wine on his breath.

He finished his prayer to Enoz, looking away from Andrada. Then his hand crawled up her inner thigh, finding its way under her skirt, to the warm spot between her legs. He grabbed her buttocks and pulled her closer. She remembered Citera's lessons, how she was supposed to please her husband, so she let him lead.

He avoided her gaze and climbed on top of her. She focused on Citera's words about the royals' duty to the gods and kept still. He was heavy on her chest, and her breath grew shallow. But she answered his impatient prodding and opened her legs.

The first thrust sucked the air out of her lungs. It was a sharp, ripping blow, followed by waves of pain in the soft matter of her belly, like a hammer striking a thumb. Again. Again. Again. Why hadn't anyone prepared her for this pain? Citera had said there might be blood, but not much, and it wouldn't hurt for long. Not true.

Neither of them wanted to perform these awful duties, but it seemed harder on her than on him. She used to be the future heir of Kerta, and now she was her husband's offer to the gods. With her eyes shut, Andrada saw Avezinas's rod, and she felt its burning pain not on her fingers but inside her. She opened her eyes and gasped for air. Nicetas was straining now, his swollen veins pulsing, a mist of sweat gathering into a trickle down his neck.

Again. Again. Then it stopped. Then it hit again, one last time, with Nicetas's loud grunt. She felt a slithering away between her legs, and he lifted his body off hers. She could breathe again. The first lungful of air reeked of sour wine and sweat, but she welcomed it.

Nicetas stood by the bed now, not looking at her but minding his trousers and belt. Andrada pulled herself up and sat on her pain, on wetness and warmth.

"Now talk to me." She felt her eyelids rimmed with heat but no tears.

"We'll have to do this again until you're with child," he said, slurring the words.

"What's wrong with you?" Andrada said. "What's wrong with us?"

"Not your concern," he said, then went out the door.

Emotions swirled inside Andrada, nameless and confusing.

A moment later, Dokina was by her side. "How was it?" she whispered.

Andrada took her hand. "I just hate my nurse." She was supposed to be there and take care of Andrada. But mothers died and nurses left.

"What on the gods' green earth does Auntie have to do with this?"

"I wish I could send soldiers all the way to Albanor to drag her from Tzintus's hut—"

"Please don't hate Auntie! Be mad at me. And your husband." Dokina took out her crystal shard and touched Andrada's shoulder with it. "Be mad at your father, who married you to a barbarian."

"It's my fault...I didn't do what Citera had taught me. I didn't remind him to respect Ea's essence in me."

Dokina sat on the bed's edge. "He shouldn't need reminding."

Andrada let go of Dokina's hand, turned away, and curled up with a pillow. "I don't love him, and he knows it. That's why he has no kindness for me. That's why he spends so little time in Zalmodava and so much time hunting in the Blue Highlands. I'm not a good wife to him, Dokina."

"He's a worse husband. I remember when Mama told me that men have a gods-given right to possess their women, as bulls do cows and roosters hens. You know what I told her? I asked her why Ea made things this way. Does She hate women? Is She not a woman Herself?"

Andrada was so tired of questions and reasoning. "Maybe women hate women the most, Dokina. Maybe a god would take better care of us than a goddess."

Maybe that was why the god of the bell hadn't brought Nicetas back home last fall when she asked: to protect her from a cruel man. She remembered his scar from the war. On their wedding night, he had called it Scorilus's branding. Today he hadn't removed his tunic. His body might be healed, but his mind was still ailing.

"Bring me the bell, Dokina."

She held out her hand until she felt the cold circle of crystal in her palm.

"Dear god of the bell, please heal Nicetas's wounds. Take away the scar Scorilus left on his body and on his mind. Make him whole again." She rang the bell.

"What about you?" Dokina said. "What about your scars?"

"Mine don't matter. Besides, I can't be a queen and have no scars."

The Valdavian Chronicle

The next morning, Nicetas woke up with a start. The shutters shook with thunder, the gods' impenetrable wrath. He passed a hand over his face, his cheek rasping against his fingertips. He was still in yesterday's clothes, his boots still on. The smell of rain was insufferable, and so was the thought of what had happened yesterday.

"Please forgive me, Enoz," he whispered. "Please put a little prince in my wife's belly, and please don't make me do it again." He wouldn't tell Una about it yet, lying to her by omission for the first time ever. He buried his throbbing head inside the fur blankets. Mating with the queen had made a mockery of his love for Una.

"My lord," Oroles called from the door, "may I come in?"

The real world, demanding Nicetas's attention again. "Yes, come in."

"I have a way out of the bind King Cothelas put us in," Oroles said, sounding hurried. "Please allow me to go to the White Fortress as your emissary."

"So Scorilus can kill you?" Nicetas got out of bed and took off his dirty shirt.

"I don't think he will."

"Right, because you're doing Ea's work." Nicetas put on a clean shirt and fidgeted with the laces at his neck. "Is that why you didn't kill him when you had the chance?"

Oroles looked pained by the question. "Human life is sacred, my lord. Only the gods can give it, and only they should take it away." As always, Oroles spoke of the gods.

"What will you tell Scorilus when you see him?"

"That we must work together to keep Emperor Vespasianus's legions off our shores."

Nicetas tightened his belt over the scar on his side. He had lost Cothelas's soldiers and could soon lose Vespasianus's gold and the Roman peace, but he had also lost that sense of righteousness that had animated him since the Night Attack. He couldn't claim he was better than Scorilus now, not after the harm done to his devotion to Una and their love.

"I know you'll never forgive Scorilus, my lord," Oroles said. "But please allow me to find a better way to serve the needs of Valdavia and Steppewynd."

There were no more clear lines separating right from wrong, so why shouldn't Nicetas send an emissary to the man who had once tried to kill him? The thought of having Steppewynder farmers back in the Valdavian fields didn't seem as loathsome as it had yesterday. Nicetas's change of heart couldn't have occurred at a better time.

Thunder picked up, and a shutter burst open. "Does this mean Beleizis agrees with us, Oroles?"

"I wouldn't dare say, my lord. But I hope this first step toward peace will be followed by others. And that King Cothelas will join us. Because alone we won't stand a chance against Roma when it comes for us."

Nicetas looked out the window. The villages across the Ozana River could one day be set ablaze by a Roman legion. A united Dhawosian front would discourage the emperor from looking north of the Danubius River for his next campaign.

"While you're in Steppewynd," he said, "travel the country and learn more about its people."

"I will, my lord. And as a sign of goodwill to Scorilus," Oroles said, his voice tentative now, "might we reopen the trading posts on our side of the border?"

"Why not, brother? Go sit at Scorilus's table, sleep under his roof, and visit his country. But don't go on and on about the Great Awakening. And, if at all possible, don't get yourself killed."

He wished Oroles had come up with this clever plan yesterday and saved him from bedding Andrada. Then again, he had only accepted the plan because of how yesterday made him feel now. *Oh, gods, why couldn't everything be as simple as roaming the forests and throwing spears?*

Oroles bowed. "My lord...may I also suggest that Queen Andrada take over Petition Day when we're both gone? The queen has already carried out a grand project—the new gardens are flourishing. Petition Day should be no trouble after raising an aqueduct to the Temple of Concord."

Nicetas hadn't expected that. "I know you think it was wrong for me to marry her, and now it's wrong for me to hide Una from her—in the name of the gods' honesty and all—but make up for it with Petition Day? Zyraxes will curse my name to his gods' heaven."

Though if Andrada were with child, she wouldn't have to rule for very long, and Zyraxes was used to waiting. The thought of angering Zyraxes felt like a balm.

Nicetas scratched his neck. Andrada had built those magnificent gardens, after all, and she might be good at sorting through people's dreary affairs for a while—something Nicetas had thought he could work on while in Twin Willows but had discovered he hated doing when he could either be with Una or go hunting instead.

"Very well," he said. His moment of peace was short-lived. Because until now, he hadn't thought how he'd take Andrada's infant son from her and send him to Cothelas.

The Book of Andrada

The day after the sacred royal duties, Andrada learned that Nicetas had left for the Blue Highlands, Oroles for the White Fortress, and that she would oversee Petition Days in their absence. But she was too heartbroken to start governing now.

During the following moon, Apollonius took care of her gardens while she locked herself in her chamber. Dokina brought meals, washed clothes, and kept her busy by asking for lessons in writing with Greek script. The quiet moments in between Dokina's chatter were the worst because of the awful memory of lying with the king. The thought of his touch made her ill, and she didn't understand why.

On midsummer morning, Andrada's twentieth birthday, she woke up from a dream where her father couldn't recognize her, and she understood why. Her life had shrunk so much since the King's Challenge that she couldn't recognize herself. She had once stared down the chieftains of Kerta, but now she couldn't get out of her chamber. Time to wake up from that bad dream. Time to get her sica. Next time Nicetas came to her chamber and refused to look her in the eye, she'd demand his respect with a blade if she had to.

Careful not to wake Dokina, she found Dapyx's riding clothes in the red trunk. She put them on, took off her earrings, and pulled down the brown fur hat, tucking the ends of her hair under the flaps. She cinched the leather belt, slipped a few coins in each pocket, and pulled on the riding gloves.

In the stable, she untied Dapyx's dapple-gray horse and mounted him. Any other horse missing would cause concern among the stable hands. She adjusted the reins and leaned down, almost hugging the horse's neck, but he wouldn't move. Of course, the carrots. After Dapple had a few, he agreed to trot out of the barn.

The city gates opened when they were still a ways away—an honest mistake on the part of the keeper, as Andrada wore Dapyx's clothes and rode his horse. She threw the man a silver coin and nudged Dapple toward the Twelve-Pier Bridge.

At the edge of the forest, the horse turned his head for another carrot. After that, he cantered of his own accord.

They crossed the muddy Ozana River at the ford and cut back into the forest. At the fork in the road, they turned right toward Erebon.

She dismounted in front of the blacksmith's. Down the slope from the shop, the smelter was quiet at that early hour. A flock of wild ducks pecked near a mound of charcoal lumps.

Andrada knocked on the open door. The blacksmith, a man with dark eyes and a shaved head, his face still clean for the day, stood by a long wooden table where a few axe handles needed new heads. The walls were lined with bare hooks.

He invited Andrada in, but she stood in the doorway, keeping her hat on.

"I don't have your sica, my lord," he said. "And I can't pay you back either. King Nicetas took all my steel. You can try your luck in another town, though you'll have to ride for days before you'll find a shop where the king's men haven't stopped before you."

In a low voice, Andrada said, "Why is the king collecting all that steel?"

"Word is he needs more weapons to protect the border with Roman Moesia."

She should have known that—had she summoned a Petition Day or talked to anyone at court.

The blacksmith scratched his chest. "I might get my hands on a load of Kertan iron ore by the full moon."

Andrada couldn't wait any longer. She'd ask Dapyx to bring her a dagger from the armory. Any blade was better than no blade.

She rode back to the square with the white oak. At the edge of the marketplace, she recognized the same Sarmatian trader she had seen the first time she came here with Dapyx. His clothes and headdress were pale as dust, his skin darkened by sun and wind.

He stared at Andrada, caressing his black beard just as he had last time. "Do you have time to look at my wares today, young master?"

Andrada dismounted. "I have time."

On his stall, glazed terra-cotta statuettes stood in neat rows. Andrada touched one, a man sitting, holding his head in his hands and thinking. She weighed it in her palm and put it back down, next to his big-bottomed wife. She admired an onyx sculpture of the Steppewynder man-and-woman hybrid deity, Napat-Dehnu, tattooed with water waves. That was worth having.

She was digging for a coin when she saw a sandstone carving of two people: a man with his arm around a woman's slender waist. Her long hair was braided and hung over her shoulder. The man was without a doubt Nicetas—his deep-set eyes, his cropped hair and shaved face, the aurochs on the hilt of his sword.

"Who's the girl?" Andrada said.

"Why, it's Una, the medicine girl," the Sarmatian said. "Who else can it be?"

Andrada picked it up. Her fingertips ran over layers of flawed sandstone. The statuette felt heavy in her hand, heavier than a sica, heavier than a Kertan shield.

The answer to all her questions.

She put down a silver coin—Nicetas's face was stamped on it—and slipped the statuette into her saddlebag.

The scattered morning clouds had turned darker and thicker in the afternoon as Andrada cantered into the stables' courtyard. Dapyx came running from somewhere and seized the reins when she dismounted.

He brought Dapple's head to his chest, patting the white spot above the big brown eyes.

"Don't you ever take my horse again," he told Andrada.

She had no time for his grievances. "Have you ever heard of a woman named Una?"

Dapyx froze with his forehead on Dapple's face. "A blessed birthday to you."

Andrada took off her saddlebag and slapped Dapple over the croup to send him back to the barn.

"Have you?" she said.

"She took care of Nicetas after the Night Attack in Twin Willows. I thought you knew."

"I knew the medicine women took care of him, yes. But I didn't know one of them is now his lover."

Dapyx rubbed his cheek, looking away.

"I thought we were friends," Andrada said.

"We are."

"Friends don't lie to each other."

"They do if there's good reason." His voice thinned as he spoke.

Andrada held her saddlebag between them, like a shield. "You and I are no longer friends. I don't need you. I won't ever trust you again."

Dapyx looked panicked. "How can I make it right again?"

"When Nicetas says he's hunting in the Blue Highlands, he's in Twin Willows, isn't he?"

He took a moment to answer. "Let's get you back into the house before people find out you were gone."

"I'm sure you'll cover our tracks well. Just like your brother."

"I'm nothing like my brother—"

"Answer my question!"

"Please, let's talk after supper. I'll tell you the whole story."

Andrada couldn't believe his nerve. "You want to come to the queen's chamber at night and tell her a story?"

He nodded. "Please."

"The whole story?"

"The truth. I promise."

Andrada had the sandstone statuette but couldn't quite grasp the face of the woman her husband loved. She didn't need to ask the crystal bell to reveal it though. Instead, she sent Dokina to get pigments: brown, green, and red.

At her table, she pulled the writing tray close, uncapped the inkwell, unrolled the parchment, put two polished pebbles over its top to weigh it open, and dipped a quill into the potash ink.

Beloved Father, I have just learned what most people in Valdavia already know, that my husband is unfaithful to me. King Nicetas's disloyalty is a grave offense to our Andori tribe, and so I request your permission to return to Sehuldava. May the Three Divines watch over you

She hesitated at the signature. *The queen of Valdavia? Devoted daughter? Rightful heir of Kerta?* Who was she to her father, now that he had given up on her and adopted Syrmos?

Dokina returned with a pitcher of water and three small clay crucibles, a layer of dark-colored powder at the bottom of each. She pulled three thin brushes and a lidded jar from her apron. The brushes were thin bristles of squirrel-tail hairs tied with thread around a stick.

Andrada opened the jar, dipped a finger inside, and licked it: mountain-flower sweetness. The cloying smell of honey and ground pigment powder overcame her, and she felt her stomach hanging heavy.

She felt better after all the shutters were open, well enough to send Dokina to the kitchen to bring supper. She removed the sandstone statuette from her saddlebag and set it on the table. Two figures were shown in tawny stone, their shape set free with each line chiseled on its surface. The girl's waist, held in the crook of the man's arm. The curve of her braid. The arch of her lips.

Andrada mixed the pigment with water and honey in each crucible. She stirred each of the paints with a brush but had to stop a few times to breathe in clean air and wait for her stomach to settle.

She dipped the first brush in the brown paint, the color of ripe chestnuts, and turned the girl's hair dark. She took the second brush to the carved circles of the girl's eyes and stabbed them green, then touched the girl's lips with red.

Without color, Nicetas's features reminded Andrada of his younger brother. After tonight, she'd be done with Dapyx. She still needed a blade though, and the armory was in the men's wing, so she'd ask Dokina to bring her a carving knife from the kitchen.

She looked at the two silhouettes again: Nicetas, pale as sand, and the girl he embraced, her face unfamiliar in features, familiar in colors. What did her voice sound like?

The Book of Dapyx

Dapyx peered in through the open door and saw Andrada at the table, facing the dark open windows. The linen tablecloth was smeared with brown, green, and red—the pigments Dokina had asked for earlier. Dapyx had rushed to the library and found the book copiers of *The Valdavian Chronicle*, who had rummaged through their desks and given him those three powders.

As he approached the table, he recognized the statuette. That explained everything.

"He's with her now," Andrada said, without turning.

"Yes." He pulled up a chair and angled it away from the cool night air.

"Is this what she looks like?"

Nicetas's image was clean sandstone, but there were running colors on Una. Andrada was trying to get the eyes painted green again. Dapyx wished Dokina had told him the pigments were meant for stone, not parchment. It might have made a difference.

"No," he said. "I mean, yes, that's what she looks like, but the colors are all wrong. Una has straw-colored hair and blue eyes."

"Ah."

Andrada picked a corner of the tablecloth and wiped Una's hair of its brown pigment, but the paint didn't come off clean. It had stained the cracks and flaws of the sandstone. She pursed her lips as if she were ready to cry, but she didn't.

She groaned, then smashed the statuette against the floor. Dapyx jerked back as shards flew everywhere.

"Tell me about Una," Andrada said in an icy tone.

Dapyx felt something burning on his cheekbone. He found a small painful cut and pressed his sleeve against the scratch.

Andrada twirled a short lock of hair around her stained finger. "I'm listening."

"She's the daughter of Rada, the Time-Giver; the granddaughter of Zia, the Family-Keeper; and the great-granddaughter of Ana, the Stardust-Harvester." He was relieved not to hide things anymore.

"Does Una have a special name?"

"Not yet." Dapyx examined his sleeve's hem and patted his cut again. No more blood.

"Tell me everything that happened in Twin Willows after the Night Attack."

"I'll tell you everything I know, but I wasn't there to see precisely what happened."

Andrada motioned for him to go on.

Dapyx took a deep breath. "Rada and Zia saved Nicetas's life, as you know. Rada opened Nicetas's belly, drained the blood, stretched muscle and skin over the wound, and sewed it all with a silver needle and lamb's wool. Zia prepared the potions and chanted the sacred incantations. And Una, who was still a young apprentice, pried Oroles's blood into glass tubes and funneled it into Nicetas's veins. They needed Oroles because Nicetas had lost a lot of blood, and Ea forbids a woman's essence to flow through a man's veins. Lucky for my brother, Oroles's blood saved him instead of killing him."

"He chose well between the twin cups," she whispered.

She looked away, and Dapyx stole a glance at the shape of her breasts in the folds of her robe. They seemed rounder and more alluring than before.

"Then Una tended to his wounds. She fed him, changed his soiled breeches, helped him get out of bed."

"And he fell in love with her?"

"Zyraxes believes she enchanted Nicetas," Dapyx said, his eyes back on Andrada's face, on her lips bitten red and raw. "That, when she snipped the wool thread of his stitches and pulled it out, she rubbed a secret love balm into the small cuts left on his skin." He scoffed. "I don't believe it. Nicetas didn't need a love balm to fall in love with Una. She was the one who healed him of the nightmares brought by Scorilus's dagger. The cold sweat, the screams...She saved him from all that. She was his friend when people judged him too young and weak for a king." He shrugged. "How could he *not* fall in love?"

Andrada spoke through clenched teeth. "Then why didn't he marry her when she was old enough?"

"He wanted to but couldn't. Una's from an ancient line of priestesses of Ea. They never marry, and they only have one child, a girl, to pass on their medicine secrets. This is the way things have been for them for centuries. But Nicetas thought he could haggle with them."

"Haggle how?"

"He thought that after Una gave birth to her daughter—Nicetas's daughter—she would've fulfilled her part of the covenant—"

"Wait, does Una have a daughter?"

"No, she's not twenty yet, the age demanded by their covenant. Nicetas thought she'd be free to marry him after the baby. Rada didn't think so, and neither did Zia, but Nicetas thought he could convince Una. He'd even made her a silver diadem with sapphires to wear on their wedding day."

Her face betrayed no emotion. "I still don't understand why he married me."

"Because your father summoned him. Nicetas couldn't say no, couldn't have his country caught between two angry neighbors and the Romans in the south. And because he needed your father to give him the soldiers Vespasianus requested on the empire's border."

Andrada picked up a sheet of parchment from the table and held it over a candle. The flames grew hungry and long, fast. She dropped the parchment on a plate before the flames could touch her fingers. The words *rightful heir of Kerta* at the bottom of the page disappeared last.

"Had I been Nicetas," Dapyx whispered to her, "I would've fought my enemies and married the woman I loved. But he's weak, my brother."

"And Una? What does Una want?"

"All she wants is Nicetas's heart. And she already has it."

There, he had told her the truth. He watched her with hope, holding his breath.

"That would be all, Dapyx," Andrada said, her green eyes burning him with pain and anger. "You and I are done."

Chapter Sixteen

The Book of Scorilus

The great hall of the White Fortress smelled of fishy brine every summer. Scorilus swatted a fly buzzing by his ear, waiting for the next petitioner. From the hilt of Phradmon's dagger at his belt, colored light reflected and scattered over the mosaic of Napat-Dehnu on the floor. Scorilus wished he had Moskon with him that day to handle the documents, but the boy had a low fever, and his mother was taking care of him.

"The Valdavian emissary," the guard announced.

Scorilus climbed back to his throne, surprised that Nicetas had sent word.

The emissary was wide in the shoulders and had a trimmed brown beard. As he stopped at the bottom of the dais, Scorilus recognized him: the man who had shot him with a barbed arrow seven years ago.

His heart started pounding. He glanced at the sica Oroles carried, a weapon that wouldn't withstand the guards' falxes and daggers. The only armor Oroles wore was a pair of studded bracers, so if Scorilus were to strike now...

Yet this was King Nicetas's blood brother, so Scorilus had to let him speak.

Oroles kneeled by the mosaic. "The blessings of Napat-Dehnu upon you and your family, King Scorilus." His Valdavian accent was grating.

"Tempting fate, I see..." Scorilus pointed to the upright arrow on the wall. "Do you remember that?"

"I do. I remember the sparrow's feathers I used for fletching and the stag's antler I used for the barbed tip."

"You know why I keep it up there?"

"I don't, no."

"To remind me that life can always turn on an arrow's point. You agree, Chief Oroles?"

Oroles wiped sweat off his brow. "I'm not a chieftain, King Scorilus. I'm only Oroles, son of Zonaras, the emissary of King Nicetas." His voice faltered. "I'm a Dhawosian man who wants to see all the Dhawosian kingdoms at peace."

Now Scorilus was more curious than riled. "Don't worry, Emissary Oroles, I won't take revenge for what happened that night. Now rise and tell me why you're here."

Oroles stood up. "My king regrets that our countries haven't spoken in years. He sends me in good faith to deliver the news that all the trading posts have been reopened on our side of the Pyretus River."

"That makes no difference to me now. I'm building a new Steppewynd, one that doesn't need the old Dhawosia."

"We're all Dhawosian folk, King Scorilus. Our countries have a common enemy. Emperor Vespasianus will crush both Valdavia and Steppewynd if we're divided."

Scorilus had developed trade ties with Roman Moesia. He didn't need Nicetas's help.

"Princess Meda," the guard announced.

Meda stood in the doorway, the sun behind her. She brought a wavy lock of red hair over her shoulder, patted it in place against the white linen of her sleeveless robe, and strode up to Oroles.

"My daughter, Princess Meda," Scorilus said. "This is Oroles, the new Valdavian emissary."

Oroles bowed, his right hand over his heart, while Meda looked him up and down.

"His king," Scorilus said, "wants a short-term alliance to fortify our border with the Roman Empire."

Meda raised an eyebrow.

"To the contrary," Oroles said. "My king wants nothing less than an everlasting alliance between our Dhawosian kingdoms."

Was Nicetas so confident in his alliance with Cothelas that he extended his generosity even to his enemies? Of course, that didn't mean Scorilus shouldn't consider it. There were rumors that the Valdavians had learned the secrets of the Roman waterwheel and aqueduct. Steppewynd could use that knowledge too.

Meda's eyes narrowed. "Is King Nicetas so desperate for Steppewynder workhands that he's willing to forget who stabbed him in the gut during the Night Attack?"

Oroles pointed to his arrow on the wall. "The king of Steppewynd let the wounds of the past heal. So did the king of Valdavia."

Meda smiled at Oroles. Her perfume, sweet and sweaty, wafted in the warm air between them.

"The gods favor those who strive for peace," she said.

"Emissary Oroles," Scorilus said, "we're honored to have you in our home."

He glanced at Meda, who continued to study Oroles in a way that troubled him.

CHAPTER SEVENTEEN

The Book of Andrada

Andrada's first Petition Day went easier than she had expected. She sat on Nicetas's silver throne and listened to her subjects, passed judgment where she could, and told them to leave their requests with her scribes where she didn't know enough about the matter to reach a fair verdict. She'd later consult with Citera, the treasurer, and other chieftains. The burden on the Valdavian court to solve disputes had lessened with the reopening of the trade routes with Steppewynd after seven years of hardship.

While Andrada stayed busy with petitioners and her gardens during the day, night spirits tormented her with vivid dreams of pain and helplessness. Since the sacred royal duties, the sandstone statuette, and Dapyx's story, her mind kept returning to Nicetas and Una. Why had the god of the crystal bell played such a cruel joke on her? She had asked Him to take away the cup of deadly water, and He had brought Nicetas to Sehuldava and made Andrada the villain in his and Una's story. An unpredictable god had made her the subject of yet another king who had no time for her, just like her father.

Nicetas had returned to Twin Willows and would stay there until after the harvest fair, at the beginning of fall. The only way for Andrada to vanquish her nightmares was to see her husband and Una together, with her own eyes. Once she decided that, she postponed Petition Day until after the harvest fair and went to the Temple of Concord's library to study the maps of Valdavia.

Before dawn the next morning, she woke Dokina with a gentle pat on the shoulder. "I need you to cover for me for a few days."

Dokina rubbed her eyes. "Going to the valley again?"

"Twin Willows. But if anybody asks, I'm ill but getting better. I need enough food for a few days on the road until I find an inn."

While Dokina was in the kitchen, Andrada prepared her saddlebag. She threw in socks, trousers, a shirt, and clean rags for bandages. She packed a jar of Citera's painkilling poultice, though she couldn't remember when she had last needed it. She put on Dapyx's riding clothes, her breasts aching a little under her chest bindings.

The flaps of her hat covered her ears and neck. Loose strands of curly hair escaped from under it, and she fiddled with them for a while but couldn't make them disappear altogether.

When Dokina returned with the food, Andrada gave her the carving knife they now kept in their chamber.

"Cut it off," she said.

Dokina recoiled. "But it's growing long at last."

"Where I go, long hair won't help. Cut it off."

Dokina sighed but took the knife and wrapped the hair around her fist. She slashed it off the way the nurse used to.

"Take the bell with you," she said, throwing the hair in the fire.

"I can't," Andrada said, putting her hat on. "The god is toying with me, Dokina. I asked Him for true love, and He showed me true love—between Nicetas and Una. I'm not touching that bell until I understand how He thinks."

"And how will you figure that out without talking to the god?" Dokina said.

"I don't know..."

With the smell of burned hair in her nostrils, Andrada grabbed her satchel and headed for the armory. The sun was not yet up, and she met no one on her way to the men's wing of the king's house.

The armory was cold, quiet, and dark. Andrada left her satchel by the door and pushed out the shutters over the tall south windows. The morning light was bright enough for her to inspect the blades mounted on the walls. She picked a Roman leaf-shaped steel dagger in a leather sheath and hooked it onto her belt. Now for a longer weapon.

She strolled past battle-axes and javelins, past maces and shields, and past a Sehul's flower made from barbed arrows pointing in all directions, until she found a falx, a wooden shaft tied to a three-foot-long curved blade. Nobody could withstand a falx wielded by capable hands. She took the polearm down and held it. Then she spun around, holding it out against an imaginary army of enemies closing in. The handle was wrapped in new leather treated with linseed oil, and the strong smell made her nauseous. She put the falx down. It wasn't a suitable weapon for the road anyway.

At the south end of the hall, an armored dummy stood on a pedestal. It held a spear in its right hand and an oval shield with charging aurochs in its left. A sica and a dagger hung from a belt over the scales. It was Nicetas's armor from the last war, the armor he wasn't wearing when Scorilus attacked him in that burning tent. No, she wouldn't take his blade on her journey.

There was a mace at the foot of the pedestal. Andrada remembered Avezinas's words from years ago.

"Most people think that skill is only for blades, and the mace is just for brawn, but they're wrong. There's an art to wielding this."

He had held a mace ready against his shoulder and, with one hand, swung it over his head, over Andrada's head, and brought it back like a whip.

"Timing is everything with a mace. You can take down a swordsman with it if you time it right. As the swordsman leans forward, he'll have to bounce back. Therefore, never aim for his head but for a hand's width behind it. That's where his head will be after he rebounds. Where his head will meet your mace. But keep your wrist loose, for a mace crushing a man's head could snap your bones like dry twigs."

The mace had been the only weapon she had not mastered back in Kerta. Now she gripped the leather-wrapped handle of the Valdavian mace and lifted, but the mace remained nailed to the floor. She groaned and tried again and again. She dropped the handle, and it knocked against the pedestal with a short echo. She didn't need a mace, anyway, but a sica.

She picked one, then another, but they were all blunt. The grindstone would make too much noise at that early hour. At last, she found a sharp one. She weighed the sica in her hand, ready to attack. The hilt was thick, but it would have to do.

She charged against an invisible enemy again. This time her imagination conjured up Nicetas standing there, smirking like Syrmos in the old days. She lunged sideways and stabbed the air as if she were going around his shield. She circled the spot where he stood and slashed at his right arm. She faced him again and thrust the sica into his chest. Maybe they'd cross blades in Twin Willows.

She hooked the sica to her belt, grabbed her satchel, and checked the cloisters outside the armory. Everything was quiet.

In the stables, Dapyx's dapple-gray let out a soft snort when Andrada passed his stall. She picked a brown mare with feathered black hooves and a white face stripe. Before putting on the harness, she removed the aurochs silver fittings from the leather straps.

She trotted out through the arched gates. At the Six-Sided Tower, the drawbridge was already lowered for her. By now, the guard knew not to ask questions.

The Book of Dapyx

Dapyx had come to the armory for the grindstone and found weapons all over the place. The armory master kept the place tidy, so Dapyx started straightening things up, wondering what had happened here. He was still an apprentice warrior, and cleaning up was his job.

He had plenty of time now that Andrada wanted nothing to do with him. She had even refused to see him on a Petition Day when he waited in line with everybody else for a chance to speak to the queen.

With his heart still heavy, he returned a falx back to its bracket on the wall. He picked up the mace someone had left lying around, its handle propped against the pedestal of Nicetas's armor dummy. Then something caught his eye. He looked closer. The back panel of the pedestal was loose, like a drawer ajar.

He slipped his fingers between the pedestal and the wooden panel, and it fell out. In its place gaped a dark hole wider than a man's shoulder span. He eased his head in. The inside of the pedestal was deeper than the floor, and from it, two tunnels headed east and west.

Dapyx couldn't believe his luck. He had found the entrance to the secret corridors of the king's house. He'd been looking for them with desperation after Andrada had cut him off. Now he had the means to watch her and learn how to get back into her good graces.

The Book of Andrada

At sunset, Andrada broke her mare's trot outside a village on the bank of the Hierasus River. The sudden change in pace made her head spin. She bent to the side, ready to throw up. Ever since Dapyx's story about Una, she had felt ill, but the anger at her weakness straightened her in the saddle.

Mehnot's moon had not yet risen when she dismounted in front of the inn. She tied her mare to a hay trough and stamped her feet to loosen her saddle stiffness. Before going in, she rubbed her hands on the sooty logs of the inn's wall, then on her face and neck so she'd be harder to recognize.

The inn was a long hall with an open hearth in the center and a roasting spit straddling the fire. A soup cauldron hung from a hook, steam rising to the smoke hole in the roof. From the ceiling beams hung garlic braids, feathered birds, and hare pelts. Guest chambers opened on all sides.

At the end of the hall, the innkeeper stood behind a counter surrounded by stuffed shelves.

"Welcome to Pirobora." His cheeks and forehead glistened with sweat. "Not from these parts, are you?"

"You have a bed for tonight?" Andrada said, keeping her voice low.

"You wear clothes from down south. I'd say, somewhere around Zalmodava? Your mare may be tired and covered in dust, but I can tell she's a good breed."

"Any beds?"

"None, but food aplenty. Porridge, roasted boar, grilled pike, wine."

"I'll have the pike with some bread and wine."

"Say, are you heading to Twin Willows? All my guests are on their way to the harvest fair."

"Master Cloilios," said someone behind Andrada. "Not good for business to pester your guests like that."

Andrada had heard that voice before. It belonged to a bearded man with sandy hair and a smile on his sunburned face. Where did she know him from?

The innkeeper waved his hands. "Just idle chat on a late night. No harm in that."

"I believe the young master here is hungry." The man put a firm hand on Andrada's shoulder. "We have a seat at our table."

"Food's coming," the innkeeper said, rushing away.

The man's breath smelled of wine and mint. Mint. Then she remembered. Ten years ago, he had captured her likeness with charcoal on parchment—a portrait she had never seen. And he had painted her horse-box in blue and gold pigments that never faded. Did he recognize her too?

She followed him to his table, where three men chatted over wooden mugs, chewed bones, and scattered crumbs. One was very young, with light hair down to his shoulders. Another had dark hair, a long beard shot with white, and a scar over his eyebrow. The third was wiry, with dark eyes and no beard. They now stared up at her, waiting.

The Cartographer pulled out a three-legged stool, and Andrada sat down, her eyes on their hands clutching their mugs. A few bronze coins were scattered on the table, some showing Scorilus's face, some the back-to-back profiles of his two lost brothers, Eptalas and Phradmon.

The Cartographer sat at her side, across the table from the other three. "What's your name, young master?"

Maybe he hadn't recognized her after all. "Lipoxais."

"Brasus here," the Cartographer said, pointing to the young man, "is a bard." He then nodded to the man with the scar. "Mucatras is a huntsman. Thiamarkos, a tentmaker. We're on our way to Twin Willows for this year's harvest fair. You can join us if you want."

He had recognized her. Why else offer her protection on the road?

The innkeeper set down a wooden mug and a plate with a loaf of bread and a thimble of salt. "The fish is coming."

"Can I sleep on a straw mat in the hall tonight?" Andrada asked him.

"All spoken for, I'm afraid. But the night should be pleasant by the campfire."

He shuffled away, and Andrada took a hearty bite of bread.

"A real traveler packs a tent," Thiamarkos said. "It's better than the vermin and vice of most inns. I have an extra one for you, Master Lipoxais, if you have five silver coins."

"I don't mind sleeping with my horse," Andrada said.

Thiamarkos counted his coins. "There're wolves in the forests around here."

"The campfires will keep them away," she said.

"Suit yourself then." Thiamarkos took a swig from his mug.

"Are you joining us at the harvest fair?" Mucatras said.

"Why would I?" Andrada said with a shrug.

"Because this is no ordinary harvest fair," Brasus said. "This year's celebration only happens every twenty years or so. The youngest of the medicine women has finished her apprenticeship and will be consecrated to Ea." He winked at the Cartographer. "I reckon she'll learn her goddess-given name soon enough."

That would happen when Una gave birth to her daughter by Nic-etas, Andrada knew.

"Watch your mouth, Brasus," the Cartographer said.

There was no way Andrada would travel to Twin Willows and not run into these four again. And the road would only become more crowded the closer she got.

"I'll take your tent, Master Thiamarkos." She set five silver coins on the table, Nicetas's shiny faces next to Scorilus's dull ones. "And join your party too."

Two days later, Andrada sat at a campfire with the Cartographer, her hands sweating on her dagger and a half-carved skewer. Beyond the fire, in the dark, the waters of the Hierasus River gurgled over the chirping of crickets. Their companions' snores rose from the tents. Bones and breadcrumbs from their supper called to night critters, whose eyes gleamed around the camp, making the party's horses and pack mules snort.

"You don't remember me, Master Lipoxais," the Cartographer said, "but we've met before."

They were alone for the first time since meeting at the inn.

"We have?" Andrada said.

"Let me tell you a story, Master Lipoxais." His sigh smelled of mint. "Years ago, I traveled to the court of Cothelas the Bald in Sehuldava."

That mention of her father jolted Andrada, especially that disre-spectful nickname, but she kept her eyes on her skewer.

"Ten years after the death of his wife," the Cartographer said, "the king had sunken into melancholy, given up food and sleep. He was obsessed with bringing back Queen Pegrina's likeness, to stop his memories of her from vanishing altogether. The few portraits painted during the queen's lifetime were as lifeless as the profiles stamped on coins. The pigments had faded..."

Andrada had thought her father was busy preparing for a Roman invasion at the time.

"The king drew with potash ink on parchment, but it was never good enough, so he started all over again. And again and again, while his body wasted away. His people tried to convince him to take another wife, but the king had vowed on his queen's deathbed to never remarry. He'd join her in the Underworld when his time came, still her husband. His people summoned physicians, but there was no wound, no illness for them to heal."

"Touched by a madness spirit?"

The Cartographer nodded. "The high priest brought sculptors and painters to give the king the image he so craved. But the sculptors chiseled faces with empty eyes. And the painters? They were merely guessing." He smiled. "The queen's eyes had been green, everybody knew that, but what shade of green? What shape?"

That explained the right alcove in the Old Temple of Sehul, filled with strange portraits and stone heads.

The Cartographer continued. "There was unrest among his chieftains, rumors of an uprising even. The king was getting worse. He believed he'd angered his late queen's spirit somehow, so he ordered his only daughter brought up as a boy from her tenth birthday on—short hair, trousers, lessons with the high priest." He threw a glance at Andrada's clothes. "He believed the memory of his wife would then return to him."

"Did it?" Andrada said, feeling bitter.

"When I brought him the likeness of his late queen—"

The portrait Andrada had set on fire in the throne chamber...

"A likeness that was not lost, but merely hidden," the Cartographer said.

"Hidden where?"

"The face of their daughter, whom he blamed for his wife's death. A child the king had refused to see since birth."

Painful words to hear, but Andrada held his blue gaze for a long moment.

He smiled. "The child had the same green eyes as her mother, same mouth, same nose. I painted the queen in the mother-goddess pose, with her daughter in her lap, like young Beleizis sitting on Ea's knee."

"That's not..." Not what the portrait had looked like.

"Because the king ordered me to erase the child from the portrait."

That was why Andrada had never seen the image she had posed for: it had been painted over.

"The gods banished the madness spirit," the Cartographer said, "and I left the king's house with a purse full of gold. For the child, I painted a whitewood box in the shape of a horse."

"Was your portrait...enchanted?" Andrada said, her throat dry.

The Cartographer laughed. "Not that I know of, though I heard it burst into flames one night."

"Why are you telling me this story?" Andrada said, staring at the fire.

"That story happened years ago, but I never forget the eyes I once painted."

The eyes in the burned portrait had been nothing like Andrada's. She gripped the hilt of her dagger tighter.

"No need for that." His voice sounded warm. "I'm your friend."

She looked up to calm her racing heart. A halo of colors shone around the moon, the arc of a ghostly rainbow bent into a diadem.

"You did good work on my whitewood box," she said.

The Cartographer grinned. "That blue pigment I used on your horse's mane? It's a rare gift from a dear friend of mine. Rada, one of the medicine women of Twin Willows." He turned to her to whisper, "But why are you going to Twin Willows?"

Andrada began carving her skewer again. "I must see something for myself."

Their horses stirred at the edge of the night.

"See what?" Brasus's voice was low and gruff as if he had just woken up. He came to squat next to Andrada.

"None of your business, Brasus," the Cartographer said.

"Oh, but it is my business." Brasus's teeth were strong, but more crooked than most. "Because something's not right with this boy. He has no bread in his satchel but plenty of coin in his pocket. You know him, Cartographer. You said you didn't."

The Cartographer heaved himself up. "Yes, I know him. He's Master Lipoxais, a scribe at the king's house in Zalmodava. He's delivering a message from High Priest Zyraxes to his brother, King Nicetas, which means he's under the king's protection and mine."

Andrada would use that cover from now on.

"It's late," the Cartographer said. "Let's all get some sleep."

"Master Lipoxais," Brasus said with a smirk, "watch out for beggars and pickpockets in Twin Willows."

His eyes stayed on Andrada until she crawled on her bedroll and closed the flaps of her new tent.

CHAPTER EIGHTEEN

The Dynastic Scrolls

On the first morning of the harvest fair, Una proudly dropped a linen sack in front of Nicetas.

"My own recipe," she said. "Throw the powder on the fire, and the flames will turn green. I sent a sack to each beacon guard from here on to Zalmodava. If I see green flames in the distance, I'll know you need me, and I'll come to you."

His face changed with warmth and love. He pulled Una into his arms. She felt at home in his embrace, with his lips on her lips, and she would have stayed for another kiss, were it not for the grape-crushing ceremony about to begin.

She let go of him and cracked the door open. The harvest fair had brought droves from all over Valdavia. They had filled the small inn and set camp under the sky oak outside the roundhouse, in the cleared fields on the other side of the cattle ditches, and on the southwestern banks of the Pyretus River.

"I don't want you out there," Nicetas said, "with all those hungry eyes on you."

Her blood stirred when he was jealous, and she would have kissed him again, but Mother Rada walked in.

"Time to go, Una."

"At least one set of eyes won't stare at me out there," Una told Nicetas. "Chief Tarbus. Have you seen how his ears turn red when he speaks to you, Mama?"

"Leave that poor man alone," Mother Rada said. "Now give me your old apron."

Una undid the red-and-white belt and took off her black apprentice's apron. Raven, Mother Rada's dog, jumped and snapped her jaws, trying to catch the wadded apron flying from Una to her mother. She yipped one grumpy bark when she missed.

"I should be the one to throw that rag into the fire," Una said. "After fourteen years, I think I've earned the right."

"We don't change the rituals, child."

Mother Rada went back out, beating a bronze pot with a spoon, making the voice of the crop goddess Enoz heard all over Twin Willows.

Una rolled up her sleeves and tied up her skirts. She looped her braid around her head and tucked its end under. Nicetas clasped her hand at the last moment and pulled her back for one more kiss.

Outside, Una shielded her eyes from the sun shimmering through the turning leaves. A path opened between her and the sacred sky oak, where a dozen boys were emptying crates of red grapes into a large wooden vat. Bronze pots and spoons hanging from the sky oak's branches chimed in the wind, channeling the voice of Enoz.

"Hail the king!" people shouted when Nicetas followed her outside.

"Let's make wine, Time-Giver," Grandmother Zia said, holding a silver flagon.

"Let's make wine, Family-Keeper," Mother Rada said, "for the gods and for the people." She hit the bronze pot one more time. "Go ahead, Una."

A fuzz of rebel golden hair flickered in the corner of Una's eye. She felt her cheeks turning hot, but she walked barefoot, humming to herself, her head held high even though her skirt was short. When she reached the round vat, she perched on its edge.

Grandmother Zia passed the silver flagon to Nicetas, who took Una's foot in his hand and washed it, sole first, then between the toes. It was cold, and it tickled, but she suffered under his touch without pulling back. As his fingers massaged her foot, he shifted in place, and she knew why. He took her other foot and washed it too.

Then she twirled around, her legs over the edge, and landed upright in the middle of the vat. Droplets of red juice from the crushed grapes under her feet peppered the pale fabric of her shift. The crowd cheered while a drum rumbled like thunder on a summer day.

Una gave a sharp shout and began dancing. Her feet followed the fast hands on the drumhead, stamping, stamping, stamping, her toes deep in mush, her knees red with juice, her tongue tasting the drops that landed on her lips. The boys around the circle slapped their knees, children jumped in the dirt, and women sang together the ancestral crop dance for the glory of Enoz.

The grapes underfoot were turning into a calf-deep pool of red. Then the drums fell quiet, and Una looked up, her heart loud in her chest.

A young man dressed in sackcloth tied with rope stood by the vat. "You laugh and dance, but the Great Awakening draws near, and you're not ready to stand in El's presence."

Una wiped her forehead and glanced at the crowd, worried.

"When El wakes up, He'll be angered by the wickedness of our world," the prophet said. "You think He'll forgive us because we sacrifice a few goats at the Festival of the Renewed Sun? He won't. Standing before El's throne, earthly kings will be as helpless as commoners. El will annihilate every authority and power—"

Nicetas grabbed the prophet and hurled him away from Una.

The prophet roared back. "Oroles's blood flows through your veins, King Nicetas, but not his wisdom!"

"Leave him, my king," Grandmother Zia said. "He's just another fool who thinks he can hear the voice of the gods."

She motioned to her people, and the villagers grabbed the prophet and shoved him out of the square while he kept shouting, "The gods speak through me...Beleizis warns us to be ready...The sleeping god will soon wake..."

The drum picked up its booming pace again, and Una her dancing, relieved that nothing worse had happened. One of Nicetas's huntsmen whispered something in his ear. He nodded back, motioned at Una to excuse himself, and followed his man through the square, toward the new king's house up the hill.

Una was now tired, but she kept dancing, the stained cloth of her shift sticking to her skin. At last, the drum stopped. Una took a deep breath, cupped her hands, and dipped them into the fresh grape must. She brought them to her lips and drank and drank and drank. When she looked up at the people on the rooftops, her heart still beating fast, she locked eyes with a boy in a brown fur hat. His cheeks were dirty. He stared at her in a way that didn't feel right.

Raven barked, and Una looked that way to see the Cartographer approaching.

"Come here, you," he said, his arms wide open.

Una shrieked with joy and hopped out of the vat. She threw herself, soaked in must as she was, into his arms.

Grandmother Zia dipped the silver flagon into the vat and held it up for the crowd to see.

"Fresh must! For the gods and for the people!"

When Una looked up again, the boy in the fur hat was gone.

The Book of Andrada

Andrada climbed off the roof into a packed alleyway, where new houses—a sign of the prosperity brought to Twin Willows by the king's regular visits—stood between old huts. The air smelled of piss, manure, and cooking fires. Soothsayers called out to read Andrada's fortune in coal lumps. Merchants offered her potions, salves, and amulets. Brothel women touched her arm, trying to pull her in. She ignored them all.

She had seen what she had come to see in Twin Willows. Here, Nicetas and Una were at home among their people, who loved them and protected them against enemies like that prophet. Andrada had no place in their story, and she couldn't compete with the woman Ea had chosen for Nicetas after lifting him from the Underworld. Una was the most powerful mortal in the universe. Una was terrifying. Una and Nicetas were blessed, while she, Andrada, was the evil queen in their love story. She was unworthy of her father's trust, her nurse's love, her husband's devotion. She lacked the vital spark that begot love, the spark Una had enough of for the whole of Valdavia.

She was close to the sky oak's clearing, where that beautiful bloody goddess had danced to the drumbeat, crushing grapes underfoot. Just as she passed the last house, a man grabbed her and slammed her against the wall, making her feel dizzy.

"You're not doing this right," he hissed in her ear.

"Thiamarkos?" Andrada said, pushing him back. "What in the gods' name you want?"

"You can't be walking around dressed in man's clothes but leaving no doubt you're a woman. Because you're a woman, right?"

"Yes, I'm a woman who needs trousers to travel the roads. I have the Cartographer's protection. What's it to you?" Her voice climbed higher with her anger.

"But he can't protect you now, can he?" Thiamarkos let her go. "You must be smarter and more careful than this. All the time. There's no sense in covering your chest with your cloak if your voice rises when you're flustered."

Andrada pulled back against the house wall and gave Thiamarkos another look. His face was lined and tanned, but there were no signs he had ever grown a beard. Yet he was a man, no doubt. Just as Citera was a woman, with Ea's blessing. Unlike Andrada, Thiamarkos didn't pretend to be someone he wasn't.

She nodded. "I understand."

"While we're in Twin Willows, you better stick around. You have a lot to learn."

"Thank you, Thiamarkos."

"Wait for me under the sky oak. I must deliver a tent, and then I'll find you there."

Andrada headed for the tree.

The wine-making vat was gone now. The sky oak's gray bark bled red sap through deep, long, rusty ridges. Hanging bronze pots and spoons clinked in the breeze. Andrada pressed her head to the furrowed bark and asked the spirit of sky oaks to forgive her for killing Zyraxes's tree back in Zalmodava. How could she have been so wrong about everything?

She first heard a breath, then the small voice of a child. "Spare a coin for the sky oak?"

A soft tug at the hem of her cloak. A little boy stood behind her, no older than five, his eyes large and brown and a bit crusty, his cheeks smudged with dirt, a daub of half-dried yellow snot over his upper lip. He wore no shoes, and his clothes were too big for his skinny shoulders. He scratched his head, no doubt crawling with lice.

"A coin?" He held out his small hand.

People bustled around—a woman with bread baskets, a boy with a rolled rug over his shoulder, an old man with an axe, a little girl pulling a cow by a rope—but no one stopped, no one looked at the little boy.

"Where's your mother, little one?" Andrada said, kneeling next to him.

"She's dead." He sniffled, his face scrunched, and he sneezed.

Andrada flinched, then wiped her cheek. She took the child's warm hand into hers. His fingers were dirty, his nails chewed short. He shivered even though it was a warm day. Andrada would have cried with pity for him if she could. She fumbled with the strings of her coin purse and fished out a silver piece.

The child grabbed it. He wiped his nose, the coin locked in his fist like a pit in a plum.

"Another one, for tomorrow?" he said.

"Leave that little bugger alone," a woman said in passing. "He's sick as a cow done grazing on nightshade."

Andrada paid her no heed and took out another coin. Children were so helpless. Could she take the boy with her to Zalmodava? She'd wash him and feed him and keep him warm.

She held out the coin, and he took it and bolted through the crowd just as she felt a sharp pull on her wrist from behind. The coin purse vanished from her hand. She snapped around, grabbed the hilt of her sica, but the thief was now just a face in the crowd. A girl with two buckets of milk on a yoke almost knocked her over. She looked everywhere, but the little boy was gone too.

Brasus had warned her of beggars and pickpockets. Now he'd be laughing at her. But maybe the little beggar had nothing to do with the pickpocket. Maybe he had told the truth, and his mother was really dead. Maybe he hadn't seen the thief sneaking behind Andrada, ready to grab her coin purse.

Maybe the thief had threatened the boy with a good whipping if he didn't help rob her. No matter, she'd find that little beggar and save him from his miserable life. She didn't know why, but she had to do it. For all her wrong decisions—sending Gerulas to his death, entering the Old Temple of Sehul, cutting down Zyraxes's tree—helping that helpless child had to be right.

The Valdavian Chronicle

The gates of the king's house opened before Nicetas. As he strode past the new watchtower with its beacon, he wondered if the message waiting for him was from Zyraxes. He hadn't heard any complaints from his brother about the queen's Petition Days. Maybe for once Zyraxes knew not to pick a fight he couldn't win.

At the well in the center of the courtyard, a servant raised the sweep and held out a cup of fresh water. Nicetas drank to erase the bitter taste on his tongue after seeing all those slacked jaws watching Una dance.

In the work chamber, the scribe Kosingas was waiting with the newest codex in *The Valdavian Chronicle* for Nicetas's approval, a volume recounting the years since the Night Attack. He had also brought a letter from Legate Lucius Flavius Magius, announcing the completion of the Temple of Iuppiter in Tomis, in the Roman province of Moesia. Payment for the defense of the empire's northern border had arrived on time, which meant Emperor Vespasianus had not yet learned of the disruption caused by the withdrawal of the Kertan troops.

Kosingas handed over a letter from Cothelas the Bald. Nobody had permission to read the Kertan king's letters. Nicetas broke the wax seal marked with a wolf head and read the short message by the window. No soldiers would return to Valdavia until Cothelas's gods-damned heir was sent to Sehuldava. Nicetas threw the parchment into the hearth and asked Kosingas what else was there.

"A scroll from Emissary Oroles."

"I hope it's not a ransom note."

"No, my king, it is not." Kosingas had no sense of humor.

"Read it."

"*To the king of Valdavia, from the emissary to Steppewynd, may Beleizis—*"

"Yes, yes, what's he saying?"

Kosingas's eyes scanned the scroll. "King Scorilus is open to creating something called the Dhawosian Alliance...With Steppewynder laborers returning to Valdavia, we should have more soldiers to send to the Roman border...And Emissary Oroles asks for permission to sell the knowledge of the Roman waterwheel to Steppewynd."

"Read that part."

Kosingas cleared his throat and began. "*King Scorilus wishes to bring a new era of prosperity upon his lands by building waterwheels and aqueducts from the Tyras River to new hill terraces where the soil is still as fertile as before the days of Queen Seba.*"

"Oroles is clever...unless Scorilus is playing him for a fool. Go on."

"*Since my arrival at the White Fortress, I came to understand that King Scorilus is not as much a warrior as a wise statesman.*"

Nicetas's hand found the scar on his side. "Fancy words from our humble Oroles's mouth. Unless he had help writing them."

"*Princess Meda, who admires our vision for peace, has joined our journey through Steppewynd. She is now a keen supporter of the Dhawosian Alliance in hopes that our corner of the world remains safe from the Roman menace that has engulfed much of the known world—*"

"Unless Scorilus uses his new crops to grow his armies. But as long as Princess Meda agrees with Oroles's bright vision of world peace…" The irony seemed lost on Kosingas.

A flock of ducks quacked and scattered in the courtyard. From the window, Nicetas saw the Cartographer approach, stirring dead leaves in his wake.

Nicetas hurried to meet him at the door. "Anything happened to Una?"

"Una's fine, no worries," the Cartographer said, and for the first time, he smelled more of wine than fresh mint. He greeted Kosingas with a nod. "But I have some news. Only for your ears."

"Go," Nicetas told Kosingas. "Leave the scroll. And write a letter to Legate Magius to congratulate him and his emperor on that new temple in Tomis." He turned to the Cartographer. "A temple dedicated to the Roman god Iuppiter, built on lands that were Dhawosian not long ago."

"I heard of it, yes." The Cartographer closed the door after Kosingas. "It shouldn't be hard to turn it into a temple of Ea when Moesia shakes off its Roman yoke, the gods willing."

Nicetas motioned at him. "Tell me the news."

"Phradmon of Steppewynd is alive."

"What? Didn't you take his severed hand to Scorilus not long ago?"

"Phradmon lost his hand, yes, but he didn't lose his life. He's now a slave, working as a scribe for Khuddan, a Sarmatian chieftain east of the Borysthenes River."

"A Sarmatian chieftain took a scribe?"

"It appears Phradmon's flattery saved his life. He told Khuddan that the Romans laugh at Sarmatians and call them barbarians, but they'd quiver with fear if only they learned the truth—"

"And for the Romans to learn about the valiant Sarmatians, Chief Khuddan needed a scribe who lost his right hand?"

"Those were Khuddan's words, more or less. Phradmon promised to learn how to write with his left." The Cartographer spit a wad of chewed leaves out the window. "The honor and joy of writing about Chief Khuddan's feats turned Phradmon into a scribe in less than a moon."

"But if Phradmon's alive...then isn't he the rightful king of Steppewynd?"

"He's a slave now. The gods of the east must be good friends with the Roman ones, for They all approve of slaves."

"Are you taking this news to the White Fortress?"

The Cartographer put a few green leaves in his mouth. "Do you want me to? Scorilus has paid me to find out about his brother, but I thought I should ask you first."

Nicetas scratched his ear, thinking. "Oroles wants to take fresh water to Scorilus's fertile terraces."

"That'd be good for Steppewynd and good for us. Trade would be booming from the Pyretus River to the Ozana."

"And I'd get some distance from Cothelas." And his need for heirs. "Things are thawing between me and Scorilus, thanks to Oroles. But wouldn't it be better to deal with a king of Steppewynd who's forever in my debt?"

"Then maybe we should see how much Chief Khuddan wants for his one-armed scribe."

"And not a word to Scorilus," Nicetas said.

The Book of Dapyx

Dapyx had to convince Andrada not to confront her husband about Una. Because it wouldn't take long for Nicetas to figure out how his wife had learned his secret.

Dapyx wished he could spy on Andrada before talking to her. Since the discovery of the secret corridors in the men's wing, he had hoped to find the entrance to the women's wing, but the two didn't seem to connect.

At midday mealtime, Dapyx followed Dokina as she left the kitchen, carrying a wooden tray with a loaf of rye, a cluster of red grapes, and a roasted duck leg. For the past few days, Andrada had been eating in her chamber.

He called her name just as she reached the queen's door, and she flinched and lost her grip on the tray. Dapyx rushed to grab it and saved the food from ending up on the floor.

"You scared me, my lord," Dokina said, her eyes lowered, her hands trembling.

"How's the queen?" Dapyx took the tray and set it down on a small table by the door. "I must see her, Dokina." His voice wavered.

"I must ask her first, my lord." Dokina searched inside her apron's pocket and took out an iron key with a round bow.

"Why is the queen locked in?"

Dokina fumbled with the key and the keyhole, her hands shaking. "My lord, please." She turned to face him, the key still in her hand.

Dapyx noticed how empty the hallway was, how quiet the entire wing was at that hour. He listened for any sound coming from behind the locked door, but all he heard was the trickling of water in Apollonius's new aqueduct outside.

He took Dokina's hand, the key sticking out from her fist. "In this light, you're as beautiful as a forest fairy." He watched the blood rush to the tips of Dokina's ears and down the paler skin of her neck. He inched closer. "Here in Valdavia, we think Kertan girls are the most beautiful in the world."

Dokina pulled back. "I'm sorry, but the queen's not...is not well." Her back was against the door.

He touched her hot earlobe with his lips. "Do you love the queen, Dokina?"

"More than I love myself."

"Then tell me what's wrong with her. Perhaps I can help. What did the physician say?"

"The...physician?"

"Don't tell me the physician hasn't seen her yet."

Dokina's lower lip trembled. "She didn't want...I only do what she tells me."

"Let me see her."

"She's not here!" Dokina blurted out, then covered her mouth.

Dapyx's stomach dropped. "Give me the bloody key!"

She opened her hand. The key was warm and clammy, and Dapyx slipped it into the keyhole. The bolt clicked, and the door squeaked open.

The chamber was empty, the beds made.

"Where is she?" Dapyx said. "And by the gods, don't lie to me now. Her life may be in danger."

Dokina grabbed a pouch at her neck and mumbled, "She went to Twin Willows. She wore her riding clothes."

Dapyx grasped the disaster. Andrada had gone there to confront Nicetas. "Both our horses are still in the stables. How long has she been gone?"

Dokina wiped her eyes. "Nine days—"

"Nine days?" Dapyx's voice climbed to a child's pitch. "Nine days?"

"Should we tell someone?"

"No, no. No one can know about this, you understand? No one."

The Book of Andrada

In a few days, Andrada had learned more from Thiamarkos about concealing her identity than in eight years of boys' school in Sehuldava. They traveled together now and never got in trouble with anyone. People greeted them as two merchant men going about their business. When Andrada's voice climbed, Thiamarkos interrupted her with a knowledgeable look that gave her a chance to adjust.

Everywhere they went, Andrada looked for the beggar child but couldn't find him. Instead, she learned more stories about Nicetas and Una. Her heart grew heavy, and her stomach was always in a ball, so she ate less and less.

On the last evening of the harvest fair, she felt bone-tired and hot to the touch. Around the fire, the Cartographer and the others waited for the call of the alpenhorns to announce the beginning of the festivities. Overhead, birds squawked, impatient to feast on the campers' scraps.

She thought again of Una. How beautiful, how terrifying the young medicine woman was. Even the thought of Una caused that strange trepidation Andrada had felt inside the Old Temple of Sehul with the crystal bell.

Thiamarkos stirred the glowing coal lumps under the spits. "Want some pike?"

Andrada shook her head. Food was the last thing she wanted when a fever spirit was toying with her. She wished for a tub of lukewarm water. She should take a bath in the Pyretus River to cool down. Her body was achy though, and she couldn't swim in her exhausted state. She wished Dokina were—

A sudden sneeze jolted her body.

"May the gods protect you, Master Lipoxais," Brasus said.

Alpenhorns and drums sounded in the distance.

"It's time," the Cartographer said.

He took a jar of salt from his satchel and lifted the lid to show everyone the beauty of the black grain. Then he and Mucatras headed to the sky oak square.

"Let's go, Master Lipoxais," Thiamarkos said. "If you miss Una's con-secration, you'll have to wait twenty years to see that of her daughter. Though it might be worth the wait. A king will be paying for that one."

For days, Andrada hadn't been able to look away from Una and Nicetas, but tonight she couldn't look on.

"You go ahead. I'm waiting for that little boy. He'll think everybody's in the square, and he'll come here to rummage through people's tents."

"There's no sense in helping a thief," Thiamarkos said. "But suit yourself." He left.

He was right, but Andrada still wanted to bring that little boy with her to Zalmodava, to safety. Except she couldn't quite remember what he looked like now, after all these days. There were dozens of boys just like him, roaming the fairgrounds of Twin Willows.

Brasus lingered with his fish skewer.

"Won't you miss the consecration?" Andrada said, her eyes on the flames.

"Somebody has to watch out for thieves. Besides, you're here..."

She could hear his breathing getting closer. She turned and met his wet mouth. His lips were soft, and his teeth were crooked, and his beard smelled of grape must.

She had never kissed anyone before, except that time she had pecked Dapyx on the cheek on her wedding day. Nicetas had never even tried.

"You're burning...with desire," Brasus whispered.

He must have seen through her disguise after all this time. Her tongue felt for his and silenced him. Her stomach balled up with revulsion, but she forced herself to go on so she could show herself—and Nicetas—that she, too, could break their wedding vows. She held Brasus's kiss and watched his eyelids lower and close.

"My tent isn't big enough for two people," she said.

Brasus's eyes opened and widened. "By Samca's army...mine is."

He opened his tent's flaps and slipped in, the end of his bedroll shifting in and out of the opening while he tugged it in place. His flushed face reappeared in the firelight. He held his unsteady hand out to Andrada, and she kneeled and entered his tent.

She sat up with her legs crossed, her head and back against the canvas.

"I want to kiss your breasts," Brasus said. "It's not fair to keep them hidden all this time." He shifted closer to her, his breath now loud and sour, his fingers on Andrada's belt buckle.

Andrada was once again standing outside a forbidden temple, but this time, her whole body screamed for her to get out of there.

"How would you like to see me dressed in proper clothes?" she whispered to him. "Undress me the right way?"

He nodded with a small whimper.

"Wait here. Don't go anywhere."

"Nowhere else I'd rather be." He lay back on his bedroll, his arms folded behind his head, his groin bulging.

Outside his tent, Andrada rubbed her face as if she had just woken from a bad dream. The harvest fair was over. Nothing more for her to do in Twin Willows, not even save one little boy among so many others. A little boy who was also not what he seemed to be.

"Are you coming, um, Master Lipoxais?" Brasus called from the tent.

"Wait there," Andrada said in her warmest voice. "You won't be disappointed."

Better get an early start to Zalmodava. Riding in the night's cool might shake the fever spirit off her back. Yes, she could make the trip on her own. She knew the way. She didn't even need to pack up her tent. How far from Twin Willows was Zalmodava again? She couldn't remember. Nicetas seemed to fly between the two. She could be home by morning if she wanted. Something was strange about that thought, but she heeded it anyway.

She gathered her saddlebags. With unsteady hands, she untied her mare's reins, put on the saddle, and mounted. She thrust her heels deep, and the mare bolted over the campfire.

They dodged tents and people and fires. They jumped over the cattle ditch. The hoofbeats drummed the ground, and the mare cut through a cleared pasture sprinkled with straw. She galloped under tight reins and heel blows, over terraces with the dirt dug out, and farther, to the edge of the Valdavian forest and into the night.

The darkness was now full. Night spirits tugged at the saddle, and it slipped on the foam on the mare's back. Andrada leaned to one side and cinched the girth strap, then to the other side, pulling strips of leather through buckles. She settled back in the saddle on waves of hoofbeats.

They rode away, guided by the mare's nose. Slope turned to hillside, hillside turned to meadow, meadow turned to forest, forest to thicket, thicket to clearing, and the sky above shifted, the gods turning Their eyes from Valdavia to Kerta through gaps in the clouds. Everything blended, sky and earth, beast and human, day and night.

Andrada rode, the hoofbeats steady as the thudding of her heart, threads of black turning gray and twisting in the corner of her eye. Was she close to home? Where was home? The fever spirit was turning the world unrecognizable.

The mare pulled right and pranced at the howling of wolves from the left, but Andrada held on to a clump of mane while her legs lost and found the sides of the saddle.

The mare pranced again, rearing.

Andrada hit the ground hard.

Chapter Nineteen

The Book of Dapyx

Two days on the road to Twin Willows, Dapyx spotted a brown horse grazing by the Hierasus River. He spurred Dapple off the road, over bumpy, patchy ground. As they drew nearer, he recognized the brown mare trotting to meet them. He dismounted, grabbed her reins, and checked them for engraved fittings. There were none, but the marks on the leather straps matched the absent shape of charging aurochs.

He scratched the mare between the ears. "Where have you left her?"

Anger brought tears to his eyes. He was alone with his horses, the Carpates Mountains belching up dark rain clouds. The mare seemed to have come from the forests in the foothills, but that was out of the way, far out. Andrada could be anywhere, and if she was wounded or sick, the coming rain could kill her.

He searched the grass, still wet with that morning's drizzle, for horseshoe prints. Wherever he found the mare's trail—snapped twigs, prints, fresh droppings along the river—he followed it. The mare pulled back again and again, toward Zalmodava, but Dapple pushed north toward Twin Willows, sniffing the air.

Night found them somewhere along the river with no light of a village in sight. Dapyx made camp on top of a flat boulder, safe from wolves if not from night spirits. He didn't tie his horses so they could protect each other through the night. All kindling was wet, so he wrapped himself in his woolen cloak, put his head down, and listened to the burbling water until he fell asleep.

Wild geese heading south woke him up before dawn. He sat up on the boulder and looked around, feeling cold and stiff. His horses were far down on the bank of the Hierasus, grazing. He whistled, and they raised their heads and trotted back to him.

The gods had shown mercy, for the rain had blown north that night. He was able to find the mare's old trail again. She had stayed close to the water, far from the road, but the forest's beasts had kept her on a predictable path. He followed the trail slowly, careful not to lose it.

He wondered what Andrada would say when he found her. Would she wrap her arms around him? Would she kiss him? Was she even alive?

He ate and drank very little that day. The signs were harder to read, and when the half-moon rose again, the trail disappeared altogether. He drenched a torch in linseed oil and lit it. He stayed close to the river, judging by the sound of the water.

Then he heard rustling—wind or wolves in the forests beyond. Dapple snorted and bolted, and the mare followed him, neighing.

Dapyx dashed after his horses, the torch flame flapping high at his side. He caught glimpses of his horses' tails—one dark, one light—just before they melted again into the night. He ran, and he stumbled, and he ran.

"Dapple! Wait!"

He couldn't see his horses anymore but could hear them in front of him, in the river.

He waded in. The water was icy on his feet, his calves, his thighs. He braced for the water to rise, but his next step took him higher. The water was shallow here.

His horses stood in the night, their heads down over the water. He walked on solid ground again, on an islet at the confluence of the Hierasus and a tributary. The muscles on his legs felt knotted and sore as he inched in.

He first saw a tree, then the back of a dark shape on the ground, the familiar riding boots, then the head with curly dark hair cut short at the neck.

The horses nuzzled the body, and Dapyx stood there for a moment, too scared to touch it. Dapple bit into the tunic and pulled it up. Andrada flopped over, her eyes open, her cheek smeared with mud.

Dapyx shrieked and jumped back.

He brought the torch closer, over his head and hers. Her pupils didn't shrink as the torch lit her face. The skin on her hands was raw from riding without gloves.

Dapyx leaned closer and heard a soft chattering of teeth.

"You're alive!" Dapyx said, his mouth dry, his heart racing. "Oh, dear gods, you're alive."

He dropped to his knees and touched her shoulder. Her clothes were cold and wet.

Dapple snorted and shook his mane.

"Good job finding her, Dapple. You can have all the carrots in the world from now on, I promise."

He shoved the end of the torch into the soft ground, between the roots of the tree, and slipped his hands under Andrada's slim body, then lifted her in his arms like a child. She was light, and she smelled like the outhouse of a crowded inn.

"Can you ride?" he asked her, but she didn't answer.

Of course she couldn't ride. She needed food, water, dry clothes, and a physician.

With Andrada in his arms, Dapyx sat on the ground, his back against the tree. He rubbed her cold hands and pressed his cheek against her forehead. They were at least two days away from Zalmodava.

He rummaged through his satchel and took out some half-eaten flatbread and the waterskin. He had to feed her somehow. Then he had to sneak her back into Zalmodava without the guards' knowledge.

He thought for a moment. Apollonius had replaced the reservoir for the courtyard well with a pipe connected to the new aqueduct. The abandoned tunnels that used to bring water from the Ozana River to the old reservoir could be their secret way into the king's house.

The Valdavian Chronicle

As soon as he arrived in Zalmodava, Nicetas headed to the women's wing. He ran into Zyraxes in the main hall.

"How ill is she?"

"Very," Zyraxes said, following along. "Fever, heaving, no food, barely any water. Could be gray fever." He paused in the middle of the hallway. "It can kill a grown man...or remove a future king from the line of succession. Our parents always said my fever was a gift from the gods, that Beleizis wanted me to be a priest, not a warrior. This fever could be just as big a blessing for your queen as it was for me."

Nicetas had no patience for Zyraxes's double-edged talk. "Just go to the temple and ask Ea and Beleizis to make the queen well again. Slaughter the fattest bull. Because I don't have to tell you what it means for us if Cothelas's daughter dies in Zalmodava."

"You want me to pray for a woman who refused to break bread with me? After she killed my sacred tree?"

"Yes. Now." Nicetas turned into the hallway leading to the queen's chamber.

Through the open doors, at the light of torches, he first saw Dapyx, his arms crossed over his chest, then the physician standing against curtains that blocked the daylight. In each corner burned the candles that kept the patient's soul from wandering into the claws of Samca's spirits. If they snatched Andrada, they'd force her to choose between Samca's twin cups of life-giving water and deadly water.

Try as he might, Nicetas couldn't remember anything from the time spent in his sickbed after the Night Attack. Maybe the sight of Samca was so terrifying that mortals were meant to forget it. Though no one doubted the story of his rescue from the Underworld, he couldn't remember Azemel or Ea either, but it served him well to say he did.

"How is she?" he asked the physician, not yet daring to go near the queen's bed. He remembered the last time he had been there and cringed.

"We tried everything, my king," the physician said, "but we need the queen to fight too."

"Is it gray fever?"

The physician shook his head. "Most likely a childhood fever we all had here growing up but the queen didn't have in Kerta."

"Or it could be a madness spirit," Dapyx said. "I found the queen in the gardens—"

"You found her?" Nicetas grabbed Dapyx's shoulder harder than he meant to.

Dapyx was on the verge of crying. "Her hair cut short...She was digging out carrots with her bare hands, her fingernails broken and bloody..."

Nicetas had to see for himself. The few shadows around the queen's bed shuffled out of the way as he approached.

A shiver of dread passed through him when he saw Andrada. She was asleep, her head propped high, her skin sallow and stretched over her cheekbones, her eyeballs sunken under ashen eyelids. Her lips were grayish green.

She looked dead already.

Could she see Samca's cups glimmering in the dark beyond? Could she hear Samca's whispering? Could she feel Her spirits' claws?

"Is she with child?" he asked the physician.

The man looked startled. "I haven't looked, my king. Should I?"

"Let her rest." Nicetas whispered another prayer to Enoz to save the queen's life. If She had heard his other prayer and put a prince in Andrada's belly, She couldn't let them die now.

Dapyx touched his arm. "Rada brought you back from the dead...Send for her, please."

"There's no time."

"I can ride to Twin Willows in two days and bring Rada back in another two. We'll change horses at each inn and outpost—"

Nicetas turned to the physician. "Does the queen have four days?"

"I'm afraid not, my king."

Dapyx teared up. "We must try, Nicetas, please."

But if they lit the beacon in Zalmodava and turned it green with Una's powder, she'd see the string of green fires along the bend of the Carpates Mountains.

It wouldn't be Rada who'd mount a horse to answer Nicetas's call though; it would be Una.

"Does she have two days?" he asked the physician, who tilted his head, as though unsure.

Andrada lay still. If her chest rose and fell, Nicetas couldn't tell.

The gods might listen to Zyraxes's prayers if They liked the blood and the smoke of the slaughtered bull.

Nicetas had promised Cothelas his firstborn son.

Yet to bring Una here?

Andrada looked dead.

"Run, Dapyx, light the beacon. And tell the watchman to turn the flames green."

The Book of Andrada

Andrada opened her eyes. She was in a bed. Two low voices—Dokina and Dapyx—whispered from beyond the footboard. The rough linen of her shift scratched her shoulder, and her legs burned under the down. Yet to move or ask for help was just too much.

On a side table, a candle flickered in a silver holder. Andrada stared at the soothing light. The flame was blurry, then sharp, swelling and rippling. She wished for the cool relief of tears in her burning eyes.

With a sputtering sizzle, the fire gnawed at the thread poking from the wax. Red and white twine? The wall of shimmering yellow and incandescent white pushed out from within, swelling the fabric of fire. Green eyes floated in a portrait devoured by flames.

She looked around for Samca's spirits and the twin cups. She had once feared a cup of deadly water. Again, she found no cups. Then she wasn't dying. She wasn't sleeping and dreaming either. She was just sailing on seas of flames. Underneath her eyelids there was sand, and under the sand was the life-giving water where the horses had found her, the tree with branches dipped into the night, Dapyx's cheek with its soft hairs, a man's shadow unclenching her jaws and pouring a bitter draft down her throat, the swaying of a covered wagon, a village at dusk, the shape of Mount Ea-El through the opening in the wagon's canvas, rats scurrying through a dry tunnel, a well with a chain hoist, narrow corridors, and torchlight.

She heard footfalls and turned her head. There was the loving face of Ea, flanked by torches, Her eyes dark as the bottom of a well, Her hair a dark braid woven with silver thread. She was a sandstone statuette painted earth-brown, and she leaned down and rested a cool hand on Andrada's forehead, with fingers rough as tree bark and smelling of mint.

Hot pain squeezed the matter inside Andrada's skull, then shrank like a hot iron tire around a carriage wheel quenched in cold oil. She screamed under the earth goddess's thumb of white pain, and the pain turned to relief, for she had seen Ea, and death was not scary but scented, and the smoke turned into a swarm of black bees that came together as a black dog, and the dog panted, a mist of warm, rusty breath wafting from its brown lips, its sharp teeth, its dangling tongue.

The goddess Enoz stood by the sickbed too, Her eyes blue, Her hair golden. The black dog's tail wagged, and the dog was licking something on the floor, brown earth dripping from between its teeth, reddish brown like thick wine.

Enoz pushed the dog away, then picked a silver tray off the floor and looked at the offering on it: a bloody hunk of meat, a bull's heart wrapped in a white towel speckled with red grape seeds.

The dog barked once, but Enoz didn't smile at the offering. Instead, She cried crystal tears.

Andrada tried to soothe Her, but she couldn't speak.

"She's losing too much blood," Ea said. "Prepare the glass tubes."

The Dynastic Scrolls

Heartbroken, Una changed the candles that kept the queen's spirit safe from Samca. Over the years, she had witnessed many patients choose wrong between the twin cups of life-giving water and deadly water, and this time she tried hard not to wish for the wrong choice.

She opened all the windows in the chamber. Nightingales trilled even here, so close to people's dwellings. The night air would help cool the patient's burning skin. Una wiped the blood off Raven's snout and sent the dog to sit and wait away from the sickbed. She added more wormwood incense to the terra-cotta altar of Ea and El. She cleaned the beeswax stubs, and she lit more candles in the shrine dedicated to the eight gods protecting the patient's internal organs.

Una tried to fulfill her duty as a medicine woman together with Mother Rada, but the limp body on the sickbed was no ordinary patient. She was Nicetas's wife. Nicetas didn't love that woman. He didn't love her, but he had bedded her when he had said he wouldn't. The child had not survived, a small wax doll with sealed eyes. Nevertheless, it was Nicetas's son wrapped in the white towel, a sick offering to the gods. His first child was supposed to be Una's. She wiped away a tear, afraid her mother would see her cry.

"She's losing too much blood," Mother Rada said. "Prepare the glass tubes."

Una rummaged through her satchel, took out the bundle of cedar ropes, and threw it to the handmaid. "Here. Tie her up."

The handmaid shook her head. "I can't do that to Queen Andrada."

"She must lie still while we do our work," Una explained. "Tie her wrists and ankles to the four corners of the bed. When you're done, we need more light around here."

The handmaid began fumbling with the ties. The patient moaned and opened her eyes. They were green. She tried to speak, but words didn't come. She tried to lift an arm, but the handmaid kept it in place and finished tying it. The patient struggled a little, then passed out, and the straps slackened around her wrists. Mother Rada pried open the patient's mouth, stuck a short stick between her teeth, and slipped a few poppy-straw pills down her throat.

Una found the brassbound wooden box in her satchel and took it to the boiling cauldron hanging over the hearth. She took out the green glass needles and tubes, which the Cartographer had bought years ago in the Roman city of Pompeii. With a pair of small tongs, she slipped them into the hot water. She then began her time-keeping song about the enchanted aurochs coming out of his cave at the call of his beloved goddess Bendis. When that was done, she picked the tubes and the needles from the water with the tongs and set them, one by one, on a clean towel on the bed table.

The handmaid had added more candles, and now the space around the sickbed was bright as day. Una pulled up the patient's bloodied shift and tied a twine around the upper thigh. Mother Rada sat on a chair and rubbed her hands with a rag soaked in wine and oil.

Una dipped her hands into a bowl of curdled milk the handmaid had brought from the kitchen, then wiped them clean. She picked a glass needle and fit it into a tapering tube, then put that into the wider end of another. She connected them end to end, running them up along the patient's leg. She then tied a twine around Mother Rada's arm and searched for a bulging blood vessel on the outside of her fist. When Una found it, she inserted the needle into the swelling.

The blood colored the cloudy glass dark as it reached the end needle. With only a few drops wasted, Una inserted it into the vein on the patient's leg.

"Ea, great mother goddess," Mother Rada said, "the people of Valdavia need their queen. We're giving her strong blood, but only You can give her life and restore her to us."

Una untied the twine on Mother Rada's arm and loosened her fist.

Mother Rada held Una's hand for a moment. "You did well. The gods are proud of you."

"Will she live?"

"The gods willing. We'll see after the blood transfer."

Una nodded and backed away from the sickbed. She put her tools away and threw the dirty linens into a basket. Sorrow she had kept deep down overcame her like a summer storm, and she rushed out the door.

In the dim hallway outside the queen's chamber, she found a dark corner away from torchlight, and there she cried her heart out.

The Book of Scorilus

Scorilus sat up in his bed and let Meda touch his forehead, though he knew he didn't have a fever. He'd been up all night, heaving over his bucket.

"What happened, Father?" Meda said.

"I tried our new salted bluefin tuna." His jaw clenched at the sound of those words. "And that garum sauce the Romans love so much." He thought of his son Moskon and his bad stomach.

Meda scrunched her beautiful face. "You ate fermented fish guts? No wonder you're sick."

"I know, I know…We can't yet compete with the Pompeiians…but don't worry, one of these days, I'll send Tymnes to Tomis…to have Legate Magius sample my garum."

"Next time, get a taster—please."

The sun shone on Meda's tanned face, on her red hair, on her gold-threaded dress.

He cleared his throat. "How's the country?" He was happy to see her after two moons of her journeying with Oroles and his Valdavian company. "Petition Day doesn't bring as much bad news as it used to."

"We reached deep into the heart of Steppewynd, Father." She sat on the edge of his bed. "Everywhere, people want peace with Valdavia, and everywhere, they could use waterwheels and aqueducts." She didn't seem tired from her journey. "I kept a journal of our travels. I'll read it to you, if you want. Oh, you should hear Oroles talking to the crowds, Father."

Scorilus didn't like her gushing tone.

"Everywhere he goes," Meda said, "people welcome him and his words of wisdom. I've met no one like him, Father—strong, and kind, and true to the gods."

"Lucretius explained the gods away with his atoms," Scorilus said, unwilling to continue the conversation. He shifted in his bed and groaned to show his daughter he wasn't feeling well.

Meda seemed to ignore that. "Oroles speaks of El's Great Awakening, Father. He believes the sky god will reward the righteous and punish the wicked when He returns."

"Sounds like Petition Day gone awry—"

"I'm not here to make jokes, Father." Meda's hands trembled as she clasped them together. "I'm here to ask you to marry me to Oroles."

Scorilus stared at her as if she had spoken the language of the Sarmatian caravan drivers: it sounded Dhawosian but had no meaning to the Steppewynder ear. He felt sick to his stomach again but couldn't tell if it was the thought of losing his daughter or the bad batch of garum.

Meda clasped her hands. "He's a good man, Father."

It pained him to see that Oroles was the man she had set her eyes on, though he wasn't surprised. Scorilus took her hand. His golden snake bracelet was still coiled around her forearm. The crystal eyes sparkled in the sunlight.

"Tell me about him," he whispered.

She smiled. "He's a lot like you, Father. You dream of a world where the people of Steppewynd aren't treated like slaves, where the resources of our three kingdoms are shared fairly, where trade routes bring peace and prosperity for all. Oroles thinks a world like that would be to El's liking at the Great Awakening."

He patted her hand. "And...you love him?" He already knew that, but he had to hear her say it.

She lowered her eyes. "I do."

"Even though he's only the son of a Valdavian builder?"

She looked hurt, and he felt sorry about his words but said nothing. He also felt locked out.

"Oroles's blood," she said, "is now the royal blood of Valdavia. He's a chosen man, Father."

"He shot the arrow that almost killed me."

She pulled back. "He didn't kill you though."

Scorilus was losing her. "Hey, hey." He caressed her hand. "I promised you'd have a say in your marriage, didn't I?"

She looked away, pouting.

"Bring him in," he said with a sigh. He'd do right by Meda.

While she was gone, he changed his tunic and put on Phradmon's dagger, as was now his habit. He was a little wobbly, his head heavy, his stomach tender, but he stood tall, gripping the back of a chair. Before long, Meda returned with Oroles, both looking uneasy.

"Do you love my daughter, Emissary?" Scorilus said.

"With all my heart, King Scorilus."

"Then who am I to stand between you two?"

Tears welled in Meda's eyes. "Thank you, Father." She took Oroles's hand.

"Today, the gods have truly smiled upon me," Oroles said.

Scorilus held on to the chair to steady himself. "I hope King Nicetas will be as happy as I am."

"As soon as the words of the Dhawosian Alliance are dry on parchment, I'll leave for Zalmodava to ask for my blood brother's blessing for our wedding."

Meda took his hand. "Please wait for me outside."

Oroles bowed and left.

"I can't wait that long," Meda told Scorilus. "Please, Father, marry us at midfall, before people can see that I'm with child."

For a moment, Scorilus couldn't breathe. His thoughts were too hectic to put into words. The brightness in Meda's eyes was also frightening.

In his flesh, the old arrow wound ached. If he did as Meda asked, he'd allow a wedding without Nicetas's blessing, which could put their budding Dhawosian Alliance at risk. But he had promised her...

"Yes," he whispered.

Meda kissed him on the cheek. "I want a ring made for him from silver and crystal, so wherever he goes, people will know he's mine."

She withdrew. The thud of the door felt more real than anything that had just happened. He had just lost his beloved daughter to the man who had almost killed him. He dropped into the chair. Meda wasn't his to keep. At least she was happy. And he still had Moskon. The boy was doing better this year, had even put some flesh on his bones. Soon, maybe they could read books together.

The door opened again. Rescuturme's robes rustled as she crossed the chamber.

"You told them yes?" she said.

Scorilus nodded.

"Good. Three married daughters out of three—all a mother can hope for. Now, I need to talk to you about something important."

Her sweet, strong perfume was more than Scorilus's stomach could take. He reached for the bucket.

"Rescuporis wants to see you," she said.

Scorilus heaved but couldn't throw up. He picked up a cup of water, but he couldn't swallow. He held the water in his mouth, swished it around, and spat it out. He didn't worry he would disgust her—he and Rescuturme hadn't shared a bed in years.

"He wants your blessing," she said. "Your son's going east in the spring to find Napat-Dehnu's promised land. He's following in your brothers' footsteps."

Scorilus wanted to stand up but feared he might crumple in front of his wife. "My brothers are dead, I'm sorry to say."

"My son will be victorious in his exploration campaign," Rescuturme said, crossing her arms. "His Tauri friends, the ones you sent him away with, along with cartloads of iron ore? They'll guide him and help him succeed where your brothers failed."

"He's putting a lot of trust in his new friends." Scorilus couldn't stifle a pang of envy. Rescuporis would become the Odysseus he had always wanted to be.

"But he needs to camp his soldiers for the winter in your empty garrisons in the valley."

"He's up to no good, I know it."

"I'm bringing you peace, Scorilus."

"I've already seized my peace. Now I'm building up my country. I'll grow crops again." He took a deep breath to ward off queasiness. "When my farmers start building Roman waterwheels and aqueducts."

She paced. "All with Vespasianus's blessing, I trust?"

"The emperor will approve."

"No matter." Rescuturme's face changed from defiant to pleasant, like in the old days. "Give him shelter for the winter, Scorilus. If he finds Napat-Dehnu's promised land, he'll settle there."

Rescuporis had been a nuisance for years. Having him chase his dreams of glory somewhere else was an unlikely break, the kind Lucretius had foreseen in his world of colliding atoms.

At last, Scorilus nodded. "Rescuporis and his men can move into my garrisons for the winter. I'd rather have him here than attacking Valdavia."

Chapter Twenty

The Book of Andrada

It wasn't Petition Day, but Andrada sat on Nicetas's throne, full of hope. A blue woolen dress embroidered with silver thread pooled around her feet, and a tasseled silver belt fell slack around her waist. Dokina was at her side to make sure she wouldn't faint.

At the foot of the dais stood Una, wearing a linen dress with simple embroidery. She was even more beautiful than in Twin Willows. A halo seemed to shimmer around her golden hair. Andrada sensed the aroma of fall flowers, and with it came the memory of two hands folding a clean dressing, a cool touch under the small of her back, lifting her while the linen was fitted between her legs.

She began trembling, and she gripped the armrests to hide it. "Have you…ever descended into the Underworld, Una of Twin Willows?"

"No, my queen."

"I thought I had crossed over, but Dokina here says it was only your mother I saw, not Ea." Speaking tired her. "I wanted to thank her for saving my life, but Dokina says she already returned to Twin Willows."

"Her work here was done, praise the gods."

"But you're still here."

"My mother wanted me to help the queen return to full health with my medicine."

Andrada tried a smile. "That vile brew Dokina forces me to drink each morning? What's in it anyway?"

"Minced carrots, beets, and herbs meant to take away nausea and weakness and bring about the yearning for food."

"Which it did, thank you." Andrada had eaten some bread and cheese that morning, the first in a long time.

Una bowed her head. "Now that the queen is better, I must return to Twin Willows."

Andrada's heart beat faster. "I want you to stay in Zalmodava for a while. Please stay...and teach me the ways of the medicine women."

Una seemed taken aback by the request. "My queen, those skills take a long time to master. I was an apprentice for many years."

Andrada didn't know why, but she wanted Una to stay. "I have time."

"But my time has been pledged to Ea."

Una had the most beautiful blue eyes Andrada had ever seen, the same color as the sapphires in the silver diadem Nicetas had once brought to Sehuldava. The same as the Cartographer's eyes—the Cartographer, who hadn't been able to hide his pride when he had watched Una dance at the harvest fair.

"Then stay and teach me about pigments, will you? How to mix my own colors. The Cartographer once told me your mother had given him a wonderful blue pigment."

Una smiled. "My queen knows the Cartographer?"

"He helped my father when he was ill."

"May I see your palm, my queen?" Una climbed the steps to the throne, and Andrada held out a cold and trembling hand.

Una's warm touch quieted the chatter in Andrada's mind. Gone were the worry and the sorrow and the doubt. Nothing bad could happen as long as Una held her hand.

"Ea allows it," Una said at last. "I'll teach my queen how to extract the colors of the rainbow from the essences of the earth. We'll need a work chamber for that. But I must leave Zalmodava at the end of winter, when the ewes give birth to their lambs."

As soon as Una let go, the weight of the world fell back on Andrada's shoulders. Through the open doors, she saw Nicetas running up toward them.

"What are you doing here?" His eyes darted from Una to Andrada. "Petition Day is not until spring."

Andrada straightened her shoulders, lifted her chin, and gripped the armrests of the throne, wishing she were back in her bed.

"Where better for a queen to express her gratitude?" she said.

"Well, you're done now." He motioned for her to descend.

"We are," Andrada said, standing, "until tomorrow."

Nicetas frowned. "What happens tomorrow?"

"I begin my apprenticeship with Una."

"What?" Nicetas glanced at Una, who stepped aside. "No, you can't."

Andrada was enjoying this. "Ea has allowed it."

"But you're still ailing."

"The best physician in the country will be at my side."

Andrada and Dokina walked from the throne chamber into the waiting hall. Andrada's forehead throbbed with every step, and she pressed her clammy hands against her temples. Was Nicetas holding Una in his arms in the throne chamber behind her? She didn't turn to see.

"Why did you ask her to stay?" Dokina said.

"I don't know...I just had to." She just had to be around Una, and she had never felt this intensity toward someone else before, not even her father.

Dokina groaned. "The god of the crystal bell has tricked us again. I should've known."

"What do you mean?"

"Forgive me, Andrada, but when Prince Dapyx brought you home, I took the bell from the whitewood box and asked the god to save your life. You said only ring it for important things. Not long after, He brought the medicine women to you. And just in time too. But now Una's here to stay. By the Three, Andrada, this god's a trickster."

Andrada felt that strange old wave of awe and terror washing over her again. The god of the crystal bell had sent the medicine women to heal her?

"He's no trickster, Dokina, but a powerful god who turns the world in ways no mortal can comprehend. I think...we should address Him as El."

"The sky god El?" Dokina gaped. "Awake and answering prayers? My prayers?"

"If He really is the sky god, then *El* is what we should call Him. And if we're wrong, I think a lesser god wouldn't mind our honest mistake."

"You're right..." Dokina clutched the amulet pouch at her neck. "We should call Him *El*. But just to be sure, could we ring the bell and ask the god to break the inkwell again if we're mistaken and He's not El?"

Andrada thought for a moment. "If you were a powerful god, would you like it if a mortal asked you to prove yourself to Them?"

Dokina blushed in an instant. "No, you're right, you're right. We'll call Him *El*, no questions asked. But if He's awake, shouldn't this be the Great Awakening?"

Andrada shook her head, overwhelmed. "I don't know, Dokina. How often do we truly understand the gods' plans?"

The Dynastic Scrolls

Una felt free without her mother and grandmother around her, alone in a Zalmodava she had dreamed of for years. Yet things were not as she had imagined, for she now walked alongside Nicetas's wife in the gardens, holding her arm, while Nicetas had gone to the Blue Highlands to stay away from them both.

Patches of dark, frozen dirt dotted the white pathway between the terraces. Leafless trees reached for the low skies. The wind had marked the icy surface of a pond with fine lines.

"I know about you and the king, but you shouldn't worry about me," the queen said without warning.

Una halted, trying to grasp the true meaning of those words. The queen didn't look angry or hostile, just tired and pale. She had spoken as if she didn't care for Nicetas, which pained Una.

"My queen, I don't know what to say..."

"Say you'll help me. Because I need your help. There was a sick little boy, not long ago...I cared a great deal about him for a while...but feeling that way was such a burden. It's gone now, but I don't want to feel that way again...I have things to do, things that..."

Of course. Even though the queen didn't know she had been with child, she had felt that powerful urge to protect small children, an urge the gods gave expecting parents.

The queen paused to catch her breath. "Can you help me avoid carrying a child...for now?" She seemed on the verge of crying. "I can't ask High Priestess Citera..."

Una nodded, though she felt hurt. The queen's children would be Nicetas's children. The queen had to be in a terrible state of mind to talk about that with a stranger. She remembered Nicetas after his ascent from the Underworld. Perhaps the queen was also going through her time of nightmares but with no one to lead her back into the light.

"Andrada! Andrada!" Una heard a call from the distance and saw Nicetas's younger brother rounding the pond toward them.

"How much longer until your work chamber is ready?" the queen said.

"Another couple of days," Una said. "We have all the seeds and mineral salts. The potter in Sanapa is sending us the earthenware we need, and the blacksmith in Erebon, the silver tools I asked for."

The prince drew closer, white vapor rising from his face.

"You're well again, thank the gods," he said when he reached them, panting. "I've been so worried about you."

The queen looked displeased. "You'll have my gratitude forever, Dapyx, but things haven't changed between us."

The prince glared at Una and took the queen's arm. "May I join you on your walk?"

"My queen," Una said, "if the prince joins us, I must remain quiet on matters regarding our apprenticeship. My words can only flow from women's tongues to women's ears. It's Ea's will."

The queen freed herself from the prince's grip. "Dapyx, you must go now."

The wounded look in his eyes, followed by a flash of anger, unsettled Una. She had laughed when Nicetas said the prince was mooning over the queen, but it didn't seem amusing now.

"Dapyx," the queen said, "do as I ask. Please." Her last word came out in a whisper. She looked tired as if she were ready to faint.

The prince grabbed her elbow. "Let me take you back to the house."

The queen shook her head. "I have my physician here with me."

Una hurried to open her satchel and found the corked vial with the gingerroot brew. She felt sorry to part with it; the Cartographer could only buy ginger when he crossed paths with the spice merchants in the south.

"Drink this," she said, "and your strength will return."

The queen emptied the vial. "I feel better already."

The prince backtracked, tears in his eyes. Una wanted to tell him not to fear, that everything would soon be as before. She wasn't there to take his place in the queen's heart. She was there only because of her goddess-given duty.

The Book of Andrada

Andrada lay in bed that morning, thinking of Una. How could it be that her whole body quivered with a strange emotion whenever she caught a glance of the medicine woman? She didn't know of any women who loved women in Zalmodava, though in some naughty songs, Enoz and Bendis, sisters as they were, pleasured each other. But those were the gods, and who could understand Them all the way?

She stood, her hand over her mouth, remembering the scroll she had once read in Sehuldava, written by a poet named Sappho of Lesbos. Those verses had stirred something inside her back then, but she hadn't known what to make of it at the time.

A look at that beautiful woman, and I can't speak any longer, as my tongue goes silent...

A bewildering hot current spread from Andrada's belly throughout her body, all tension and no aim, like a bow with no arrow.

She rushed out of bed, panting. No, she couldn't allow herself to think of Una and love. She was a married woman who had pledged an oath to Nicetas before the gods. And she had to work on becoming a great queen, for one day she'd return to Kerta and take over her father's throne.

The Book of Dapyx

It took days for Dapyx to find a good time to explore Andrada's work chamber, but here he was at last, early in the morning. It was a large hall on the corner of the east and north wings of the king's house, across the courtyard from the armory. Women used to dye fabric here, back when they didn't buy colored cloth from the merchants in the Ozana Valley. The place still had a faint smell of piss from the mix used to bind pigments to fabric. A large hearth sat in the center, with a generous smoke hole above. Tall east-facing windows let the draft run through the clotheslines hanging from the ceiling.

Dapyx had learned from Dokina—his new ally since Andrada's illness—that those windows were the reason Una had chosen this chamber for her lessons. She needed them for the morning sun or the rising moon or whatever light her recipes required. Thick woolen curtains hung from high rods, ready to close when the formula needed the flickering light of a single beeswax candle.

Dapyx had explored this place once, before Una's arrival, while searching for an entrance to the secret corridors in the women's wing. At the time, he hadn't found anything other than a long redwood table nailed to the floor under the windows. Now the chamber was furnished, and there was fresh firewood stacked in the hearth. On the west wall, opposite the table, cupboards framed the door. On the south wall, there was a terra-cotta altar of Ea and El.

Dapyx listened to the door he had left ajar. No one came from the courtyard, so he set to work, learning everything he could about how Andrada spent her time without him. On the table were clay beakers and tin cups on linen towels. He lifted lids, revealing small saucers holding powders made of dried herbs or...insect shells? He recognized the potash he used in his nature studies and the Kertan salts, white for the body, black for the spirit.

He turned again to the door, listening. Silence.

He searched the open shelves of a cupboard and found hemp bags of seed and dried fruit. He opened the drawers and found wicker baskets, tin flagons, and hemp pouches. His nose grew numb to the pungent smells.

He pulled open another drawer: wax tablets. One had three panels bound with leather strips on the left side. Disciplined narrow handwriting, Dhawosian words in Greek characters. Lists of ingredients, lines drawn to separate inventory from instruction, with writing in the margins. Sheets of parchment were stacked next to the tablets, written by what looked like a child's hand: Dokina's copies of Andrada's tablets.

One page was a list of ingredients for a potion named *wellness gargle for women*. Was Una now teaching Andrada medicine too? Another page talked about making pigments stick to the painting surface, with ingredients such as egg yolk and Valdavian honey. One was called *mixture to ease the pain of a bleeding womb*, another *potion to bring about sleep to the restless mind*, and another *how to stop the womb from catching seed*. Women were such strange creatures.

Dapyx wondered if he could mix a potion for Una that would make her homesick for Twin Willows. Then she'd just leave here, and he could win Andrada back. But there was no recipe for homesickness in that drawer. Maybe a potion for nightmares? Or a bad rash? No, she wouldn't teach Andrada any of those things—

"What are you doing here?"

Dapyx flinched. How had Dokina sneaked up on him like that?

"They're coming," she said. "You must go."

With no time to reach the door, Dapyx skidded across the chamber and hid behind the curtains, peering out. Dokina tried to say something, but now footfalls drew closer, and she just motioned for him to stay quiet.

First Una, then Andrada came into Dapyx's line of sight, both wearing black aprons. Andrada's short hair poked out from under a woolen cap. She was so pretty this morning.

"Because a blade covered in blood or dirt brings more than its sharpness to the blow," she said as if answering a question. "In a day or two, the wound boils over with pus, and the victim falls prey to a fever spirit, even if the blade hit no vital organs."

"And so," Una said, "the arrows gathered from dead bodies are deadlier than new ones." She unrolled a square of deerskin. "Dokina, don't start the fire in the hearth yet."

"What's that?" Andrada said, pointing at the deerskin.

"A map of the heavens. What the gods allow us to glimpse of their divine kingdom. Dokina, draw the curtains."

Dapyx stood still while Dokina, her hands trembling, moved the curtains around him.

"If we can see the gods' light by looking at the sky," Andrada said, "can we also hear the gods' voices somehow?"

"After much practice," Una said, "I now hear Enoz's voice in the chiming of bronze pots and spoons hanging from our sky oak in Twin Willows."

"What does She say?"

"She mostly sings the songs of my childhood..."

Dapyx eased to the slit in the curtains, careful not to let daylight into the darkened chamber. He couldn't see much, other than the soft glow of an oil lamp on the floor.

Una stretched the deerskin over the lamp using a wooden frame, and the ceiling was now covered in yellow dots.

"The midsummer night sky," she said, "when many medicinal plants are ready for harvest. I trust my queen still remembers the words of the Stardust-Harvester?"

"The fruit is for food, the leaf is for medicine," Andrada answered in a singsong voice.

A good time for Dapyx to get out of there. He slipped from under the curtain and was crouching behind the women gathered around the lamp, when Una stood up, heading to the cupboards by the door. Dapyx scurried back and landed on his knees under the table, where the darkness was deepest. He slowed his breath to silence.

Una and Andrada now blocked his path to the door, so he had to stay put and listen to their talk of constellations and medicinal plants. He felt his way around to pass the time: the curtain, the underside of the table, the flagstones. One of the table legs fit into a tight hole in the floor. The leg could keep the table anchored or—

He almost gave a shriek. That could be the key to the secret corridors. The entrance to the men's wing was in the armory, where women never set foot, so it made sense for the entrance to their wing to be in the old dyeing chamber, right under this table.

Una's sandals shuffled toward the terra-cotta altar, away from Dapyx. "My mother taught me this chant at the beginning of my apprenticeship. As with all songs, we use it to keep time while we clean a wound or boil a cauldron." Her voice dropped to a hum.

"There's no healing the eyes without healing the head,

"Or healing the head without healing the body,

"Or healing the body without healing the heart,

"For the head and the body and the heart are one.

"If the whole is sick, the part can't be healthy.

"To restore health to the head and the body,

"You must first hear the words that bring wisdom.

"Once Ea's wisdom is rooted in the heart,

"The head and the body will obey the medicine women's potion."

Una stopped chanting. "Repeat after me, my queen, just as I repeated after my mother when I was her apprentice.

"Don't ever give a potion to a patient who

"Won't put his heart into your hands

"And lend his ear to your words of wisdom..."

Andrada repeated the words, but Dapyx also heard Dokina whisper, "*Don't ever give a potion to a patient...*"

Time to sneak out for good. He'd wait for nightfall, come back here, move the table, and inspect the hole in the floor. He wished to all the gods that it was the secret entrance.

"*Give me your heart first, and I'll heal it,*" Una said.

"*First, the words of wisdom, and only then the potion.*"

"*Give me your heart first...*" Andrada said.

"*...and only then the potion...*" Dapyx heard Dokina whisper as he crept along the wall to the door.

"Should I open the curtains now?" Dokina asked Una, glancing at Dapyx.

Una nodded.

Under the cover of sudden daylight, Dapyx cracked open the door and ran out.

The Book of Andrada

Andrada finished scribbling another recipe on black wax, while Una brought a small clay jar from the hearth fire to the table. At Una's request, Dokina wasn't in the work chamber today, and Andrada couldn't hide her joy at having Una all to herself. She still didn't know what to make of these strange new feelings. She hadn't thought about her father in quite a while, she realized, or about becoming the next queen of Kerta. It was as if her illness had shaken her free of past and future, teaching her to cherish only the present.

Una dipped a finger into the yellow pigment she had just prepared and drew a line on the side of the jar. "Mixed with honey, it's the best yellow pigment there is. Stays bright over time, without fading or browning."

A weak ray of winter sun brightened her face, throwing the shadow of a loose lock of hair on her cheek. Andrada wanted to touch that lock of golden hair, tuck it behind Una's delicate ear, but only a mother could do that. Or a lover.

"The pigment I'll show you next comes from El Himself, through Ea and the first medicine woman. You must promise you won't speak of this recipe to anyone else."

"I promise," Andrada said, feeling herself blush. Now she and Una had a secret.

"What would the world be without El's blue pigment?" Una lit a taper from the hearth and brought it to the two hollowed heads of the terra-cotta altar on the south wall. White smoke of wormwood incense rose to the clotheslines.

Andrada picked up her silver stylus.

"This sacred recipe can't be written down," Una said, sounding stern.

Andrada felt the familiar pang of guilt for doing something wrong in Avezinas's presence. She put the tablet aside and reminded herself that Una was nothing like Avezinas. She was kind, she was spellbinding, and she was beautiful.

From her satchel, Una took an object wrapped in a pelt. It was a crystal cup without a beak or handle, with a translucent pestle inside.

"A wooden mortar won't do if we want to recreate the work of the gods." Una held out a bronze coin stamped with Scorilus's profile. "First, we must pay."

The coin clinked twice against the crystal and fell to the bottom, but the mortar continued to ring like the buzz of a bumblebee. Like the crystal bell from the Old Temple of Sehul.

Andrada had thought of showing the bell to Una, since a medicine woman might know how it worked, but what would Una ask El if she had the chance? To be free to marry Nicetas? Would El make the king a widower? Andrada wouldn't dare tempt that unpredictable god.

Una opened a brassbound wooden box, removed the first tray, and took out three ceramic vials, all sealed with small corks. With the smallest of the measuring spoons on a brass ring, she scooped a light-green powder from the first vial.

"Green vitriol, left over from forging steel blades," she said.

She took the largest spoon on the ring and measured a gray powder from the second vial. "Potash, but it has to be the right kind, leached ashes of sea plants."

She opened the third vial and poured all the dark-brown liquid into the mortar. "Goat liver oil from the kitchen."

She began mixing the ingredients with the pestle.

Maybe Zyraxes was right about Una. Maybe she was a witch who put love spells on people, for how else to explain the fire burning in Andrada's heart?

"We keep time with another sacred story." Una's voice turned into a chant. "During earth's first age, the young Bendis, goddess of animals, and the older Enoz, goddess of plants, got into a quarrel. To punish Her sister, Bendis unleashed the rats upon the fields to eat all the seeds. When there was almost no seed left, Mother Ea began to worry for the world the sky god El had left in Her care. But She didn't want to wake Him from His slumber or set His anger against Their children."

Andrada wondered for a moment why Ea was a worse overseer of Her realm than El had intended, same as Queen Seba, same as Andrada, who had failed the King's Challenge.

Una's beautiful voice brought her back to the story. "Rats are cunning creatures. They know how to take a small first bite, then wait and only take a second bite if it's not poisonous. So Ea made a salt that smelled of nothing, tasted of nothing, and killed long after the rats took their first bite. We call it Ea's poison."

Andrada caught Una's blue gaze for a moment, and her heart raced.

"Ea gave the poison to Enoz, and Enoz sprinkled it over the fields. The rats died a few days after, but it didn't kill only the rats. The poison also killed the deer, and the bees, and the fish in the streams. This time, the stench of rotting corpses reached El in Heaven, and He woke from His slumber. One of His Small Awakenings. And when He saw the desolation of His world, He cried. His tears brought down a blue rain that cleared the fields of poison and healed both plants and animals. And after He scolded Ea and His children, He went back to sleep."

Una was now stirring a pale red viscous substance in the translucent mortar. "Right on time."

"Could He be awake now?" Andrada whispered. "Some prophets think that time is near."

Una tilted her head as if suspecting Andrada had meant the prophet from Twin Willows.

"When He wakes," Una said, "we'll know, because He'll set the world right. He'll vanquish the Romans and cleanse His kingdom of injustice and pain."

The pestle was now coated in a thick purple balm.

Una kept stirring. "My mother once took me to the cave where Ea hid Her poison. I remember the bleeding helmets in the clearing outside."

"Bleeding helmets?"

"Mushrooms good for red pigment."

A scraping sound, short as a cough, came from the walls around them.

Una put down the crystal pestle. "What was that?"

"Could it be rats?" Andrada thought of Dokina's fear of rats.

They listened to the silence while the coating on the pestle turned deep blue.

"For rats," Una said, "I have a pinch of Ea's poison right here in my satchel."

"You brought Ea's poison with you to Zalmodava?"

"I didn't mean to, my queen, but when the beacon lit up green, I stuffed everything I had in my satchel—"

Andrada didn't want to talk about her illness again. "Now, the salt we used yesterday for the sleeping potion, it had no smell and no taste."

"But it had a tinge of pink in the sunlight. Don't worry, my queen, I know Ea's poison, and I won't mistake it for anything else. Here, the blue pigment is now ready. As close to El's blue rain as we can make it."

Andrada was startled. The paste in the crystal mortar was almost the same shade of blue as the one on her whitewood horse-box, painted by the Cartographer years ago.

"It's so beautiful..." Like Una's eyes. "Like El's blue sky. May I have it?"

Una seemed to weigh the request for a moment, then said, "When I leave Zalmodava, my queen can have it, yes."

The Valdavian Chronicle

Nicetas had to return to Zalmodava for the Ceremony of the Renewed Sun. He wasn't happy to see Una in her chamber here, getting ready and humming her familiar tune. The flames in the hearth scattered, and in that light, she looked different for a moment. He hadn't noticed until then, but she was dressed like one of the court ladies now, in an embroidered dress with tight sleeves and a high waist. She gazed at him in a new way. She had a new half-smile. The sapphire diadem he had kept on a shelf in his chamber would go well with this new Una.

She caught his glance. "I'm only wearing this because of the festivities tonight. I don't want to stand out." She pulled at one of her sleeves. "You've been gone a long time."

"Hunting..." And keeping away from Una and Andrada, from their unsettling new friendship that felt like a dark path laid with snares. "I'm here for the year-end ceremonies."

"Are you leaving again after you light the new year's fires?"

"There's word the great aurochs came out of his cave to feed."

"Don't you dare kill Bendis's lover!"

"Gods are good at guiding arrows. She can stop me if She wants."

"That's a mean thing to say. You're angry with me for staying in Zalmodava." She took his hand. "Nicetas, I'm here because it's time."

He felt his throat dry as he swallowed. "Is it?"

"Yes, but you have to be willing."

"Willing?" He shook his head. "How would any man be willing? A little girl who'd never call me *Father*. A little girl who'd look like you. A little girl who'd have her own little girl one day, without ever asking me for my blessing."

Una touched his cheek. "Yes."

"Was it this hard for you when I...married Andrada?"

"The hardest. And even harder when you took her to your bed."

Nicetas felt the cold wind through the smoke hole descend upon him. He hadn't told Una about that wretched night because Andrada wasn't with child, but had the queen spoken of it? By Bendis's bees, their friendship was wrong in so many ways.

"Don't make that face," Una said. "She didn't tell me. You did. Just now." She shrugged. "You hide things from me, I understand. You're a king, and I'm a medicine woman. We're both born to it. We both do what we must."

"What if we don't?" He sounded and felt desperate.

She gave him a sad smile, but it was her old smile. "I don't know why you're afraid. It won't hurt at all. I'll be the one who won't be allowed to eat my favorite food, handle blood, or hear certain incantations. I'll be the one growing big—"

"It'll hurt more than you think." He pulled her to him and buried his head against her neck. It was Una he held, but gone was the scent of sweet flowers from her skin and hair. Now she smelled of beeswax and tallow soap. Her hair was softer, her skin paler.

"Shush now." She took his hands and kissed his fingers. Her lips were dry and hot, like the breath of the hearth. "*I choose you and no other for as long as I live*," she chanted.

Nicetas couldn't utter those words. He'd have to lie with Andrada again, for his own offspring if not for Cothelas's heir.

A strange thought crossed his mind. "If I give you a girl, will you give me a boy to adopt like the Roman emperors?"

"If I give birth to a boy, I'm sworn to send him to the gods." She must have seen the dismay on his face, for she sealed his mouth with a warm kiss.

He closed his eyes and let her search for the buckle on his belt, as she had done so many times before. He thought of the great aurochs holding his enormous head high, with those thick, sharp horns.

Una's hands had found their way between his legs, and his breath turned warm and fast. He pulled her up to him and kissed her, hurt her lips with his teeth, crushed her breasts with his chest. But he wanted to be outside, in the cold, in the thickness of black trees, throwing his spear at the aurochs.

Una clung to him, her kiss on his cheek feeling rushed. He set her down on the fur rug by the fire, and she opened for him, the flower of her dress's hem blooming around her pale belly. Then she opened again, light-brown hairs curling around the entrance to what he knew was home—and he sank into her.

The loud wind through the smoke hole touched the small of his back with icy fingers. He pressed his face against the bear pelt on the floor and smelled its greasy hairs.

Soon he'd mount the steps of the Temple of Concord with Andrada at his side, and Citera would give the sign. The temple servants would kill the sacrificial goat for the dying year. Then all lights would be put out, and in the darkness, Nicetas would strike fire with the flint, set the pyre ablaze, and ask the gods for light and warmth in the year to come. With the kindling of that fire, all of last year's wrongdoings would be erased, and the world would start anew.

And a new life would blossom inside Una's womb.

Chapter Twenty-One

The Dynastic Scrolls

Una's life in Zalmodava was dull without Nicetas, who was always away on hunting trips. The days spent teaching the queen simple medicine concepts crawled by. She missed Twin Willows, but she couldn't go home until the end of winter. At least the sun was shining into the work chamber this morning.

She watched the queen at the table mix a pain balm in a wooden mortar, while her handmaid copied the recipe from a wax tablet onto a piece of parchment. The queen frowned, her tongue sticking out. Color had returned to her cheeks, but she still looked thin.

"What are you humming, Una?" the queen said, stirring the balm.

Una hadn't realized she did that. "A song about Bendis, who fell in love with a prince and turned him into a great aurochs. His haunt is now a cave where the two lovers meet on the full moon. My mother took me there once—a long ride south, close to where the Ozana River springs from the mountain." She missed her mother.

"The cave with the bleeding helmets?" the queen said.

Una cut her a hard glance. They shouldn't speak of Ea's poison or the blue pigment in the handmaid's presence. The queen nodded, blushing. For a moment, she looked lost, even though she was the queen of Valdavia and Nicetas's wife, even though, like Nicetas, she had been touched by the gods—while Una still struggled to comprehend Enoz's voice.

"Let's see that." Una pointed to the mortar.

The balm had the right brown color and the right thickness. Grandmother Zia would be proud.

"This recipe comes to us from the first medicine woman," Una said.

"Who was the first medicine woman?" the queen said. The handmaid looked up too.

Una drew a chair and sat down. "Centuries ago, Ea used to come down to earth and attend to the needs of Her mortal children. One late-winter morning, just after the ewes had their lambs, She stopped in a shepherds' village on the right bank of the Pyretus River, carrying a baby girl in a white lambskin bunting. The ewes in their pens smelled them from afar and woke up the village with their bleating. When people came out of their huts, they saw Ea lay the bundle on the snow-covered ground between two leafless willow trees, but they couldn't utter a word or take a step until She disappeared into the morning mist."

"The first of your line was a gift from Ea?" the queen said.

"That she was. The people in the village took her in, gave her a rag soaked in sheep's milk to suckle, and cared for her as if she were one of their own. And after six years, they understood Ea's gift, for the girl knew how to heal wounds and ease pain."

"What was her name?" the queen said.

"In the beginning, they called her Twin Willows."

"Like your village," the handmaid said.

"But she later received another name, a sacred name," Una said. "She was called the Root-Setter."

"That's an ugly name," the handmaid said.

What a silly thing to say. "Our goddess-given names aren't meant to be beautiful. They're meant to be meaningful."

"Meaningful how?" the queen said.

How to explain it? Una clasped her hands so she wouldn't rest them on her belly. She'd been doing that lately, even though she wouldn't be showing for quite a while.

"After we…bring forth the next girl in our line, Ea gives us two things: one is painful, but both are purposeful. The first is fear for our child's life, red-blooded fear we've never known before, to keep us and our line safe.

The second is the name that reveals our purpose in life. Twin Willows was born to set the roots of our line. My grandmother's name is the Family-Keeper, a name she learned when Ea first spoke to her, on the day Mother Rada was born. Ever since, she's been keeping watch over our family."

"Why is your mother the Time-Giver?" the handmaid said.

"She doesn't know yet. Sometimes our purpose isn't revealed to us until the right moment."

"What happens if you have a baby boy?" the queen said.

Una rubbed her forehead. "The boys...they're put to sleep on Ea's altar, and She takes them from us."

The queen grimaced. "And...if you don't have a baby at all?"

"We adopt a young woman and bring her into our bloodline."

"Wait," the queen said. "Am I your mother's blood sister now?"

"No, because she didn't chant the sacred words to bring you into the line."

"So your line can never be broken?" the handmaid said.

Una wondered if she should put an end to these questions. In her state, she was supposed to protect her mind from harmful thoughts.

"We've never tried," she said. "If our line is broken, a thousand years of darkness will swallow Dhawosia and the known world."

"A thousand?" the handmaid said. "That's a lot of years."

"Why did your mother leave you here?" the queen said with an intense look on her face. "Isn't she worried that something bad could happen to you away from home, endangering the line?"

Time to put an end to that ungodly conversation. "We trust the goddess to keep us safe, my queen. As long as we follow Her rules, She always—always—keeps us safe."

Una wrapped her arms around herself and the little seed growing inside her.

She nodded at the mortar. "The pain balm looks ready."

The Valdavian Chronicle

On Beleizis's holy day, the first full moon of the year, Nicetas was in the hunting quarters of the king's house—as far away from Una and the queen as possible. He waited at the table with Zyraxes as two kitchen servants hauled in a large tray with a roasted wild boar. Nicetas had roused it from its den and speared it that morning.

A servant sliced into the boar along a rib. There wasn't much fat under the skin, and the insides were ashen from being roasted on a bed of coals for too long.

Nicetas broke a loaf of bread. He inhaled the steam of dough as he sank his teeth into the crust.

Neither he nor Zyraxes talked during the meal, both angry with the world for different reasons.

"Emissary Oroles," a guard announced, interrupting their uncomfortable silence.

Zyraxes scowled as Oroles strode in and greeted them.

Nicetas put his knife down. "My blood brother, first councilor, and emissary, welcome home. Traveling in the thick of winter? That means pressing news from Steppewynd."

Oroles sat down and poured himself some wine. "I bring you the Dhawosian Alliance, my lord. May the gods bless the peace we're forging here."

Zyraxes rolled his eyes in disbelief. Nicetas picked up the boar leg on his plate and took a dry bite.

"More good news, my lord," Oroles said. "King Scorilus will join our defenses against a possible Roman invasion. And this coming spring, the gods willing, Steppewynd will start building hill terraces and aqueducts in the Tyras River Valley."

Zyraxes scoffed and shook his head, while Nicetas tried to ignore his antics.

"I'm disappointed in Scorilus," he said. "This is so unlike the king who once thrust a dagger into my gut."

"If I may, my lord, during my time in Steppewynd, I learned that their war with us was the wish of old King Thiaper. King Scorilus is now heeding the words of the prophets who say the gods favor those who strive for peace."

Zyraxes groaned and spoke at last. "Mark my words, if we allow Scorilus to grow his own crops, he'll make war on us in less than three years."

"Are these words of prophecy?" Nicetas said.

Zyraxes looked offended but didn't claim prophecy.

Nicetas felt an itch to press the matter. "It's not war on us, Zyraxes. Together, Steppewynd and Valdavia will stand strong against Roma. I'm sure I'll approve the Dhawosian Alliance as soon as I read it."

Zyraxes cackled. "Beleizis has always kept us safe from the Romans, even got Iulius Caesar killed before he could lead a campaign against us."

Nicetas sucked his teeth. "I'm sorry, Zyraxes, but this matter is as good as settled. My brother is just giving me the details."

If Beleizis had struck Zyraxes on the spot, the high priest wouldn't have looked more hurt.

He hissed into Nicetas's ear, "What did I ever do to you other than make you a king?"

"You keep reminding me of it. But there's only one king in Valdavia."

"You don't even care about ruling, but I do. I care about my country. I worry about its future all the time."

For a moment, Nicetas felt the truth in his brother's words. Yes, the throne should have been Zyraxes's. They both hated their place in life—and each other. He could end their strife by giving Zyraxes his birthright. A tempting thought. Then he remembered that this arrangement had been Beleizis's will. He crossed his arms and lifted his chin, holding his brother's eye.

Zyraxes sat up tall. "You enjoy hurting me, don't you?"

"If you'd stop walking right into it..." Nicetas turned back to Oroles. "Anything else you wanted to tell me, brother?"

Oroles glanced at Zyraxes, then shook his head. "It can wait, my lord."

Nicetas called for more wine and took another bite from the cold boar's leg. The next morning, he'd go hunting again—for a stag, if not an aurochs.

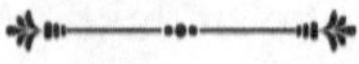

The Book of Andrada

Andrada had never been happier in her life. Every day, she was either with Una or studying to impress Una with her command of medicine and alchemy. She hadn't seen Nicetas since the Ceremony of the Renewed Sun, and she didn't seek him out. She wished winter would never end.

"The ewes in the pens will soon give birth to their lambs," Una told Andrada one morning in their work chamber. "My queen, it's time for me to return to Twin Willows."

Andrada froze with the stylus in one hand and the tablet in the other. She listened for the call of ewes outside but heard nothing.

She sat up in her chair, her heart pounding. "You can't leave now. It'd be..." She wanted to say it would be harder to part with Una than it had been to part with her father, her nurse, her country. "It'd be bad for my studies..."

"I've already taught you more than we agreed on." Una looked more peaceful than ever, her hair, her eyes, her cheeks full of life and color.

It pained Andrada to look at such beauty. "You've never shown me how to use your glass tubes..."

Una shook her head. "I can't do that."

Andrada rounded the hearth and cracked open the window—she needed air. The gardens were still covered in snow. It was too early for lambs. "Did I do something to upset you?"

"It's just time, my queen."

"I won't allow it."

"It's Ea's will, I'm afraid."

Andrada closed the window. "How do you know Her will, Una? You know what I want because I tell you, in words. But how do you know what the gods want?"

"I sometimes hear their words in my mind."

"But how do you know you're hearing Their words and not your own?"

"I just do." She sounded impatient with Andrada's questions. "I wouldn't dare upset Ea with my doubts."

Still. "Could it be that...you're placing your trust in the wrong god?"

Una frowned. "I don't understand..."

"If El is awake and—"

"I must go now." Una hung her apron on the back of the door and picked up her satchel.

Andrada felt a rush of panic. "No, please, Una...You see, I'm drowning in doubt. Ea loathes doubters. I need your guidance."

Una hesitated. "These questions are indeed strange—and dangerous if they upset the gods."

"Then give me until the new moon. Help me clear my mind of doubt. The ewes won't give birth until then, will they?"

For a moment, Una was silent. "Ea wouldn't want me to ignore someone in need...Very well then, until the new moon."

Nine days wasn't much, but Andrada was grateful for them.

The Book of Dapyx

Since discovering that the table's leg hole in the floor could be fit with a hook to reveal a trapdoor through the flagstones, Dapyx had used the secret corridors to spy on every chamber in the king's house, with two exceptions. The queen's chamber in the women's wing and the king's in the men's remained hidden for now. But he had drilled holes in the work chamber's floor to eavesdrop on Andrada's lessons with Una.

He was there when Andrada begged Una to stay and help her with her doubts. He heard Una promise to do so out of fear of the goddess. If Una wouldn't fight back, it was up to Dapyx to send her home. Otherwise, Andrada would keep coming up with reasons to keep Una around.

After supper, he entered the secret corridors with a lantern and watched Una through a peephole. Every night before bed, she'd have a cup of warm milk brought from the kitchen, but tonight Nicetas sent for her, and she left. Dapyx waited a while, and when she didn't return, he knew she'd be gone until morning.

He lifted the beam that barred the secret door from moving and found the iron ring in the center. He pulled the block along the grooves on the floor. Dust that hadn't been disturbed in ages sifted down from the open seams. Dapyx broke into a cough he struggled to muffle with the crook of his elbow.

On the back of a chair hung Una's satchel. He grabbed it, ducked out of the chamber, and turned to sweep away a few dust prints. He then slid the block back into its place and bolted it. Rats scurried from his path, startled by his lantern.

Back in his chamber, he opened Una's trove of women's secrets. He didn't need the linen wrap with utensils, nor the sky map on the deer-skin. Jars of balm, corked ceramic vials, boxes of seeds and powders—he lined them on the table next to the scrolls he'd been smuggling from the work chamber to copy. Some of the ceramic vials and jars had one, two, or three brushstrokes of different widths painted on in different colors.

He opened each container, looking for the ingredients of the potion to bring about sleep to the restless mind. When he found a liquid, he poured some into one of the clay cups he had brought from the kitchen. If it was a balm, he scooped it with a spoon, scraped it on a wooden plate, and wiped the spoon clean. He took a pinch from each box of seeds and powder the recipe required, and he snapped the ends of dried twigs. Throughout, he dipped his quill and noted descriptions and quantities on a sheet of parchment. He took more than the recipe required—in case his potion didn't work the first time.

Tomorrow he'd go to the kitchen and lace Una's cup of nightly milk, then wait for her to fall into a deep sleep. He'd get Una out of Zalmodava and put her on a carriage to Twin Willows. Getting her out of the fortress shouldn't be hard. He had brought Andrada back into the city through the old reservoir tunnels, hoisting her up the abandoned well and carrying her to his chamber through the corridors in the men's wing. He'd do the reverse now, using the women's wing corridors. *Praise the gods for making girls lightweight.*

In the carriage, he'd tell Una he had freed her from the queen. Nicetas would follow his lover to Twin Willows, and they'd be together for moons, as always. To Andrada, Dapyx would say that Mother Rada had sent for Una. It would take a long time for Andrada to sort out what had happened, if ever, and by then it might not even matter. By then, Dapyx would have won back her friendship. A perfect, gods-inspired plan.

He still needed the last ingredient for the potion. He opened a brassbound wooden box to find a shallow compartment with green glass tubes. Under the top tray, he found a leather pouch. He loosened the strings. White powder. It smelled of nothing, tasted of nothing. He poured some of it into a jar and wrote *white powder for sleep potion* on his parchment.

The Book of Andrada

Andrada received Una in her chamber with a heavy heart. Today was their last day together, for tomorrow would be the new moon.

Una's breath was loud and labored as if she had run here, but her cheeks were pale.

"Are you feeling ill, Una?"

"Nothing to worry about. It'll pass." She held on to the satchel on her shoulder.

"I will not see you in the morning, so this is farewell. But before you go, I want to ask you something."

In the candlelight, the shadows under Una's eyes seemed inked in soot.

"You said you'd give me the sky god's pigment, remember?" Andrada hoped she wouldn't need to beg or demand.

An image of Una in the right colors would help her cope with her loss for a while. The very next morning, she'd gallop to Erebon to find the statuette merchant.

Una reached into her satchel, pulled out a small clay jar marked with a blue brushstroke, and handed it over. Andrada opened her horse-box on the table and set the jar beside the yellow and the red pigment jars.

"One last thing." She picked up the comb of her childhood, every bone and sinew in her body vibrating beyond control. She whispered, "Please, let me comb your hair."

Una twitched, her brow furrowed.

"You see, I've never had long hair like yours." Andrada pulled at a curly lock that only reached halfway down her neck.

Una nodded and sat in a chair, her satchel in her lap. Andrada came around, comb in hand. She eased out Una's braid. It was soft as the pelt of a hare. The tassel at its end curled with the brightness of melted gold. Andrada untied the string.

The roots of Una's hair were darker, almost brown, but as the strands cascaded down her back, they ran bright with yellow. Her hair smelled of milk and honey.

The comb slid down as if parting water. Andrada tried to keep her hand steady. True love—she had once asked the crystal bell for true love. She had never felt like this before. This must be what true—

"I think my hair is well combed now," Una said.

Her cheek was pale, but her forehead glistened with sweat. She stood from the chair.

"Farewell, my queen. I hope your knowledge of pigments and women's medicine will serve you well."

Andrada didn't move for a long time after Una walked out. She wished she could cry. All she had left of Una was a long golden hair hanging from the teeth of the comb. She spooled it around her forefinger and opened the horse-box to lay it inside.

She could ask El to keep Una at court until midspring. With renewed hope, she set Una's ring of hair in the box and picked up the crystal bell. She hesitated. What if El twisted her honest request again? He might hurt Una in ways Andrada couldn't foresee. No, she didn't dare put Una in danger. She returned the bell to the box.

Something caught her eye: a golden wad of loose hairs on the floor by the empty chair. She picked it up with care. The pale cheeks, the sweaty forehead, this fallen hair—could Una be ill? Maybe she couldn't travel tomorrow. Maybe she'd delay her leave until she felt better. Hope bloomed in Andrada's heart.

The Dynastic Scrolls

Back in her chamber, Una opened the window and took a deep breath, like a gulp of cold water. The spell of nausea she'd had in the queen's chamber was fading.

The night was dark. The air was crisp and smelled of spring, of melting snow and ripe soil underneath. The whisper of the wind wrapped her in a soothing cold embrace. With another deep breath, she felt better. But she began to shiver, so she pulled back inside.

The hearth was ablaze. On the table, there waited a clay mug filled with goat's milk, still warm. She sat on the bearskin, sipping milk sweetened with honey. She rested her left hand over her womb, where that new shoot of life grew as Ea wished it.

She loved that tiny girl more than she loved Nicetas now. But if that love could be upended, who was to say Nicetas wouldn't love a son by Queen Andrada more than he'd love Una's daughter? She dismissed that thought. There would be no half brother or sister for Una's daughter, at least for now. Nicetas hadn't lain with the queen since last summer, and Una had taught the queen how to keep Nicetas's seed from taking root inside her womb, as requested. But a day would come when Nicetas would need his heir.

The curtains fluttered, and the flames in the chamber cowered. Una went to the window to close it. She felt a shiver down her back, a shiver of fire instead of ice, a shiver that stuck to her like a spiderweb and burrowed into her flesh. She rolled her shoulders and shook her head, but the shiver was still there.

The air was made of water now, deadly water, and she was drowning in it. She gripped the windowsill—the wood frozen—and forced herself to breathe. Her fingers, her hands, her arms were cold and tingled with a thousand pricks of ice. Her chest ached, her tongue grew thicker and filled her mouth, her eyes burned in their sockets.

This couldn't be. She grabbed her satchel, turned it upside down, and shook it. She combed through vials and pouches, opened the box, and clawed at the top tray with the glass tubes until she held up the empty pouch.

No, no, no...The illness that had gripped her was not the weakness brought about by the new life inside her womb. It was Ea's poison. Una needed the antidote, but she had just given the sky god's blue pigment to Queen Andrada.

What of the baby? Ea wouldn't let anything happen to the baby.

Una had to return to the queen's chamber. Now. But her legs didn't follow her mind's command. They stood with ashen toes on the bearskin rug in front of the fire. She heaved, and out poured curdled milk spiked with tendrils of blood.

Her knees gave way. Her arms didn't feel the body they hugged. Her body curled by the cold fire.

Ea protected the line, and Una was the last in line. She couldn't die. She was *the* line.

Why had Ea forsaken her?

She hadn't. She couldn't have.

Una tried to pray but couldn't remember the words.

A flock of white hares hopped in through the window and lay down around Una, their pelts stretching and stitching together around and underneath her. Cuddling her. Wrapping her. Smothering her.

Una surrendered without sound, without struggle—without and within.

The Valdavian Chronicle

A flurry of snowflakes swayed around the waterwheel's clearing, obscuring the bleak gardens beyond. But bleakness didn't touch Nicetas's heart this morning. He and Una were finally returning to Twin Willows, and she needed fresh water for an incantation seeking Ea's blessings on their journey there.

He rubbed his hands and stomped his feet in the snow as Oroles unfastened a frozen bucket from the double chain.

White vapor rose from Oroles's mouth. "My lord, there is something I must ask you before I leave for the White Fortress to work on the new Dhawosian Alliance with King Scorilus. I need your blessing to marry, for I love someone."

"I thought you only loved the gods," Nicetas said, laughing. He couldn't hide his joy at having Una all to himself, at long last. "And who is this special someone who stole my brother's pious heart?"

"Princess Meda of Steppewynd," Oroles said, switching the bucket from one hand to the other.

"And what does her father say about that?"

"The king has already given us his blessing. Will my brother give us his too?"

Nicetas rubbed his cold hands, his laugh now gone. "Are we talking about Princess Meda of the Tyrageti tribe, whose father once gutted me like a fish?"

Oroles grimaced but nodded. "Yes, my lord."

"An alliance, yes, but now we're to become family?"

Nicetas felt a painful tightness in his throat. It wasn't just the memory of that long-ago attack that hurt him. Had it ever occurred to Oroles that his marriage would create trouble at the Valdavian court? After all, as the king's blood brother, he was a legitimate heir to the Valdavian throne, though after Dapyx. Oroles was an heir who would now have the Steppewynder army on his side.

Oroles's eyes shone with anxious expectation, but Nicetas needed to think about his answer.

"Go ahead," he said, "take the ice to the kitchen and melt it. We'll talk soon."

"But, my lord—"

"Don't push your luck, brother," Nicetas said.

He waited for Oroles to leave. Snow swirled in the icy wind, sticking to his face. The more he thought about Oroles's request, the less he liked it.

At last, he started walking, eager to get to the warm house and to Una. She always did what was right by the gods. She'd point him to the right answer.

The Book of Andrada

Andrada put on her riding gloves. The statuette merchant wouldn't be in Erebon on such a snowy day, but she'd ride there anyway. If she left now, she might even catch a glimpse of Una in her carriage crossing the valley.

She reached for the sheathed sica on the table to hook to her belt when the howling began. It came from inside the house, but what kind of beast could scream like that?

She opened the door. People were running down the hallway.

Dokina skidded to a halt. "Una's dead, frozen solid in her chamber..."

Her voice broke, her chin trembled. She clutched the amulet pouch at her neck.

"What?" Andrada's blood chilled.

The howling returned, wailing from the walls, the hallways. Then...silence.

"Was that Nicetas?" she whispered.

"Yes." Dokina covered her face. "The king is with her now."

Dread gripped Andrada like never before, not even when there had been a cup of deadly water waiting for her. She needed divine intervention.

"Bring me incense, Dokina." She swiped the table clean around the terra-cotta altar of Ea and El she had brought here from the abandoned work chamber.

If there was a way to bring Una back from the Underworld, Andrada couldn't leave it to her newfound faith in El, who might or might not be awake, might or might not answer her prayer. No, she had to ask Ea for salvation. Ea had brought Nicetas back from the Underworld. She could save Una too.

Andrada took the jar of sweet-basil incense Dokina gave her and spilled it over Ea's open head.

"Leave me," she told Dokina while grabbing a lit candle off the table.

Red terra-cotta flickered crimson with the new flame. Andrada stared at Ea's hollow head, smoke rising white and thick from the burning incense. She saw an angry face, thick eyebrows dug over the hole of the nose. Terror sank into the pit of her stomach.

She dropped to her knees, clasped her hands together, and recited the words of Ea's prayer, "Oh, loving mother who watches over Her children and gives life to the world. You feed us, heal our wounds, comfort our sorrows. You stamp out the storms of our lives and save us from the misfortunes written in the stars." Her fingers tightened on her knuckles. "Mother Ea, I've strayed from Your path with the crystal bell, and I deserve to be punished. So punish me, not Una. Don't let Samca drag her to the Underworld. Take me instead, I beg You."

Her words dried up, but still, she begged in silence for Ea to turn Una back on the threshold, stop her from setting foot into the Underworld.

"You're praying to the wrong god," a voice whispered inside her head.

Andrada forced herself to look at the angry face of the terra-cotta goddess, to breathe the smoke of incense. She remembered the sweet smell of Una's clothes when she had first arrived—

Her mind was wandering. "Forgive me, Mother."

Like crawling uphill on ice, Andrada had little to cling to. Her gaze slipped from Ea to the quiet god at Ea's side.

No, she couldn't risk angering Ea. Her adoration and devotion should be pledged to the goddess if Ea were to ever answer.

"Please, please, please, Mother...You returned Nicetas from the dead. Please bring Una back. Please, bring her back..."

If the goddess could see her tears, maybe She'd answer, but Andrada's eyes had been dry for years.

The voices charging through the walls rose to such a din, Andrada knew Ea couldn't hear her now. She rushed to the window, opened the latch, and shoved her shoulder against the shutters until the seal of snow and ice broke.

"Ea, where are You?" she screamed into the morning haze.

She listened, but the goddess was not in the whisper of the wind. She looked up, but the goddess was not in the gray clouds. She took a trembling breath, but the goddess was not in the incense smoke around her. Andrada was alone with her despair. Her last hope to save Una was now the crystal bell.

She turned from the window and gave a shriek when she bumped into a broad-shouldered guard. Two more men stood behind him.

"Sorry to startle you, my queen, but I must escort you to the Six-Sided Tower."

"The tower?" Andrada said. "Why?"

The guard glanced away, embarrassed. "By the order of High Priest Zyraxes. Please, my queen."

"Zyraxes? He can't do this. I'm the queen."

"He wants to make sure we keep you safe until we know there's no danger to you."

Andrada's sica was still on the table, in its sheath. "Let me...change my clothes first."

"No time." He touched her shoulder to guide her. "I'll bring a change of clothes to the tower."

"I need to take some things with me."

"Later, my queen." He clasped her arm and pulled her along.

"No, you don't understand," Andrada said, shaking him off.

Another guard also grabbed her. She kicked him in the shin, and he let go, but the third one locked her in his grip. She groaned and struggled but couldn't free herself.

"I got it from here," the first guard said, pressing a blade against her side.

She didn't care if she died in the heat of the fight. But nothing mattered more than asking the crystal bell to bring Una back. She'd go with the guards to the Six-Sided Tower, and Dokina would bring the bell there.

They left the women's wing and crossed the courtyard. Andrada looked everywhere for Dokina but couldn't find her.

The muscles in her legs burned when she reached the top landing. Of the three cell doors before her, the one in the middle was wide open.

"High Priest Zyraxes will visit soon," the first guard said, nudging her in.

He closed the heavy door but kept watch through the cutout window.

The chamber was oddly shaped. The floors were flagstones covered in bear pelts. There was a bed with a chamber pot next to it. A small hearth, not yet lit. A table and two chairs. A candle wheel hanging from a chain in the ceiling. Cold air blew in through the window slits. This had to be where the Valdavian kings locked their important prisoners.

Andrada shivered, her back wet with chilled sweat.

"What's your name?" she asked her guard.

"Calidrones, my queen."

"Tell my handmaid to bring me the bell, Calidrones. It's a matter of life and death."

"Only if High Priest Zyraxes orders me to."

He closed the cutout window.

Andrada sat down on the hard bed. She was a prisoner. Ea had let Una die, and the bell that might bring her back from the Underworld was out of reach.

PART THREE

"Andrada the Wicked..."

—from a Dhawosian nursery rhyme

129 LE

Chapter Twenty-Two

The Valdavian Chronicle

Another morning without Una. The sun still rose, spring brought nature back to life, and Nicetas kept breathing.

A knock on his door reminded him he was alive in this world while Una wasn't. An older woman stepped in, and it took him a moment to recognize Una's grandmother.

"Zia?" Nicetas said, coming to greet her. "What are you doing here?"

She looked like a night spirit. She had rubbed ash in her white hair, and soot ran down her face like black ink. Her sheepskin cloak shone heavy with rain. The floor around her turned dark with dripping water.

"Where is she?" Zia said.

"Not far." Tears welled in Nicetas's eyes. "I buried her next to Ea's high priestesses at the Temple of Concord."

Zia shook her head. "She didn't belong here when she was alive, and she doesn't belong here now. Take me to her now."

Nicetas picked his cloak from the back of his chair and followed Zia.

Outside the house, Rada and the Cartographer waited by a donkey-drawn cart. Rada, too, had dark lines of ash on her face. She held Raven by a rope collar, and the dog was frantic, whimpering and wagging her tail. Her black fur was a mass of prickly wet tufts.

"This way," Nicetas said.

The cart rumbled on the graveled path to the Temple of Concord. The puddles boiled with rain. Zia walked next to Nicetas, wiping black drops off her forehead. Raven skipped ahead, her paws crunching pebbles underneath. Once in a while, she stopped to shake, a whirl of drops flying around.

Una's grave, marked by two leafless willow saplings, was in the north corner of the Sanctuary of the Dead. Raven ran ahead, her howl cleaving the quiet morning. At Una's grave, she whimpered and howled and dug her claws into the mud.

Nicetas couldn't believe it when the Cartographer took a long-handled shovel from the cart.

"You can't..." Dread gripped him. "This is sacred ground."

"We're taking Una home," the Cartographer said, rain dripping from his hair.

To Nicetas's dismay, Zia began mouthing a prayer. But Rada stood to the side, silent in the rain. The Cartographer thrust the shovel into the ground. Raven kept digging too.

"No!" Nicetas grabbed the slippery handle of the shovel.

The Cartographer jostled Nicetas to the side. "You won't stand between me and my child."

Nicetas got up again. "She was mine too." He wiped rain and tears off his face and curled his hands into fists.

Raven bristled and growled, while the Cartographer scooped up another clump of black soil.

"I said no!" Nicetas hurled himself at the Cartographer.

Raven barked and lunged. Her teeth burned into Nicetas's leg. He fought to regain his balance while shaking off the snarling dog. They were at a standstill: he, leaning onto his unharmed leg, and Raven, baring her teeth.

Rada stepped between them. She put her hand on Nicetas's chest but spoke no words.

His heart snapped inside. "Please don't take her..." He'd never go back to Twin Willows to see Una's grave there. Twin Willows was dead to him without her. "Say you won't take her from me."

"Rada won't say anything for thirty days," Zia said, referring to the mourning vow of silence. "Now stand back. This is Ea's will."

Ea's will...

Nicetas kneeled in the mud by the gravestone of a long-dead priestess, closed his eyes, and listened to the pain in his injured leg and the sound of the shovel. The ground trembled beneath him with each thrust.

Rada and Zia picked up shovels from the cart and started digging. After a while, the Cartographer jumped into the hole to dig there.

"There she is," he said at last. He had reached the shrouded body.

Zia landed with a thud inside the hole. Nicetas heard a knife slit through the fabric. The Cartographer moaned. Zia called for Ea's mercy.

Nicetas hid his face in his hands and waited. He had seen Una frozen, the burst veins in her skin covering her face—seen her body thawed in the Hall of the Dead, her hair limp under a linen shroud. He didn't want to see it again. Already he had trouble remembering her alive after finding her snow-covered body curled up by the frozen hearth. He dug his heels into the mud and waited.

The smell of rotting flesh was faint but there.

"Her hair..." Zia said from the grave. "Her fingernails...This was poison."

Rada let out a whimper that made Nicetas's blood chill.

"What kind?" the Cartographer said.

"Something only we medicine women know of," Zia said.

Only the medicine women. And Andrada, Una's apprentice. The tears on Nicetas's cheeks were warm, and the rain was cold. It felt good to cry together with the sky. He promised those cruel gods he'd make Andrada pay with her life for Una's murder.

Once Una's family had left with her body, Nicetas wandered without purpose, limping, a jug of wine in hand, and somehow ended up in the armory. He collected a few dull blades to sharpen and sat at the grindstone. After another swig of wine, he picked up a sica and stepped on the treadle.

The pumice wheel turned slowly, then faster and faster, sparks flying from the edge of the blade, burning the skin on his hands and piercing his shirt and trousers. The wine couldn't take away Nicetas's pain, but the screech of the grindstone, like mourners' wailing, soothed him.

A shadow grew on the flagstones. A tall figure with a staff. Zyraxes.

Nicetas threw the sica into the water trough, where it sank with a hiss.

"I can't go on living while that murderer still breathes," he whispered. "She killed Una, Zyraxes."

That was why she had kept Una at court, close to her, pretending to be her apprentice, so she could find the best way to poison her and cover it up.

"I know, brother," Zyraxes said, patting him on the back. "Just like she felled my sky oak. But we need her father on our side."

"Do we?" The air tasted of metal. Nicetas took a few gulps of wine, wine made by Una at the harvest fair, then wiped his mouth on his sleeve. "We now have Steppewynd...and Oroles's alliance."

"Spring is coming," Zyraxes said. "Roma is planning its next campaign. Divided, Dhawosia will become its target. We don't have enough gold and soldiers to fight it alone."

"What if we give Cothelas what he wants?" Nicetas's words came out slurred.

"And what does Cothelas want? The part of the marriage alliance he complained you didn't keep?"

Nicetas nodded. "My firstborn son to..." He waved his hand, searching for the word. "Groom...as the next king of Kerta."

"You don't say..." Zyraxes chewed on his gray bristles. "Who else knows about this?"

"Just me...And now, you."

"It's not every day that you trust me, brother. I'm grateful—"

"This is not me unburdening my heart, Zyraxes. I'm telling you this because I need the queen...to bear a son for Cothelas before she dies...Because she must die." He took another swig of wine.

Zyraxes tapped his chin. "I thought Cothelas had an heir, one Syrmos of the Bear-Hunters tribe. But if he still wants one from his precious bloodline, well, we can send him any newborn child and have the queen die of childbed fever soon after."

"Yes, yes…" Nicetas said, hope for revenge warming his heart.

"We'll make sure justice is done, yes." Zyraxes's face changed. "By Beleizis's thunder, Nicetas. We're working together at long last, like true brothers…"

Nicetas had no use for that kind of talk. He picked up a falx from the pile of blades on the floor and balanced it on the pumice wheel. The falx screeched as he pressed his foot on the grindstone's treadle. He stepped harder, his foot aching, his fingers burning, his ears ringing.

The light grew brighter once Zyraxes left.

After sharpening the falx, Nicetas went for a battle-axe. After the axe, he picked up a skinning knife. The blade made a sharper sound, but the sparks still stung.

The light around the grindstone dimmed again. Nicetas stopped the wheel and looked up.

"My lord," Oroles said, "I'm due to return to the White Fortress."

Nicetas couldn't look at Oroles, so eager to go back to his woman, who was alive and well.

"I can't give you my blessing to marry the princess, Oroles. Not while my heart is bleeding."

"I can wait, my lord." Oroles cleared his throat. "There's something else, more pressing. The queen is still locked in the tower. If anything happens to her, we'll have war with Kerta. Legate Magius will alert his emperor, and Roman legions will be on our shores by summer."

"I know what I'm doing, Oroles. Just go away…"

Nicetas set the skinning knife against the wheel and began grinding. The blade retreated, screaming, one glowing red wisp at a time, the edge fluttering like the wing of a butterfly, red, orange, gone. And so was Oroles.

Nicetas looked at the blade in his hand. One slash at his own throat, and he'd be down in the Underworld with Una. Except he wouldn't be. The gods didn't let mortals pick their own time to die. They'd keep him away from Una until the Great Awakening.

He threw the knife into the trough. He'd have to wait here alone, go on living alone, be a king alone. Cothelas the Bald had gone mad with grief after his wife died...Nicetas hoped for a madness spirit now to take away the gutting pain—

"Nicetas," a girlish voice sounded in his ear.

For a moment, he imagined that the hand on his shoulder was Una's as she leaned down, whispering his name. But the voice didn't quite belong to a girl.

He turned, and the pain of disappointment sucked the air from his chest.

Dapyx pulled back with a frightened look on his face.

"What do you want?" Nicetas's eyes burned, no matter how much he rubbed them.

"Please set Andrada free," Dapyx whispered. "She didn't kill Una."

"How would you know?"

Nicetas was certain of Andrada's guilt, just as he was certain of the wheel turning when he stepped on the treadle. What he wasn't certain of was how to make her suffer before she died.

"More people than you imagine wanted Una gone. Just think about it. Zyraxes hated her for keeping you away from Zalmodava. Citera hated her because you broke the marriage vows she had guaranteed in front of Ea. Even Oroles—"

"No, no, and no..." Nicetas's words rolled out like heavy pebbles off a wooden tongue.

"What if there's a simpler reason?" Dapyx went on. "What if Una just fell asleep with the windows open and froze to death?"

That meant blaming the gods, who had no reason to hurt Una.

"No. Andrada hated Una. But you can't see that...because you're in love with my wife." Nicetas rubbed his forehead. "You have been since that kiss...at our wedding."

"No, that's not it." Dapyx clasped his hands together. "Trust me, she's innocent. Una was her tutor and her friend."

Nicetas raised his jug and drained its last drop.

The armory was now spinning, and he felt like throwing up.

Dapyx teared up. "Please, brother, you'll anger the gods if you spill innocent blood."

Nicetas burst into laughter. "But They love innocent blood. That's why we give Them our white bulls."

"Please, Nicetas...maybe Una...killed herself."

Nicetas felt those words like a punch in the stomach. "What did you just say?"

He pounced at his little brother, the knife against Dapyx's neck, so soft a neck, so easy to carve. The skin gave in, tiny beads of red blooming up and down the knife's edge.

Dapyx squeezed his teary eyes shut, panting.

Nicetas groaned. "Get out of here...before I offer the gods your innocent blood."

Dapyx pressed his hands on his bleeding neck, turned, and ran away. The way he ran was funny somehow, and Nicetas started laughing. The laughter broke the dam of his heart, and he laughed and laughed and cried until he could no longer tell one from the other.

The Book of Dapyx

Dapyx pressed a kerchief to the cut on his neck as he headed to the queen's chamber, looking for Dokina. Maybe she had seen Andrada and had news. The guard had turned Dapyx away that morning, just like yesterday.

He couldn't confess to Nicetas that he had poisoned Una. His brother had almost killed him just now. No, he could tell no one he had poisoned her. Besides, poison was a woman's weapon. A warrior would never kill his enemy in such a sneaky way. It had all been an accident anyway. All he had wanted was to send her back to Twin Willows.

The sleeping potion hadn't taken on the first day, so he had kept trying different ingredients for Una's nightly milk. But she never fell into that deep sleep he had hoped for. Somehow, he poisoned her after a few days. Yet Una was a medicine woman. Why couldn't she have healed herself?

The door to the queen's chamber was open, and two male voices spilled into the hallway, one low and commanding, the other submissive and curt. What was Zyraxes doing in Andrada's chamber? Dapyx peered in. Clothes, wax tablets, and an empty chamber pot were strewn over the floor. A broken inkwell lay in a black puddle at the foot of the table.

The voices came from deeper into the chamber, where the beds were.

"Have you looked in that red trunk over there?" Zyraxes said.

"It's locked, Your Holiness," his servant said.

"Open it, handmaid," Zyraxes said.

"I can't." Dokina's voice. She was there too. "The queen won't allow it."

"The queen is in the Six-Sided Tower," Zyraxes said. "Open the trunk, or you'll join her."

"Happy to be with my queen," Dokina said.

Zyraxes cackled. "You won't be going to the top of the tower but straight to the dungeon with the rats."

There was a long silence. Zyraxes was probably smiling.

"There's nothing inside the trunk but women's things," Dokina said, her voice hesitant.

Dapyx could hear her tinkering with the lock on the trunk, wood and metal clicking, a clasp, a creak. He took another step in and could now see them. Zyraxes was bent over an open red trunk painted with gold wolf heads. He pulled out and threw on the floor shawls, tunics, breechcloths, an embroidery frame, a headscarf. He tossed a bag from which two spools of colored thread unrolled. Then he flung woolen socks, another headscarf, a gold thimble. He straightened his back, holding the whitewood carving of a horse painted gold and blue. He flipped the lid and dug inside with his bony fingers, picking up something Dapyx couldn't see.

"What's this, handmaid?" Zyraxes said. "Neither you nor your queen has golden hair."

He then took out a crystal bell, turning it this way and that in the sunlight. The bell rang with the purest sound, a sound that kept going until Zyraxes smothered it in his fist.

"The queen uses it," Dokina said, "during certain times of Mehnot's dance in the sky—"

"Ugh." Zyraxes dropped the bell in Dokina's hand, and she slipped it inside her apron's pocket. "Take the handmaid to the tower," he told his servant.

"You can't." Dapyx dashed in. "She didn't do anything."

"Whatever do you want?" Zyraxes said.

"You leave her alone."

"She knows things."

Dokina dodged the servant and rushed to Dapyx, slipping him the crystal bell.

"Give it to her," she whispered as the servant grabbed her and pushed her out.

"Don't worry," Dapyx called after her. "I'll get you out of there."

"You'll take care of her, won't you?" Zyraxes said. "Just like you took care of my sky oak?"

Dapyx wanted to scream. Both his brothers were in the grip of madness spirits. It was up to him alone to save Andrada. He'd bring Cothelas the Bald to his daughter's rescue, no matter what that did to Valdavia.

He'd have to steal Nicetas's signet ring for the letters of passage along the way to Kerta. The ring was in his brother's work chamber, which connected through a removable granite block to the secret corridors in the men's wing of the king's house. He also needed enough time for Cothelas's armies to gather and cross the Norland Pass into Valdavia. Praying to the gods was always Zyraxes's job, but Dapyx would now pray to Them to keep Andrada safe until he brought help.

The Book of Andrada

Andrada watched Mehnot's moon every night to keep track of time. Una had died with the new moon, and now another crescent waned with every passing day. Unlike the moon, Andrada's pain of losing Una only grew and deepened. She had no words for what she felt—and no tears. She didn't have her crystal bell, Dokina wasn't allowed to see her, and Dapyx had abandoned her. Meanwhile, Ea hadn't answered any of her prayers.

One evening, she sat on her bed and tried to remember Una's voice. There was a song Una used to hum, but the voice escaped her. She ached for anything of Una's, but the only things she'd had—the wad of hair and the color pigments—now belonged to Zyraxes, as he had told her when he last visited.

She had dreamed of Una the night before and the night before that. Una was walking through a dark forest, and Andrada followed, dressed in heavy skirts that slowed her down. She called after Una, but her words came out as broken shards of crystal dropping from her mouth on the dusty path. No sound. Dreams were messages from the gods, and Andrada wished her nurse were there to help interpret hers.

The candles in the wheel overhead sputtered, and their long shadows licked at the mossy walls. The wind whispered through the window slits, mixing the scents of beeswax and spring rain. Andrada's dress wasn't warm enough, and she wrapped her cloak around her shoulders.

The outside crossbar fell with a thud, and the door opened.

"A visitor," Calidrones said.

Another visit from Zyraxes, most likely another plea for her confession. In the time she'd been locked in the tower, she had grown to agree with the high priest. Yes, she was guilty of Una's death. Had Andrada not asked her to stay in Zalmodava last fall, Una would have been safe at home with her mother and grandmother. She wouldn't have frozen to death.

But Zyraxes said Andrada had poisoned Una, and that wasn't true. She couldn't confess to that. How Una had ended up taking in Ea's poison, Andrada couldn't fathom. Una had promised she'd never make such a terrible mistake.

From the dark, the shape of a man in a bearskin cloak appeared.

Andrada stood up. "Cartographer?"

Zyraxes had told her Una's family had taken her back to Twin Willows. Yet here he was, walking into the light, his blue eyes sunken, his hair disheveled, his beard untrimmed.

She was about to tell him of that first heavy breath she took every morning when she woke up and remembered that Una was dead.

"You killed Una," the Cartographer said in a growl. He stepped closer, as if ready to grab her and snap her neck. He didn't smell of mint anymore.

"My queen?" Calidrones asked from the door.

"Go, Calidrones."

The door thumped shut.

"I should've known." The Cartographer sounded like a wounded beast. "When I met you on the road last fall. I should've known you were after Una. If it hadn't been for Brasus scaring you away, you might've gotten close enough—"

"No, that's not why—"

"And when your plan didn't work, you pretended to be sick, so Nicetas would bring Una to you."

Andrada took a step back. "I was sick."

He inched closer to her. "And after she came here, you ordered her to stay at court—"

"To be my tutor."

"You kept her here so you could plot her murder!"

Andrada closed the distance between them. "Then kill me. Now. Here. If you truly believe I murdered your daughter."

He squeezed his eyes shut for a moment.

"Yes, I know you're her father," Andrada said. "You're not the only one who remembers faces. She had your blue eyes."

He covered his face, and his shoulders trembled.

"I know you're hurting," Andrada said. "I am too. Sometimes I can't even breathe...that's how much I miss her."

"No, no..." He wiped away tears. "You poisoned her, and you'll pay for what you did. And I'll be there to see it."

Had he offered Andrada a cup of deadly water, she would have emptied it without another thought.

She turned away from him, to the drifting clouds in the pale sky through the window slits. If he tried to kill her now, she wouldn't fight him.

The door opened, closed, and the outside crossbar fell back into place.

The Valdavian Chronicle

A whole moon after Una's death, Nicetas sat next to Zyraxes at the table in the council chamber, waiting for the others to arrive.

Zyraxes cracked his knuckles. "Cothelas received his heir and named him Pegrinus, after his late queen." He meant the blue-eyed bastard he had taken from a young woman in Sanapa on a promise the child would become a temple servant someday. "Your queen can now die of childbed fever. Cothelas won't question it. It happened to his wife."

Una wouldn't approve, but she wouldn't know what it felt like to be left behind.

Nicetas rearranged the objects on the silver tray in front of them: the two confession scrolls and Andrada's horse-shaped box.

"What about the soldiers Cothelas owes us?" he said.

"They should cross the Norland Pass any day now."

An old man wearing rich clothes and a fine sheepskin cloak walked in. Chief Petoporus had long white hair, and his face was marked by the pox. Nicetas hadn't seen him in ages. He and his tribesmen from the banks of the Pyretus River hadn't helped with the last war.

Three other men soon joined him: Chief Arpoxais from the Blue Highlands, who had lost an ear during the Night Attack; Chief Tarbus from the Alutus River Valley, a constant admirer of Rada's; and High Priest Daizus, who dwelled in the foothills of Mount Ea-El.

"Chief Bikilis is still on his way here from the Iron Gates," Zyraxes said. "He should arrive in the next few days. Chief Arpoxais, how were your plum orchards last summer?"

"Your Holiness won't regret entrusting the Upper Pyretus estate to my family. To show my gratitude, I brought a dozen jugs of the best firewater in Valdavia for the king's pleasure."

His words reminded Nicetas of the harvest fair, a time when Una had been alive and full of life, another jab at his pain.

"Council of Six," Zyraxes said, "we called you here today because we face a matter of grave importance for our country."

Daizus sucked his teeth. Tarbus's face was set. Arpoxais turned his good ear to Zyraxes.

"We need a Council of Six so the verdict comes down from the gods of our tribes and not from the king. We ask you to be this council. You must speak to no one of its existence, and on midspring day, you must pass a fair sentence."

"For what sin?" Daizus said. "And what sinner?"

"Murder," Zyraxes said. "Queen Andrada poisoned Una of Twin Willows."

"I've known Una since she was a child," Tarbus said through clenched teeth. "Her death should not go unpunished."

Nicetas leaned back in his chair, his arms crossed over his chest. He needed a deep breath to get out the words. "Una is dead. The queen is to blame. I need you now to pass the verdict."

"Of course," Petoporus said. "As long as there's proof of guilt."

The others nodded in approval, except Tarbus, who kept his eyes on his clasped hands.

"The proof of guilt," Zyraxes said, "is right here on this tray. This whitewood box belongs to the queen. In it, there's a small clay jar with the antidote to the poison that killed Una. Zia, the oldest medicine woman, revealed this secret knowledge to me."

He pointed to the scrolls. "We also have the words of the queen's handmaid, who confessed that Una had been in the queen's chamber the night she died. That's when the queen slipped her a deadly dose of Ea's poison."

"Ooh," Daizus said, "that's a bad way to go. But doesn't Ea's poison kill slowly?"

"Why does it matter how it kills?" Tarbus said without raising his eyes. "It just kills."

"But how did the queen get the poison?" Daizus said. "Only the medicine women of Twin Willows know where to find it, and they always guard their secrets."

"The queen stole it from Una," Zyraxes said.

"Una brought this poison to Zalmodava?" Daizus said, making a disbelieving face.

"Are you saying it's Una's fault?" Nicetas said, his voice on edge.

"No, no, I just don't understand why Ea let Una die, and by Her own poison."

"Una had the antidote," Zyraxes said, "but that night, the queen stole it from her."

"Why did the queen keep the antidote after the murder?" Arpoxais said, picking at his ear stub. "Why not get rid of it?"

Zyraxes threw him an annoyed glance. "Because, Chief Arpoxais, the antidote to Ea's poison happens to be a beautiful blue pigment. This pigment." He tapped the mane on the horse-box. "We know from her handmaid that the queen studied pigments with Una."

Petoporus spread open the confession. "Is the handmaid Kertan?"

"Yes," Zyraxes said.

"Then why did she speak against her own queen?"

"So many questions," Nicetas whispered, glaring at Zyraxes. They had assembled the council to pass a verdict, not to attack Una's precious memory.

Zyraxes took the scroll from the chieftain and handed it to High Priest Daizus. "It only matters that she did." He then turned back to Petoporus. "Read this other scroll, the testimony of Zia of Twin Willows, Una's grandmother, who looked at Una's body and is certain her granddaughter swallowed Ea's poison. Since the antidote that could have saved Una's life was found in the queen's chamber, together with a wad of Una's hair, there's no doubt Una died at the queen's hands."

"Why did the queen want Una dead?" Daizus said.

"You really need to ask?" Tarbus said.

No one met Nicetas's eyes. They all busied themselves with the proof of guilt on the table. Arpoxais spread some of the blue pigment between his thumb and forefinger and smelled it. Daizus followed the words on the scroll with his stubby finger.

"Is it possible," Petoporus said, "that someone wanted to make the queen look guilty?"

"Was the handmaid forced to confess?" Arpoxais added.

"By Beleizis's thunder, the queen is guilty," Zyraxes said, slamming his fist on the table. "She's been angering the gods with her repugnant ways for far too long. Not only did she fell my sky oak, but when the guards arrested her, she was wearing men's clothes—"

"Zyraxes, enough." Nicetas propped his elbows on the table. "My lords, it pains me more than I can say that the queen did such evil. Nobody wants this stain on the name of Valdavia. That's why there'll be no public trial. But the gods won't allow us to ignore such a heinous crime."

"We won't ignore it," Tarbus said.

"I brought you the proof of guilt," Zyraxes said, "so I must withdraw from the Council of Six. High Priestess Citera will take my place, and I ask Chief Arpoxais to be the head of the council."

"No," Nicetas said. "I want Chief Tarbus."

Arpoxais frowned, but Tarbus's pained gaze told Nicetas he had made the right choice. Tarbus, who cared about Rada, wouldn't let Una's murder go unpunished.

"With Chief Bikilis on his way," Tarbus said, "the Council of Six will be gathered on midspring day to pass its verdict."

The Book of Dapyx

Dapyx arrived in Sehuldava late in the afternoon. A courtier escorted him to the king's house, to a chamber with a small hearth and a table. Shelves stuffed with scrolls and codices lined the walls.

"Prince Dapyx of Valdavia," King Cothelas said in the same clear Dhawosian accent as Andrada's. "You don't look much like your brother."

He looked fierce: his shaved head, his thick arms crossed over his broad chest, his wide shoulders. More than anything, it was his voice. Dapyx hadn't heard such a voice—deep, calm, and firm—since his own father's death years ago.

Under the king's gaze, he became aware of his dusty riding clothes, the muddy hem of his cloak, his disheveled hair and unwashed face. He stepped forward and set the letter of passage on the table.

"It has my brother's seal," he said. "But he doesn't know I'm here."

"And why are you here?"

"To ask King Cothelas to come to Queen Andrada's rescue."

"Rescue?"

"My brother has been touched by a madness spirit. He locked the queen in the Six-Sided Tower."

Cothelas smiled. "You don't understand these things, Prince Dapyx. Andrada needs to be in isolation for a while, in her condition."

Dapyx frowned. "What condition?"

"The real Prince Dapyx would know what I'm talking about." He leaned back in his chair. "You're not who you say you are."

"But I am, and this"—he pulled down the collar of his tunic—"is the scar my brother gave me when I asked him to spare your daughter's life."

"Spare her life?" The king raised an eyebrow.

"She was accused of killing Nicetas's lover, but she's innocent. The punishment for murder is death."

Cothelas stood up and came around the table. He rested a heavy hand on Dapyx's shoulder. "Prince, what you're telling me makes no sense. Are you looking for revenge for some squabble with your brother? Trying to lure me into a fight with my son-in-law?"

"I swear." Dapyx felt his whole frame shake under the weight of the king's hand.

"Very well," Cothelas said, letting go of Dapyx. "I'll summon my Valdavian emissary and confirm your story."

"There's no time—"

The knock on the door startled Dapyx.

"Time for your grandson's bath, my king," said a woman in a black headscarf.

She had an old scar on her cheek and a baby in her arms. A small boy held on to her skirts.

"Would my king like to be there?" she said.

"Yes." Cothelas's face brightened with joy. "How's our little Pegrinus today, nurse?"

"Getting used to us, my king. And hungry all the time."

"By the gods, then feed him," the king said with a chuckle. "And don't start the bath without me."

The nurse threw a glance at Dapyx. "Are you a messenger from Zalmodava, perhaps?"

"He brings us troubling news of Queen Andrada," the king said.

"Is she not getting better from her childbed fever?" the nurse said, sounding worried.

"I'll find out soon enough," the kind said, motioning for her to go.

The nurse bowed, and the small boy did too, and they left.

Cothelas's eyes were red-rimmed. "A fine nephew you have here, Prince Dapyx."

A nephew? "King Cothelas..." Dapyx didn't know how to say this. "Queen Andrada...she has not been with child."

Cothelas's expression turned from smile to stone. "Guard!" The door opened at once. "Throw this proven liar in jail."

A surge of dread slashed through Dapyx's gut. He scrambled to open the pouch on his belt and pull out the crystal bell. It rang in that clear voice he had listened to many times on his way to Sehuldava, while praying to all the Valdavian gods, big and small, to grant him enough time to save Andrada.

"She gave this to me," he lied, panicking, "so you'll believe me."

The guard put a dagger at Dapyx's throat, but Cothelas motioned him to withdraw. Dapyx felt hot tears on his cheeks as he gave the bell to the king.

"There's no little prince?" Cothelas said, turning the bell in his hand.

"Not by Queen Andrada, no," Dapyx whispered, sniffling his tears. "I swear. And she wasn't ill with childbed fever when I left."

"They're planning to put her to death, but she's still alive. My spies would have sent word otherwise."

"Then we must hurry."

Cothelas turned to his guard. "Send word to all my chieftains to gather in Sehuldava for a war council on midspring day."

Dapyx's lungs filled with air for the first time since his arrival. But midspring was twelve days away. A lot could happen to Andrada until then.

"Give me your sica," Cothelas told the guard.

The man unhooked his blade and offered it to his king with both hands.

"Prince Dapyx," Cothelas said, taking the sword, "are you a warrior yet? I can't tell, judging by your tears."

"Apprentice." Dapyx wiped his face with the back of his hand. "But I'm sixteen, my king."

"Not yet a man, but kneel. I need all the warriors I can find."

Chapter Twenty-Three

The Book of Andrada

On midspring morning, Andrada put on a linen shift and the woolen cloak Calidrones had brought her, then followed him to the Temple of Concord to face the Council of Six. On the way there, she begged El to spare her life despite knowing He only answered prayers through the crystal bell.

She kept praying to El as Calidrones left her at the statue of Ea with the child Beleizis in Her lap. Ea had never granted Andrada's prayers, not even for Una's life.

At the foot of the statue, six people sat at a long table, while Zyraxes paced around. Among the councilors, Andrada saw High Priestess Citera and the Cartographer. What was he doing here? Did the others know he was Una's father? Would Citera, who had always been good to her, help her today? Andrada could barely breathe as she came to stand before their table.

Nicetas walked in, shut the doors, and bolted them, and only then did Andrada realize there were no guards present, just the six councilors, Zyraxes, and now Nicetas, who walked past her without a glance and joined his brother.

Andrada's knees went weak when she recognized her horse-box on a silver tray on the councilors' table. The council had her crystal bell. Maybe that was a sign that El had heard her prayers.

Zyraxes rang another bell, a brass one, the sound echoing under the dome of the empty temple. "May your minds be clear and your hearts be just."

"The gods and our ancestral spirits are watching," said the man seated in the middle. Andrada knew him from somewhere. He wore a heavy silver chain with a crystal medallion around his neck.

"The gods' blessings upon your council, Chief Tarbus," Zyraxes said.

Tarbus. Andrada had seen him in Twin Willows, with Rada and Zia. He'd be her enemy then. She clasped her cold, clammy hands together, her breath shallow.

"I call upon King Nicetas," Tarbus said, "to speak first on this matter."

Nicetas stood before the council, a foot away from Andrada. "My lords, I was wronged. I was wronged by someone I loved and trusted. I will not carry judgment, for it is not for the king to do so, but I ask the Council of Six to bring the gods' justice to us."

"My king," Tarbus said, "we judged this woman by the fair laws of Valdavia. We looked at the proof of guilt and reached our verdict." Tarbus tapped the silver tray in front of him. "And the fair laws of Valdavia demand us to condemn a murderer to death. The sentence is beheading on the sundial, and it will be carried out tomorrow at dawn."

Andrada shuddered, unable to breathe. "No..."

"I thank the council for its wisdom," Nicetas said.

"I stand by the verdict," Citera said. All eyes turned to her. "But before the sentence is carried out, the king must first hear the words of the Time-Giver."

Andrada felt faint. Citera headed to the door to the underground vaults and returned with Rada, her face smeared with soot. Nicetas and Zyraxes exchanged angry glances. The Cartographer clasped his hands on the tabletop, while Chief Tarbus seemed resigned.

"Before you decide when the sentence is to be carried out," Rada said, "I'm bound by the laws of Valdavia to reveal to you that, like myself not long ago, the queen owes Ea thirty days of silent mourning."

Andrada didn't follow. Her mouth was dry. Were Citera and Rada trying to save her life?

Nicetas glared at Rada. "What in Beleizis's thunder are you saying, woman?"

"The queen is not at fault for not observing Ea's law," Rada said. "She doesn't know. It happened when Una and I saved her life last fall."

"Happened? What happened?" Zyraxes said.

"The king has lost a son," Rada said, motioning to Nicetas. "He was born before his time. Una wrapped him in a linen shroud, carried him out on a silver tray, and buried him in the Sanctuary of the Dead."

Andrada began to shiver. Air didn't reach her lungs, though she kept breathing.

"No, no, no." Nicetas looked at her for the first time that morning.

Andrada held his hateful gaze, and his face changed to rage. In a few steps, he was at her side, gripping her arm.

"Was it Dapyx's child?" he whispered in her ear.

Andrada unclenched her chattering jaws. "If there was a son...it was yours and no one else's."

"You lost Cothelas's heir?" He pushed her away and started laughing.

Andrada regained her footing. She wished she could cry. Nothing made sense to her. Nothing.

"As an act of mercy," Rada said, "Una kept that child a secret to be revealed one day, when the mother was ready. But now we're out of time, and this mother still owes Ea thirty days of silent mourning before she can die. Councilors, let her mourn her child."

"A parent should be allowed to mourn," Citera said.

"It should be so," another judge said.

The Cartographer nodded too.

"It will be so," Tarbus said. "Queen Andrada, any last words before you take the vow of silence for your thirty days of mourning?"

She'd soon die, but not yet. The Time-Giver had given her time. Thoughts hurt and made no sense. Maybe if she wrote them down, they'd somehow make sense.

"I...ask for parchment, quills, inkwell, and an ink block," she whispered.

"But she's a woman," Zyraxes told the council. "Only men of valor and wisdom may bring to Azemel a written account of their earthly lives."

What did he know about Andrada's valor and wisdom? Throughout much of her life, she had followed the path meant for highborn men. She had the right.

"Give her what she wants," Nicetas said, "and take her from my sight."

Zyraxes slammed his staff against the floor. "You're making a mistake. Words on parchment are more powerful than words spoken."

Tarbus ignored him. "Queen Andrada, be grateful for the time given to you. And show remorse before the gods."

"Remorse?" Zyraxes said. "Look at her dry eyes. She's just learned she lost a son, and she won't even shed a tear."

Tarbus shook his head. "Go with the gods, Queen Andrada, and remain silent for the rest of your time on earth—under penalty of early death."

That she would do, for she had nothing left to say to anyone. Not even to El, who had abandoned her in her hour of need.

The Valdavian Chronicle

Between swigs of wine, Nicetas paced around his chamber. Andrada should have been dead by now, but thanks to Rada and the gods, he had to wait thirty days to taste justice, a time he resolved to spend hunting down Bendis's great aurochs. Since the weather had turned, his scouts had spotted the beast in the foothills of Mount Ea-El. He wished Una were there to stop him, but she wasn't. Nobody could stop him now, not even Bendis, who'd now see what heartbreaking loss felt like. He'd set off with his hunters as soon as he was done with Oroles.

At last, his blood brother arrived.

"I sent you to the White Fortress to be with your woman, didn't I?" Nicetas said.

"I know, my lord, but—"

"Then why were you at the sundial this morning, rousing the rabble with fiery words about the Great Awakening? You want my people to rise against me?"

"No, my lord. An argument with Chief Bikilis got out of hand—"

"Because it was you who delayed his arrival, wasn't it?" Nicetas yelled into Oroles's pained face. "You hoped to stop the Council of Six."

"Yes, my men stole Chief Bikilis's horses at the inn in Tiason and delayed his arrival here. I did that to serve peace, and I failed. If King Cothelas's daughter dies, he'll seek revenge. Then the Romans—"

"The Romans, the Romans..." Nicetas passed a hand through his hair. "Every haranguer since the times of Iulius Caesar has used the Roman threat to make his point."

Since becoming an emissary, Oroles had kept a close eye on Valdavian state matters. Zyraxes had been right to distrust him.

"Please, my lord. Why do you think the gods sent Una's mother to offer Queen Andrada a stay of execution? They want us to preserve the peace in Dhawosia."

Nicetas balled his hands into fists. "Bendis has lost Her mind. Ea too. All of Them."

"The gods don't want the queen to die, my lord. Never repay evil with evil. Killing Queen Andrada will bring evil upon our world, and El will judge us harshly after the Great Awakening."

"Is that what you told the crowd during your sundial sermon?" Nicetas groaned. "Next you'll tell me to love my enemy."

"Yes, my lord. If we stop fighting one another, El will be pleased with us when He awakes."

Nicetas shook his head. "You've lost your mind too. This peace of yours? All it takes is one man to undo it."

"I beg you, brother, don't be that man."

Nicetas couldn't take it anymore. With a growl, he punched Oroles in the chest.

Oroles stumbled back but regained his footing. Nicetas rubbed his fist, where his knuckles had hit something small and hard under Oroles's tunic. A medallion maybe.

Oroles moaned but stood tall.

Nicetas couldn't stop now. The pain he felt was good, in his knuckles, in his arm, in his shoulder. Pain was better than the cold abyss in his chest.

He rubbed his knuckles, stretched his neck, and charged again. Again, his fist hit something small and hard. With his other hand, he grabbed, pulled, and ripped the fabric of his brother's tunic.

There, glimmering on Oroles's chest, against curled brown hairs, hung a ring on a silver chain. It was silver and crystal, and it could only mean one thing.

"You...married Princess Meda?"

Oroles clasped the chain and the ring in his hand. "I've been trying to tell you, my lord. Our son was born not long ago."

Such betrayal. Nicetas couldn't have Oroles as his councilor and emissary now.

"You gave me back my life once," he said, "and I'm giving you yours now. But I never want to see you again."

Oroles pulled his ripped tunic over his chest. "My lord, don't let our fight destroy the Dhawosian Alliance."

"Go see your son...Go before I repay your evil with my evil."

As soon as Oroles left, Nicetas fell to his knees. The pain in his heart was back. He didn't want to be king. He wanted to be dead and for Una to be alive.

"I'm glad you're still here." Zyraxes's maddening voice. "I'll need your signet ring while you're out hunting, but it's not in your work chamber."

"Will I ever be whole again?" Nicetas whispered. Una had put him together once, after the Night Attack. He stood and wiped his eyes. "Who can rid me of my torment now?"

Zyraxes frowned. "You mean what Oroles did this morning at the sundial?"

That too. "He's married Meda of Steppewynd...They have a newborn son."

Zyraxes's eyes bulged, his nostrils flared. "Oroles has a claim to your throne, however small. And now he has Scorilus's army and a bloodline?"

"No, he won't hurt me. He's on a gods-given mission to prepare the world for the Great Awakening..."

"If he thinks he's on a divine mission, he'll kill you if you're in his way."

Nicetas shook his head. "I won't hurt him. He's my blood brother."

Zyraxes clasped Nicetas's arm. "Well, he's not mine."

Chapter Twenty-Four

The Book of Dapyx

On midspring day, Dapyx entered the great hall of Sehuldava, hoping Andrada was still alive. He wondered what had happened to little Pegrinus after the revelation that he wasn't Andrada's son. King Cothelas had seemed fond of the child, so maybe Pegrinus was still in the care of that scarred nurse and doing well.

The throne chamber was full of chieftains and warriors from all over Kerta and even farther, from the Germanic lands of the Great Plains in the west. They had gathered under the strangest standard Dapyx had ever seen: Andrada's green eyes, painted on a scorched panel mounted on a wall. Those warriors had assumed they'd return to Valdavia to help guard the northern borders of the Roman Empire. Instead, they had learned they'd be fighting the Valdavians.

"You know, I used to tease her when she was a little girl," said a young man with flaxen hair and dark eyes, a few years older than Dapyx. "But I won't stand for what your brother is doing to her." He bowed his head. "Syrmos of the Bear-Hunters tribe. Kerta's chosen heir."

Dapyx had heard of him, yes. Syrmos had a trimmed beard, which made Dapyx aware of the thin hairs growing on his own face. He felt the familiar blush spread from his ears to his neck, but just then, Syrmos turned away as King Cothelas entered the throne chamber.

"How will we pay our soldiers, my king?" said someone in a husky voice. "The treasury isn't ready for a war with Valdavia."

"The soldiers will keep their plunder," King Cothelas said on his way to the dais. "Chief Boruistas, are you forging blades?"

"Ever since you sent word, my king."

"That's King Cothelas's treasurer," Syrmos explained to Dapyx.

A tall man called in a Germanic accent, "The Romans will attack us all if we make war on Valdavia."

Syrmos grunted in disgust and shouted back, "Letting our princess die at the hands of a Valdavian because we fear the Romans?" He turned to those around him. "Imagine the songs the bards will sing at harvest fairs for years to come."

King Cothelas stood by his throne, facing the gathering. "I hear you, my good people, but the Romans are moons away from us. We'll be swift."

"How will we be swift?" a chieftain said. "Word came back this morning that the Valdavians have taken over the Norland Pass."

Dapyx wondered if Nicetas had figured out where his little brother had gone and was taking measures to defend his borders against a possible attack from the Kertan army.

"There's another way into Valdavia," King Cothelas said. "But we'll need to build ships. Hollow ships—long, light, and fast. Ships with fifty oars and no decks."

"Ships won't help us," the same chieftain said. "They've also seized the Red Tower Pass."

"Besieging Fort Norland Pass or the Red Tower," Syrmos explained to Dapyx, "or cutting new roads through thick forests across the mountains will take moons or even years. We're locked inside the bend of the Carpates Mountains with no way into Valdavia."

"We'll build ships," King Cothelas said. "Because there is another way into Valdavia."

Dapyx glanced at Syrmos, who seemed just as confused as he felt.

The king opened a codex bound in the same whitewood as Andrada's painted horse-box, pulled out a piece of parchment, and gave it to a high priest, an old man in dark robes, wearing a gold chain with a crystal pendant.

"In three days' time at dawn," the high priest read from the parchment, "we'll load three thousand men on sixty ships and take them down the Marisus River. They'll sail along the Theiss River and the Danubius into Valdavia. They'll march north along the Alutus River and take over the Red Tower Pass. The rest of our troops will then cross the mountains."

"But," a man in the crowd said, "the Danubius cuts through the Iron Gates."

"That's Chief Comosicus," Syrmos whispered to Dapyx. "Brave man, but so cautious."

"Do you have knowledge of a secret passage alongside the Iron Gates?" Chief Comosicus said.

"No secret passage," King Cothelas said. "We'll sail right through."

The reaction was an instant grumble throughout the throne chamber. Dapyx had learned about the terrible Iron Gates from his tutors.

"Chief Gerulas drowned sailing through Azemel's Gorge there," an older man said.

"Chief Gerulas sailed at fall's end, Chief Rubobostes," the high priest said, "after the waters of the Danubius had waned and exposed the sharp rocks of the riverbed. We'll be sailing on melted snow that will raise us above the highest rocks."

"But all that water will be swift and dangerous," Chief Rubobostes said.

"Easier to siege Fort Norland than sail across the Iron Gates," a tall chieftain said.

"That's Chief Wodan," Syrmos whispered. "Braver than Comosicus, but not as wise. If King Cothelas can get them both on his side, he'll prevail."

"Easier, yes, but not as fast," King Cothelas said. "Avezinas, read on!"

The high priest read from his parchment, "West on the Marisus for two hundred miles, down on the Theiss River for another one hundred and fifty, then three hundred miles more on the Danubius, with eighty miles inside the Iron Gates."

This was the first time Dapyx witnessed a king's court, and if the stakes weren't as high as Andrada's rescue, he would have enjoyed it more.

"Your Highness," the Germanic voice called, "those strong currents will pull down any vessel, no matter how nimble."

King Cothelas raised his arm, and the men fell silent. "Just like the Danubius breaks through the mountains, we'll break through the Iron Gates. Or we'll die trying."

"Why should we die at all?" a young man said. "The future of Kerta now lies with the Bear-Hunters tribe and Syrmos, not with the queen of Valdavia and Cothelas the Bald."

The crowd parted, and he advanced to the base of the dais.

Syrmos whispered to Dapyx, "My uncle Piepor. His mouth will get him killed one day."

The silence stretched. Glances darted around. Men weighed their options. Dapyx saw Chief Rubobostes slink away. Chief Wodan stepped forward.

King Cothelas spoke again. "We are Kertans, and our standard is a wolf. We won't let one of ours be slaughtered like a lamb. What say you, Chosen Heir Syrmos?"

"I'm with the king," Syrmos said, "on behalf of the Bear-Hunters tribe."

His uncle looked crestfallen.

"Chief Piepor," King Cothelas said, "I'll spare your life, for your nephew's sake. But you're banished for life from Kerta, and all your lands will pass on to Syrmos."

"Thank you, my king," Syrmos said, his hand over his heart.

Dapyx would have stricken the traitor on the spot, but the chieftains nodded in approval of their king. Chief Piepor was swallowed by the same ranks that had just opened for him. Dapyx glanced at Syrmos, who seemed unmoved by his uncle's fate and by his new fortune.

"Here's the plan for reopening the Red Tower Pass," the high priest said. "After you beach your ships, you have a four-day march north to the pass. You'll get there without making yourselves known, marching by night and hiking through the forest by day. At sundown, you'll storm the Red Tower before Nicetas can bring down reinforcements. Then the rest of our armies will cross the mountains into Valdavia."

Around Dapyx and Syrmos, some men nodded, while some shook their heads and furrowed their brows.

"From then on," the high priest said, "you'll have another nine days to Zalmodava. But we expect to meet Nicetas's armies earlier. As soon as word spreads that we've crossed into Valdavia."

"He might think twice about imprisoning our princess then," Chief Comosicus said.

Dapyx felt his blood rush to his face. "If we want to delay the news from the south," he said, his voice shaking, "we could send a few swift soldiers ahead to take out the beacons."

Everybody turned to the small voice that came from Dapyx's throat. They probably already knew about the chain of firelit beacons that ran from the southern border of Valdavia all the way north.

"Make use of those beacons, Avezinas," King Cothelas said. "Chief Wodan—now Army Chief Wodan—will lead the three thousand brave soldiers who'll sail through the Iron Gates and reopen the Red Tower Pass from the south. I'll lead the rest of the army—twenty thousand strong and growing—across Kerta to the Red Tower. We leave in three days." He waved a hand, and the council ended.

Syrmos patted Dapyx on the shoulder. "Good thinking with those beacons. It'll save us time and a world of pain. Andrada would approve." He spoke Andrada's name with unsettling familiarity. "Are you sailing with us, Prince? May the gods keep us alive out there."

Dapyx couldn't say no. He'd sail through the Five Gorges of the Iron Gates and fight in battle for Andrada. If everything went well, they'd be in Zalmodava in about thirty days. Had the gods been keeping her alive all this time? He didn't dare imagine otherwise.

At sunrise three days later, the sound of axes and adzes carving out the charred wood of burned cedar logs echoed against the mountains on both sides of the Marisus River. Priests chanted around sacrificial fires, asking the gods of forest and water to bless the new ships. Young warriors dressed in wolf skins and masks danced and howled. The noise put Dapple on edge, so Dapyx took him down to the river and let him graze on beach grass.

The valley was full of soldiers: young men in search of adventure, strong men with too many mouths to feed at home, graybeards ready to show the youngsters the ways of war. Some would row across the Iron Gates, but most were headed to the Upper Alutus River to wait for the reopening of the Red Tower Pass. Some spoke Kertan Dhawosian; some spoke a Germanic tongue and wore their hair in a high bun. Many had been in the valley since the king's first call went out. They had found a commander and fastened their war gear on cross-shaped marching poles: tents and bedrolls, pickaxes for digging trenches, iron pots for cooking, and satchels with three days' worth of food and water.

Many would go to their deaths, but they sang of the glory of battle and the Valdavian riches awaiting them. Dapyx cringed, but those men were there for Andrada, and that was all that mattered.

Mules with hemp sacks on their backs descended the slopes from neighboring villages, heading to the riverbank, where dozens of anchored ships waited. They were long and narrow vessels with a row of oars on each side and a square leather sail. The lower part of the bow jutted out like the head of a snake to cut the water from beneath, and the stern curved up like the tail of a fish. At its tip was a one-man platform for a lookout.

"My lord," a tall boy said, approaching. "I'm here for the horse." He wore a short wolf pelt tied around his neck.

It took Dapyx a moment to remember the stable boy from Sehuldava. "Bring him to me at the Red Tower and take good care of him until then. A large coin purse will be waiting for you, larger than anything Dapple would fetch at the market." He kissed his horse's white forehead, then handed the reins and the last of his carrots to the stable boy.

Dapple's nostrils flared, and his ears flattened against his head—he was spooked by the wolf pelt scent. But the stable boy held out a carrot while whistling a low tune. After a while, Dapple relented and took the carrot. He'd be fine among those wolf-loving people.

The sun was still behind the mountains when Dapyx, a marching pole over his shoulder, walked up the gangplank. His ship was the eleventh in a long line of vessels. A priest was there, two buckets at his feet, one with water and one with dirt. He scooped water with a tin mug and threw it in front of the men's boots. He dug out a lump of dirt from the other bucket and pressed it into their hands. Like the men before him, Dapyx put the dirt in his pocket and begged the gods of air and water to let him set foot on dry land again.

The captain, a graying man with huge arms, stood by the stern-mounted steering board. "Those of you who know how to row, I want you at stern and bow. The others, sit in between, keep your eyes peeled, and learn fast."

There was no deck, only wide beams set into the hull that spanned the width of the ship.

"Sit with me, Prince," Syrmos of the Bear-Hunters called to him.

Dapyx took the opposite end of their common bench, then stuck his marching pole and sica in the tight space underneath. His oar was tied with rope to the railing. He rolled his hands over it and felt the knuckles of cutoff branches. He put on his leather riding gloves.

Syrmos muttered, "Valdavians," and shook his head as he wrapped a brown lamb pelt around the end of his oar.

Dapyx felt his cheeks warm up but followed Syrmos's lead and pulled his oar out of the water. On the bank, dozens of hands pushed together, and the ship rolled off logs and slipped into the stream with a thud and a splash.

Pulled by donkeys, the ship began its descent on the Marisus River, oars up, along the slow-moving waters by the banks, to the place a few miles down where it would anchor and await Army Chief Wodan's orders.

When the sun rose over the mountains, six ships fanned out from the shallow waters near the banks of the Marisus. The oars adjusted course until the ships were far enough apart, then the leather sails swelled as they caught the west wind.

Dapyx dipped and scooped in time with the captain's chant of "hey-ho-hey-ho." Sometimes the tip of Dapyx's oar skipped across the water, sometimes it bounced back without dipping, and sometimes the end of his oar slipped from his wet gloves. But he was learning how to hit the water and dig in. After half a day of gentle rowing, with the wind doing most of the work, Dapyx was in lockstep with Syrmos and the others. He had also learned how to pull his oar in when he needed food or drink or a quick piss overboard.

At sunset, they rowed to the bank. When the bottom grazed rocks, they climbed out and pulled the ship halfway up the sloping ground, parallel to other vessels. They hauled out the mast, steering board, anchor, oars, planks, and cargo, and used the smooth logs from the bottom of the ship to roll it all the way up on dry land. They made camp on the sand and pebbles of the narrow bank and started again the next day at sunrise.

On the third day, Dapyx saw the clear waters of the Marisus River joining with the murkier ones of the Theiss. That same day, they reached the Danubius. Where the Theiss was a light brown from the rain falling in the western fields of Kerta, the Danubius was dark brown from the clay, silt, and sand tributaries brought from their floodplains.

Syrmos pulled up his oar and cupped his hands. He brought a mouthful of Danubius water to his lips and drank. "To make me as strong as the river that cuts through the mountains."

Dapyx took his gloves off, cupped his shaking hands, and dipped them into the murky water. He held his breath and swallowed. It tasted cold and gritty and powerful.

The sky was dark blue, and the stars were pale. Dapyx rowed, one stroke for two breaths, his eyes on the lamp mounted on the bow of the vessel behind. The water was loud and swift. They might still make it in time to save Andrada.

The captain was nothing but a barking voice in the dark. "Today's the day, my little wolves. Behold, the Iron Gates!"

The ships went in single file, rowing close to the inner bend of the Danubius River, hugging a limestone wall streaked with waterfalls. Before long, Dapyx lost sight of the stars, and his heart sank. The river twisted, and the opposite bank swung away into the distance. Then the stars reappeared, and the sky expanded, but before he could relax, the ship skidded toward a large rock jutting up from the water.

The captain yelled something. Dapyx strained to row. He couldn't see in the dark but felt the current trying to suck them in and crush them against the rock. Oars snapped on the other side of the ship. The hull hit the rock. Syrmos cursed. Dapyx was terrified. The captain called to the gods. Men pushed against the tower of stone rising from the dark water. They pushed with oars, with hands, with shoulders, with foreheads. Blood from cuts made everything slicker.

At last, the ship snapped from the rock's grip and straightened its course. Syrmos spit out blood. Dapyx was soaked but elated as they rowed away from the deadly whirlpool. Soon the light would be brighter, and they'd spot such traitorous rocks and currents from a distance.

Azemel's Gorge, the first of the Iron Gates, was upon them. Vessels ahead and behind approached the huge jaws of stone that forced the rising waters of the Danubius River through the narrow canyon. The captain rolled up the sail, and half the oars came out of the water as the current pulled the ship up a liquid hill.

Dapyx remembered his geography lessons. After El had created the world, He unleashed the Danubius River upon the unbroken mountain range that snaked its way across Dhawosia. It cleaved the range in two, from summit to bottom, forming the Carpates Mountains in the north and the Haemus Mountains in the south, with the Iron Gates in the middle.

As Dapyx surveyed the muddy waters boiling around the ship, he wondered what good geography did him now. How was it helpful to know that those forceful rapids were due to an uneven riverbed cut into granite? Why hadn't his tutors taught him how to sail over underwater streams and boulders, instead of having him memorize the names of the Five Gorges? He had no idea how to stop the currents that dived down and spiraled up to the surface from sinking a ship.

The choppy waters kept him hopping on the back of his bench. His arms were limp, his arse sore. The ship shot up in the air and skipped over the waves before landing with a thud.

A cracking noise froze his hands on the oar. Dapyx and Syrmos craned their necks. A nearby ship had snapped in half. Men fell into the churning waters and sank fast. The damaged vessel drifted away, while Dapyx and the rest brought their own ship back on course. The roaring of the river muffled the calls for help that Dapyx couldn't answer. All he could focus on right now was the oar in his hands.

The wind buffeted Dapyx's eyes and ears. The limestone cliffs were closing in to form the next gorge, the Twin Crests, so deep that sunlight couldn't reach the water.

Tied to the mast with his belt, the captain cupped his hands around his mouth. "Keep to the inside bend, away from the deep-water channel! Away from the cliffs!" He pointed to the slanting wall of the gorge. "Don't want my mast caught up in tree limbs or crushed against—" The roar covered his voice.

The Danubius shrank further. Waves crashed downstream and upstream, left and right. River spirits popped their heads from the foam and disappeared again in the blink of an eye. A mast with a torn sail flew by Dapyx's ear and splashed somewhere beyond the stern of his ship. A man's face bobbed out of the water, gasping for air. Dapyx froze for a moment, his hands on his oar, afraid he'd smash the drowning man's head. Before he could lend a hand, the face disappeared, flotsam taking its place. Pieces of oars, sections of planks, dead bodies—everywhere.

Dapyx pulled his oar from the water and held on to the railing while the ship slammed around the waves. His legs were numb, and his spine shot icy shards of pain to the crown of his head. He prayed to Beleizis as they slid from chamber to chamber, until the waters grew tamer and the walls of the gorge opened.

After they pulled the remaining ships onto the bank, Dapyx wrapped a cut on his head with a strip of linen. Syrmos and the others still on their feet began felling trees for new oars, railings, and masts. The bloodied ones nursed their wounds and set broken limbs with splints. Many of them would have to stay behind.

Dapyx curled up by a boulder and fell asleep.

When everything was tallied up, Chief Wodan had lost five ships and four hundred men across multiple vessels. And there were three more gorges to cross: the Three Divines, the Golden Carriage, and the Hand. Three men in Dapyx's ship had been swept away by the current, and two new faces took their places from ships that had sunk.

They set off again at sunrise. The din grew louder as the mountains on either side drew together once more. Toothlike rocks broke the water, snapping at hulls. Dapyx rowed faster, while Syrmos pulled his oar from the water. Sweat and fog covered their faces.

Dapyx felt the bench underneath him yank to one side, like a fast sleigh on ice. A rush of fear choked him. He thrust his oar in, and the water spit it out. Wood chips flew everywhere. Around him, faces scrunched in effort and frustration as the river roared.

He was numb, clutching the bench, his muscles weak, his neck like a rope, his hands raw inside his soaked gloves.

The end of Syrmos's broken oar, still wrapped in its lamb's pelt, stuck out through the broken railing. The bench was empty.

"Syrmos?" Dapyx yelled, "Syrmos!"

The low sun broke between peaks as they sailed out of the Hand, the last of the Five Gorges, and into the open. The water leveled like a lake, and Dapyx's ship glided, surrounded by mountains, with gulls squawking and circling the evening sky. His left eye was swollen shut, his forehead cut open again. His arms and legs ached, but they weren't broken, and he was alive and grateful to the gods of Valdavia.

The vessels that still had a mast and a sail fanned out at the front of the fleet. Dapyx's ship had only half a mast left, so they had to make do with the oars. He was too exhausted to speak, and his muscles quivered each time he dipped his damaged oar into the water.

The ship halted, grinding into a sandbar that ran along the middle of the Danubius. The captain ordered them to get out and push. With his last drop of strength, Dapyx pulled the oar in and heaved himself out onto the sand, his face landing in the cold water. Then he got up to help his mates.

They all pushed, but the ship pushed back. Another ship was stranded behind them. Men poured out and lent them a hand until, at last, Dapyx's ship skidded down the edge of the sandbar into deeper waters. He grabbed the railing but had no strength to pull himself into the ship.

Tears of frustration stung his eyes when the captain grabbed him by the armpits and pulled him in.

"Valdavians," the captain growled, dropping him on the bench.

Dapyx took the oar and started rowing, but the ship didn't move. He glanced at the stern. Three ropes connected their vessel to the other stranded ship.

"Faster!" the captain cried. "You're rowing for two now."

The winds picked up without warning, turning the river into another boiling cauldron. Dapyx's ship made land with the remaining half of Chief Wodan's army, a dozen miles down from the Iron Gates, on the Valdavian bank. They salvaged whatever they could from the broken ships and mounted their gear on marching poles. Their waterlogged bows and shields were of no use for now. Dapyx had lost all his weapons.

Fewer than two thousand men marched north as fast as their tired legs could carry them, to the thick forests up the hill. In their wake, angry river spirits ripped into the empty ships, snapped the masts like twigs, blew them back into the water, and smashed them against one another, hurtling them to the depths.

Taking down beacons along the way might stop the news of dead bodies and wreckage floating downstream from spreading.

Dapyx slouched toward the dark forest ahead, praying that the gods of Valdavia would forgive him for bringing an invading army home.

"Please keep Andrada safe until we get there," he whispered.

Chapter Twenty-Five

The Book of Andrada

It was past midnight, judging by the black sky through the window slits and the long time since supper. Andrada dipped her quill into the inkwell and started a new page.

The nurse once told me there would come a day when I'd understand what it meant to lose a child. Taking a knife and carving the memory of that loss on one's cheek doesn't seem so incomprehensible now.

Andrada was still trying to make sense of her brief and bewildering life. She deserved to die for her part in Una's death, but her heart loved staying alive. Yet she was glad to meet Una in the Underworld, ask for forgiveness, and maybe become her loyal companion there.

The crossbar outside the door went up. Were they coming for her already? But it wasn't time yet, and *The Book of Andrada* was not yet finished. She had to bring that story with her to the Underworld to show it to the gods and denounce Their heartless treatment of mortals. Especially El's cruel abandonment and betrayal.

The door opened, its hinges creaking, and Zia, the medicine woman from Twin Willows, stepped in. Andrada sighed with relief. She still had time to finish her story.

"We haven't much time, child," Zia said.

Andrada stood, trying to quiet her heart, and straightened her black headscarf.

"I know you can't talk, or they'll kill you, but please listen," Zia said.

Andrada glanced past her at the open door. No sounds came from the hallway. Where was Calidrones?

"Don't worry about the jailer. He'll be fast asleep for a while. Listen, child, I've been praying for guidance, together with the high priestess of the Temple of Concord, and today Ea revealed to us in the limestone bowl that you didn't kill Una."

Andrada nodded, though she felt she was at least responsible for Una being in Zalmodava, her place of death.

Zia wrung her hands. "Come with me, child, and help me mend our line."

Andrada pulled back. She was not Zia's child, and she wasn't going anywhere, even though the door to her jail cell now stood open. She'd keep writing her story—the story of a girl who'd let her father down, the story of a mother who'd lost her son without realizing it—until the guards took her to the sundial and chopped her head off.

"Our line is broken," Zia said. "If the line dies, a thousand years of darkness will descend upon the known world."

Andrada had no use for the known world.

"Rada is the last of the medicine women. Her body is spent, her spirit crushed. She thinks her purpose on earth is fulfilled, now that she gave you time. But the Time-Giver saved you for a reason, child. Her blood is flowing through your veins."

Andrada didn't follow. Rada had done what she would do for any patient.

"Did Una teach you about pigments?" Zia said.

Andrada didn't move, but Zia seemed to read something on her face.

"She did. What about blood transference?"

Andrada remained still.

"She didn't. Did she teach you Ea's oath to do no harm?"

A queen couldn't keep an oath to do no harm.

"I know you're angry," Zia said. "I'm angry too. But everything that happened, has happened by Ea's will. I don't know why She had no use for Una, but I know why She had no use for your boy. You're meant to give birth to a girl...to mend our line."

Andrada locked her hands over her empty womb. Her body would never give birth to a girl or any child. Her body would part with her head soon.

"Please, come with me to Twin Willows, the place where Ea anoints Her chosen priestesses."

Andrada didn't care for any of that. She returned to the table and dipped her quill in ink. She had a story to write.

"You think your pain is the worst in the world?" Zia's voice was now shrill. "Your pain is nothing compared to what I felt when I climbed down in Una's open grave, when I touched her head and her hair fell like dandelion fuzz." Zia grabbed Andrada's arm. "And now Ea leads me to...you. As if you could ever replace my Una. Una, who was already with the child the goddess had asked her to carry."

Another lost child. Like the nurse's, like Andrada's. Nicetas's child.

A faint noise came from the open door. Maybe Calidrones was waking up.

"Ea has chosen you." Zia kept hold of Andrada's arm. "I don't know why. But you must come with me."

Andrada stared at the old woman's face and shook her head.

Zia's dark gaze changed as she let go of Andrada's arm. Again, she had read something on Andrada's face, and now she looked stunned.

"May the gods have mercy on us." She took a step back. "I was mistaken. You're not the one to mend our line. You're already dead to the goddess."

She left the door open on her way out, while Andrada went back to writing.

The Book of Scorilus

In his chamber at supper, Scorilus raised his cup to Meda and took a sip of the Falernian wine. Cispius had bought it in Pompeii last fall and brought it to the White Fortress in resin-coated amphoras. It was sweet and had a strange flowery flavor. Dhawosian wine was only called *wine*, but this Falernian one was called *white wine*. Another marvel of ingenuity from the Roman Empire, Scorilus's newest trading partner.

Meda pushed her cup away. "Oroles should've returned by now."

She looked more like her mother since giving birth to her little boy, whom she hadn't named yet, without her husband there.

"Something's wrong," she said.

"The road from Zalmodava is still flooded in two places." Scorilus sliced through a piece of ham with Phradmon's dagger. "He'll be here soon." He didn't really feel like having a long conversation, but Meda needed comfort. "Pickled olives?" He pointed to the jar on the table. "From my friend Lucius Flavius Magius, who appreciates my garum."

Meda held up a hand. "Just the thought makes me gag. What I need is Oroles. Here. Now. Our son needs a father and a name."

"You said he's Ea's chosen man, so don't worry—Ea will protect him." Scorilus didn't believe it himself, but maybe Meda would, and she'd feel better. "I'll send another messenger—"

"Yes, before dawn, with coin to buy a new horse at each outpost. And, just this once, would you please join me in the sanctuary tomorrow for the sacrifice?"

The gods, Lucretius had written, *with their endless lives of peace and joy, are far removed from our affairs. Unlike us, they feel no pain and fear no danger. They need nothing from us, and we won't win their love with services and gifts, nor will we rouse their anger with our earthly deeds.*

"Yes, my little redhead, we'll sacrifice the finest steed to Nap-at-Dehnu."

A knock on the door interrupted Scorilus's thoughts.

It was Rescuporis, already out of the garrisons. He took a few tense steps around, his legs not what they used to be before those arrows had pierced them.

"Good news, Father," he said.

Scorilus stood, wiping his dagger on his sleeve. "You've decided not to go east, and you're disbanding your armies?"

"Better." Rescuporis grinned. "Cothelas the Bald is marching on Zalmodava."

Scorilus had not expected that. "How do you know?"

"Oroles might still be in Zalmodava," Meda said, looking even more worried.

Rescuporis shrugged. "I've always said we must foster alliances, Father. I'm friends with a Kertan chieftain named Piepor, who fled his country and crossed the Carpates Mountains using footpaths known only to his Bear-Hunters tribe. Cothelas banished him, and he thought to find me in hopes I might hurt his king. Piepor said Cothelas has split his armies and sent some down the Danubius, through the Iron Gates, to invade Valdavia."

"That's madness," Meda said.

Rescuporis patted his leg. "I've learned the hard way that a man would do anything for his daughter."

Scorilus frowned. "What about his daughter?"

"Nicetas has decided to shorten her by a head. Cothelas is coming to rescue her. I say we let them fight but watch from a distance, then go in when they've weakened each—"

"Watch?" Meda said. "We must get Oroles out of there!"

"We're not going to war!"

Scorilus had just improved his garum recipe and was ready to sell it in Pompeii through Cispius. His trade with Roma was flourishing. He was preparing to build his first aqueduct from the Tyras River to a terraced hill in the north. He wasn't about to throw it all away.

"I have your army ready, Father," Rescuporis said. "Ten thousand Tauri riders and Steppewynder footmen waiting on the east bank of the Pyretus River."

"How soon can we leave?" Meda said.

"I'm not taking you with me," Rescuporis said. "You have a child to nurse."

"Both of you, out." Scorilus pointed at the door with his dagger. "I must think."

"Don't take long, Father," Meda said, clinging to the doorjamb. "Oroles's life depends on us."

"I'll be in the great hall at dawn, Father, waiting for your word." Rescuporis closed the door behind him.

At dawn, Scorilus sent for Moskon. He needed to craft a message of neutrality to his two neighbors, Cothelas and Nicetas. Steppewynd would stay on its hard-won path of peace and prosperity. Oroles would find his way back to Meda somehow—he was resourceful.

Rescuporis was not yet in the great hall. He'd be angry to hear there'd be no war, but Steppewynd's future lay with Roma and with itself.

A servant entered the hall. "Prince Moskon is not in his chamber." The servant handed Scorilus a piece of parchment. "The prince left this letter."

Where would Moskon go so early in the morning?

Scorilus squinted but couldn't read the tight Greek script. He wouldn't reveal his weakness to a servant and ask for help.

He had a bad feeling. He rubbed his forehead, pacing around.

On the mosaic of Napat-Dehnu, he halted and stared at the wall with Oroles's arrow.

The arrow was gone. That could mean only one thing.

Scorilus ran from the great hall, crossed the square, and climbed the Tyrine Tower, his heart bursting inside his chest when he reached the top.

His legs shook as he gasped for air. He hurtled to the rampart in time to see the last of Rescuporis's troops disappearing over the hills in the west.

Rescuporis and his army were gone, and Moskon had joined them. Scorilus had no army to bring to their rescue. His sons' fates now lay with Lucretius's atoms and their power to turn even the most sensible plans into chaos.

The Book of Dapyx

From the cover of trees at that evening hour, Dapyx studied the redbrick stronghold on the east bank of the Alutus River. The Red Tower—the fortress Chief Wodan's army needed to take in order to open the mountain pass and allow the rest of King Cothelas's army into Valdavia.

The fortress guarded a submerged river gate that stopped vessels from passing if they didn't pay their fares. Between the mountain wall on the other side of the Alutus, the river gate, and the fortress, the Red Tower looked impenetrable. But there was a way in from the south, over a short bridge and a moat, overlooking the market road.

Chief Wodan's army, hiding in the forest half a mile from the Red Tower, was ready to storm the south gate. They only had a dozen horses, mostly draft animals stolen from the villages they had encountered on the way here. The animals were better at pulling a plow than charging into battle, but they could still carry soldiers to the south gate faster than the men would run across the field from the forest.

At dusk, the south gate was still open, the moat bridge still lowered, as a lonely ox cart rolled up the market road half a mile away. Chief Wodan would order the attack any moment now, under the cover of darkness. But if anything went wrong, the Red Tower would go into lockdown. A siege would drag on, and who knew what would happen to Andrada then?

The scene with the lonely cart looked familiar to Dapyx. He had lost track of time as the army had trudged through the forest along the banks of the Alutus River. But now he remembered. Market day was twice every moon in his home country, which gave him an idea.

He eased along the army lines until he found Chief Wodan.

"Ah, the little prince." Wodan turned his back to Dapyx and continued to survey the Red Tower. "How's the eye?"

"Better, thank you, my lord." Dapyx's hands trembled, but his voice was steady. "If I could have a moment of your time—I know how to take the fortress without bloodshed."

Bloodshed was what he'd been preparing for since he had held his first wooden blade ten years ago. Bloodshed was expected of him after so much practice with the armory master in Zalmodava. Bloodshed was the warrior's gift to the gods.

"I'm listening," Wodan said.

"Tomorrow's market day."

"All I care about is tonight," Wodan said.

"But tomorrow, villagers from ten miles around will arrive here. We can travel on horseback up the road and join them, pretending to be mer-chants. Then we take over a few of their carts and hide our swords under their loads. Once inside the fortress, we disarm the guards, capture the river gate, and let King Cothelas's army sail through."

"If we fail," Wodan said, "the fortress will lock down, and we'll have a siege on our hands. I believe they have hidden tunnels to restock food, arrows, and tar."

"We'll have a better chance tomorrow than tonight."

There was a long silence. Wodan paced, stroking his beard. Dapyx held his breath.

At last, Wodan said, "Get ready for battle now and wait for my order."

Dapyx's heart sank. He stepped back and rejoined the other soldiers, who weren't as friendly to a Valdavian as Syrmos used to be.

The light was fading. A relentless woodpecker hammered the tree Dapyx was leaning against. Still, the order to move did not come.

The bell at the south gate of the Red Tower rang. The ox cart rolled in. Still no order.

The drawbridge came up behind the cart.

Chief Comosicus, Chief Wodan's right hand, rejoined his troops. "You, you, and you, take down the beacons in the chain toward Zalmodava. The rest of you, I want the horses ready before dawn. We'll ride a mile down the road, past the bend, where the forest hides us from the Red Tower. Thank the gods, tomorrow is market day in Valdavia."

They were using Dapyx's plan after all! Light-headed, he backed away from the restless soldiers, deeper into the dark woods. He swung around a thick hackberry tree, unfastening his belt. He had steered an army that day. No one would recognize his role in taking the Red Tower, but if he had proven himself to be a strategist once, he could do it again.

Someday Andrada would see that she had married the wrong brother. For it was Dapyx who had saved her life after Twin Willows. It was Dapyx who'd soon free her from the Six-Sided Tower. She'd see, and then he might stand by her side one day as her husband. That last thought was intoxicating, a wave of heat after the chill of fear.

He slipped farther into the forest, hurting with desire, to where the only sound was that of night owls and his own labored breath.

Chapter Twenty-Six

The Book of Andrada

Andrada's absent father. Queen Pegrina's burned portrait. Syrmos. The King's Challenge. The crystal bell. Nicetas. The sky oak. The waterwheel. The nurse's new baby. The new gardens. The sacred royal duties. The sandstone statuette. The sick beggar child in Twin Willows. Dapyx's rescue. Andrada's illness. Una's teachings. Una's death. Ea's silence. The Council of Six. The dead baby. El's betrayal.

Andrada had written everything down in *The Book of Andrada*, so she closed her eyes and fell asleep.

She was done with this world.

She woke up to the hard bed underneath her and the pain in her belly, the same pain she had known in Sehuldava, when she had used hot bricks wrapped in towels, before Citera's potions and Una's balms. Her body was still going through its mindless life cycle, even though in the morning it was condemned to lie on the sundial and part with its head.

She hugged the pain in her belly. The window slits were dark blue. The moldy odor of the cell couldn't smother the sweet perfume of spring flowers coming from her gardens.

There was a sound, an eerie faraway sound, like drums or hoofbeats. She sat up in bed. A few embers still glowed in the hearth, helping her see around the cell.

The noise grew louder. The floor trembled, and the water in the mug on the table rippled.

After a while, the door opened. "My queen," Calidrones said, "King Cothelas and his army are down in the valley. They're demanding your freedom."

Andrada was supposed to die with the sunrise. Now her father was here?

She didn't move until she heard the crossbar fall into place. The awe and terror she had felt in the Old Temple of Sehul seized her again, and she started shivering.

No, her father wouldn't come to save her because of the goodness of his heart. He had never truly cared for her and, after adopting Syrmos, had no use for her.

She stared down at her trembling hands. Had someone else rung the crystal bell and asked El to save her?

Then she remembered the word engraved on the bell. ONE. All became clear as crystal.

The sky god El had revealed Himself to Andrada little by little, answering her prayers the way He saw fit, guiding her steps, waiting for her to understand.

Now she understood. At long last, she understood.

El wasn't one of the many gods of Dhawosia. He was the one and only god, a heavenly father who was now using Andrada's earthly father as His instrument for her rescue.

The stories about Him being asleep while Ea and Her children ruled the world were just that: stories. He'd been watching over His earthly children. And it had taken Andrada a long time to recognize El's love because she had never known what a father's love felt like—strong, unwavering, everlasting. She'd been done with the world and done with El, but He would never be done with her because she was His beloved child who needed rescuing. He had summoned armies and sent them to save her.

The pain in her belly fell quiet as she embraced His love. That love could heal. Awe and terror dwindled and vanished, replaced by a sense of security. Her life was now in El's hands.

The Valdavian Chronicle

Nicetas had arrived in Zalmodava without the head of the great aurochs but certain he'd at least have the queen's head that morning. Instead, he found himself in the saddle at the forefront of his army, beside Chief Tarbus.

Zalmodava looked dark and depthless against the forest on the hill. A column of smoke rose into a gray cloud in the brightening sky above the Temple of Concord. Citera must have sacrificed a bull, yet Nicetas didn't feel heartened. He needed Bendis to help those who stood with their king, for this invader was worse than Scorilus. Cothelas was so disciplined that he had broken through the Iron Gates. So shrewd that he had taken out the beacons, leaving Nicetas to learn about the attack only when a young man from a sacked village had made his way north.

Zyraxes arrived and brought his mount to a halt. "Have you seen Dapyx?"

"No," Nicetas said.

He hadn't seen his little brother since he had held a dagger to his neck, but he knew Dapyx liked to mingle with the common folk. What if he'd been in one of the villages in Cothelas's path? Nicetas hoped he was safe, for he was skilled with a falx and fast with a horse.

Zyraxes drew closer and put a chain in Nicetas's hand. In the predawn light, he recognized Oroles's silver-and-crystal ring. He breathed a sigh of relief, knowing Oroles wasn't headed to alert Scorilus. One invading army was more than enough.

"What did you do with him?" he said.

"Locked him in the Boulder Hut on Mount Ea-El."

Nicetas hung the chain around his neck. "We'll have a Council of Six for him after the war."

"I'll be at the temple," Zyraxes said, "praying with Citera for your victory."

He clicked his tongue, and his horse set off for the hills.

Last night, Nicetas had been on the back of his hunting horse, cursing Bendis for hiding Her aurochs lover from him. Now he was on a warhorse in the Ozana River Valley, praying for Her help again while leading an army Zyraxes had gathered in just a few days.

At least the valley was an open battlefield with only a few scattered willow trees, so no hidden troops could ambush them. To get here, Cothelas would have to squeeze his troops between the bend of the river and the steep northern slope of Zalmodava Hill. In the case of a retreat, he'd have little space for a maneuver.

Nicetas turned to Tarbus. "Reinforcements still coming?"

"The south of the country is cut off, but the north should be trickling in all day. We have eighty thousand footmen and six thousand horses, my king. With Beleizis's help, we'll force their forty thousand back and drown them in the river before sunset."

Nicetas shook his head. "Our flanks aren't evenly matched. And our scout says they have ten thousand horsemen."

"Our archers will take them out before they can do us harm."

"What if the Romans get wind of this?"

"Let's get through today, my king. We'll worry about the Romans tomorrow."

Nicetas yanked the reins and turned his horse for the river. The right flank was his weakest: cavalry made of villagers on mules, carrying hunting bows, slings, and hammers. Few of them had armor, only fur coats, hide shields, or cloaks with hoof slices sewn on. A few lucky men had leather tunics with scales made of scraps their women had found around the house: bronze coins, pieces of iron pots, points of shovels.

On the banks of the Ozana, Nicetas pulled up in front of a large group of peasants having their first meal of the day. They didn't look like soldiers, with their downcast eyes and beards dotted with crumbs. They rose to their feet, wine spilling from leather flasks like drops of blood. Those who wore felt caps took them off.

"My good men," Nicetas said, "Ea once showed me Her divine face." After all those years, he almost believed the legends about his descent into the Underworld. "As long as my arm swings, it will take down Kertans.

Today we'll be victorious, by Ea's will, by the grace of Beleizis, and by the guile of Bendis."

"Yes, my king," the peasants answered in weak voices.

He wanted to whip them into formation but worried they might run away. "Remember to keep your mounts in a tight rein when the Kertans' dracos go up. Our horses aren't used to their wolf howling."

"Yes, my king."

Nicetas prayed his right flank would withstand the Kertan attack. He nudged his warhorse and turned around. The strength of his army was in its left flank, a cavalry company of battle-hardened chieftains and their men. They had iron shields and helmets, hide and bronze armors, and bronze-plated boots, and they carried longbows, falxes, sicas, and battle-axes.

"King Nicetas." The chieftains at the front of the flank saluted him.

Nicetas pulled hard on the reins, and his horse pranced. "My good men, today I'll have the heart of Cothelas the Bald on the point of my spear."

The Book of Dapyx

Dapyx was happy to ride his beloved stallion again. Their reunion at the Red Tower had been heartwarming. Dapple hadn't even asked for a carrot, he'd been so excited to see his master again.

From the saddle, Dapyx looked up at the dark fortress on Zalmodava Hill. No doubt Dapple could hear his horse friends in the Valdavian army up ahead, but Dapyx couldn't see much from where he was, at the back of King Cothelas's left flank, on the bank of the Ozana River. With the falx he had picked up at the Red Tower and his leather tunic sewn with iron scales, he hoped to make it to Andrada. There had been no news of her death yet.

"Sehul, Mehnot, and Heusos," a man prayed behind him, "keep me alive for the sake of my little children."

Would praying to the Kertan gods on Valdavian soil work? Dapyx wondered.

Dapple sniffed the air—smoke, coming from the other side of the river—but Dapyx couldn't tell if it was Erebon and Sanapa burning or the forests beyond them. He pressed through a tight group of riders, nudging Dapple to the edge of the flank, where he could glance across the water.

"I bet one gold coin I'll cut more tongues than you," a stout Kertan told another.

"You get the tongues," the taller one said. "I get the ears. Double the fun for me." He laughed and banged the hilt of his sword against the shield strapped over his chest.

Dapyx couldn't help staring at the man. His laughter was too loud, and there was sweat on his forehead, even though it was chilly this close to the riverbank. At least Dapyx wasn't the only one frightened of the battle to come.

"Behold the little prince," said a bearded man in hide armor, carrying a battle-axe. "Ready to rip out some guts, my lord?"

"Some Valdavian guts?" someone else added.

A young man with broken teeth pretended to throw his spear at Dapyx, who flinched and forced Dapple to backtrack. Once he was far enough, he turned to them.

"Ready since the Iron Gates," he said in his shrillest voice, the one he hated.

"That was water," a graybeard said. "This will be blood upon your home."

Zalmodava was the place where Andrada was held captive, the place where she'd be put to death. This was no home for Dapyx.

There were lights on the parapets of the Six-Sided Tower, torches blinking in the gray morning. Maybe Andrada was awake, watching the soldiers in the valley through a window slit in her cell. His heart swelled, for he would save her.

The horse in front of Dapple lifted his tail, and a pile of dung fell with a steamy plop.

The Book of Andrada

Andrada banged on the door, three loud fists against the blackened wood. She waited. Calidrones's eyes appeared through the cutout window.

"I'm going up to the roof," Andrada said, her voice hoarse after her silence of thirty days. "There's a battle out there, and I must see it."

"By Beleizis's thunder, the high priest—"

"Whom do you answer to in times like these, the high priest or the queen of Valdavia?"

The crossbar came off. "My queen, I beg you—"

"Don't worry, Calidrones, when it's all over, you'll either take me back here or back to King Cothelas. Either way, you'll be obeying your king, whoever that will be."

They climbed to the platform at the top of the tower. Andrada held on to the parapet, and Calidrones stood by, gripping her arm. Below, on a lower walkway, guards and house servants had gathered to watch the armies in the valley.

The wind brought with it the smell of horses and iron and dust. Laced over everything was the smell of smoke. At first, Andrada thought it came from the fires in the valley, where Erebon and Sanapa were burning, but they were too far away. This smoke didn't smell of wood or hay or wool, but sizzling fat—it came from the Temple of Concord. Zyraxes and Citera must have sacrificed a bull to Beleizis. Their sacrifice was in vain though. They should have prayed to El instead.

The valley between the Ozana River and Zalmodava Hill was a battle-field capped at both ends by soldiers and horses. The Valdavian army in the west was broken into three flanks. All carried linen standards painted with charging aurochs in whatever colors they could find. The right flank, close to the river, was made of people from the valley on foot or on mules. The left, close to the steep hill, was also cavalry, but well armed and armored. So was the infantry in the center, ranked deeper than it was wide because of the tight space between the river and the hill. Nicetas had to be the rider in silver armor at the front. She hadn't seen him since the Council of Six.

She smiled. Nicetas didn't stand a chance, for El had summoned the Kertan army to Andrada's rescue. Her soldiers were at a good distance east, along the river, the dracos lowered and quiet. Almost no one used chariots in battle anymore, not even the Romans, because they were slow to turn and no match for nimble mounted archers, but King Cothelas looked glorious in his gold-plated chariot, like a god coming down to earth, and that must count for something.

His army was split into five distinct companies, fronted by another motley unit. A weak front, but why? She shook off Calidrones's hold on her arm and tiptoed along the parapet, her breath hazy. Something about that strange formation seemed familiar. Nicetas had the advantage in numbers and in knowing the terrain, but his troops were crowded between the river and the hill, and the wind was blowing in their faces, carrying the dust raised by the Kertan horses and the smoke of the burning villages.

Then she saw it. She remembered Avezinas's lesson about the Battle of Cannae in the Second Punic War between Roma and Carthago. If King Cothelas was using Hannibal Barca's strategy, then the Kertan center only looked weak but wasn't. Judging by Nicetas's lack of interest in anything but hunting and Una, he wouldn't recognize the trap.

Andrada watched, her hands clasped and her breath shallow, as the Kertans began their advance. The center marched faster than the flanks, and the army swelled into a crescent, with the cavalry at the two points by the river and the hill.

It was Hannibal Barca's strategy, of course. El was leading King Cothelas to victory.

The Valdavian Chronicle

Nicetas ran his tongue over his teeth, then spit out the dust in his mouth. "Tarbus, move some of the good riders from the left to the right flank to keep the peasants from fleeing."

A scout arrived on horseback. "Cothelas's flanks are cavalry, stronger than ours, at least on the riverside. The middle is made of three infantry companies, and the center is light-armored, but the sides are heavy. Cothelas the Bald drives a chariot at the front of a unit of light-armed slingers and spearmen on foot and on horses. They all wear fur capes."

"Fur capes to make the blade slip in hand-to-hand combat," Tarbus said. "Light-armored soldiers move faster. But where would they use that advantage? Their numbers are half ours."

"You keep saying that." Nicetas spit out more dust with his words.

The Kertans seemed ready for battle, while his army had just scrambled into formation. Yet the Kertans were surely tired from the long march north, while the Valdavians were well-fed and rested.

If Cothelas had a plan, Nicetas couldn't see it, and that made him nervous.

The sun broke through the clouds, right into his eyes. Behind him, soldiers groaned, and horses whinnied.

"We must stall until the sun climbs higher," he said. "Chief Tarbus, gallop ahead and ask Cothelas for a conference. Make it sound like we might surrender—anything to stall him."

Tarbus did that and soon brought back word that Cothelas was on his way.

"Finish sorting out the flanks," Nicetas told him, then trotted into the open field between the two armies.

Cothelas drove a gold-plated chariot. In his shining armor with the sun at his back, he looked like Sehul's own champion.

Nicetas squared his shoulders, but his muscles felt weak. He had to remind himself he had survived the Night Attack. Ea had rescued him from the Underworld. The goddess must have a plan for him today.

Cothelas grew taller in his chariot of light. His black cloak flapped in the wind. Behind him, the Kertan center columns swelled at a steady pace.

Nicetas's stomach quivered. He felt his bowels turning to liquid. Ea had forgotten to take away his fear.

He could now see Cothelas's dark eyes under his gold helmet, his shaved face. Nicetas reined in his warhorse, holding up his aurochs standard.

A few feet away, Cothelas stopped his chariot.

"You wronged me, King Nicetas," Cothelas said.

"You've made your anger quite clear, King Cothelas." Nicetas nudged his horse forward. "But what is its cause?"

"Where's my daughter?"

"Queen Andrada belongs to me now."

"Is she dead?"

"With the rising of the sun."

"If my daughter's dead, how will you keep your word?"

"I kept my word. You have your heir."

Cothelas threw the hem of his cloak to the side. He held a large bundle in the crook of his arm. He threw it at Nicetas.

"This is not my heir," he said.

Nicetas flinched, and his horse hopped back.

In the dirt, the bundle came undone, and a small, shriveled foot poked out.

He felt sick to his stomach. "You killed your own grandson?"

"If a dead son is lying in the dirt, then why is there no tear in the father's eye?"

The sun had risen just enough for its glare to move past the Valdavian army.

"Let there be war then," Nicetas said, turning his horse.

The Book of Dapyx

The swords ahead of Dapyx rose. Thousands of Kertan soldiers hailed their returning king. All around, bearded faces strained to see what happened ahead. Horses crept in, pressing forward, grazing each other's withers with nervous muzzles. Dapple turned his head, his mouth open. Dapyx dug inside the saddlebag and pulled out a carrot.

"My horse feasts on Valdavians, not carrots," a man said.

It was the broken-toothed Kertan who had threatened Dapyx with his spear earlier. He now grinned and raised his draco, pretending to throw again.

A howl followed. Dapple's ears flattened against his head. The Kertan, too, seemed surprised, as a breeze rang the wolf's brass tongues and swelled its linen bag. He let out a curse and lowered his standard.

But another standard went up, then another, farther away. They'd been kept down since the army had crossed into Valdavia. Dapyx patted his stallion between the ears. He hoped the stable boy from Sehuldava had taught Dapple how to handle the fake wolves' howling.

At some distance, a chieftain yelled, though nobody could hear his words, and gestured for the standards to stand down. Dapple crow-hopped and tried to prance, but there was no space. He neighed in utter terror, kicking his hind legs. Dapyx held on. Around him, horses jerked their heads in their bridles, their ears pricked, their tails ruffled.

Hundreds of standards went up, howling. A bronze bell rang to stop the call to arms, but the horses were now spooked by each other's fright. A moment later, a drumbeat sounded, ordering the attack after all.

Though Dapyx had started the battle unawares, he now threw himself into it. Yet he couldn't see much around him, only the rumps of horses and the backs of soldiers. Dapple trotted now, calming down. But in an instant, the horses ahead stalled, shifting around, pulling Dapyx forward and sideways.

He needed to be near the battle, but the soldiers who pushed ahead also pushed back. He gripped his falx in one hand and held the reins in the other. He pushed forward, but there was still no battle there, just more horses crammed together, and more soft ground and wolf howls.

The world became blurred through his hot tears. He was wasting time. He had to get out of there and save Andrada.

The Book of Andrada

Andrada leaned over the cold rock of the parapet. The Valdavians weren't in complete formation—a chieftain was still shuffling troops around—and now their horses pranced and neighed in panic. Andrada had never seen the dracos in battle, but the legends were true. The Valdavian horses were afraid of the wolf howls. But they weren't real wolves, just gaping brass heads with bodies made of hollow linen bags.

The Kertan army, where the ripple had formed, was now advancing, their horses used to the wolf din. For a moment, Andrada worried that Hannibal's brilliant battle plan would be undone by a wretched soldier in the back ranks starting the attack too soon. But now she understood that even that mishap had been part of El's plan—for the Valdavian mounts at the other end of the battlefield were frantic. The horses caught in the center of their flanks pushed forward, and those on the front lines had no choice but to slip closer and closer to the source of their terror.

The earth shook with the sudden burst of the Valdavian cavalry. They didn't charge ahead, instead scattering in all directions.

Meanwhile, the two mounted Kertan flanks poured forward, as the central company stayed in a bow-shaped formation, just like Hannibal's.

Under El's watchful eye, Kertans and Valdavians clashed on both sides, but the Valdavian villagers and their horses turned tail and fled along the riverbank. On the hillside, the Valdavians fought harder but gave way when the Kertans dismounted and began slashing the Valdavian horses and stabbing their fallen riders.

Andrada didn't blink, afraid she might miss something. From where she stood, looking down over the forest, to the bottom of the hill, she was as close to the battle as possible without being in the thick of it. The cries of agony rang clear, but she couldn't see the wounds and the blood. She could only hear death.

The Book of Dapyx

The horse before Dapple fell aside, and there was the battle Dapyx had been searching for. A Valdavian soldier shouted and swung a falx, cutting down horses at the knees.

Dapyx pulled on the reins, and Dapple leaped from the falx's path just in time. Dapyx thrust his pole arm through the crazed man's shoulder, into his torso, and the man fell. Dapyx bent over, pulling the hilt of his falx, and the blade escaped with a geyser of blood.

It was his first slaying, but—may the gods forgive him—not his first kill.

Another Valdavian foot soldier charged. Dapyx let go of the reins, squeezed his saddle with his knees, and gripped his falx with both hands. The blades clashed, but Dapyx had the advantage of height. His falx cleaved the head of his attacker, slid down through to the man's clavicle, and bounced back to Dapyx.

The slippery dirt under Dapple's hooves turned from brown to red. The air stank of sweat, iron sparks, warm blood, opened guts, and emptied bowels. Anchored in his saddle, Dapyx swung the falx around. Another Valdavian fell, blood gushing from his chest.

A dreadful thought gripped Dapyx. He looked back at the man he had just killed—and sighed with relief. No, he wasn't any of the merchants from Sanapa and Erebon Dapyx knew well, but he could have been. Dapyx was killing Valdavians, his people, villagers Master Balius had talked to on market day.

He didn't want to kill them. He was there to save Andrada.

He leaned into Dapple, clicking his tongue, but couldn't hear himself, his ears ringing with the clamor of battle. Two foot soldiers climbed over fallen bodies, trying to pull Dapyx from his saddle. Both men fell backward when Dapple bounded and kicked them in the face.

Dapyx spurred his mount, always leftward, along the flank, until they splashed into the river. They swam deeper into the water, to where no Valdavian could stand and fight at the same time, and they began their wade against the cold stream to find a way around the battlefield, toward the Six-Sided Tower.

The Book of Andrada

Andrada watched as the Kertan cavalry shaved off the mounted flanks of the Valdavian army, then chased and slaughtered what was left of them along the river and the bottom of the hill. Nicetas still had his large infantry though. Armored in silver, he spurred his horse forward, but the animal buckled. He prodded it again, but nothing happened. He dismounted, and his war horn called for his infantry-men to follow.

He knew nothing of Hannibal Barca. He led his men forward against the seemingly weak center of the Kertan light-armored sol-diers, who pretended to fight back but only for a short time. Their bow-shaped frontline flattened, then dipped, and the Valdavians crowded in. The heavy-armored troops on the wings of the Kertan infantry attacked the flanks of the Valdavian army. The Kertan cavalry closed the circle, blocking the Valdavian rear.

Now the Valdavian army was squeezed on all sides, shields trapped between soldiers' bodies, blades stuck, aurochs standards falling aside. The gilded chariot was in the rear, outside that circle of death, and Nicetas was somewhere inside. King Cothelas raised his sword, gave the order, and the butchery began.

The trapped Valdavian army slimmed down like a log on a lathe. In the valley, idling Kertan riders kept watch for Valdavian soldiers escaping the grinding. They chased the fugitives, killed them, and returned at a trot for more.

"By all the gods in heaven," Calidrones said after a while, "this is carnage. How can They allow it?"

"There's only one god, Calidrones," Andrada said.

"Beleizis? But then, why are our people getting killed?"

Andrada took in the whole battlefield. The sun was a deep orange behind the haze of smoldering villages across the river. From the mountains, a large company on horseback approached a sloping funnel that opened into the battlefield. It was a late Valdavian arrival, one that could sway the battle.

Andrada looked the other way. Rounding the east end of Zalmodava Hill, positioned to attack the Kertans from the rear, a new army had appeared. It had cavalry on the flanks, with infantry and longbow archers in the middle. The two-headed snake adorned their standards. They could only be Steppewynders—and King Cothelas couldn't see them from ground level.

So far, Andrada had been a witness to El's plan, but now she had a part in it. She had to warn the king about the looming danger.

She turned to Calidrones. "Give me your cloak. I'm cold."

Calidrones held up his cloak, and Andrada turned her back to him. As Calidrones laid his cloak on her shoulders, she took half a step back, her hand feeling for the hilt of the dagger at Calidrones's belt, the way Syrmos had once taught her on a winter day.

Calidrones looked shocked when she turned with his own blade and pressed it against the stubble on his neck.

He staggered back, his palms up. "By Beleizis's thunder…"

"Do as I say, and I won't hurt you. Give me your keys."

She needed armor and a better blade from the tower's storage chamber.

The Book of Dapyx

The red sun shone through the smoke. Dapyx was still on the lookout, his legs numb in the cold water. The battle to his right was getting sparser, a sign that he was close to the end of the battlefield.

As he drove Dapple out of the river, a spear hit Dapyx above the right knee. The scales on his long tunic kept it from piercing his flesh, but his upper leg took the blow. With a pained groan, he spurred his horse forward, broke through a last row of fighters, and found himself at the rear of Nicetas's flank, in the open.

Dapyx glanced up at Zalmodava Hill, beyond the soldiers. The Six-Sided Tower seemed so close.

He clicked his tongue, but Dapple slumped on his hind legs, and Dapyx slid back from the saddle. He bounced back on his feet just in time to parry a falx that came swinging at him. He bent down, sucked in his stomach, but the hooked tip of the falx still snapped a few ribs under his armor.

He screamed in agony. Daylight turned bright with pain, and he couldn't see around him for a moment. Still, he swung his falx, keeping his attacker at a distance, though he didn't know anymore where anything was, except for the ache in the center of his body.

He took another throbbing breath. Another swing. He heard a scream as he hit someone with his blade. There was a loud thud, a groan, then a curse. He blinked until he saw the man he had taken down, one leg cut clean just below his hide armor. The man dropped his weapon and grabbed his thigh, blood spurting out in beats.

Dapyx turned away and called for Dapple. Every step hurt. He pressed his arm over his broken ribs and limped on.

He found Dapple lying on one side, his hind leg slashed deep into the hamstring, bleeding. Dapyx forgot all about his own pain. He fell to his knees next to his beloved horse.

"Don't worry, Dapple, Bendis will make you whole again..."

All around them, horses and men lay in a red ooze. That day, the goddess of animals favored only the flies and the vultures.

Dapyx pulled a broken carrot from a pocket on his belt. He brought it to Dapple's lips, but the horse didn't sniff the hand as he used to. He blinked, and his lids came back up slowly. Dapyx caressed that beloved face. His fingers trembled over the white forehead, down to the wet nostrils.

"Please don't die...You saved her once, remember? She's waiting for us..."

The big brown eyes watched him until they could see him no more.

Dapyx wiped his tears, rage filling his chest. He dragged his falx to where the man who had killed Dapple lay, but he, too, was dead, his eyes open to the sky.

The wind blew the smoke in from the water. There was no one left alive on that gods-forsaken riverbank. The battle raged east of there, judging by the clangor and the shouts.

Dapyx took out his dagger and slashed at his cloak. He tied a strip of cloth around his torso, over his armor. He couldn't quite breathe now, but his broken ribs moved less when he walked.

He looked up, through tears, at the fortress on the hill. He'd save Andrada, despite the agony of crawling through the abandoned water tunnels. Once inside the dry well, he'd hoist himself up into the courtyard, then break into the Six-Sided Tower somehow.

The Book of Andrada

The storage chamber was shaped like Andrada's old cell but had more furniture and no bed. On a shelf, she found a close-fitting leather helmet and a messenger's wooden tube for *The Book of Andrada*. She looked through drawers and found foot wrappings, breeches, buckles, buttons, and gloves belonging to former prisoners. She picked a pair of studded leather bracers, a wide leather belt with pouches, and a wooden sheath for Calidrones's dagger.

Inside a trunk, she found a scaled leather tunic, with slits in the front and back for riding, and a pair of loose woolen pants. From a hook on the wall hung a red-dyed woolen cloak—a Roman cloak, and it looked new too. No matter how it had gotten there, it would be useful to her in battle.

She cut through the fabric of her own shift, around her hips, until the linen skirts fell at her feet. Her lower body was naked in the cold cell, except for the T-shaped bandage that went between her legs and around her waist. She slashed the shift's extra fabric into wide strips and stacked a few together. The dry linen pad replaced her old bandage.

The riding pants were too long, so she cut them to size. She slipped into the scaled tunic and tightened the belt. The remaining linen strips went into her belt pouches.

She tried a few boots and found a bearskin pair with pointed spurs and rusty iron plates on the shins. With foot wrappings stuffed inside, they were about the right size.

She looked around one more time for a longer blade, but prisoners didn't come armed to the Six-Sided Tower. She slung the messenger's tube over her back and tied the red Roman cloak around her neck.

"By Bendis's bees, my queen, please don't leave me here." Calidrones's muffled voice came from Andrada's old cell.

She dropped his keys by the locked door and clunked down the stairs in her iron-plated boots. She stopped when she heard footsteps ahead and slinked back to the top floor to wait there, her hand on the hilt of her dagger.

"My queen, please," Calidrones said.

The woman who reached the landing was Zia, in a black headscarf and cloak. Andrada sheathed her dagger. If Zia was surprised to see Andrada dressed for battle, she didn't show it.

"My child," she said, "please come with me to Twin Willows. Last time we talked, I was angry, I was hurt, I was proud, and I was wrong. I'm the Family-Keeper, and my family saved your life with our blood. Una shared our family's secrets with you, and Rada gave you precious time. It has to be you, child. Only you can mend our line."

Andrada had to warn King Cothelas about the Steppewynders.

She pointed to the key ring on the floor. "After I'm gone, let Calidrones out of his cell." She started down the stairs.

"Thank you, my queen," Calidrones's muffled voice sounded from behind his door. "Beleizis bless you. And Bendis too."

"In fact, let them all out," Andrada called up as she descended the stairs.

When she reached the stables, she searched every stall, but there were no horses left except for a white mare and her days-old foal, a light bay with a white blaze. Andrada found a harness on a peg and a bucket of oats. The mare raised her head, her nostrils flaring. Andrada held out a handful of oats. The mare stretched her neck and sniffed them, then sucked them in with arched lips.

Andrada offered more oats and waited for the mare to relax. The foal pressed his skinny body against his mother's belly and began to suckle.

After a while, Andrada held her left hand to the mare's face. With her right, she put on the saddle, and the mare didn't fight it. Andrada slipped the bit in and pulled the bridle over the mare's head, then tightened the girth strap, pulled herself up, and was now in the saddle. She nudged the mare out of the barn, and the foal followed.

They trotted onto the bridge, and when they passed the twelfth pier, Andrada spurred the mare to a canter, then a gallop down the winding road through the forest, with the foal falling behind. They were going into battle, and that was no place for a baby.

They thundered down the road, trees flashing past, to the bottom of the hill, where they reached the clamor of war: the swishing of arrows, the knell of blades on shields, and the ghastly screams. They were at the northern edge of the battlefield, but the fighting had drifted east. Between them and the river, there now was a wasteland of dead and dying. Horses lay on their sides. Flies landed on open eyes. Vultures and crows pecked at bloody flesh.

Andrada remembered the harvest fair in Twin Willows, when Una had danced, crushing red grapes in a large wooden vat. Now El Himself danced, crushing people underfoot, splattering their blood on the thirsty ground.

Most of the dead looked Valdavian, some with aurochs standards nearby, but Andrada also spotted Kertan wolf pelts and trampled dracos. The Valdavians had broken Hannibal's stranglehold and fought back, at least for a while.

She had to find King Cothelas and warn him about the Steppewynders. She spurred her mare toward the battle in the east, toward the taunting and the curses of men in the rear ranks. The mare's hooves slid on blood-logged mud, on broken limbs, soft stomachs, crushed-in faces. Blades and shields rang underfoot.

Andrada dismounted and patted her white mare on the neck. "Go to your child now."

The mare snorted and took off.

Andrada undid the belt of a dead young man with an arrow sticking out from his neck. She buckled his sica beneath the wooden tube on her back. From a white willow tree, she scraped some bark, in case she needed to ease her pain later. A few feet away, she found an oval Kertan shield, which she knew how to use.

She now had to pass through the last standing fighters ahead, but with El by her side, she wasn't afraid. With her red Roman cloak, no one would mistake her for the enemy they should worry about.

There was no method to the fighting anymore, just every man for himself. She dodged a few tired blows not meant for her and kept searching the battlefield for King Cothelas. Then she saw Nicetas in his silver armor, his shield in hand, his face covered in sweat, dust, and blood.

He parried a blow from a mace and thrust his sica into a Kertan enemy, who doubled over. Nicetas turned, his eyes the same cold blue as ever, and came straight for her.

"You," he growled. "You're supposed to be dead."

El had guided Andrada there.

"Then fight me," she said. "Let's end this here and now."

She held her shield up and gripped her sica.

Her voice made soldiers turn and gape at the strange sight of a woman on the battlefield. Weapons were lowered. Nicetas began treading a circle around Andrada, as the surrounding crowd formed a bigger circle, watching.

Nicetas scowled. "I'll never cross blades with a woman."

She took a step toward him. "But you'll betray a woman. You'll force yourself on her. You'll sentence her to death."

"Don't let her speak to you like that," a man called in a thick Germanic accent.

"Fight me, Nicetas," Andrada said. "Or are you too scared? You don't have Una now to hold your hand."

"Don't you dare speak her name!" He charged, his sica aimed at her chest.

She stepped aside, her back arched. Pivoting on one leg, she crossed her blade with his. A glint of surprise showed in his eyes, but he didn't lose his footing.

The crowd gasped each time Andrada backed away under Nicetas's heavy blows she blocked with her shield. She remembered her sword skills, but her muscles had grown weak since her days in Sehuldava.

Their blades parried, and the curved tip of his sica almost pulled the weapon from her hand once. His sword came close to her face, but each time she blocked with her shield and shoulder and all the strength she could muster. Yet she wasn't scared. This fight had already been written by El, the ending settled.

The muscles in her blade arm stiffened, and her shield shoulder ached with each blow she blocked. He grunted with each strike, his face hard like a fist. Sparks flew from the clashing steel, stinging their faces. She heard nothing but the sound of their blades and shields, their grunts, her shrieks, his panting.

Nicetas slashed. The blade bounced off Andrada's shield. Instead of retreating, she lunged forward. Her blade rebounded from the scales of his armor on his shoulder, but the sharp tip cut his right cheek. He cursed and fell back, then charged again.

Her back was now up against the wall of onlookers. She could smell the wine and onions on the men's breath.

Andrada was trapped. She waited until Nicetas was close enough and blocked his blow. Then she lowered herself on her knees and pivoted away to the center of the tightening circle of soldiers. She gripped the handle of her shield and was lifting it to block his next blow, when she stumbled on the leg of a slain Kertan and fell. The wooden tube under her cloak hit her hard, and her shield and sica flew from her hands.

Nicetas strode the few steps between them. She lifted her head from the muddy ground. The people around the circle closed in. She groped for her lost blade. Her fingers wrapped around the handle of an abandoned weapon. Nicetas raised his sica.

The weapon she had grabbed was heavy. She couldn't lift it.

Nicetas was going to slash her throat.

She grunted, her hand on that hilt that wouldn't budge. It was a full-size mace, the only weapon she had never mastered. She groaned. She cried out. Her weak arm muscles hardened.

Nicetas's sica was lower now.

This was the Night Attack in broad daylight, and Andrada was Nicetas, and Nicetas was Scorilus, but the blade wouldn't miss this time. Dread choked her. She rolled over, grabbed the mace with both hands—releasing one last shriek of strenuous effort—but still couldn't lift it.

She closed her eyes, waiting for Nicetas's sica to hit her, when she felt an unearthly power flowing through her arms. She clasped the mace, and it bobbed up from the ground. It was in her hands, but she knew El was lifting it for her. She swung it through the air with all her might.

One of the mace's flanges caught Nicetas's throat. He dropped his sica and grabbed his neck. He fell on his knees, blood spouting from his open throat, through his fingers, onto his chest. That was El's will, Andrada thought, as she closed her eyes and lay in the bloody mud.

"No, no, no," cried a young voice. Dapyx dropped next to his brother and propped him up. "A physician!" he called, but there was no physician in that wasteland.

Nicetas stared at Andrada with those eyes that had never shown her any love. A low gurgle came from his mouth, blood dripping through his parted lips. His throat was open, and his face was ashy. Not even Una could have saved him now.

Andrada crawled up to him, took a few linen bandages from a belt pouch, and covered his neck. When Nicetas saw Una in the Underworld, he'd look like himself again, only paler.

She wondered who this man had really been. He hadn't been a good king nor a good husband, but had he been a gentle lover to Una? Maybe he had hoped to live and love, but he had been born a prince, without a choice, much like Andrada.

His eyes closed. The gurgling in his throat stopped.

She spread blood on his forehead like black salt, remembering she had once asked El to take away her husband's scars. Around them, people muttered prayers for the fallen king. Dapyx let his brother's body slide from his arms and set it on the ground with care.

A part of Andrada, the one that used to ask Avezinas all those questions, wanted to find out if Nicetas no longer had Scorilus's scar on his body, as proof of El's power. Another part wanted to just trust that El had answered her old prayer.

Andrada heard King Cothelas's voice. "She's here, Wodan. The red cloak."

Soldiers everywhere remembered there was still a war going on. Their weapons went up again, and their battle cries followed.

Andrada had to see the healed scar with her own eyes. She tried to turn Nicetas's limp body to the side, to search for the hooks and eyes that fastened his armor. Her fingers kept missing though, slipping on the silver of his bloodied armor.

Clashes picked up all around her. She had undone three armor hooks and had three more to go when King Cothelas grabbed her elbow.

"Leave him," he said.

She shook him off. "Listen, Scorilus is bringing an army around the hill. Your back flank is defenseless."

Her fingers dug underneath the neck opening of Nicetas's armor and caught something. In her right hand, on a snapped silver chain, she held a ring made of silver and crystal. Inside, the word MEDA was engraved in Greek letters. What did that mean?

"You're coming with us," King Cothelas said. "Wodan, help me!"

Andrada felt herself grabbed from behind, squeezed inside Wodan's grip, the strap of her messenger's tube strangling her. He lifted her, and she landed on her knees on the royal chariot's wooden floor. Dapyx, grimacing with pain, hopped on just as the reins whipped the horses and the chariot jolted forward.

Andrada rested her forehead against the side guard. She'd never know if Nicetas's scar had vanished. It was time to forget all doubts and just believe in El.

The Dynastic Scrolls

Dokina wrung the neck of a rat and flung its body away from her corner of the dark cell. A torch lit the narrow hallway outside the floor-to-ceiling iron bars. Dapyx had said he'd free her, but he had never come.

The dark was when the rats attacked, so she had to stay awake now that the light grew dimmer as the torch ran out. But she was ready for them. She'd show them all, and she'd show Zyraxes, who had thrown her in with the rats and the night spirits. Nothing he had forced her to confess would hurt Andrada, for Andrada had the crystal bell and the sky god El watching over her. Still, she begged Sehul, Mehnot, and Heusos to forgive her for speaking even a word to that rotten priest.

Another torch added its light to the entrance of the vault. Dokina reached for the crystal at her neck, but it had long been gone, ever since Zyraxes's first visit to her cell.

"Anybody here?" a woman called.

"I'm here." Dokina's voice was but a whisper. "Here...I'm here."

She heard steps and the jingling of keys. The light grew brighter. An old woman in a black headscarf stopped before the iron bars with a torch.

"You're the last one," she said.

Dokina stood up. The woman set her torch in the bracket and tried key after key until one fit into the padlock, and the cell door squeaked open.

Dokina hurried out of her cell. The woman took her torch and started up the hallway between empty cells.

"Please..." Dokina tried to keep up with the woman, but she felt dizzy. "What happened to Queen Andrada?"

"She's alive and well. What's it to you?"

"I'm her...handmaid."

The woman stopped and raised her torch over Dokina's head. "Have you ever met Una of Twin Willows?" she said.

"Yes." Dokina grabbed the bars of a cell to steady herself.

"Were you there when Una spoke of medicine with the queen?"

"I copied the queen's wax tablets onto parchment..." She felt light-headed but forced herself to focus. "And I mixed potions with Una..." She squinted when the torch came close to her face again.

"Do you remember anything about pigments?"

"I...think so..."

"Incantations?"

Dokina wanted to sit down.

"Incantations," the woman said. "The songs? Think, child."

"Yes, yes...I know the songs." She felt so weak, she wanted to throw up.

"Are you twenty years of age?"

"Not yet."

She felt the woman's arm wrap around her back. Together, they started up the stairs.

"You're taking me to my queen?" Dokina said.

"No, I'm taking you to the goddess. We'll give you our blood, and you'll mend our line."

CHAPTER TWENTY-SEVEN

The Book of Andrada

The sun had begun its descent beyond the Carpates Mountains. Andrada bounced in the back of King Cothelas's golden chariot, her legs dangling out, her arm wrapped around the side guard. Across from her, she saw Dapyx moaning but couldn't hear him over the din of the battlefield.

"Fall back to the Norland Pass," the king called to Wodan, who rode alongside the chariot.

How they planned to march their army through an impenetrable fort that spanned from one mountain wall to the other, Andrada didn't know. The fort would be guarded by Nicetas's soldiers, who didn't yet know their king was dead.

"And leave Zalmodava to Scorilus?" Wodan shouted.

"Our soldiers can't fight anymore," the king explained. "They're wounded. They need food and water. Our horses are spent. The Steppewynders are rested. They'll crush us, now that we vanquished the Valdavians. We must retreat for the night."

Wodan raised his draco. "Fall back! To the Norland Pass!" A dozen wolf heads went up, the Ozana Valley echoing with their howls.

Kertan troops led by Comosicus peeled off from the battlefield. The chariot headed toward the setting sun, where Andrada saw more Kertan wolf pelts.

They reached the west end of the Ozana Valley. The funnel-shaped road Andrada had seen from the tower was the one leading up to the

Norland Pass. At its base waited an army of riders carrying black banners with the white double-headed snake. Steppewynders and Tauri archers had encircled Zalmodava Hill on both sides.

Their leader barked an order, and chants of "Napat-Dehnu!" resounded in the distance.

"Take cover!" Wodan shouted, galloping past the chariot.

The enemy archers sat up in their saddles, fitting arrows to their short bows. The air trembled as they shot a volley.

King Cothelas raised his oval shield overhead, against the cloud of arrows. Andrada grabbed Dapyx, and together they crouched close to the king's gold-shinned boots, under the shield, as arrows rained down on them.

Around the chariot, horses buckled, and riders fell. An arrow landed by Andrada's knee, its shaft burning, and she scrambled to put it out.

The archers shot another volley, and another, and another. Andrada kept her head down. The chariot didn't move. The hailstorm of arrows didn't ease, nor did the surrounding cries. One of the chariot's two horses fell, then the other, and the carriage tipped forward. Andrada hugged her knees and waited.

After the sixth volley, the sky above fell silent.

"Run out of arrows yet?" Wodan shouted, still on the back of his horse. "That's all you've got?"

Andrada lifted her head, while King Cothelas lowered his shield, which was pierced by dozens of arrows. The archers were now charging the short distance from the foothills of the Carpates Mountains to where the chariot was trapped with its dead horses. King Cothelas unsheathed his sica and brandished it. The setting sun glinted off his gilded-steel breastplate. He looked like a war god, fearless and victorious.

Andrada heard a sharp whiz, then a gasp and a grunt. King Cothelas dropped his sword. He leaned over the front guard of the chariot, the feathered shaft of an arrow sticking out from his neck, just above his breastplate.

He groaned through gnashing teeth, grabbed the arrow with both hands, and pulled it out. Blood gushed from his throat, over his shining armor, trickling on the floor of the chariot. Andrada scrambled to catch him as he sank. The small pool of blood at her feet grew bigger, rippling as the Steppewynder riders drew closer.

Andrada remembered Una's words about war wounds, how arrows could be poisoned with other people's old blood. *No time to worry about it—just stop the bleeding.*

She took a bandage from her pocket and pressed it over the king's wound, as she had done for Nicetas. She tore a piece of her cloak and tied the dressing around his neck.

The enemy riders were only a few yards away. Their armor was made of slices of horse hooves that looked like fish scales. There were women among them, shouting. These were the famed Tauri riders. Their leader was a man with dark hair and a trimmed beard.

Andrada seized King Cothelas's sica and prepared to fight.

Another group of Steppewynder riders was moving in from the banks of the Ozana. At their head was a young man, around Dapyx's age. A nobleman, judging by his tanned-leather armor.

The Tauri leader slowed his black warhorse and reached for an arrow but didn't aim it at the chariot. He turned toward the river.

His arrow hit the young Steppewynder leader in the eye.

Andrada was stunned. Weren't the Steppewynders and the Tauri allies? Why were they killing each other? The Steppewynder squad by the river halted and scrambled. Was this El's hand on the battlefield, confounding Andrada's enemies and saving her yet again?

Kertan soldiers took a defensive position around the chariot, blocking Andrada's line of sight. Hoofbeats drifted toward the river. Horses neighed, and soldiers cried in the distance. Weapons clashed.

The sun was now behind the mountains. The chariot jolted forward—sometime during that chaos, Wodan had changed the horses.

"Take the reins," he ordered Dapyx, who stood and did as asked, even though he seemed to be in pain.

Andrada put down the sica and helped the king sit up against the chariot's side guard. His eyes were closed, but he was breathing. She didn't understand how a wounded king fit into El's plans, but she had vowed to never doubt Him again. Now her part was to use the medicine knowledge she had learned from Una and care for the wounded.

Wodan slapped one of the horses, and the chariot with Dapyx at its reins was on the move again, racing up the path into the mountains. What was left of the Kertan army followed.

The Book of Dapyx

For a while, Dapyx feared the Steppewynders or the Tauri would pursue them, but nightfall saved them. The moon broke once through the clouds but vanished soon. Dapyx's broken ribs hurt. Torches lit the road for the chariot, and the horses followed them without prodding. Andrada and her father rode in the back.

After a while, Chief Wodan brought a new mount for Dapyx and relieved him of the chariot's reins. This new Valdavian warhorse had a black mane, a white forelock, and a crusty slash across his breast. He was no match for Dapple but was sturdy enough to carry Dapyx up the narrow mountain path.

It was close to midnight now. Wrapped in his cloak, Dapyx slumped over the warhorse's warm neck, a position that lessened the pain of riding on the bumpy mountain road. His stomach growled.

He heard Andrada's voice from behind him. "Dapyx!"

He didn't want to stop for her. She had killed his brother. Yes, Nicetas had almost slain her while she was down, but he hadn't succeeded, and now he was gone. Dapyx wiped his eyes.

"Let me look at your wounds." Andrada hurried up the path, holding a torch.

Bone-tired and in pain, Dapyx weighed her offer. That day, he had killed his share of people who would have killed him otherwise. This was the first time she had called his name in what felt like forever. He still loved her.

He reined in his warhorse and slid off the saddle. Andrada caught up with him, and they stepped to the side of the path. She thrust the torch into the ground, and he sat next to her by the mountain wall, moaning.

"My ribs are broken," he said.

She finished mixing something inside a leather helmet with a stick. "Pain balm. I learned the recipe from Una."

He undid his armor and lifted his tunic to reveal his bruised left side. She scooped out a thick dollop of aromatic balm and spread it with cold fingers over his tender rib cage. Where the remedy touched his skin, he felt warm and tingly. It should have made him breathe easier, but he choked with Andrada's hand on his body. She was so close to him now. Her clothes stank of battle, but her hair—short, wavy, tucked behind her ears—still carried a sweet perfume from the oils the temple servants had rubbed in before her scheduled execution that morning.

She wrapped his torso in strips of fabric. The pain settled into a wieldy ache, with no more sharp jabs.

"Thank you." He lowered his tunic over the bandage.

"Chew this. It's white willow bark. It also helps with the pain."

The bark was bitter and juicy, and Dapyx chewed it to a pulp before swallowing.

"Now eat this."

Andrada gave him a piece of flatbread, and he took a bite.

"Drink," she said, handing him a small flask.

The water was cool and bitter and smelled like the balm she had just spread on his ribs. His thirst vanished after the first sip, and his stomach felt warm and full. A wave of gratitude warmed his heart.

He remembered his big plans before the battle, how he'd free Andrada and be her hero. Instead, while he had been slowly crawling up the hill to the Six-Sided Tower, she had freed herself. She had killed Nicetas in battle like a true warrior, and now she took care of the wounded, like a true medicine woman. He didn't dare tell her of his sad rescue attempt. He wanted her love, not her pity.

"Here comes King Cothelas," she whispered, and Dapyx wondered why she hadn't said *my father.*

The torchlit chariot rumbled up the path, covered by a makeshift canopy of cloaks. Its floor had been extended with tree branches roped together so the king could lie as in a bed.

"Will he live?" Dapyx said. His tongue felt spongy and strange in his mouth.

"I don't know. I couldn't boil his bandages, the way Una had taught me, but I washed his wound with firewater. He lost a lot of blood. Una knew how to take blood from one man's veins and put it inside another's, but I don't. And even if I tried, I'd need glass tubes."

Dapyx had seen glass tubes in Una's satchel. "Can't we use reeds instead or something else?"

"No, it has to be glass, or the blood curdles."

She seemed sad, but she wasn't crying. Had he ever seen her cry? Never, he realized.

"Maybe we'll find glass at the fort," she said with a sigh.

She stood to leave, but he wanted her to stay a little longer.

"Andrada, what does the crystal bell mean to your father? He only believed me when I showed it to—"

"You have my bell?" she said.

"Your father has it. I went to Sehuldava to tell him you were in danger—"

"How did you get it? I thought the bell was inside my horse-box at the Council of Six."

Andrada didn't seem impressed by his good deed at all.

"There was a Council of Six?" Dapyx said.

"Answer me!"

Dapyx got back on his feet. "Dokina took it from Zyraxes. She gave it to me."

Andrada nodded a few times as if she understood. "Do you know where she is?"

"Zyraxes locked her in the dungeon, but it was empty today."

She smiled. "Zia must've freed her and the other prisoners." She started after the chariot.

Dapyx didn't know if their brief encounter meant they were friends again, but he dared to hope. He touched his left side: the pain was now distant. He let his warhorse take him up the winding path between the mountain walls, and he fell asleep in the saddle, thinking of Andrada.

Dapyx was jolted awake by pain in his rib cage. It took him a moment to grasp where he was. The sun was rising. The convoy had stopped in a clearing on a plateau, for people and horses to rest. If they pressed on, they could reach Fort Norland by sundown. Nicetas's signet ring might open the gates for them.

Dapyx found Andrada, and she gave him more white willow bark to chew and mixed more balm for his broken ribs. He asked her about the Kertan king and learned he was in a deep sleep. He asked her about the pain balm and learned she had used arnica and chamomile flowers gathered from the side of the road. Now that they were higher up on the mountain, the flowers were harder to find, so she'd be digging for valerian root next.

They stopped again at midday along a narrow path to eat bread and fill their flasks from a waterfall. Dapyx's warhorse was weary and angry, so he left him on his own to graze and nap. Dapyx sat with his back against the mountain wall and fell asleep.

He woke up with a start, his heart pounding.

"Riders coming up the mountain," a scout yelled from a high tree. "Half a day away."

Chief Wodan gave the order to start up the mountain but left Chief Comosicus with a group of soldiers behind to dig a hole in the path, deep enough to hide wooden spikes covered with leaves. Dapyx wanted to help, but his broken ribs didn't let him lift a shovel.

At sunset, Andrada redid his dressings. She didn't talk much before she left. The king was not doing well. The fever spirits had found him, and he was growing weaker.

Dapyx was holding the warhorse to climb into the saddle when he saw Chief Wodan and two soldiers coming his way.

"You've been of great help to us, Prince," Chief Wodan said. "I'm sorry for what I'm about to do." His soldiers seized Dapyx. "We're upon Fort Norland. Your brother's guards are sure to deny us entry without an order from their king. But maybe they'll let us through in exchange for their young prince."

Dapyx groaned in pain, the medicine's relief still a while away.

"No need for this." He kept still for his ribs' sake. "I can write a letter of passage. They'll let me in, and I'll persuade them to open the gates. Queen Andrada will have a bed to sleep in tonight."

In the wavering torchlight, Chief Wodan had the same doubtful expression he'd had outside the Red Tower.

"Fine," he said at last. "I'll give you parchment and wax, and I'll keep the convoy back."

As soon as he sealed the letter of passage with Nicetas's signet ring, Dapyx mounted. He took a torch with him and started up the path, hoping Andrada's remedies would keep him free of pain for a while.

Soon the road turned, and Fort Norland appeared in the dark ahead. Its walls spanned the width of the gorge. A few braziers burned high on the parapets.

Dapyx dismounted at the east gates. With his torch, he examined the dirt for prints of horseshoes or boots. A party of riders had come through not long ago and was still inside. Dapyx had to think fast. The Tauri riders on the battlefield—they had come down the mountain. Had there been more of them, going up? At the rest stop, he had overheard Chiefs Wodan and Comosicus saying that the Tauri riders fought for Prince Rescuporis of Steppewynd.

He took out his letter of passage, broke the wax seal, and scraped the charging aurochs off the parchment, praying to Beleizis, Bendis, and Enoz that he was right that the men inside were Rescuporis's Tauri riders, and that they didn't know how to read Greek script.

The cutout window at the gate opened. Two squinting eyes—from sleep, wine, or anger?—appeared, a side flame lighting a bearded cheek.

Dapyx said, "Prince Rescuporis wants to know how many men you lost taking the fort."

He hoped they understood Dhawosian because he didn't know one iota of Sarmatian or whatever tongue they spoke in the Tauris Peninsula.

"Who are you?" the man said in the throaty Sarmatian accent.

Dapyx held up the letter of passage. "Prince Rescuporis's emissary. How many men?"

"None at first, because we had an aurochs standard we captured on the battlefield. But before we walked through the gate, a cursed Valdavian with a keen ear picked up on my men's accent. They all pulled their blades, but they were not that many, with most of them down on the battlefield. Still, they killed one of us."

"How many left?"

"Three."

Dapyx held the letter for the guard to see. "This is the prince's letter to you."

"Will not do me much good..."

"I'll read it to you then. Let me in."

The man's face turned away. He spoke in a foreign tongue to the others, and the only word Dapyx understood was *Rescuporis*. The window closed, and the door opened.

Dapyx stepped inside. Two bearded shadows with lowered battle-axes stood behind the first man. Tauri fighters, whose clothes had seen battle. Dapyx swallowed his fear and held up the letter. The men huddled so close under the gate torch that he couldn't reach his sica if he had to.

He pretended to read. "Prince Rescuporis of Steppewynd praises the valiant soldiers who seized Fort Norland..."

The men's faces stretched into grins of pride.

"And rewards each of them with a hundred acres of land near the Valdavian village of their choosing."

"You hear that?" The man on the left slapped his friend's shoulder. "We are rich."

"I will breed my own steeds," the one on the right said. "But first, I will sell the villagers to the Roman slave merchants—"

Before he finished his sentence, Dapyx's sica slashed his throat. The man in the middle turned and met Dapyx's blade with his chest, but the third man's axe was coming down. Dapyx ducked and skidded toward the courtyard, stumbling against trestle tables in the dark. The guard was coming after him, roaring.

Dapyx found some steps and followed them up. He tripped on a dead body on a landing but kept climbing the zigzagging staircase to the ramparts, where he hid behind some tar barrels. He then heard the guard reach the ramparts, panting and cursing.

Pain-free thanks to Andrada's medicine, Dapyx kneeled in the dark. He heard the heavy steps of his enemy approaching. He waited with his blade ready.

The Book of Andrada

Andrada's convoy reached Fort Norland around midnight. Dapyx had the east gates open, and the chariot entered the fortress and pulled up under an awning.

Andrada listened to King Cothelas's heart. It was still beating. She touched his burning brow and felt the short hair growing since his last head shave. She took a waterskin and poured a few drops between his parted lips.

"Look for glass tubes," she told Dapyx. "Merchants stop here all the time. We might get lucky."

He nodded and disappeared into the crowd, looking happy to be back in Andrada's good graces. As much as she wanted to, she couldn't push him away again. The crystal bell had gone to him. He had brought King Cothelas to Zalmodava and captured Fort Norland. He was part of El's plan.

"Are we home?" the king whispered, awake at last.

"Not yet. We're at Fort Norland. The horses must rest for the night."

He closed his eyes. "Give me..." She put her ear close to his face. "My handful of dirt." A warrior's last request.

She found the pouch on his belt and untied it. She loosened the strings, scooped out the lump of Kertan dirt, and pressed it into his hand. He rested his fist over his heart and closed his eyes.

"Don't go to sleep," she said. "Tell me, please, where is my crystal bell?"

"Not yours..." He turned to her and whispered, "Pegrina's...wedding bell..."

Andrada remembered the crystal bell Citera had rung at the end of the royal wedding. King Cothelas seemed to believe the crystal bell from the Old Temple of Sehul was a simple wedding trinket.

"Do you know what happens when it rings?" she said.

"When it rang in the old temple...you failed me."

His words stung, but she brushed them aside. The king didn't seem to know that El answered prayers whispered to the bell. For the first time, she felt sorry for him. He didn't know what an astonishing power he had once held in his hand. King Cothelas of Kerta—Cothelas the Bald—was just a man, as ignorant as any.

His eyes closed, but Andrada shook his shoulder. "Where's the bell now?"

He grimaced. "Back in Pegrina's shrine...where it belongs..."

Of course, the old temple served as a shrine to Queen Pegrina—Andrada could see that now.

"No glass tubes in the guards' quarters," Dapyx said, skidding back under the awning.

People bustled around them with torches, unloading and settling down for the night, while the fort gates grated and creaked shut. A thud told Andrada the fortress was now bolted. The pursuers the scouts had seen earlier were locked out.

"Where else should I look?" Dapyx said, panting.

"Nowhere," Andrada said.

What happened to King Cothelas from now on was El's will.

Chapter Twenty-Eight

The Book of Andrada

Andrada had hoped El would keep King Cothelas alive, but he died of blood poisoning from his arrow wound a day away from Sehuldava, twelve days after the Battle of Zalmodava.

"No news of Syrmos?" Andrada said, following Avezinas around the Hall of the Dead in the New Temple of Sehul.

Her tutor shook his head. He had grown old over the past two years. His beard was all white, his eyes deeper under thick eyebrows. There were no windows in the Hall of the Dead, only burning torches, glowing braziers, and candle stands around empty stone tables. All but one of the dead had been left on the battlefield or burned along the way home. At the other end of the hall, Avezinas's aides prepared the king's body for tomorrow's funeral pyre.

"Is it true?" Andrada said. She waited for a temple servant to walk by with a jar of black salt. "King Cothelas never adopted Syrmos?"

"The adoption was a useful rumor," Avezinas said. "Syrmos was well-loved among the tribes. And the king needed to make peace with the Bear-Hunters after Gerulas's death at the Iron Gates. Yes, Syrmos was the chosen heir, but your son by Nicetas was to surpass him as King Cothelas's true heir."

Andrada's stomach turned to ice. *You lost Cothelas's heir?* Nicetas had asked her that at the Council of Six. The two kings had made an agreement about her womb without her knowledge. She felt humiliated. But they were both dead, and she was alive, with El by her side.

"Then little Pegrinus arrived," Avezinas said. "I had never seen the king so happy as when he was around that little boy. As if he'd found Queen Pegrina again."

King Cothelas had never been happy around his own daughter.

"Where is the boy now?" Andrada said.

Avezinas sighed. "When Prince Dapyx arrived, he told us it was all a lie. The king was angrier than when you failed the King's Challenge."

Andrada didn't need reminding, but Avezinas went on, sounding bitter. "The king had been so proud of you that midsummer day. A smart, strong heir he'd groomed himself..."

A familiar shiver ran down Andrada's spine, as when she had held up her palm for the rod. His words burned, but she wasn't his student anymore. She remembered the bundle King Cothelas had thrown at Nicetas on the battlefield but couldn't bring herself to believe it.

"What happened to the baby?" she asked again.

Avezinas looked away for a moment. "So many things are lost in a war...And some are found. Remember the crystal bell? The word ONE was your parents' promise to each other on their wedding day. To be together forever, in life and in death. The bell was returned to us, and I'll ring it at the king's funeral. Queen Pegrina will hear it in the Underworld and prepare for their long-awaited reunion."

Andrada didn't care about her parents now. El had been guiding her steps since saving her life, but she had to forge her path forward.

"The country still needs an heir, Avezinas. I can be that heir—if you support me."

"Not after you failed the King's Challenge." His voice was shrill. "Be grateful you're still alive. You should be dead."

"But I'm not. I've been on a battlefield and slain Nicetas in single combat. I was the queen of Valdavia, and I can be the queen of Kerta—if you help me."

"The chieftains won't have you. They'll demand a new King's Challenge."

"So be it then." Andrada reminded herself she didn't need his help, now that she had her faith in El. "I want to be alone with the king."

She left Avezinas behind and approached the stone table at the other end of the hall. The temple servants withdrew into the shadows.

King Cothelas rested with his arms folded on his chest, dressed in a black woolen tunic, a linen shirt, and woolen trousers. His boots were tied together with rope. His sica was ritually bent and set aside. His head and cheek were shaved clean, marked by a few bloodless cuts from the barber's blade. Black salt was smeared on his forehead. Up close, he smelled of death. Andrada looked at his torchlit face: the tall forehead, the deep-set eyes, the strong chin. She might see that face again on old coins.

She touched his shoulder to remember how his presence in this world had felt, and her fingers found a split seam in his tunic. She called for thread and needle, and a needle threaded with gray wool was put in her hand. She bent over King Cothelas's body and pinched the split seam. The needle went into the thick cloth, and the thread made a loop.

Fire hissed and crackled around them as she sewed his tunic. She added stitch after stitch, thinking of the king's glance she had longed for as a child, then his embrace she had never received. She had tried so hard to be this man's daughter, but he had always wanted a son. She knotted the thread and snapped it, then straightened his tunic. When he walked in front of his beloved Queen Pegrina in the Underworld, he'd look like a king.

Staring at the fallen king, Andrada whispered a prayer to her true father. "God El, make me as tough as the toughest Roman emperor. Show me how to defeat the Steppewynders who've taken Valdavia from me. Make me the queen of these three Dhawosian kingdoms, and I'll turn my people into Your faithful worshippers."

And just like that, she knew what she had to do. Her heart raced. El had just revealed His plan to her. She would be queen over the free Dhawosian realms. And for the first time, He had answered her prayer without the crystal bell. Words failed her, but she didn't need words for the sense of oneness she felt with El.

She found Avezinas, who was preparing the funeral bowls, and told him, "After you ring the crystal bell tomorrow, return it to the shrine together with the king's ash urn."

El had used the bell to make Andrada perceive Him, but it had outlived its usefulness.

"The burned portrait from the throne chamber?" she added. "Move it to the rightmost alcove in the temple, with the rest."

Avezinas seemed taken aback by her orders but nodded.

Andrada stopped at the door with one last request. "Once you're done, seal the old temple so that no one can disturb my parents' tomb."

She walked out of the Hall of the Dead into fresh air and blue sky. She felt El's presence everywhere around her, in the shimmer of snowy peaks, in the song of the birds, in the bustle of the square.

At the bottom of the stairs, the nurse was waiting, her arms extended for a hug. Andrada ran down and locked into that embrace of her childhood, her head resting on the nurse's bony shoulder. She breathed in the familiar scent of sage. Rough fingers caressed the back of her neck, under the line of her short hair.

"My child," the nurse whispered. "My child…"

It was good to be called *child* again.

"Is Dokina here too?" the nurse said.

"She's still in Zalmodava." Andrada let go. "But we'll see her again soon."

The nurse let out a sob. "I'm sorry, child, I don't know who I'm weeping for: the king or that poor little babe. I took care of him, and now he's gone."

"Your son is…?"

"Not my son, praise the Three Divines. Little Pegrinus. The one the king thought was yours. He took the child with him when he went to war."

Andrada was now certain the bundle on the battlefield had been Pegrinus.

"I'm sorry, I don't know of any child," she whispered, wiping a tear off her nurse's scarred cheek.

After the funeral pyre, Andrada and Dapyx went to the great hall. Warm sunlight poured through the open windows of the throne chamber. King Cothelas's gilded chair was empty, and chieftains, noblemen, and priests debated who should sit in it next.

"Wait here," Andrada told Dapyx, then walked up the steps to the throne.

From up high, she surveyed the loud gathering. The wall across from her was bare. Avezinas had been fast.

Comosicus, with fresh scabs on his face, stopped talking and looked up. So did Wodan. More men turned to the throne, their faces set in tense expectation.

"My lords," Andrada said, "I'm here to claim the throne of Kerta."

"Queen Andrada of Valdavia," Wodan said, "we only recognize as our ruler a man who has shown valiance in battle, or a man of great wisdom, or a man the gods have chosen for us. You are none of those things."

Andrada smiled. "I'm all of them and much more."

"You're a woman," somebody shouted from the crowd. "Last time a woman ruled Dhawosia, garden turned into wasteland."

"Who spoke?" she said, her voice louder than all.

Old Rubobostes pushed through, climbed the first two steps, then turned his back to Andrada.

He shouted over the others, "The ancestral spirits of my tribe will never allow this woman on the throne of Kerta."

The men grumbled, most of them in approval.

"My lords," Dapyx said, though Andrada didn't need his help. "Those of you who've been at the Battle of Zalmodava have seen Queen Andrada fight better than a man. She...she killed a king in single combat—"

"That battle ended in retreat," Rubobostes said.

"A battle you did not see, my lord," Andrada said.

"That's true," someone said.

"Throw her out," another yelled.

People began arguing all at once, their voices rising and overlapping and echoing. Andrada saw those men for what they were: a flock of frightened sheep in need of a shepherd. She began to laugh, a loud cackle that lasted until it was the only sound in the chamber.

"The woman has scared you, my lords?" She touched the armrest of the throne. "Answer me this: Who's your real enemy?"

Wodan stepped forward. "Scorilus of Steppewynd."

"That's right," Andrada said. "Scorilus of Steppewynd—and now of Valdavia. Do you have a plan to defeat him?"

Wodan stared at her, waiting. The rest kept quiet.

"Well, I do," she said. "I'll take a small group of trusted guards on a moon-long journey north. While I'm gone, Chief Wodan will be in charge. He'll raise another army. Because, when I'm back, we'll cross the Norland Pass, march into Zalmodava, and conquer Valdavia and Steppewynd."

"I'm missing something here," Wodan said. "We have Fort Norland, yes, but Scorilus has an army camped in the Ozana Valley."

"A new King's Challenge, my lords," Andrada said. "If I destroy King Scorilus's army, will I have your allegiance, as King Cothelas had it before me?"

Wodan scratched his beard. Comosicus shook his head.

It was now or never. "All of you men standing before me, listen carefully," Andrada said. "King Scorilus is the enemy of my people, and I'll bring the gods' vengeance upon him. And when I sit upon this throne, I'll be the judge of your courage or cowardice at this decisive moment." The chamber was so quiet, she could hear the fire crackling in the hearth. "If I deliver upon my word, you'll know I have heaven and earth on my side. And you, Chief Wodan, will pledge your allegiance to me."

At last, Wodan said, "I will. If you deliver."

Comosicus nodded. Around him, others nodded too. Rubobostes looked around, shook his head, and retreated into the crowd.

Dapyx stared at Andrada and mouthed, "You're letting him go?"

She gave him the smallest nod, though she didn't expect him to grasp how a wise leader chose her battles.

The Book of Scorilus

Scorilus received a letter from Rescuporis a moon after both his sons had left the White Fortress and gone west with a mercenary army. In the letter, his stepson wrote of a magnificent victory in which the Kertans and the Valdavians counted ten dead or wounded for each Steppewynder or Tauri lost—a feat never heard of in known history. Rescuporis had waited for the two armies to destroy each other, then stepped in with his soldiers and vanquished them. He was now the caretaker of Valdavia. *Behold, Father, Napat-Dehnu's promised land.*

Rescuporis regretted that King Cothelas had escaped to Kerta through the Norland Pass. He also wrote of Moskon, shot through the eye with a barbed Valdavian arrow and given the funeral of a Steppewynder hero. *I lay this victory at your feet, Father, as your faithful heir.*

Heartbroken, Scorilus arrived with Meda and her baby in Zalmodava fourteen days later, and Rescuporis welcomed them to a deserted fortress. The locals had fled, with no one left to tell what had happened to Oroles. Rescuporis had already ordered the dead buried and the battlefield combed for armor and weapons. They hadn't discovered Oroles's body among the corpses. But they had found King Nicetas, armored in silver, and had given him a royal funeral, to appease the Valdavian folk.

Scorilus sent Rescuporis and a group of chieftains on a journey around the country to establish the Steppewynder occupation of Valdavia. The demands of governing a conquered country kept his mind off Moskon—little Moskon with a frown on his thin face, young Moskon trying to hide his sickly nature, brave Moskon going into battle.

Steppewynder soldiers moved into tents pitched outside Valdavian towns, and some took over houses and turned them into command centers. In every marketplace, a Steppewynder official who knew how to read and write Greek script met with local priests and landowners to learn and record their needs.

The population was restless under their new conquerors, as the country had long profited off cheap Steppewynder labor. But some locals hoped the new rulers would improve their lot in life. Scorilus would make it happen. He'd join the two countries through a network of paved roads, and he'd widen the one through the Danubius Delta to Roman Moesia, to strengthen the trade ties with the empire.

Day after day, he sat on Nicetas's throne and listened to complaints from defeated chieftains and embittered priests. He extracted as much as he could from them without taking all their lands and turning them into a fired-up army of outlaws. Yet outlaw settlements were bound to pop up all over Valdavia. The families of dead chieftains whose lands Rescuporis had taken would soon build alliances.

The work ahead was Sisyphean, and not only in Valdavia. In the west, Kerta was biding its time behind the Carpates Mountains. This was the moment to conquer it and take over its mines, full of gold and iron and lead, but the mountain passes were blocked, and the Steppewynder army couldn't sail up the Danubius through the Iron Gates even if it tried. Besieging Kerta would take years. Meanwhile, Cothelas the Bald would get help from the Germanic tribes and even from Roma. Had he rescued his daughter, or was she still in Valdavia? Was Prince Dapyx with them? Where was High Priest Zyraxes, the oldest brother of the Carpi tribe? And where was Oroles?

Scorilus often remembered Lucretius's wise words: *Better be a subject and at peace than hold the throne and rule the world.*

Chapter Twenty-Nine

The Book of Dapyx

They had been journeying north to find the cave of the great aurochs for half a moon. Dapyx didn't know why, but he trusted that Andrada's plan to defeat the Steppewynders would make sense when she chose to reveal it. The only clue he had about it was that Apollonius of Damascus, the architect, was traveling with them.

That afternoon, Dapyx reached the snow-covered plateau first and waited there for Andrada and the rest. The border between Kerta and Valdavia was an invisible line over the mountaintop. The few pine trees in the clearing threw no shadow under the gray skies. From the open eastern edge of the plateau, Dapyx surveyed the lower mountain ridges, the hilltops covered in greening forests, and the streams gathering speed toward Valdavia. It was the same view out west: ridges, hills, forests, streams, as if Kerta and Valdavia were mirror images of each other.

"We should rest here for the day," Ismarus the guide said, "and plot our descent."

He was maybe five years older than Dapyx but talked with the poise of a graybeard, his voice deep and confident, his eyes dark and inscrutable. He had a slender frame but carried his bearskin cloak like a feather mantle.

Andrada seemed to trust him more than she had trusted Dapyx on their trips to the Ozana Valley. Every time she asked for Ismarus's opinion, Dapyx felt a prick of jealousy, even though Andrada never smiled at the guide. She had abandoned the mourning dress and wore trousers instead, but she still didn't smile. Dapyx needed to see her laugh again before he could open his heart to her. *Leave the dead with the dead,* he'd tell her one of these days.

Andrada dismounted and called for Ismarus. They headed to the eastern edge, while the servants began setting up camp on the frozen ground under a lone pine tree.

Clenching his teeth, Dapyx followed Andrada, close enough to eavesdrop. Being around her kept him from thinking about the nightmares tormenting him since the Battle of Zalmodava.

"Which one is the Ozana though?" she said. "They all look the same from up here."

Streams fed with melting snow headed downhill into Valdavia. Creeks and rivulets soon disappeared into the forests on the eastern slopes of the Carpates Mountains.

Ismarus narrowed his eyes toward the shaded chasm at their feet and pointed. "The one running closest to the beacon."

Dapyx came to Andrada's side and strained to see what Ismarus pointed to: the stone structure of a Valdavian beacon sticking out from snow and rock.

"The watcher mustn't see us," Andrada said.

"Don't worry, he won't," Dapyx said, emboldened by a sudden rush of bravery.

He hadn't felt that way since the battle, before the nightmares. Without waiting for Andrada's word, he bent down, his right hand on the ground, his foot sliding down the slope. He'd show her who she could truly count on.

"Dapyx," she called after him, "what are you doing?"

The descent was abrupt, and Dapyx felt the jolts in his mended ribs. The bearskin soles of his boots slipped on ice-covered rocks. He braced himself as he landed a few feet down. He picked himself up and continued his descent, using roots for footholds and handholds.

He slid down, small rocks tumbling around him with the sound of hailstorm, when he spotted a footpath below. He jumped toward it, his cloak flapping on his back. The ground hit him hard, his ankles and wrists taking the brunt of it. His ribs hurt. He glanced back at the heights he had come down from. He hoped Andrada had watched him, her hand over her mouth, but the mountain wall was too tall for him to see the ridge or her.

The skin on his knees burned, but he kept going, his eyes set on the beacon. Soon he arrived at the stone tower. With one hand on the hilt of his dagger, he ducked under the low archway. He climbed the first flight of stairs to a narrow landing, then up again. Just enough daylight filtering through the arrow slits in the walls helped him see the stone stairs ahead. He crept up the icy steps and emerged on the south side of a platform covered in pristine snow.

The wind howled. No sign of a watchman here or in the clearing around the tower. Kertan scouts must have killed him when they broke the beacon chain that would have alerted Nicetas of King Cothelas's invasion. A full moon after his victory, King Scorilus of Steppewynd and Valdavia hadn't yet replaced this watchman.

As Dapyx climbed down the stairs, ready to return to Andrada with the news that all was clear, a shadow covered the watchtower's entrance. He peered outside and froze.

Through the beacon's arch, the great aurochs stood a few paces away in the snow. The beast was enormous, bigger than the biggest bull, with shaggy black fur around his shoulders. His horns were larger than sicas. His brown eyes were human, like those of a prince enchanted by a goddess. Dapyx held his breath, trying to clamp down the chatter of his teeth. That beast would shred him to pieces.

The aurochs snorted, stomping his hoof in the snow, then turned and vanished from sight. After a long moment, Dapyx followed him outside. Where the beast had stood, the crushed snow was reddish like there was blood on it.

Dapyx scooped some of the dark snow in his warm hand, but it didn't melt. He broke the morsel in half, and it opened to a section of crushed reddish-brown gills. The great aurochs had stepped on bleeding helmets, a kind of mushroom Dapyx had read about in Una's notes on red pigments. He could now track the great aurochs for Andrada—an easier job than when he had rescued her in the foothills of the Carpates

Mountains. She would be so impressed when he took her to the cave she wanted.

Dapyx heard Ismarus's voice nearby. "The great aurochs was here."

The guide and Andrada approached the beacon.

"He left smears of bleeding helmets in his wake," the guide said.

Bitter tears appeared in Dapyx's eyes. The great aurochs was his discovery, not Ismarus's.

"How long until sundown?" Andrada said.

"Not long," Ismarus said. "We'll track him tomorrow."

Andrada's shoulders slumped. She probably wanted to find the cave tonight.

"I found the aurochs first," Dapyx said, to no one's reply.

Andrada called to her servants, "Move my camp here but don't build a big fire. The other beacons might see it. Dapyx, don't you dare run away like that ever again."

Dapyx smiled to himself. At least she had been worried about him.

The Book of Andrada

In the morning, Andrada thanked El again for sending her the aurochs to point the path to the cave Una had told her about. She still needed Ismarus to follow the trail but was certain they'd find it soon. Full of vigor, she strode ahead of everyone else, probing the path with a pikestaff.

The sun was on their side of the Carpates Mountains, shimmering over treetops and speckling the ground. Ismarus lit a lantern, for good measure. The trail of the aurochs descended, sometimes following a mild slope, sometimes tumbling down through a thicket of pine trees, until they saw oak trees growing side by side with the evergreen.

"Here is the Ozana again," Ismarus said around midmorning.

He measured the surroundings in silence. There was no more snow on the ground. Oaks had replaced pine trees. It seemed like a different forest than the one at sunrise.

Ismarus kneeled at the edge of the water and looked at a large print stamped on the soft mud.

"This way," he said, picking up a tuft of black fur hanging from the thorns of a blackberry vine.

"It could be any aurochs," Dapyx grumbled.

Just ahead, a ravine of beech trees opened. Ismarus climbed down first, and Andrada followed him. Clusters of purple and pink-brown mushrooms grew from dead leaves and branches all around the narrow clearing on the doorstep of a cave.

Andrada slid down, swinging around her pikestaff for the last leap of her descent. She knew this was the cave of the aurochs but relished the proof. She kneeled by a log and plucked one of the bleeding helmets. The bell-shaped cap was plum-colored, growing paler toward its wavy edge. Andrada snapped the thin stem between her forefinger and thumb. It was hollow and brittle, but the broken flesh oozed tiny red drops. Just like Una had once described.

From the other side of the cave mount, she heard a stream gushing downhill.

"The Ozana?" Andrada said.

"Yes, my queen," Ismarus said.

"Bring two torches," he called to his people.

The servants lit and carried torches, and one of them followed Ismarus and his lantern inside the cave. Andrada and Dapyx entered next, trailed by another servant with a torch. Apollonius and the rest remained outside to keep watch.

Somewhere inside was the vein of Ea's poison: one last gift from Una.

Andrada's eyes discerned nothing but the torchlight flapping on a draft that blew from the pitch-dark cave ahead. The ceiling was low, and the ground under her feet was slippery and uneven. It reminded her of the corridor in the Old Temple of Sehul, which reassured her. That was where she had first experienced El's power.

She scraped the closest wall with her dagger, looking for the poison vein, but only found solid rock.

They went through a passage, keeping close and squeezing between boulders. The surrounding walls were also hard stone.

They passed through a narrow archway, then Ismarus halted, and everyone else did too.

He was on the doorstep of another chamber. He raised his lantern, ducked in, and disappeared from Andrada's sight. In the opening he left behind, a faint glow dimmed further, then brightened again.

Ismarus reappeared and motioned for them to follow.

The chamber they emerged into had a high ceiling, and the torchlight didn't reach the far wall. Ismarus probed the ground with his pikestaff for hidden holes. He started at the right of the entrance, keeping a hand on the wall, and walked around until he arrived back.

"Is this the end of the cave?" Andrada's disappointed voice echoed from the walls.

"Looks like it." Ismarus advanced to the center of the chamber. "The draft is stronger here. Torch!"

His servant gave him the flame. Ismarus held it high while walking in a circle. The flame burned upright no matter which direction he turned. Ismarus looked up, wiping something off his face. He smelled his hand.

"Bat piss," he called to Andrada just before the chamber filled with clatter. "Watch out!"

The ceiling was falling. A swarming army of bats exploded into an earsplitting commotion.

Andrada cried out and covered her face. Dapyx ran to her, but a large shrieking shadow hit him over the head. Andrada grabbed his arm and dragged him close to the wall.

They all kneeled and huddled inside a low niche. Their torches fought to stay lit in the gale, but Ismarus held out his lantern so they could all stare at the flying beasts. Large bats with wings spanning an arm's length, young bats that flapped twice as fast—they all flew around, chittering, hanging for a moment on the walls before diving again, soaring. Some clashed and fell on the ground, flailing and squirming.

"They're more afraid of us than we're of them," Ismarus shouted.

Somehow, the bats' numbers thinned, and the din died down. Rumpled moss and fern leaves lay on the ground at the end of a new shaft of sunlight. There was a hole in the ceiling now. In their panic, the bats must have broken through the outside foliage covering it.

Ismarus squeezed out of the niche first. Andrada ran into the sun, glad to feel its warmth on her face.

Dapyx kicked an injured bat out of his way, raising a puff of dust. Its screech made the air vibrate with sound now that the rest of the bats were gone.

Andrada kneeled and scraped the dirt under their feet with her dagger. It was white. She brought the blade close to her nose. It smelled of nothing.

Dapyx grabbed her wrist. "Don't touch it." His trembling voice echoed around them.

Andrada frowned. How could he know of Ea's poison?

"What is this white dust, my queen?" Ismarus said.

"Can you tell me how deep this vein runs?"

Ismarus scratched the dirt with his knife. "More than a foot deep."

"Let's see this cave from above," Andrada said.

They returned to the clearing full of bleeding helmets, the sun now shining above the mountain crests.

"Apollonius," she called the architect, motioning to the abrupt slope above.

He hurried to her side. Andrada grabbed roots and branches to pull herself up. Ismarus helped her and Dapyx at times, until they all reached a wide plateau covered in beech trees, where bats hung from the top branches. Water gurgled close by.

They searched the ground and found the fresh hole in the cave's ceiling.

"How long will it take us to build an aqueduct that brings the Ozana spring through this hole into the cave?" Andrada asked Apollonius.

"For a temporary structure," Apollonius said, "just a few days. We'll use wood instead of stone."

"And to return the stream to its riverbed downhill?" Andrada said.

"No more than a day."

"What are you trying to do?" Dapyx said with a terrified look on his face.

"Altering the essence of the river spirit will anger the gods," Ismarus said. "They'll send Fever, Cough, Jaundice, and other spirits to punish us."

"Don't worry, Ismarus—they won't."

But El would be pleased because Andrada had fulfilled His plan. Some of Scorilus's soldiers would be in the fortress of Zalmodava, but most of them would still be camping on the banks of the Ozana River in the valley. Ea's poison would take days to make them sick, but then thousands would die.

Back when she had unknowingly been with child, Andrada had recoiled at the thought of hurting another human being, even one as dreadful as Brasus. But now that she had seen war and killed Nicetas in battle, she knew she was strong enough to carry out El's plan for victory.

The Ozana Valley would again be covered in rotting corpses, as it had been after the Battle of Zalmodava, corpses that had once been young boys like Dapyx, wise graybeards like Avezinas, peace-loving men like Oroles. Sons, fathers, husbands—all speaking the same Dhawosian as Andrada.

Her throat tightened. No, she couldn't think of them that way. She remembered Una's story, how Ea's poison had been meant for rats unleashed upon the fields to eat the seeds. Yes, it was better to think of Scorilus's army that way.

Andrada took a deep breath. Zalmodava itself would be safe from the poison, for it had the sky oak's aquifer and her new waterwheel. As for Sanapa, Erebon, and the other villages downstream, King Cothelas had already burned them to the ground. There were no people left there. The heart of Sanapa, the heart of Erebon—gone. Poison strength would diminish as the Ozana gathered tributaries, so people farther downstream would get sick but wouldn't die.

And if they died?

Andrada pushed that thought away. The last time she had allowed doubt to creep in, she had asked Ea to save Una's life instead of asking El—a terrible mistake.

And if they died?

Andrada had pledged allegiance to El, as His loving daughter. She couldn't waver now. She couldn't say no to a loving father who had saved her life. This was El's plan for peace in Dhawosia. The way to unite these warring realms against the looming Roman menace.

Andrada felt her heart turn to stone.

And if those innocent souls died...it would be El's will.

Chapter Thirty

The Book of Scorilus

Lucretius had once warned that small atoms could ruin the most righteous dreams. An unknown plague had laid ruin to Scorilus's plans for the prosperity of Valdavia and Steppewynd together. The beginning of summer brought with it the stench of corpses from the Ozana Valley and the sharp smell of lime poured into mass graves. Now there was news of the Kertan army gathering at Fort Norland, and Scorilus had no soldiers to defend Zalmodava against the attack. Rescuporis's last letter had arrived a moon ago from Tomis in Roman Moesia, where he had gone to discuss a new alliance with the empire's Legate Magius.

Scorilus had to convince his daughter to let him take her and little Thiaper back to the White Fortress.

"I'm not leaving without my husband," Meda told him as soon as he entered the queen's chamber, where she stayed. She wore a magnificent gold necklace with a crystal pendant—a piece of jewelry she had found in the temple in a box shaped like a horse. She looked regal and unyielding.

"You won't find Oroles if you're dead. And he'll be looking for you at the White Fortress. Please, my little redhead, come with me. Think of your child." He motioned to the crib by the open window.

"Our lives aren't in danger, Father." She went to check on her son.

Scorilus looked over her shoulder, his heart melting with love and sadness. Thiaper was swaddled in light linen and babbling to himself.

"Cothelas won't hurt me, a mother with a child. I'll ask to be his guest while I wait for Oroles here." She pointed at the door, the snake bracelet gleaming on her forearm. "But you must go, Father. Steppewynd still needs its king."

Meda was probably right, but that hardly mattered. Scorilus left her chamber, looking for a guard or two to give him a hand to restrain her. He'd have to take her against her will.

The hallway outside and the entire wing were deserted. Since the news about the Kertan army, his people had been filing out of the fortress and making their way east. Scorilus turned a corner, then another.

"King Scorilus, praise the gods!" said a deep voice in a Valdavian accent.

Scorilus strained to make out the features of the man walking toward him, but the light was dim without torches. The man carried a stuffed bag across his chest and looked strong and healthy.

"Cartographer? What are you doing here? You're not afraid of the plague?"

"There's something strange about this illness," the Cartographer said, bowing. "It should've reached the fortress by now, but it didn't. It stayed in the valley."

"Have you seen anything like it before?"

The Cartographer nodded. "A young woman died here at the end of winter." His voice caught. "But she didn't die of plague; she died of poison."

"Poison? Are you saying the entire valley has been poisoned? How?"

"I don't know, but I've been drinking wine and eating last year's nuts and grain, and I'm not sick."

Scorilus sighed. "I'll let Cothelas the Bald sort it out. When he arrives, he'll find a valley full of mass graves and dead trees."

"King Cothelas died soon after the Battle of Zalmodava. It's his daughter who's leading the army."

While the news was surprising, it didn't make much difference to Scorilus.

"There's a way to defeat Queen Andrada," the Cartographer said.

"Too late for that...Most of my army is dead. The rest have fled."

"You can raise another army, King Scorilus," the Cartographer said. "Here, take these." He pulled a wooden tube from his satchel. "Use them to make war on the Kertans."

"What are these?" Scorilus said.

"My maps. They show more than just little-known passes over the mountains. They show watering holes, paths through thick forests, and where rivers are shallow and can be pushed from their beds."

He held the tube but did not release it when Scorilus reached out and grasped it.

"Will you make war on Queen Andrada and kill her?"

The Cartographer cared more about killing the Valdavian queen than about his precious maps. Scorilus didn't have time for that intrigue. He needed to take Meda and Thiaper to safety. He let go of the tube, but the Cartographer pushed it back at him.

"She took something from me, and I need justice," he said with tears in his eyes. "Last year, when I returned Princess Meda safe to the White Fortress, I said I'd ask for a favor of King Scorilus when the time comes. Now is that time. Will you grant it? I can't surrender my life's work for anything less than a king's word."

Scorilus hated being dragged into something he didn't understand. "If your maps show me the way, I'll follow it. That's my promise."

The Cartographer let go of the tube and left without another word.

Scorilus hurried back to Meda's chamber. Those maps might give her hope of finding Oroles by other means, and she might agree to leave here. She wasn't around though, and the baby was not in his crib. Scorilus would rather not peer past the wooden screen to where Meda's bed was. She might be changing the baby or, judging by the silence, nursing him to sleep.

He opened the wooden tube, pulled the maps from their linen wrap, and spread them on the table. The parchment was cracked here and there, but some of the blurry ink marks looked fresh. He couldn't read the writing—too small—but Meda could.

He thought he heard hoofbeats down the hallway. A rider in the Valdavian king's house?

"Stay there, Meda, don't come out," he whispered.

He pulled out Phradmon's dagger and sidled by the open door, waiting. He glanced back, hoping Meda would listen and stay hidden.

The rider's pace was steady, as if inspecting the house, one door at a time. Scorilus raised his blade. Meda and her child were in danger. In his hand, the hilt of Phradmon's dagger was slippery with cold sweat.

The low muzzle of a bay foal appeared in the doorway, then the white blaze down its nose, then the large brown eyes. There was no rider. Scorilus peered outside, around the foal's tail. The hallway was empty. The foal backed out, and the sound of hoofbeats restarted.

Relieved, Scorilus returned to the table, set down the dagger, and wiped his clammy hands on his trousers.

"Meda? Are you there?"

No answer. His stomach turned cold. He went around the screen. No one was there. He groaned. She knew he wouldn't leave without her, so she had run away. Despite his anger, he felt proud of his strong-willed daughter.

He reached out to roll up the maps, and his hand froze over the dagger. In the sunlight, through the hilt's polished crystal, the letters on the map were bigger, large enough for him to read with his bad eyes.

The atoms of light Lucretius had once talked about, the crystal spread them out somehow, allowing Scorilus to see them better. He picked up the dagger by the blade and moved its hilt over the map. The carving of the two-headed snake got in the way, but still, Scorilus could see red dotted lines for borders between chiefdoms. Green lines ending in arrows for trade routes. Blue lines over the waves of the Black Sea for currents. His brother Eptalas had sailed by Heusos's eyes at night and by headlands and mountaintops by day. Had he known of these currents, he might have still been alive.

Scorilus was shaken. For an entire year, he'd had the means to see better, right there, in his hand. He took out the letter he had been carrying with him since Moskon had left with Rescuporis. Meda had read it to him a few times. He unrolled the small piece of parchment with trembling hands and held the crystal hilt over the Greek script.

...vow to be brave...i'm not an invalid...better die on a battlefield than in a sickbed...i'll be with my brother, who'll protect me...make you proud, father...

He couldn't read anymore for the tears in his eyes and the knot in his throat. He wiped his face and beard, then pulled another sheet from the Cartographer's pile—a map of the land of the Sarmatians. Across the Borysthenes River, a chiefdom was marked with the name KHUDDAN. Next to it, another word: PHRADMON. His heart beat faster. That place was far from the Old Salt Road, where the dagger and the severed hand had been pinned to the well for travelers to see. The Cartographer had learned something about Phradmon. Scorilus thought to run after him and ask, but he could be anywhere by now.

He made up his mind to travel east and find his brother. He'd start by searching for a Tauri tribe with good steel blades—Rescuporis's old allies—and ask them for shelter and guidance. There was no future for him in Dhawosia, except as a prisoner of war or a diminished vassal king, but with maps and a magnifying crystal, he could be an explorer now, like Odysseus. After years of being either a failed warrior or a failed king, and with a lot of luck from Lucretius's atoms, Scorilus might one day triumph in his quest to return Phradmon, Steppewynd's rightful king, to his people.

The Book of Andrada

The gates of Zalmodava stood open, a white flag flying over the Six-Sided Tower. Andrada sat in the saddle of a brown horse at the foot of the Twelve-Pier Bridge with Wodan at her side and her army behind her, waiting for the scout.

"Chief Wodan, you're in charge of my fortress. When you find High Priest Zyraxes, remember he's still Dapyx's brother and mine, and he should be treated with respect."

This high up the hill, the summer wind carried the scent of pine trees and fresh grass, not the sharp odor of lime pits and the stench of rotting corpses from the valley. It had been El's will, all those deaths. It had all been El's will—not just a cup, but a whole valley full of deadly water. Now it was over, the river back in its bed and the cave of the aurochs guarded by Andrada's soldiers.

The scout galloped back across the bridge. "The fortress is yours, Queen Andrada. Princess Meda is waiting for you."

The very fortress where Andrada had almost died was now in her hands.

"Are there any dead bodies in the fortress?" she said.

"None, my queen."

Andrada nudged her horse up the bridge. In the distance, a woman in colorful robes walked through the gates, followed by a servant holding a baby in her arms. When they were close enough, Andrada dismounted, sore from the saddle and stiff inside her armor.

"Welcome home, Queen Andrada," Princess Meda said in the harsh accent of the steppes. Everything about her was stunning: her lush red hair falling in thick waves over her shoulders, her round bosom, her dark eyes and full lips. Around her neck hung the necklace that had once belonged to Queen Pegrina. A beautiful bracelet of pure Kertan gold shaped like a snake with heads at both ends looped half a dozen times around her forearm.

"Where is King Scorilus?" Andrada said.

"He returned to the White Fortress a few days ago." Princess Meda cleared her throat as if trying to keep herself from crying.

Andrada looked away from the princess's trembling lips. "And Prince Rescuporis?"

"He left after the battle to establish wardens of peace in Southern Valdavia on behalf of my father."

"Why are you still here?" Andrada said.

A tear rolled down Princess Meda's cheek. "I don't care if I'm your hostage, as long as I find Oroles, my husband."

"You married Emissary Oroles?" Andrada said, surprised by this news.

The princess nodded. A silver-and-crystal band twinkled on her finger when she wiped her eyes.

The other ring, the one around Nicetas's neck...Andrada had been carrying it with her since the Battle of Zalmodava. She scrambled to find it in a pocket on her belt, pulled out the silver chain, and held it out.

"Oroles's ring..." Princess Meda said, her brown eyes wide. "He wouldn't part with it alive. You killed my husband?"

"No, I didn't know what this ring meant until now. Nicetas had it around his neck when he died on the battlefield."

"Then Nicetas killed his blood brother?" Princess Meda covered her face. "I must know. I must be able to tell his son what happened to his father."

She turned to the servant with the baby to hide her sobs. Andrada waited for the princess to collect herself, then gave her the chain.

"I always respected Oroles. For his sake, I'll help you learn the truth, Princess."

"Thank you," Princess Meda whispered.

"And you're not my hostage. You're welcome to stay in Zalmodava as long as you like." She thought of Una. "If you choose to stay, you'd do me a great favor if you were my councilor in all matters regarding Steppewynd."

Princess Meda bowed. "It will be an honor, Queen Andrada." She then unclasped the gold chain with its crystal pendant from her neck and gave it to Andrada. "I think this belongs to you."

Unable to say no to someone so vulnerable and beautiful, Andrada accepted Queen Pegrina's necklace with a quick nod.

On her journey back to Kerta, Andrada was greeted by all as a victorious general. The heart of her country—the Kertan people—welcomed her home.

Dressed as a warrior but without her armor, she entered the throne chamber of Sehuldava, and a path opened before her to the dais. She climbed the stairs, expecting some chieftains to protest when she reached the gilded chair, but no one did. They all waited for her to speak.

"The King's Challenge is over," she said, standing tall. "And I demand your allegiance."

"You have mine, Queen Andrada." Comosicus stepped up to the dais.

Wodan was in Zalmodava with Dapyx, but Comosicus was the army chief's right-hand man. With him on her side, her claim to the throne was secure.

The others voiced their approval, some more eager than others. "Hail Queen Andrada!"

Avezinas brought her King Cothelas's whitewood codex. "This now belongs to the queen of Kerta."

Andrada sat on the throne but didn't feel the joy and pride she had once expected. After staring death in the face and receiving deliverance from El, being queen of Kerta didn't seem as significant. Still, she had to rule her country. She'd start with Petition Day.

She undid the leather strips of the codex with reverence, opened it, and looked through. A map, a tally of taxes, a decree commuting someone's death sentence, a market license, and more. Everything King Cothelas had collected on his chieftains and priests—their debts, their weaknesses, their plans—was now Andrada's. She could start rewarding her allies and punishing her enemies, forgiving debts, negotiating the opening of new markets, and assigning the profits of trade routes. Someone had to command her armies, govern her provinces, and run her grain and water supplies. Granting new honors and new powers—or withholding them—was what a ruler did.

She lifted a few more sheets of parchment, only to find a request from Chief Rubobostes for a new windmill to help turn rock salt into fine powder. Another windmill would secure his place as the main salt merchant in the country, since he already owned the largest mines.

"Is Chief Rubobostes here?" Andrada said.

"Here," the old man answered while others moved from his way.

He didn't seem as confident as the last time she had seen him.

"Are the ancestral spirits of your tribe now allowing a woman to sit on the throne of Kerta, Chief Rubobostes?"

"Y-yes, my queen," he said.

"I'm happy to hear that. Now, your new windmill?" She paused and let him squirm a little. "Denied. And the other one will be torn down. From now on, you'll send your salt and grain to the windmills of your neighboring tribes, to share your prosperity with them."

The man's face turned to an angry grimace, but people around the hall burst into cheers. Andrada hadn't expected that reaction, but she wasn't surprised Rubobostes was hated among the chieftains. She closed King Cothelas's codex and clasped it to her chest like a shield.

In her old childhood chamber, Andrada sat on her bed with the codex. She started taking out documents and laying them beside her. Permits and licenses in one pile, debts in another, and courthouse documents in a third. The water levels of the Danubius River, amounts of salt and gold extracted from the western mines after the Night Attack, and so on.

The last sheet in the codex didn't belong in any pile though. The parchment was yellowed and crumbling and covered in a jumpy hand-writing in Greek script. The words were smudged in places. Dried droplets of water had cleared the writing here and there, pushing the potash ink toward the jagged edges of small empty circles.

It began with *my beloved andrada.*

She couldn't imagine who had written that. She had never been *beloved* to King Cothelas. The nurse always called her *child.* Could it have been Avezinas? She skipped the rest of the letter, looking for a signature.

Where a piece of the parchment was now gone, she saw scribbled at the bottom of the page, *your loving mother pegr.*

She didn't know how to feel about her discovery. She went back to the top of the letter.

my beloved andrada

listen with your eyes closed and you'll hear my voice

in the whisper of the wind
in the rumble of the ground
in the crackle of the fire
in the stillness of your breath
you'll know my voice because you heard it before you were born
follow my voice
and you'll know the fresh breeze over the life-giving river
from the dusty gale over the deadly stream
follow my voice
and you'll know the hoofbeats of thirsty deer
from the footfalls of samca's hordes
follow my voice
and you'll know the rustling of turned leaves
from the hissing of molten rock
all you have to do is close your eyes and listen for my voice
it will always be there my child to keep you safe
your loving mother pegr

Andrada read those rambling words again. Queen Pegrina had not kept her promise to watch over her daughter from the Underworld and guide her with her voice. But now that Andrada had carried a life in her own womb—even for the shortest time—she understood the queen's promise. No one knew what the Underworld held in store for mortals, but for a moment, on her dying bed, Queen Pegrina had imagined she'd be able to reach out for her daughter and keep her safe. Andrada was that daughter. Queen Pegrina was her mother.

Andrada touched the discolored spots on the letter. She didn't need anyone to tell her that those were marks of tears.

"My mother," she whispered, caressing the parchment in her lap.

The anger she had felt for Queen Pegrina all these years vanished like fog under the summer sun.

"Mother..."

She'd had a mother once. Her mother had asked King Cothelas to let Andrada be like a son to him because that was what a mother would do, of course. Her mother had died loving her.

Andrada's eyes burned without tears. A wave of sorrow overcame her. She had once set fire to her mother's portrait, her mother who had loved her and died after giving birth to her. The knot in Andrada's throat was painful. She squeezed her dry eyes shut and gasped for air through silent sobs.

She was sad for her mother, who couldn't see her daughter grow up and sit on the throne today. Heartbroken for wasting years hating the only person in the world who had loved her completely. Glad to have found this love letter from beyond the grave. Remorseful to have destroyed her mother's last earthly image. Other than this piece of old parchment, Andrada had nothing left of her mother. Everything else was sealed in the Old Temple of Sehul.

No, that wasn't true. She searched around the chamber until she found the saddlebag from the trip to Valdavia. She turned it upside down on the floor and shook it. Many things tumbled out, but on top of it all fell the gold chain with a crystal pendant Princess Meda had returned at the gates of Zalmodava.

Andrada clasped it around her neck, the way the nurse had always wanted her to. The weight of the pendant on her chest felt like a mother's gentle embrace.

She picked up the letter and read it again in a whisper. The burning in her eyes faded as if taken away by El's divine touch. A droplet fell on the parchment in her lap.

CHAPTER THIRTY-ONE

The Book of Andrada

Andrada's anointment ceremony as queen of Dhawosia took place in Zalmodava on midsummer day, on her twenty-first birthday. She stood before Ea's statue in the Temple of Concord, the same place where the Council of Six had once given her the death sentence. The granite goddess sat in the same pose as Andrada's mother in the old portrait made by the Cartographer.

Andrada clasped the crystal pendant at her neck the way Dokina used to clasp her mama's pouch. She wished her friend were there to see her become the queen of Kerta, Valdavia, and Steppewynd on that glorious day, but no one knew what had happened to Dokina.

All around the sanctuary, the priests and priestesses of the gods and ancestral spirits of the three realms stood. Behind them, people of all ages had gathered to witness the anointment of their new queen. In the sacred precinct, robed in black and flanked by two temple servants, Citera waited. Andrada would have liked Avezinas to perform the ritual today, but he was back in Sehuldava, as the new governor of Kerta.

Citera raised her arms. "Welcome, Queen Andrada. May the god El bless you on this holy day."

Andrada kneeled in front of three stone drums on which the Queen's Sword, the Queen's Whetstone, and the Helmet of the Kin lay. The sword was a pattern-welded sica, the whetstone was crystal, and the helmet was solid gold decorated with wolves, aurochs, and snakes.

More drums rumbled, making the ground vibrate under Andrada's knees. The same tingling sensation she had once felt in the Old Temple of Sehul spread over her face and hands. Even her heart altered its beating. That was how she knew she was in the presence of El.

"Great mother goddess—" Citera began. "I mean, great sky god El," she added, flustered, "bless our new queen."

It had been an honest mistake, and Andrada nodded for the high priestess to continue.

"God El," Citera said, "let your sacred black salt touch upon our queen's head, descend into her heart, and enter her spirit."

She rubbed Andrada's forehead with an ointment that stung. "And let her, by your grace, be worthy of her ancestors so she may reign with strength and honor."

The two temple servants raised the Helmet of the Kin over Andrada's head and lowered it. The gold felt cool on her warm face.

"Queen Andrada," Citera said, "receive this helmet as the seal of El's blessings upon you and the strength of your ancestors within you. With this helmet upon your head, may you rule justly over your people. May you defeat your enemies. May you unite those whom you rule, and conquer and bind them all to the worship of the god El." She paused. "And to the worship of all the gods of Dhawosia," she added in a whisper.

Citera took the sword and put its steel hilt in Andrada's right hand. She set the whetstone in the crook of Andrada's left arm.

"Queen Andrada, descend through the Underworld to the beginning of time, shed your spirit like an old skin, and return to us as a queen reborn."

A drumbeat like a heart made the whole sanctuary pulse. Andrada felt a new emotion choke her, an unfamiliar one: bliss.

"You may now rise, Queen Andrada of Dhawosia."

Andrada rose, the Helmet of the Kin heavy on her head, forever holding her to a sacred bond with the heart of Dhawosia, her people.

The Book of Scorilus

On midsummer day, Scorilus saw the Tauris Peninsula appear at the bow of his ship in the distance. He hadn't been sailing for long with this crew, but he had already forgotten what it felt like to be king. No Petition Day, no trade routes, no Roman emperor to worry about—just the bright sun above and the shimmering waters around him. He remembered Lucretius, who had spoken of gentle pleasures and peace of mind as the main purposes of human life.

> When the strong winds of storm boil the waters of an angry sea,
> It's pure joy to watch from shore the troubles of a mighty ship.
> It's not the anguish of the sailors that gives you pleasure, no,
> But seeing the ills from which you're being spared,
> The relief of seeing armies locked in battle from a distance,
> While you yourself are free from danger.

On a barrel table before him lay one of the Cartographer's maps. He pulled a small bundle wrapped in hide from a pocket and unwrapped his invention: two pieces of polished crystal in a wooden frame, which he put on his nose and tied with leather straps around his head. Like magic, the markings on the map became clear. There was a Greek harbor ahead by the name of Chersonesus, where he could buy more food and supplies for his journey east.

"Prepare to drop anchor," he called over his shoulder to his captain. "I'll need six men and a loaded boat lowered before sunset."

While they readied the expedition party, Scorilus wrote a few more words in the codex he had started after leaving Steppewynd. For now, he called it *The Book of Scorilus*, though he didn't write it for the Underworld god to read but to record his life as a king, a warrior, and an explorer—a small bout of order in the chaos of Lucretius's atoms.

❖⊪────•••────⊪❖

The Book of Dapyx

In the courtyard of the Queen's House in Zalmodava, Dapyx sat to the right of the throne, sweating in his ceremonial clothes under the midsummer sun. The walkways and balconies around the courtyard were full of people of all stations, from drab-looking peasants to armored warriors and red-cloaked Romans who called their hosts *barbarians* behind their backs. A group of Steppewynder merchants prattled within earshot. There hadn't been a woman ruler in Dhawosia since Queen Seba, and they all knew how that had ended.

Dapyx felt another wave of malaise. The Battle of Zalmodava was hard to forget. He had seen death: men drowning at the Iron Gates, soldiers falling under his falx, his brother Nicetas gagging for air, his horse Dapple lying in the bloody mud. There was no glory in that or in the poison victims' gasping for air in the Ozana Valley. The image of Una lying on a stone table in the Hall of the Dead, her body prepared for her funeral, slipped in among the rest, and Dapyx felt his heart racing again. He took a few deep breaths and wiped his clammy hands on his trousers.

The battle, and everything that had come before it—he should set it down in writing for posterity. Under Andrada, there would be no *Valdavian Chronicle* but a *Dhawosian Chronicle* written by many scribes, which would free Kosingas, the main Valdavian scribe, to write *The Book of Dapyx*. He leaned back in his chair, holding that thought for a while.

It would be wiser not to write down what had happened after the battle though. Andrada's actions had killed all those Steppewynders. She had taken those lives. Enemies—they had all been enemies—and Dapyx was loyal to Andrada, now more than ever. He looked around for something else to think about.

Andrada's empty throne, at his side, was topped with gold finials. Next to it, there was a chair meant for Prince Rescuporis of Steppewynd. Dapyx understood why Andrada wanted Rescuporis there—the three of them signifying the three kingdoms—but he had a strange feeling every time he laid eyes on that man. As if he had seen him before and not in the best of circumstances.

People trickled in through the festooned gates of the queen's house, returning from the Temple of Concord, where Andrada had by now received her Helmet of the Kin and her blessings from High Priestess Citera. Dapyx wished he had been at her side, but her orders had been clear: wait in the courtyard and oversee the last preparations for her arrival.

He wasn't the only important person missing from the queen's consecration ceremony. Dokina wasn't there. Some of Andrada's fiercest Kertan opponents from before the war—Chief Piepor and Chief Rubobostes among them—had not traveled to Zalmodava either. No one knew what had happened to Oroles. Zyraxes, whom Andrada had pardoned for all his offenses against her, had nonetheless refused to come down from the Boulder Hut on Mount Ea-El.

Dapyx was here though. Now that Una and Nicetas were gone, nothing would stand between him and Andrada. Just that morning, she had told him she had Una's satchel and wanted to go back to the work chamber to study the green glass tubes. Would he be her helper? Then she asked him about the secret tunnels and corridors he had made use of to bring her inside Zalmodava after her fateful trip to Twin Willows. He promised to show them to her but wondered if Andrada was prodding him to confess to what he had done to Una. Never.

Out of nowhere, the image of his first slaying on the battlefield flashed before his eyes. He flinched and cursed so loudly, a passing guard stopped walking and looked his way.

These flashes of terror must have been what Nicetas had struggled with after the Night Attack. But Nicetas had had Una. Who would help Dapyx now? He'd been praying to Beleizis, who had helped him bring the Kertans to Andrada's rescue. Nothing. He didn't understand what Andrada's woken El could do for mortals like him, and he didn't much care for Bendis, the goddess who had let Nicetas die on the battlefield under Andrada's mace. Zyraxes could tell him which god to pray to, but he wasn't there.

Dapyx took another deep breath…

Everything was in place for Andrada's arrival: the flowers, the alpenhorns, the drums. Empty jugs and wooden panels had been placed around the courtyard to make the queen's voice carry farther into the crowd. The wolf, the aurochs, and the snake standards flapped side by side with the new banner, the black triangle on a white canvas, a symbol of the three provinces of Dhawosia coming together again under one ruler. It reminded him of Andrada's crystal bell.

Two men in togas and red cloaks crossed the courtyard, chatting like old friends. One was Quintus Domitius Cispius, a Roman merchant from Tomis, and the other was Lucius Flavius Magius, the emperor's diplomatic legate to the new kingdom of Dhawosia. If the Romans were already in the courtyard, Andrada's procession was soon to follow.

Dapyx straightened in his chair. At the foot of the stairs, three women ranted about the ceremonial prayers. They had left the Temple of Concord early because they couldn't stand the way the high priestess now replaced *goddess* with *god* in her invocations. The word *god* was shorter, they said, and it ruined the rhythm of the prayers they had known since childhood. It was certain the goddess would soon punish Queen Andrada for her sacrilege.

More people trickled in from the gardens. Dapyx saw Princess Meda and Oroles's younger sister Olma, who was carrying her baby nephew. A new life, after so many had died in such a short time, starting with Una and that botched potion. Was there not enough space on the gods' earth for all mortals to live together? Was this carnage a competition for their amusement? Whose place on this crowded earth was Dapyx taking up now? How soon was he meant to relinquish it? He felt sick to his stomach. His hands were cold despite the hot day.

Prince Rescuporis arrived and took his seat on the other side of Andrada's throne. He waved to a Tauri woman in trousers, then turned to Dapyx.

"I finally get to meet you, Prince," he said. "Too bad I won't be in Zalmodava for long. I must head back to Steppewynd, to take over my duties as Queen Andrada's provincial governor. I know, the honor she did me is beyond words."

Dapyx was searching for a reply when the drumbeat swelled, and the flow of people into the courtyard doubled. Through the festooned arches of the garden gates, the royal procession finally appeared. Army Chief Wodan led a dozen guards who parted the crowd. Then came Andrada, dressed in white robes like a bride but wearing a silver breastplate like a warrior. Upon her head, she wore the newly forged Helmet of the Kin.

Dapyx swallowed the lump in his throat and forced himself to pay attention. The alpenhorns joined with the drums. The crowd roared, and the entire fortress trembled. Hats flew high in the air as Andrada climbed to her throne. She didn't look at Dapyx, but he was there, guarding her back.

In that moment, he remembered where he had seen Rescuporis before. On the battlefield in the Ozana Valley, at the head of the Tauri riders, charging the Steppewynders led by the young nobleman. An arrow through the eye—that was how Prince Moskon had died, wasn't it?

Rescuporis had killed his own brother...so he could become Scorilus's heir to the Steppewynder throne. Now that Andrada was queen, he wouldn't stop there.

It was hard to keep still, but Dapyx stood at Andrada's right, his every sense alert, while Rescuporis waved at the cheering crowd with her, nodding and smiling. Any disruption now would invite chaos, and chaos would allow Rescuporis to murder Andrada, the way he had murdered Prince Moskon.

Dapyx waited, his breath shallow. The familiar claw of dread grabbed his chest again. The crowd vanished, and a ringing sound filled his ears. He saw Una's blue-gray face framed in snow on a fur rug. That was how she had looked that night when Dapyx's poison had overwhelmed her for good.

Unable to breathe, Dapyx didn't dare to blink.

He knew he was Andrada's only shield.

The Book of Andrada

"People of Dhawosia," Andrada said when they all fell silent, "you are the heart of our beloved country."

Her voice rang clear inside the walls of the packed courtyard. She glanced at the people—some were frowning—and her throat tightened. If they all charged up the stairs to her throne, they could seize her and throw her over the parapet into the chasm below.

No, El wouldn't have brought her all this way for such a meaningless end.

"By the grace of our god El, peace is once again restored in Kerta, Valdavia, and Steppewynd. Emperor Vespasianus has deemed Dhawosia *friend and partner of the Roman people.*"

She nodded at Legate Magius, who bowed to her, his fist over his heart, saying, "Long live Pax Romana!"

She needed her people on her side without telling them that their entire lives, they had mistaken the actions of the one true god El for those of Ea, Sehul, Mehnot, Heusos, Beleizis, Bendis, Enoz, Napat-Dehnu, Azemel, Samca, and all the other spirits. They'd see that someday, though not today.

"Today marks the beginning of a new era of prosperity, for El has awoken and is watching over His flawed creation with love, not wrath. He's giving us a second chance to live as Oroles, son of Zonaras, once taught us: helping those in need, respecting our neighbors, and never repaying evil with evil."

Princess Meda nodded, wiping a tear, but Legate Magius shifted in his place, looking uncomfortable. Andrada knew he wouldn't be the first foreign emissary to leave Zalmodava if he felt offended. But he might put up with this new god in exchange for Dhawosian gold, salt, iron, and lead—as long as Andrada paid respect to his false gods and the claimed divinity of his emperor.

With El's help, a day would come when Roma wouldn't see the belief in a single god as a threat. A day when it wouldn't cross the Danubius

River to crush the Temple of Concord as they had done to the temple in Ierusalem. A day when it would join Dhawosia in worshiping the one true god—or face El's wrath, maybe even with Andrada at the head of El's armies.

"Today we come together as one country striving for a world worthy of our creator. A world in which widows and orphans and the sick find solace and protection at temples. A world where merchants find shelter no matter which guild they belong to. A world where, in years of drought or pest or plague, temples see everyone through until the next harvest."

People now looked more intrigued than hostile, but an angry shout rose from the back, the words garbled by the distance.

Andrada's heart raced. Sweat trickled under her helmet. "As your queen, I will forgive all debt, so we may all start anew with El's Great Awakening."

She paused to let that sink in, and a wave of approving murmurs rippled.

"Together, we'll work the mines of Kerta. We'll tend the fields of Valdavia. We'll build aqueducts to the terraced hills of Steppewynd. We'll tie our provinces together with paved roads. We'll move goods from the Black Sea up the rivers of Dhawosia, and we'll build a fleet to feed our trade with Roma."

She locked eyes with Legate Magius. "From now on, there'll be peace along the northern border of the Roman Empire."

Andrada didn't mention Moesia, the other Dhawosian kingdom under Roman rule. If El wished it, the reunion of all four realms would happen one day.

"And now, as your queen, I command you to bow your heads and pray to El."

Time crawled...

The crowd's wall of silence pressed against Andrada. She began to tremble, and she touched the crystal pendant on her necklace to ground herself. If a riot happened, it would be now, and not even the guards at the bottom of the dais could protect her. She could hear her ragged breath inside her helmet.

Then, at the front of the crowd, Wodan kneeled and uncovered his head. One by one, uncomfortable-looking people kneeled around him, and then those around them followed, as far as the gates to the gardens.

"May El make Dhawosia more prosperous than ever before," Andrada said, her voice strong.

She felt powerful like never before, a true queen. She took in the crowd from one end to the other.

"Say it with me, people of Dhawosia, praise our mighty god El!"

And the crowd answered in one thundering voice: "Praise El!"

"*Andrada Evermore.*"

—from a Dhawosian nursery rhyme

If you enjoyed *The Exiled Queen*, explore the far-future world shaped by Andrada's alternate history in my novel *The Regolith Temple: A Sci-Fi Thriller*, also in the Delight of Humans and Gods series.

Sign up for my newsletter at roxanaarama.com/newsletter to receive a FREE copy of *The Last Time I Held You: A Prologue to The Exiled Queen*. This is where the story begins, when Andrada's birth destroys her father.

If you leave a review for *The Exiled Queen* on the retail platform where you purchased the book, on Goodreads, or on your own website, I'd love to read it. Email me the link at roxana@roxanaarama.com. Thank you!

Afterword

Andrada's story began a long time ago, when I was in seventh grade in my hometown of Galați, Romania. In December 1989, people took to the streets to protest our communist regime. When we kids recessed for our winter break, the large portrait of President Nicolae Ceaușescu was up on the wall behind the teacher's desk. When we returned in January 1990, the portrait had been removed, and in its place, someone had hung a small icon of Jesus Christ. It was centered inside the rectangle of darker wall paint where the old frame used to be. I didn't know much about Jesus at the time, but I remember staring at the discolored wall and thinking:

Why do we need another portrait up there?

That question made me want to understand how history gets rewritten and what stays true. What should I believe in as an adult, when as a child I was told to discard everything I had known until then and adopt a new canon?

As Romania took a sudden turn from secularism to Orthodox Christianity, I tried to keep up. I learned my prayers, but I had questions no one could answer. I didn't doubt the faith, but I struggled with it. Prayers for myself went unanswered, so I figured that divine intervention only worked if we prayed for one another. There was so much injustice in the world, so I started there but didn't make much of a dent.

In high school, I couldn't feel the support and comfort some of my friends found in our religion. They seemed to have a trusted ally in the sky, one who unfortunately didn't hear me. I was stuck, so I focused on computer science instead.

When I moved to the United States with a job in software development, I encountered different traditions, and I accepted that Romania's official creed wasn't widely shared. I picked up philosophy and psychology books, and I studied biblical history, hoping to discover a unifying theory of it all. No surprise: I couldn't find it. But in the process, I started building my own worldview, which is still evolving.

Andrada's quest to understand how her world worked draws from my own lifelong journey. When I started writing her story in 2011, I turned to novels such as *War and Peace* by Leo Tolstoy to find models of characters who change their religious beliefs. I was disappointed when the debauched Count Pierre Bezukhov embraced Orthodoxy in just a few pages, so I resolved to do better than Tolstoy in my novel. (I know how that sounds, but that's what I thought back then.) Years later, I had a finished manuscript that took Andrada from the belief in many gods to one through small investigative steps followed by gradual changes in her faith.

What I realized while writing her story was that we all have a deep desire to feel safe and protected. Parents sometimes provide that sense of security, but for most of human history, the gods have filled that soothing role. At the end of Andrada's story, she abandons her need for an earthly father and embraces a heavenly parent. She's still searching for the protection and love of someone more powerful. She's a fierce queen who has seen battle and death, but her childhood desire to be loved and protected is as alive as ever in her heart. It's still alive in many of us.

Her Dhawosian subjects struggle to worship a different god, and I don't think I spoil the sequel by telling you that Andrada's religion will splinter and gather enemies. Which creates plenty of drama for a new historical fantasy adventure. I hope you'll follow me there—as I write and rewrite (and rewrite) *The Foreign King*—by signing up for my newsletter. Thank you for reading!

I'd like to add a word of thanks to my fellow writers at Louisa's Café in Seattle, who helped me get this book's words down on the page in forty-five-minute sprints when my life was hard to manage otherwise. Authors Robert J. Ray and Jack Remick welcomed me to their writing group where I made lifelong friends: Mindy Halleck, Karen Phelps Heines, Beth Maxey, Pamela Hobart Carter, Lori Pohlman, Melanie Childers, Jerry Jaz, Arleen Williams, Anne Herman, Elise Stephens, Isla McKetta, Betsy Bell, Zack Hoffman, Janet Lynn Yoder, Nancy-Lou Polk, Stacy Lawson, Vladimir Vulovic, Laura Nelson, and many more wonderful writers I was lucky to sit with at the tables over the years. Thank you all!

Thank you, Cristina, for being my trusted friend through the ups and downs of my writing and life journey.

And thank you, Tracy, for being such a supportive and understanding life partner. This book wouldn't exist without you.

About the Author

Roxana Arama is an award-winning Romanian American author. She studied computer science in Bucharest, Romania, and moved to the United States to work in software development. She is the author of two other novels: *The Regolith Temple: A Sci-Fi Thriller* (also in the Delight of Humans and Gods series) and *Extreme Vetting: A Thriller*. Her short stories and essays have been published in many literary magazines. She lives in Seattle, Washington, with her family.

Subscribe to her newsletter at roxanaarama.com/newsletter to receive free content and updates.

ALSO IN

WHAT DOES IT MEAN
TO BE HUMAN?
complex worldbuilding...thrilling
narrative...frequent twists..."
—Kirkus Reviews
"A must-read for sci-fi fans."
Publishers Weekly
THE
REGOLITH
TEMPLE
A SCI-FI THRILLER
ROXANA ARAMA